INTERPRETER OF MALADIES

———

THE NAMESAKE

BOOKS BY JHUMPA LAHIRI

Interpreter of Maladies
The Namesake
Unaccustomed Earth

Interpreter of Maladies

The Namesake

JHUMPA LAHIRI

Houghton Mifflin Harcourt

BOSTON • NEW YORK

2010

For information about permission to reproduce
selections from this book, write to Permissions,
Houghton Mifflin Harcourt Publishing Company,
215 Park Avenue South, New York, New York 10003.

www.hmhbooks.com

Library of Congress Cataloging-in-Publication Data
Lahiri, Jhumpa.
Interpreter of maladies ; The namesake / Jhumpa Lahiri.
p. cm.
ISBN 978-0-547-44781-0
1. East Indian Americans — Fiction. I. Lahiri, Jhumpa. Namesake.
II. Title.
PS3562.A316A6 2010
813'.54 — dc22   2010025827

Book design by Melissa Lotfy

Printed in the United States of America

DOC 10 9 8 7 6 5 4 3 2 1

Some of the stories in *Interpreter of Maladies* have appeared
elsewhere, in slightly different form: "A Temporary Matter"
in *The New Yorker*, "When Mr. Pirzada Came to Dine" in
The Louisville Review, "Interpreter of Maladies" in the *Agni
Review*, "A Real Durwan" in the *Harvard Review*, "Sexy" in
The New Yorker, "Mrs. Sen's" in *Salamander*, "This Blessed
House" in *Epoch*, and "The Treatment of Bibi Haldar" in
Story Quarterly.

A portion of *The Namesake* appeared in slightly different
form in *The New Yorker*.

Interpreter of Maladies

For my parents and for my sister

WITH THANKS TO

The Fine Arts Work Center in Provincetown,
Janet Silver, and Cindy Klein Roche

Contents

A Temporary Matter

T HE notice informed them that it was a temporary matter: for five days their electricity would be cut off for
one hour, beginning at eight P.M. A line had gone down in the
last snowstorm, and the repairmen were going to take advan-
tage of the milder evenings to set it right. The work would affect only the houses on the quiet tree-lined street, within walking distance of a row of brick-faced stores and a trolley stop,
where Shoba and Shukumar had lived for three years.

"It's good of them to warn us," Shoba conceded after reading
the notice aloud, more for her own benefit than Shukumar's.
She let the strap of her leather satchel, plump with files, slip
from her shoulders, and left it in the hallway as she walked into
the kitchen. She wore a navy blue poplin raincoat over gray
sweatpants and white sneakers, looking, at thirty-three, like the
type of woman she'd once claimed she would never resemble.

She'd come from the gym. Her cranberry lipstick was visible
only on the outer reaches of her mouth, and her eyeliner had
left charcoal patches beneath her lower lashes. She used to look
this way sometimes, Shukumar thought, on mornings after a
party or a night at a bar, when she'd been too lazy to wash her
face, too eager to collapse into his arms. She dropped a sheaf of

mail on the table without a glance. Her eyes were still fixed on the notice in her other hand. "But they should do this sort of thing during the day."

"When I'm here, you mean," Shukumar said. He put a glass lid on a pot of lamb, adjusting it so only the slightest bit of steam could escape. Since January he'd been working at home, trying to complete the final chapters of his dissertation on agrarian revolts in India. "When do the repairs start?"

"It says March nineteenth. Is today the nineteenth?" Shoba walked over to the framed corkboard that hung on the wall by the fridge, bare except for a calendar of William Morris wallpaper patterns. She looked at it as if for the first time, studying the wallpaper pattern carefully on the top half before allowing her eyes to fall to the numbered grid on the bottom. A friend had sent the calendar in the mail as a Christmas gift, even though Shoba and Shukumar hadn't celebrated Christmas that year.

"Today then," Shoba announced. "You have a dentist appointment next Friday, by the way."

He ran his tongue over the tops of his teeth; he'd forgotten to brush them that morning. It wasn't the first time. He hadn't left the house at all that day, or the day before. The more Shoba stayed out, the more she began putting in extra hours at work and taking on additional projects, the more he wanted to stay in, not even leaving to get the mail, or to buy fruit or wine at the stores by the trolley stop.

Six months ago, in September, Shukumar was at an academic conference in Baltimore when Shoba went into labor, three weeks before her due date. He hadn't wanted to go to the conference, but she had insisted; it was important to make contacts, and he would be entering the job market next year. She told him that she had his number at the hotel, and a copy of his schedule and flight numbers, and she had arranged with her friend Gillian for a ride to the hospital in the event of an emergency. When the cab pulled away that morning for the airport, Shoba stood waving good-bye in her robe, with one arm resting on the mound of her belly as if it were a perfectly natural part of her body.

Each time he thought of that moment, the last moment he saw Shoba pregnant, it was the cab he remembered most, a station wagon, painted red with blue lettering. It was cavernous compared to their own car. Although Shukumar was six feet tall, with hands too big ever to rest comfortably in the pockets of his jeans, he felt dwarfed in the back seat. As the cab sped down Beacon Street, he imagined a day when he and Shoba might need to buy a station wagon of their own, to cart their children back and forth from music lessons and dentist appointments. He imagined himself gripping the wheel, as Shoba turned around to hand the children juice boxes. Once, these images of parenthood had troubled Shukumar, adding to his anxiety that he was still a student at thirty-five. But that early autumn morning, the trees still heavy with bronze leaves, he welcomed the image for the first time.

A member of the staff had found him somehow among the identical convention rooms and handed him a stiff square of stationery. It was only a telephone number, but Shukumar knew it was the hospital. When he returned to Boston it was over. The baby had been born dead. Shoba was lying on a bed, asleep, in a private room so small there was barely enough space to stand beside her, in a wing of the hospital they hadn't been to on the tour for expectant parents. Her placenta had weakened and she'd had a cesarean, though not quickly enough. The doctor explained that these things happen. He smiled in the kindest way it was possible to smile at people known only professionally. Shoba would be back on her feet in a few weeks. There was nothing to indicate that she would not be able to have children in the future.

These days Shoba was always gone by the time Shukumar

woke up. He would open his eyes and see the long black hairs she shed on her pillow and think of her, dressed, sipping her third cup of coffee already, in her office downtown, where she searched for typographical errors in textbooks and marked them, in a code she had once explained to him, with an assortment of colored pencils. She would do the same for his dissertation, she promised, when it was ready. He envied her the specificity of her task, so unlike the elusive nature of his. He was a mediocre student who had a facility for absorbing details without curiosity. Until September he had been diligent if not dedicated, summarizing chapters, outlining arguments on pads of yellow lined paper. But now he would lie in their bed until he grew bored, gazing at his side of the closet which Shoba always left partly open, at the row of tweed jackets and corduroy trousers he would not have to choose from to teach his classes that semester. After the baby died it was too late to withdraw from his teaching duties. But his adviser had arranged things so that he had the spring semester to himself. Shukumar was in his sixth year of graduate school. "That and the summer should give you a good push," his adviser had said. "You should be able to wrap things up by next September."

But nothing was pushing Shukumar. Instead he thought of how he and Shoba had become experts at avoiding each other in their three-bedroom house, spending as much time on separate floors as possible. He thought of how he no longer looked forward to weekends, when she sat for hours on the sofa with her colored pencils and her files, so that he feared that putting on a record in his own house might be rude. He thought of how long it had been since she looked into his eyes and smiled, or whispered his name on those rare occasions they still reached for each other's bodies before sleeping.

In the beginning he had believed that it would pass, that he and Shoba would get through it all somehow. She was only thirty-three. She was strong, on her feet again. But it wasn't a consolation. It was often nearly lunchtime when Shukumar would finally pull himself out of bed and head downstairs to the coffeepot, pouring out the extra bit Shoba left for him, along with an empty mug, on the countertop.

Shukumar gathered onion skins in his hands and let them drop into the garbage pail, on top of the ribbons of fat he'd trimmed from the lamb. He ran the water in the sink, soaking the knife and the cutting board, and rubbed a lemon half along his fingertips to get rid of the garlic smell, a trick he'd learned from Shoba. It was seven-thirty. Through the window he saw the sky, like soft black pitch. Uneven banks of snow still lined the sidewalks, though it was warm enough for people to walk about without hats or gloves. Nearly three feet had fallen in the last storm, so that for a week people had to walk single file, in narrow trenches. For a week that was Shukumar's excuse for not leaving the house. But now the trenches were widening, and water drained steadily into grates in the pavement.

"The lamb won't be done by eight," Shukumar said. "We may have to eat in the dark."

"We can light candles," Shoba suggested. She unclipped her hair, coiled neatly at her nape during the days, and pried the sneakers from her feet without untying them. "I'm going to shower before the lights go," she said, heading for the staircase. "I'll be down."

Shukumar moved her satchel and her sneakers to the side of the fridge. She wasn't this way before. She used to put her coat on a hanger, her sneakers in the closet, and she paid bills as soon as they came. But now she treated the house as if it were a hotel. The fact that the yellow chintz armchair in the living room clashed with the blue-and-maroon Turkish carpet no longer bothered her. On the enclosed porch at the back of the house, a crisp white bag still sat on the wicker chaise, filled with lace she had once planned to turn into curtains.

While Shoba showered, Shukumar went into the downstairs bathroom and found a new toothbrush in its box beneath the sink. The cheap, stiff bristles hurt his gums, and he spit some blood into the basin. The spare brush was one of many stored in a metal basket. Shoba had bought them once when they were on sale, in the event that a visitor decided, at the last minute, to spend the night.

It was typical of her. She was the type to prepare for surprises, good and bad. If she found a skirt or a purse she liked she bought two. She kept the bonuses from her job in a separate bank account in her name. It hadn't bothered him. His own mother had fallen to pieces when his father died, abandoning the house he grew up in and moving back to Calcutta, leaving Shukumar to settle it all. He liked that Shoba was different. It astonished him, her capacity to think ahead. When she used to do the shopping, the pantry was always stocked with extra bottles of olive and corn oil, depending on whether they were cooking Italian or Indian. There were countless boxes of pasta in all shapes and colors, zippered sacks of basmati rice, whole sides of lambs and goats from the Muslim butchers at Haymarket, chopped up and frozen in countless plastic bags. Every other Saturday they wound through the maze of stalls Shukumar eventually knew by heart. He watched in disbelief as she bought more food, trailing behind her with canvas bags as she pushed through the crowd, arguing under the morning sun with boys too young to shave but already missing teeth, who twisted up brown paper bags of artichokes, plums, gingerroot, and yams, and dropped them on their scales, and tossed them to Shoba one by one. She didn't mind being jostled, even when she was pregnant. She was tall, and broad-shouldered, with hips that her obstetrician assured her were made for childbearing. During the drive back home, as the car curved along the Charles, they invariably marveled at how much food they'd bought.

It never went to waste. When friends dropped by, Shoba would throw together meals that appeared to have taken half a day to prepare, from things she had frozen and bottled, not cheap things in tins but peppers she had marinated herself with rosemary, and chutneys that she cooked on Sundays, stirring boiling pots of tomatoes and prunes. Her labeled mason jars lined the shelves of the kitchen, in sealed pyramids, enough, they'd agreed, to last for their grandchildren to taste. They'd eaten it all by now. Shukumar had been going through their supplies steadily, preparing meals for the two of them, measuring out cupfuls of rice, defrosting bags of meat day after day. He combed through her cookbooks every afternoon, following her penciled instructions to use two teaspoons of ground coriander seeds instead of one, or red lentils instead of yellow. Each of the recipes was dated, telling the first time they had eaten the dish together. April 2, cauliflower with fennel. January 14, chicken with almonds and sultanas. He had no memory of eating those meals, and yet there they were, recorded in her neat proofreader's hand. Shukumar enjoyed cooking now. It was the one thing that made him feel productive. If it weren't for him, he knew, Shoba would eat a bowl of cereal for her dinner.

Tonight, with no lights, they would have to eat together. For months now they'd served themselves from the stove, and he'd taken his plate into his study, letting the meal grow cold on his desk before shoving it into his mouth without pause, while Shoba took her plate to the living room and watched game shows, or proofread files with her arsenal of colored pencils at hand.

At some point in the evening she visited him. When he heard her approach he would put away his novel and begin typing sentences. She would rest her hands on his shoulders and stare with him into the blue glow of the computer screen. "Don't work too hard," she would say after a minute or two, and head off to bed. It was the one time in the day she sought him out, and yet he'd come to dread it. He knew it was something she forced herself to do. She would look around the walls of the room, which they had decorated together last summer with a border of marching ducks and rabbits playing trumpets and drums. By the end of August there was a cherry crib under the window, a white changing table with mint-green knobs, and a rocking chair with checkered cushions. Shukumar had disassembled it all before bringing Shoba back from the hospital, scraping off the rabbits and ducks with a spatula. For some reason the room did not haunt him the way it haunted Shoba. In January, when he stopped working at his carrel in the library, he set up his desk there deliberately, partly because the room soothed him, and partly because it was a place Shoba avoided.

Shukumar returned to the kitchen and began to open drawers. He tried to locate a candle among the scissors, the eggbeaters and whisks, the mortar and pestle she'd bought in a bazaar in Calcutta, and used to pound garlic cloves and cardamom pods, back when she used to cook. He found a flashlight, but no batteries, and a half-empty box of birthday candles. Shoba had thrown him a surprise birthday party last May. One hundred and twenty people had crammed into the house—all the friends and the friends of friends they now systematically avoided. Bottles of vinho verde had nested in a bed of ice in the bathtub. Shoba was in her fifth month, drinking ginger ale from a martini glass. She had made a vanilla cream cake with custard and spun sugar. All night she kept Shukumar's long fingers linked with hers as they walked among the guests at the party.

Since September their only guest had been Shoba's mother. She came from Arizona and stayed with them for two months after Shoba returned from the hospital. She cooked dinner every night, drove herself to the supermarket, washed their clothes, put them away. She was a religious woman. She set up a small shrine, a framed picture of a lavender-faced goddess and a plate of marigold petals, on the bedside table in the guest room, and prayed twice a day for healthy grandchildren in the future. She was polite to Shukumar without being friendly. She folded his sweaters with an expertise she had learned from her job in a department store. She replaced a missing button on his winter coat and knit him a beige and brown scarf, presenting it to him without the least bit of ceremony, as if he had only dropped it and hadn't noticed. She never talked to him about Shoba; once, when he mentioned the baby's death, she looked up from her knitting, and said, "But you weren't even there."

It struck him as odd that there were no real candles in the house. That Shoba hadn't prepared for such an ordinary emergency. He looked now for something to put the birthday candles in and settled on the soil of a potted ivy that normally sat on the windowsill over the sink. Even though the plant was inches from the tap, the soil was so dry that he had to water it first before the candles would stand straight. He pushed aside the things on the kitchen table, the piles of mail, the unread library books. He remembered their first meals there, when they were so thrilled to be married, to be living together in the same house at last, that they would just reach for each other foolishly, more eager to make love than to eat. He put down two embroidered place mats, a wedding gift from an uncle in Lucknow, and set out the plates and wineglasses they usually saved for guests. He put the ivy in the middle, the white-edged, star-shaped leaves girded by ten little candles. He switched on the digital clock radio and tuned it to a jazz station.

"What's all this?" Shoba said when she came downstairs. Her hair was wrapped in a thick white towel. She undid the towel and draped it over a chair, allowing her hair, damp and dark, to fall across her back. As she walked absently toward the stove she took out a few tangles with her fingers. She wore a clean pair of sweatpants, a T-shirt, an old flannel robe. Her stomach was flat again, her waist narrow before the flare of her hips, the belt of the robe tied in a floppy knot.

It was nearly eight. Shukumar put the rice on the table and the lentils from the night before into the microwave oven, punching the numbers on the timer.

"You made *rogan josh*," Shoba observed, looking through the glass lid at the bright paprika stew.

Shukumar took out a piece of lamb, pinching it quickly between his fingers so as not to scald himself. He prodded a larger piece with a serving spoon to make sure the meat slipped easily from the bone. "It's ready," he announced.

The microwave had just beeped when the lights went out, and the music disappeared.

"Perfect timing," Shoba said.

"All I could find were birthday candles." He lit up the ivy, keeping the rest of the candles and a book of matches by his plate.

"It doesn't matter," she said, running a finger along the stem of her wineglass. "It looks lovely."

In the dimness, he knew how she sat, a bit forward in her chair, ankles crossed against the lowest rung, left elbow on the table. During his search for the candles, Shukumar had found a bottle of wine in a crate he had thought was empty. He clamped the bottle between his knees while he turned in the corkscrew. He worried about spilling, and so he picked up the glasses and held them close to his lap while he filled them. They served themselves, stirring the rice with their forks, squinting as they extracted bay leaves and cloves from the stew. Every few minutes Shukumar lit a few more birthday candles and drove them into the soil of the pot.

"It's like India," Shoba said, watching him tend his makeshift candelabra. "Sometimes the current disappears for hours at a stretch. I once had to attend an entire rice ceremony in the dark. The baby just cried and cried. It must have been so hot."

Their baby had never cried, Shukumar considered. Their baby would never have a rice ceremony, even though Shoba had already made the guest list, and decided on which of her three brothers she was going to ask to feed the child its first taste of solid food, at six months if it was a boy, seven if it was a girl.

"Are you hot?" he asked her. He pushed the blazing ivy pot to the other end of the table, closer to the piles of books and mail, making it even more difficult for them to see each other. He was suddenly irritated that he couldn't go upstairs and sit in front of the computer.

"No. It's delicious," she said, tapping her plate with her fork. "It really is."

He refilled the wine in her glass. She thanked him.

They weren't like this before. Now he had to struggle to say something that interested her, something that made her look up from her plate, or from her proofreading files. Eventually he gave up trying to amuse her. He learned not to mind the silences.

"I remember during power failures at my grandmother's house, we all had to say something," Shoba continued. He could barely see her face, but from her tone he knew her eyes were narrowed, as if trying to focus on a distant object. It was a habit of hers.

"Like what?"

"I don't know. A little poem. A joke. A fact about the world. For some reason my relatives always wanted me to tell them the names of my friends in America. I don't know why the information was so interesting to them. The last time I saw my aunt she asked after four girls I went to elementary school with in Tucson. I barely remember them now."

Shukumar hadn't spent as much time in India as Shoba had. His parents, who settled in New Hampshire, used to go back without him. The first time he'd gone as an infant he'd nearly died of amoebic dysentery. His father, a nervous type, was afraid to take him again, in case something were to happen, and left him with his aunt and uncle in Concord. As a teenager he preferred sailing camp or scooping ice cream during the summers to going to Calcutta. It wasn't until after his father died, in his last year of college, that the country began to interest him, and he studied its history from course books as if it were any other subject. He wished now that he had his own childhood story of India.

"Let's do that," she said suddenly.

"Do what?"

"Say something to each other in the dark."

"Like what? I don't know any jokes."

"No, no jokes." She thought for a minute. "How about telling each other something we've never told before."

"I used to play this game in high school," Shukumar recalled. "When I got drunk."

"You're thinking of truth or dare. This is different. Okay, I'll start." She took a sip of wine. "The first time I was alone in your apartment, I looked in your address book to see if you'd written me in. I think we'd known each other two weeks."

"Where was I?"

"You went to answer the telephone in the other room. It was your mother, and I figured it would be a long call. I wanted to know if you'd promoted me from the margins of your news-paper."

"Had I?"

"No. But I didn't give up on you. Now it's your turn."

He couldn't think of anything, but Shoba was waiting for him to speak. She hadn't appeared so determined in months. What was there left to say to her? He thought back to their first meeting, four years earlier at a lecture hall in Cambridge, where a group of Bengali poets were giving a recital. They'd ended up side by side, on folding wooden chairs. Shukumar was soon bored; he was unable to decipher the literary diction, and couldn't join the rest of the audience as they sighed and nodded solemnly after certain phrases. Peering at the news-paper folded in his lap, he studied the temperatures of cities around the world. Ninety-one degrees in Singapore yesterday, fifty-one in Stockholm. When he turned his head to the left, he saw a woman next to him making a grocery list on the back of a folder, and was startled to find that she was beautiful.

"Okay," he said, remembering. "The first time we went out to dinner, to the Portuguese place, I forgot to tip the waiter. I went back the next morning, found out his name, left money with the manager."

"You went all the way back to Somerville just to tip a waiter?"

"I took a cab."

"Why did you forget to tip the waiter?"

The birthday candles had burned out, but he pictured her face clearly in the dark, the wide tilting eyes, the full grape-toned lips, the fall at age two from her high chair still visible as a comma on her chin. Each day, Shukumar noticed, her beauty, which had once overwhelmed him, seemed to fade. The cos-metics that had seemed superfluous were necessary now, not to improve her but to define her somehow.

"By the end of the meal I had a funny feeling that I might marry you," he said, admitting it to himself as well as to her for the first time. "It must have distracted me."

The next night Shoba came home earlier than usual. There was lamb left over from the evening before, and Shukumar heated it up so that they were able to eat by seven. He'd gone out that day, through the melting snow, and bought a packet of taper candles from the corner store, and batteries to fit the flashlight. He had the candles ready on the countertop, standing in brass holders shaped like lotuses, but they ate under the glow of the copper-shaded ceiling lamp that hung over the table.

When they had finished eating, Shukumar was surprised to see that Shoba was stacking her plate on top of his, and then carrying them over to the sink. He had assumed she would retreat to the living room, behind her barricade of files.

"Don't worry about the dishes," he said, taking them from her hands.

"It seems silly not to," she replied, pouring a drop of detergent onto a sponge. "It's nearly eight o'clock."

His heart quickened. All day Shukumar had looked forward to the lights going out. He thought about what Shoba had said the night before, about looking in his address book. It felt good to remember her as she was then, how bold yet nervous she'd been when they first met, how hopeful. They stood side by side at the sink, their reflections fitting together in the frame of the window. It made him shy, the way he felt the first time they stood together in a mirror. He couldn't recall the last time they'd been photographed. They had stopped attending parties, went nowhere together. The film in his camera still contained pictures of Shoba, in the yard, when she was pregnant.

After finishing the dishes, they leaned against the counter, drying their hands on either end of a towel. At eight o'clock the house went black. Shukumar lit the wicks of the candles, impressed by their long, steady flames.

"Let's sit outside," Shoba said. "I think it's warm still."

They each took a candle and sat down on the steps. It seemed strange to be sitting outside with patches of snow still on the ground. But everyone was out of their houses tonight, the air fresh enough to make people restless. Screen doors opened and closed. A small parade of neighbors passed by with flashlights.

"We're going to the bookstore to browse," a silver-haired man called out. He was walking with his wife, a thin woman in a windbreaker, and holding a dog on a leash. They were the Bradfords, and they had tucked a sympathy card into Shoba and Shukumar's mailbox back in September. "I hear they've got their power."

"They'd better," Shukumar said. "Or you'll be browsing in the dark."

The woman laughed, slipping her arm through the crook of her husband's elbow. "Want to join us?"

"No thanks," Shoba and Shukumar called out together. It surprised Shukumar that his words matched hers.

He wondered what Shoba would tell him in the dark. The worst possibilities had already run through his head. That she'd had an affair. That she didn't respect him for being thirty-five and still a student. That she blamed him for being in Baltimore the way her mother did. But he knew those things weren't true. She'd been faithful, as had he. She believed in him. It was she who had insisted he go to Baltimore. What didn't they know about each other? He knew she curled her fingers tightly when she slept, that her body twitched during bad dreams. He knew it was honeydew she favored over cantaloupe. He knew that when they returned from the hospital the first thing she did when she walked into the house was pick out objects of theirs and toss them into a pile in the hallway: books from the shelves, plants from the windowsills, paintings from walls, photos from tables, pots and pans that hung from the hooks over the stove. Shukumar had stepped out of her way, watching as she moved methodically from room to room. When she was satisfied, she stood there staring at the pile she'd made, her lips drawn back in such distaste that Shukumar had thought she would spit. Then she'd started to cry.

He began to feel cold as he sat there on the steps. He felt that he needed her to talk first, in order to reciprocate.

"That time when your mother came to visit us," she said finally. "When I said one night that I had to stay late at work, I went out with Gillian and had a martini."

He looked at her profile, the slender nose, the slightly masculine set of her jaw. He remembered that night well; eating with his mother, tired from teaching two classes back to back, wishing Shoba were there to say more of the right things because he came up with only the wrong ones. It had been twelve years since his father had died, and his mother had come to spend two weeks with him and Shoba, so they could honor his father's memory together. Each night his mother cooked something his father had liked, but she was too upset to eat the dishes herself, and her eyes would well up as Shoba stroked her hand. "It's so touching," Shoba had said to him at the time. Now he pictured Shoba with Gillian, in a bar with striped velvet sofas, the one they used to go to after the movies, making sure she got her extra olive, asking Gillian for a cigarette. He imagined her complaining, and Gillian sympathizing about visits from in-laws. It was Gillian who had driven Shoba to the hospital.

"Your turn," she said, stopping his thoughts.

At the end of their street Shukumar heard sounds of a drill and the electricians shouting over it. He looked at the darkened facades of the houses lining the street. Candles glowed in the windows of one. In spite of the warmth, smoke rose from the chimney.

"I cheated on my Oriental Civilization exam in college," he said. "It was my last semester, my last set of exams. My father had died a few months before. I could see the blue book of the guy next to me. He was an American guy, a maniac. He knew Urdu and Sanskrit. I couldn't remember if the verse we had to identify was an example of a *ghazal* or not. I looked at his answer and copied it down."

It had happened over fifteen years ago. He felt relief now, having told her.

She turned to him, looking not at his face, but at his shoes —old moccasins he wore as if they were slippers, the leather at the back permanently flattened. He wondered if it bothered her, what he'd said. She took his hand and pressed it. "You didn't have to tell me why you did it," she said, moving closer to him.

They sat together until nine o'clock, when the lights came on. They heard some people across the street clapping from their porch, and televisions being turned on. The Bradfords walked back down the street, eating ice-cream cones and waving. Shoba and Shukumar waved back. Then they stood up, his hand still in hers, and went inside.

Somehow, without saying anything, it had turned into this. Into an exchange of confessions—the little ways they'd hurt or disappointed each other, and themselves. The following day Shukumar thought for hours about what to say to her. He was torn between admitting that he once ripped out a photo of a woman in one of the fashion magazines she used to subscribe to and carried it in his books for a week, or saying that he really hadn't lost the sweater-vest she bought him for their third wedding anniversary but had exchanged it for cash at Filene's, and that he had gotten drunk alone in the middle of the day at a hotel bar. For their first anniversary, Shoba had cooked a ten-course dinner just for him. The vest depressed him. "My wife gave me a sweater-vest for our anniversary," he complained to the bartender, his head heavy with cognac. "What do you expect?" the bartender had replied. "You're married."

As for the picture of the woman, he didn't know why he'd ripped it out. She wasn't as pretty as Shoba. She wore a white sequined dress, and had a sullen face and lean, mannish legs. Her bare arms were raised, her fists around her head, as if she were about to punch herself in the ears. It was an advertisement for stockings. Shoba had been pregnant at the time, her stomach suddenly immense, to the point where Shukumar no longer wanted to touch her. The first time he saw the picture he was lying in bed next to her, watching her as she read. When he noticed the magazine in the recycling pile he found the woman and tore out the page as carefully as he could. For about a week he allowed himself a glimpse each day. He felt an intense desire for the woman, but it was a desire that turned to disgust after a minute or two. It was the closest he'd come to infidelity.

He told Shoba about the sweater on the third night, the picture on the fourth. She said nothing as he spoke, expressed no protest or reproach. She simply listened, and then she took his hand, pressing it as she had before. On the third night, she told him that once after a lecture they'd attended, she let him speak to the chairman of his department without telling him that he had a dab of pâté on his chin. She'd been irritated with him for some reason, and so she'd let him go on and on, about securing his fellowship for the following semester, without putting a finger to her own chin as a signal. The fourth night, she said that she never liked the one poem he'd ever published in his life, in a literary magazine in Utah. He'd written the poem after meeting Shoba. She added that she found the poem sentimental.

Something happened when the house was dark. They were able to talk to each other again. The third night after supper they'd sat together on the sofa, and once it was dark he began kissing her awkwardly on her forehead and her face, and though it was dark he closed his eyes, and knew that she did, too. The fourth night they walked carefully upstairs, to bed, feeling together for the final step with their feet before the landing, and making love with a desperation they had forgotten. She wept without sound, and whispered his name, and traced his eyebrows with her finger in the dark. As he made love to her he wondered what he would say to her the next night, and what she would say, the thought of it exciting him. "Hold me," he said, "hold me in your arms." By the time the lights came back on downstairs, they'd fallen asleep.

The morning of the fifth night Shukumar found another notice from the electric company in the mailbox. The line had been repaired ahead of schedule, it said. He was disappointed. He had planned on making shrimp *malai* for Shoba, but when he arrived at the store he didn't feel like cooking anymore. It wasn't the same, he thought, knowing that the lights wouldn't go out. In the store the shrimp looked gray and thin. The coconut milk tin was dusty and overpriced. Still, he bought them, along with a beeswax candle and two bottles of wine.

She came home at seven-thirty. "I suppose this is the end of our game," he said when he saw her reading the notice.

She looked at him. "You can still light candles if you want." She hadn't been to the gym tonight. She wore a suit beneath the raincoat. Her makeup had been retouched recently.

When she went upstairs to change, Shukumar poured himself some wine and put on a record, a Thelonious Monk album he knew she liked.

When she came downstairs they ate together. She didn't

thank him or compliment him. They simply ate in a darkened room, in the glow of a beeswax candle. They had survived a difficult time. They finished off the shrimp. They finished off the first bottle of wine and moved on to the second. They sat together until the candle had nearly burned away. She shifted in her chair, and Shukumar thought that she was about to say something. But instead she blew out the candle, stood up, turned on the light switch, and sat down again.

"Shouldn't we keep the lights off?" Shukumar asked.

She set her plate aside and clasped her hands on the table. "I want you to see my face when I tell you this," she said gently.

His heart began to pound. The day she told him she was pregnant, she had used the very same words, saying them in the same gentle way, turning off the basketball game he'd been watching on television. He hadn't been prepared then. Now he was.

Only he didn't want her to be pregnant again. He didn't want to have to pretend to be happy.

"I've been looking for an apartment and I've found one," she said, narrowing her eyes on something, it seemed, behind his left shoulder. It was nobody's fault, she continued. They'd been through enough. She needed some time alone. She had money saved up for a security deposit. The apartment was on Beacon Hill, so she could walk to work. She had signed the lease that night before coming home.

She wouldn't look at him, but he stared at her. It was obvious that she'd rehearsed the lines. All this time she'd been looking for an apartment, testing the water pressure, asking a Realtor if heat and hot water were included in the rent. It sickened Shukumar, knowing that she had spent these past evenings preparing for a life without him. He was relieved and yet he was sickened. This was what she'd been trying to tell him for the past four evenings. This was the point of her game.

Now it was his turn to speak. There was something he'd sworn he would never tell her, and for six months he had done his best to block it from his mind. Before the ultrasound she had asked the doctor not to tell her the sex of their child, and Shukumar had agreed. She had wanted it to be a surprise.

Later, those few times they talked about what had happened, she said at least they'd been spared that knowledge. In a way she almost took pride in her decision, for it enabled her to seek refuge in a mystery. He knew that she assumed it was a mystery for him, too. He'd arrived too late from Baltimore—when it was all over and she was lying on the hospital bed. But he hadn't. He'd arrived early enough to see their baby, and to hold him before they cremated him. At first he had recoiled at the suggestion, but the doctor said holding the baby might help him with the process of grieving. Shoba was asleep. The baby had been cleaned off, his bulbous lids shut tight to the world.

"Our baby was a boy," he said. "His skin was more red than brown. He had black hair on his head. He weighed almost five pounds. His fingers were curled shut, just like yours in the night."

Shoba looked at him now, her face contorted with sorrow. He had cheated on a college exam, ripped a picture of a woman out of a magazine. He had returned a sweater and got drunk in the middle of the day instead. These were the things he had told her. He had held his son, who had known life only within her, against his chest in a darkened room in an unknown wing of the hospital. He had held him until a nurse knocked and took him away, and he promised himself that day that he would never tell Shoba, because he still loved her then, and it was the one thing in her life that she had wanted to be a surprise.

Shukumar stood up and stacked his plate on top of hers. He carried the plates to the sink, but instead of running the tap he looked out the window. Outside the evening was still warm, and the Bradfords were walking arm in arm. As he watched the couple the room went dark, and he spun around. Shoba had turned the lights off. She came back to the table and sat down, and after a moment Shukumar joined her. They wept together, for the things they now knew.

When Mr. Pirzada
Came to Dine

I N THE autumn of 1971 a man used to come to our house, bearing confections in his pocket and hopes of ascertaining the life or death of his family. His name was Mr. Pirzada, and he came from Dacca, now the capital of Bangladesh, but then a part of Pakistan. That year Pakistan was engaged in civil war. The eastern frontier, where Dacca was located, was fighting for autonomy from the ruling regime in the west. In March, Dacca had been invaded, torched, and shelled by the Pakistani army. Teachers were dragged onto streets and shot, women dragged into barracks and raped. By the end of the summer, three hundred thousand people were said to have died. In Dacca Mr. Pirzada had a three-story home, a lectureship in botany at the university, a wife of twenty years, and seven daughters between the ages of six and sixteen whose names all began with the letter A. "Their mother's idea," he explained one day, producing from his wallet a black-and-white picture of seven girls at a picnic, their braids tied with ribbons, sitting cross-legged in a row, eating chicken curry off of banana leaves. "How am I to distinguish? Ayesha, Amira, Amina, Aziza, you see the difficulty."

Each week Mr. Pirzada wrote letters to his wife, and sent comic books to each of his seven daughters, but the postal system, along with most everything else in Dacca, had collapsed, and he had not heard word of them in over six months. Mr. Pirzada, meanwhile, was in America for the year, for he had been awarded a grant from the government of Pakistan to study the foliage of New England. In spring and summer he had gathered data in Vermont and Maine, and in autumn he moved to a university north of Boston, where we lived, to write a short book about his discoveries. The grant was a great honor, but when converted into dollars it was not generous. As a result, Mr. Pirzada lived in a room in a graduate dormitory, and did not own a proper stove or a television set. And so he came to our house to eat dinner and watch the evening news.

At first I knew nothing of the reason for his visits. I was ten years old, and was not surprised that my parents, who were from India, and had a number of Indian acquaintances at the university, should ask Mr. Pirzada to share our meals. It was a small campus, with narrow brick walkways and white pillared buildings, located on the fringes of what seemed to be an even smaller town. The supermarket did not carry mustard oil, doctors did not make house calls, neighbors never dropped by without an invitation, and of these things, every so often, my parents complained. In search of compatriots, they used to trail their fingers, at the start of each new semester, through the columns of the university directory, circling surnames familiar to their part of the world. It was in this manner that they discovered Mr. Pirzada, and phoned him, and invited him to our home.

I have no memory of his first visit, or of his second or his third, but by the end of September I had grown so accustomed to Mr. Pirzada's presence in our living room that one evening, as I was dropping ice cubes into the water pitcher, I asked my mother to hand me a fourth glass from a cupboard still out of my reach. She was busy at the stove, presiding over a skillet of fried spinach with radishes, and could not hear me because of the drone of the exhaust fan and the fierce scrapes of her spatula. I turned to my father, who was leaning against the refrigerator, eating spiced cashews from a cupped fist.

"What is it, Lilia?"

"A glass for the Indian man."

"Mr. Pirzada won't be coming today. More importantly, Mr. Pirzada is no longer considered Indian," my father announced, brushing salt from the cashews out of his trim black beard. "Not since Partition. Our country was divided. 1947."

When I said I thought that was the date of India's independence from Britain, my father said, "That too. One moment we were free and then we were sliced up," he explained, drawing an X with his finger on the countertop, "like a pie. Hindus here, Muslims there. Dacca no longer belongs to us." He told me that during Partition Hindus and Muslims had set fire to each other's homes. For many, the idea of eating in the other's company was still unthinkable.

It made no sense to me. Mr. Pirzada and my parents spoke the same language, laughed at the same jokes, looked more or less the same. They ate pickled mangoes with their meals, ate rice every night for supper with their hands. Like my parents, Mr. Pirzada took off his shoes before entering a room, chewed fennel seeds after meals as a digestive, drank no alcohol, for dessert dipped austere biscuits into successive cups of tea. Nevertheless my father insisted that I understand the difference, and he led me to a map of the world taped to the wall over his desk. He seemed concerned that Mr. Pirzada might take offense if I accidentally referred to him as an Indian, though I could not really imagine Mr. Pirzada being offended by much of anything. "Mr. Pirzada is Bengali, but he is a Muslim," my father informed me. "Therefore he lives in East Pakistan, not India." His finger trailed across the Atlantic, through Europe, the Mediterranean, the Middle East, and finally to the sprawling orange diamond that my mother once told me resembled a woman wearing a sari with her left arm extended. Various cities had been circled with lines drawn between them to indicate my parents' travels, and the place of their birth, Calcutta, was signified by a small silver star. I had been there only once and had no memory of the trip. "As you see, Lilia, it is a different country, a different color," my father said. Pakistan was yellow, not orange. I noticed that there were two distinct parts to it, one much larger than the other, separated by an expanse of Indian territory; it was as if California and Connecticut constituted a nation apart from the U.S.

My father rapped his knuckles on top of my head. "You are, of course, aware of the current situation? Aware of East Pakistan's fight for sovereignty?"

I nodded, unaware of the situation.

We returned to the kitchen, where my mother was draining a pot of boiled rice into a colander. My father opened up the can on the counter and eyed me sharply over the frames of his glasses as he ate some more cashews. "What exactly do they teach you at school? Do you study history? Geography?"

"Lilia has plenty to learn at school," my mother said. "We live here now, she was born here." She seemed genuinely proud of the fact, as if it were a reflection of my character. In her estimation, I knew, I was assured a safe life, an easy life, a fine education, every opportunity. I would never have to eat rationed food, or obey curfews, or watch riots from my rooftop, or hide neighbors in water tanks to prevent them from being shot, as she and my father had. "Imagine having to place her in a decent school. Imagine her having to read during power failures by the light of kerosene lamps. Imagine the pressures, the tutors, the constant exams." She ran a hand through her hair, bobbed to a suitable length for her part-time job as a bank teller. "How can you possibly expect her to know about Partition? Put those nuts away."

"But what does she learn about the world?" My father rattled the cashew can in his hand. "What is she learning?"

We learned American history, of course, and American geography. That year, and every year, it seemed, we began by studying the Revolutionary War. We were taken in school buses on field trips to visit Plymouth Rock, and to walk the Freedom Trail, and to climb to the top of the Bunker Hill Monument. We made dioramas out of colored construction paper depicting George Washington crossing the choppy waters of the Delaware River, and we made puppets of King George wearing white tights and a black bow in his hair. During tests we were given blank maps of the thirteen colonies, and asked to fill in names, dates, capitals. I could do it with my eyes closed.

The next evening Mr. Pirzada arrived, as usual, at six o'clock. Though they were no longer strangers, upon first greeting each other, he and my father maintained the habit of shaking hands.

"Come in, sir. Lilia, Mr. Pirzada's coat, please."

He stepped into the foyer, impeccably suited and scarved, with a silk tie knotted at his collar. Each evening he appeared in ensembles of plums, olives, and chocolate browns. He was a compact man, and though his feet were perpetually splayed, and his belly slightly wide, he nevertheless maintained an efficient posture, as if balancing in either hand two suitcases of equal weight. His ears were insulated by tufts of graying hair that seemed to block out the unpleasant traffic of life. He had thickly lashed eyes shaded with a trace of camphor, a generous mustache that turned up playfully at the ends, and a mole shaped like a flattened raisin in the very center of his left cheek. On his head he wore a black fez made from the wool of Persian lambs, secured by bobby pins, without which I was never to see him. Though my father always offered to fetch him in our car, Mr. Pirzada preferred to walk from his dormitory to our neighborhood, a distance of about twenty minutes on foot, studying trees and shrubs on his way, and when he entered our house his knuckles were pink with the effects of crisp autumn air.

"Another refugee, I am afraid, on Indian territory."

"They are estimating nine million at the last count," my father said.

Mr. Pirzada handed me his coat, for it was my job to hang it on the rack at the bottom of the stairs. It was made of finely checkered gray-and-blue wool, with a striped lining and horn buttons, and carried in its weave the faint smell of limes. There were no recognizable tags inside, only a hand-stitched label with the phrase "Z. Sayeed, Suitors" embroidered on it in cursive with glossy black thread. On certain days a birch or maple leaf was tucked into a pocket. He unlaced his shoes and lined them against the baseboard; a golden paste clung to the toes and heels, the result of walking through our damp, unraked lawn. Relieved of his trappings, he grazed my throat with his short, restless fingers, the way a person feels for solidity behind a wall before driving in a nail. Then he followed my father to the living room, where the television was tuned to the local news. As soon as they were seated my mother appeared from the kitchen with a plate of mincemeat kebabs with coriander chutney. Mr. Pirzada popped one into his mouth.

"One can only hope," he said, reaching for another, "that Dacca's refugees are as heartily fed. Which reminds me." He reached into his suit pocket and gave me a small plastic egg filled with cinnamon hearts. "For the lady of the house," he said with an almost imperceptible splay-footed bow.

"Really, Mr. Pirzada," my mother protested. "Night after night. You spoil her."

"I only spoil children who are incapable of spoiling."

It was an awkward moment for me, one which I awaited in part with dread, in part with delight. I was charmed by the presence of Mr. Pirzada's rotund elegance, and flattered by the faint theatricality of his attentions, yet unsettled by the superb ease of his gestures, which made me feel, for an instant, like a stranger in my own home. It had become our ritual, and for several weeks, before we grew more comfortable with one another, it was the only time he spoke to me directly. I had no response, offered no comment, betrayed no visible reaction to the steady stream of honey-filled lozenges, the raspberry truffles, the slender rolls of sour pastilles. I could not even thank him, for once, when I did, for an especially spectacular peppermint lollipop wrapped in a spray of purple cellophane, he had demanded, "What is this thank-you? The lady at the bank thanks me, the cashier at the shop thanks me, the librarian thanks me when I return an overdue book, the overseas operator thanks me as she tries to connect me to Dacca and fails. If I am buried in this country I will be thanked, no doubt, at my funeral."

It was inappropriate, in my opinion, to consume the candy Mr. Pirzada gave me in a casual manner. I coveted each evening's treasure as I would a jewel, or a coin from a buried kingdom, and I would place it in a small keepsake box made of carved sandalwood beside my bed, in which, long ago in India, my father's mother used to store the ground areca nuts she ate after her morning bath. It was my only memento of a grandmother I had never known, and until Mr. Pirzada came to our lives I could find nothing to put inside it. Every so often before brushing my teeth and laying out my clothes for school the next day, I opened the lid of the box and ate one of his treats.

That night, like every night, we did not eat at the dining table, because it did not provide an unobstructed view of the television set. Instead we huddled around the coffee table, without conversing, our plates perched on our knees. From the kitchen my mother brought forth the succession of dishes: lentils with fried onions, green beans with coconut, fish cooked with raisins in a yogurt sauce. I followed with the water glasses, and the plate of lemon wedges, and the chili peppers, purchased on monthly trips to Chinatown and stored by the pound in the freezer, which they liked to snap open and crush into their food.

Before eating Mr. Pirzada always did a curious thing. He took out a plain silver watch without a band, which he kept in his breast pocket, held it briefly to one of his tufted ears, and wound it with three swift flicks of his thumb and forefinger. Unlike the watch on his wrist, the pocket watch, he had explained to me, was set to the local time in Dacca, eleven hours ahead. For the duration of the meal the watch rested on his folded paper napkin on the coffee table. He never seemed to consult it.

Now that I had learned Mr. Pirzada was not an Indian, I began to study him with extra care, to try to figure out what made him different. I decided that the pocket watch was one of those things. When I saw it that night, as he wound it and arranged it on the coffee table, an uneasiness possessed me; life, I realized, was being lived in Dacca first. I imagined Mr. Pirzada's daughters rising from sleep, tying ribbons in their hair, anticipating breakfast, preparing for school. Our meals, our actions, were only a shadow of what had already happened there, a lagging ghost of where Mr. Pirzada really belonged.

At six-thirty, which was when the national news began, my father raised the volume and adjusted the antennas. Usually I occupied myself with a book, but that night my father insisted that I pay attention. On the screen I saw tanks rolling through dusty streets, and fallen buildings, and forests of unfamiliar trees into which East Pakistani refugees had fled, seeking safety over the Indian border. I saw boats with fan-shaped sails floating on wide coffee-colored rivers, a barricaded university, newspaper offices burnt to the ground. I turned to look at Mr. Pirzada; the images flashed in miniature across his eyes. As he watched he had an immovable expression on his face, composed but alert, as if someone were giving him directions to an unknown destination.

During the commercial my mother went to the kitchen to get more rice, and my father and Mr. Pirzada deplored the policies of a general named Yahyah Khan. They discussed intrigues I did not know, a catastrophe I could not comprehend. "See, children your age, what they do to survive," my father said as he served me another piece of fish. But I could no longer eat. I could only steal glances at Mr. Pirzada, sitting beside me in his olive green jacket, calmly creating a well in his rice to make room for a second helping of lentils. He was not my notion of a man burdened by such grave concerns. I wondered if the reason he was always so smartly dressed was in preparation to endure with dignity whatever news assailed him, perhaps even to attend a funeral at a moment's notice. I wondered, too, what would happen if suddenly his seven daughters were to appear on television, smiling and waving and blowing kisses to Mr. Pirzada from a balcony. I imagined how relieved he would be. But this never happened.

That night when I placed the plastic egg filled with cinnamon hearts in the box beside my bed, I did not feel the ceremonious satisfaction I normally did. I tried not to think about Mr. Pirzada, in his lime-scented overcoat, connected to the unruly, sweltering world we had viewed a few hours ago in our bright, carpeted living room. And yet for several moments that was all I could think about. My stomach tightened as I worried whether his wife and seven daughters were now members of the drifting, clamoring crowd that had flashed at intervals on the screen. In an effort to banish the image I looked around my room, at the yellow canopied bed with matching flounced curtains, at framed class pictures mounted on white and violet papered walls, at the penciled inscriptions by the closet door where my father recorded my height on each of my birthdays. But the more I tried to distract myself, the more I began to convince myself that Mr. Pirzada's family was in all likelihood dead. Eventually I took a square of white chocolate out of the box, and unwrapped it, and then I did something I had never done before. I put the chocolate in my mouth, letting it soften until the last possible moment, and then as I chewed it slowly, I prayed that Mr. Pirzada's family was safe and sound. I had never prayed for anything before, had never been taught or told to, but I decided, given the circumstances, that it was something I should do. That night when I went to the bathroom I only pretended to brush my teeth, for I feared that I would somehow rinse the prayer out as well. I wet the brush and rearranged the tube of paste to prevent my parents from asking any questions, and fell asleep with sugar on my tongue.

No one at school talked about the war followed so faithfully in my living room. We continued to study the American Revolution, and learned about the injustices of taxation without representation, and memorized passages from the Declaration of Independence. During recess the boys would divide in two groups, chasing each other wildly around the swings and seesaws, Redcoats against the colonies. In the classroom our teacher, Mrs. Kenyon, pointed frequently to a map that emerged like a movie screen from the top of the chalkboard, charting the route of the *Mayflower*, or showing us the location of the Liberty Bell. Each week two members of the class gave a report on a particular aspect of the Revolution, and so one day I was sent to the school library with my friend Dora to learn about the surrender at Yorktown. Mrs. Kenyon handed us a slip of paper with the names of three books to look up in the card catalogue. We found them right away, and sat down at a low round table to read and take notes. But I could not concentrate. I returned to the blond-wood shelves, to a section I had noticed labeled "Asia." I saw books about China, India, Indonesia, Korea. Eventually I found a book titled *Pakistan: A Land and Its People*. I sat on a footstool and opened the book. The laminated jacket crackled in my grip. I began turning the pages, filled with photos of rivers and rice fields and men in military uniforms. There was a chapter about Dacca, and I began to read about its rainfall, and its jute production. I was studying a population chart when Dora appeared in the aisle.

"What are you doing back here? Mrs. Kenyon's in the library. She came to check up on us."

I slammed the book shut, too loudly. Mrs. Kenyon emerged, the aroma of her perfume filling up the tiny aisle, and lifted the book by the tip of its spine as if it were a hair clinging to my sweater. She glanced at the cover, then at me.

"Is this book a part of your report, Lilia?"

"No, Mrs. Kenyon."

"Then I see no reason to consult it," she said, replacing it in the slim gap on the shelf. "Do you?"

As weeks passed it grew more and more rare to see any footage from Dacca on the news. The report came after the first set of commercials, sometimes the second. The press had been censored, removed, restricted, rerouted. Some days, many days, only a death toll was announced, prefaced by a reiteration of the general situation. More poets were executed, more villages set ablaze. In spite of it all, night after night, my parents and

Mr. Pirzada enjoyed long, leisurely meals. After the television was shut off, and the dishes washed and dried, they joked, and told stories, and dipped biscuits in their tea. When they tired of discussing political matters they discussed, instead, the progress of Mr. Pirzada's book about the deciduous trees of New England, and my father's nomination for tenure, and the peculiar eating habits of my mother's American coworkers at the bank. Eventually I was sent upstairs to do my homework, but through the carpet I heard them as they drank more tea, and listened to cassettes of Kishore Kumar, and played Scrabble on the coffee table, laughing and arguing long into the night about the spellings of English words. I wanted to join them, wanted, above all, to console Mr. Pirzada somehow. But apart from eating a piece of candy for the sake of his family and praying for their safety, there was nothing I could do. They played Scrabble until the eleven o'clock news, and then, sometime around midnight, Mr. Pirzada walked back to his dormitory. For this reason I never saw him leave, but each night as I drifted off to sleep I would hear them, anticipating the birth of a nation on the other side of the world.

One day in October Mr. Pirzada asked upon arrival, "What are these large orange vegetables on people's doorsteps? A type of squash?"

"Pumpkins," my mother replied. "Lilia, remind me to pick one up at the supermarket."

"And the purpose? It indicates what?"

"You make a jack-o'-lantern," I said, grinning ferociously. "Like this. To scare people away."

"I see," Mr. Pirzada said, grinning back. "Very useful."

The next day my mother bought a ten-pound pumpkin, fat and round, and placed it on the dining table. Before supper, while my father and Mr. Pirzada were watching the local news, she told me to decorate it with markers, but I wanted to carve it properly like others I had noticed in the neighborhood.

"Yes, let's carve it," Mr. Pirzada agreed, and rose from the sofa. "Hang the news tonight." Asking no questions, he walked into the kitchen, opened a drawer, and returned, bearing a long serrated knife. He glanced at me for approval. "Shall I?"

I nodded. For the first time we all gathered around the dining table, my mother, my father, Mr. Pirzada, and I. While the television aired unattended we covered the tabletop with newspapers. Mr. Pirzada draped his jacket over the chair behind him, removed a pair of opal cuff links, and rolled up the starched sleeves of his shirt.

"First go around the top, like this," I instructed, demonstrating with my index finger.

He made an initial incision and drew the knife around. When he had come full circle he lifted the cap by the stem; it loosened effortlessly, and Mr. Pirzada leaned over the pumpkin for a moment to inspect and inhale its contents. My mother gave him a long metal spoon with which he gutted the interior until the last bits of string and seeds were gone. My father, meanwhile, separated the seeds from the pulp and set them out to dry on a cookie sheet, so that we could roast them later on. I drew two triangles against the ridged surface for the eyes, which Mr. Pirzada dutifully carved, and crescents for eyebrows, and another triangle for the nose. The mouth was all that remained, and the teeth posed a challenge. I hesitated.

"Smile or frown?" I asked.

"You choose," Mr. Pirzada said.

As a compromise I drew a kind of grimace, straight across, neither mournful nor friendly. Mr. Pirzada began carving, without the least bit of intimidation, as if he had been carving jack-o'-lanterns his whole life. He had nearly finished when the national news began. The reporter mentioned Dacca, and we all turned to listen: An Indian official announced that unless the world helped to relieve the burden of East Pakistani refugees, India would have to go to war against Pakistan. The reporter's face dripped with sweat as he relayed the information. He did not wear a tie or a jacket, dressed instead as if he himself were about to take part in the battle. He shielded his scorched face as he hollered things to the cameraman. The knife slipped from Mr. Pirzada's hand and made a gash dipping toward the base of the pumpkin.

"Please forgive me." He raised a hand to one side of his face, as if someone had slapped him there. "I am—it is terrible. I will buy another. We will try again."

"Not at all, not at all," my father said. He took the knife from Mr. Pirzada, and carved around the gash, evening it out, dispensing altogether with the teeth I had drawn. What resulted was a disproportionately large hole the size of a lemon, so that our jack-o'-lantern wore an expression of placid astonishment, the eyebrows no longer fierce, floating in frozen surprise above a vacant, geometric gaze.

For Halloween I was a witch. Dora, my trick-or-treating partner, was a witch too. We wore black capes fashioned from dyed pillowcases and conical hats with wide cardboard brims. We shaded our faces green with a broken eye shadow that belonged to Dora's mother, and my mother gave us two burlap sacks that had once contained basmati rice, for collecting candy. That year our parents decided that we were old enough to roam the neighborhood unattended. Our plan was to walk from my house to Dora's, from where I was to call to say I had arrived safely, and then Dora's mother would drive me home. My father equipped us with flashlights, and I had to wear my watch and synchronize it with his. We were to return no later than nine o'clock.

When Mr. Pirzada arrived that evening he presented me with a box of chocolate-covered mints.

"In here," I told him, and opened up the burlap sack. "Trick or treat!"

"I understand that you don't really need my contribution this evening," he said, depositing the box. He gazed at my green face, and the hat secured by a string under my chin. Gingerly he lifted the hem of the cape, under which I was wearing a sweater and a zipped fleece jacket. "Will you be warm enough?"

I nodded, causing the hat to tip to one side.

He set it right. "Perhaps it is best to stand still."

The bottom of our staircase was lined with baskets of miniature candy, and when Mr. Pirzada removed his shoes he did not place them there as he normally did, but inside the closet instead. He began to unbutton his coat, and I waited to take it from him, but Dora called me from the bathroom to say that she needed my help drawing a mole on her chin. When we were finally ready my mother took a picture of us in front of the fireplace, and then I opened the front door to leave. Mr. Pirzada and my father, who had not gone into the living room yet, hovered in the foyer. Outside it was already dark. The air smelled of wet leaves, and our carved jack-o'-lantern flickered impressively against the shrubbery by the door. In the distance came the sounds of scampering feet, and the howls of the older boys who wore no costume at all other than a rubber mask, and the rustling apparel of the youngest children, some so young that they were carried from door to door in the arms of their parents.

"Don't go into any of the houses you don't know," my father warned.

Mr. Pirzada knit his brows together. "Is there any danger?"

"No, no," my mother assured him. "All the children will be out. It's a tradition."

"Perhaps I should accompany them?" Mr. Pirzada suggested. He looked suddenly tired and small, standing there in his splayed, stockinged feet, and his eyes contained a panic I had never seen before. In spite of the cold I began to sweat inside my pillowcase.

"Really, Mr. Pirzada," my mother said, "Lilia will be perfectly safe with her friend."

"But if it rains? If they lose their way?"

"Don't worry," I said. It was the first time I had uttered those words to Mr. Pirzada, two simple words I had tried but failed to tell him for weeks, had said only in my prayers. It shamed me now that I had said them for my own sake.

He placed one of his stocky fingers on my cheek, then pressed it to the back of his own hand, leaving a faint green smear. "If the lady insists," he conceded, and offered a small bow.

We left, stumbling slightly in our black pointy thrift-store shoes, and when we turned at the end of the driveway to wave good-bye, Mr. Pirzada was standing in the frame of the doorway, a short figure between my parents, waving back.

"Why did that man want to come with us?" Dora asked.

"His daughters are missing." As soon as I said it, I wished I had not. I felt that my saying it made it true, that Mr. Pirzada's daughters really were missing, and that he would never see them again.

"You mean they were kidnapped?" Dora continued. "From a park or something?"

"I didn't mean they were missing. I meant, he misses them. They live in a different country, and he hasn't seen them in a while, that's all."

We went from house to house, walking along pathways and pressing doorbells. Some people had switched off all their lights for effect, or strung rubber bats in their windows. At the McIntyres' a coffin was placed in front of the door, and Mr. Mc-

Intyre rose from it in silence, his face covered with chalk, and deposited a fistful of candy corns into our sacks. Several people told me that they had never seen an Indian witch before. Others performed the transaction without comment. As we paved our way with the parallel beams of our flashlights we saw eggs cracked in the middle of the road, and cars covered with shaving cream, and toilet paper garlanding the branches of trees. By the time we reached Dora's house our hands were chapped from carrying our bulging burlap bags, and our feet were sore and swollen. Her mother gave us bandages for our blisters and served us warm cider and caramel popcorn. She reminded me to call my parents to tell them I had arrived safely, and when I did I could hear the television in the background. My mother did not seem particularly relieved to hear from me. When I replaced the phone on the receiver it occurred to me that the television wasn't on at Dora's house at all. Her father was lying on the couch, reading a magazine, with a glass of wine on the coffee table, and there was saxophone music playing on the stereo.

After Dora and I had sorted through our plunder, and counted and sampled and traded until we were satisfied, her mother drove me back to my house. I thanked her for the ride, and she waited in the driveway until I made it to the door. In the glare of her headlights I saw that our pumpkin had been shattered, its thick shell strewn in chunks across the grass. I felt the sting of tears in my eyes, and a sudden pain in my throat, as if it had been stuffed with the sharp tiny pebbles that crunched with each step under my aching feet. I opened the door, expecting the three of them to be standing in the foyer, waiting to receive me, and to grieve for our ruined pumpkin, but there was no one. In the living room Mr. Pirzada, my father, and mother were sitting side by side on the sofa. The television was turned off, and Mr. Pirzada had his head in his hands.

What they heard that evening, and for many evenings after that, was that India and Pakistan were drawing closer and closer to war. Troops from both sides lined the border, and Dacca was insisting on nothing short of independence. The war was to be waged on East Pakistani soil. The United States was siding with West Pakistan, the Soviet Union with India and what was soon to be Bangladesh. War was declared officially on December 4, and twelve days later, the Pakistani army, weakened by having to fight three thousand miles from its source of supplies, surrendered in Dacca. All of these facts I know only now, for they are available to me in any history book, in any library. But then it remained, for the most part, a remote mystery with haphazard clues. What I remember during those twelve days of the war was that my father no longer asked me to watch the news with them, and that Mr. Pirzada stopped bringing me candy, and that my mother refused to serve anything other than boiled eggs with rice for dinner. I remember some nights helping my mother spread a sheet and blankets on the couch so that Mr. Pirzada could sleep there, and high-pitched voices hollering in the middle of the night when my parents called our relatives in Calcutta to learn more details about the situation. Most of all I remember the three of them operating during that time as if they were a single person, sharing a single meal, a single body, a single silence, and a single fear.

In January, Mr. Pirzada flew back to his three-story home in Dacca, to discover what was left of it. We did not see much of him in those final weeks of the year; he was busy finishing his manuscript, and we went to Philadelphia to spend Christmas with friends of my parents. Just as I have no memory of his first visit, I have no memory of his last. My father drove him to the airport one afternoon while I was at school. For a long time we did not hear from him. Our evenings went on as usual, with dinners in front of the news. The only difference was that Mr. Pirzada and his extra watch were not there to accompany us. According to reports Dacca was repairing itself slowly, with a newly formed parliamentary government. The new leader, Sheikh Mujib Rahman, recently released from prison, asked countries for building materials to replace more than one million houses that had been destroyed in the war. Countless refugees returned from India, greeted, we learned, by unemployment and the threat of famine. Every now and then I studied the map above my father's desk and pictured Mr. Pirzada on that small patch of yellow, perspiring heavily, I imagined, in one of his suits, searching for his family. Of course, the map was outdated by then.

Finally, several months later, we received a card from Mr. Pirzada commemorating the Muslim New Year, along with a short letter. He was reunited, he wrote, with his wife and children. All were well, having survived the events of the past year at an estate belonging to his wife's grandparents in the mountains of Shillong. His seven daughters were a bit taller, he wrote, but otherwise they were the same, and he still could not keep their names in order. At the end of the letter he thanked us for our hospitality, adding that although he now understood the meaning of the words "thank you" they still were not adequate to express his gratitude. To celebrate the good news my mother prepared a special dinner that evening, and when we sat down to eat at the coffee table we toasted our water glasses, but I did not feel like celebrating. Though I had not seen him for months, it was only then that I felt Mr. Pirzada's absence. It was only then, raising my water glass in his name, that I knew what it meant to miss someone who was so many miles and hours away, just as he had missed his wife and daughters for so many months. He had no reason to return to us, and my parents predicted, correctly, that we would never see him again. Since January, each night before bed, I had continued to eat, for the sake of Mr. Pirzada's family, a piece of candy I had saved from Halloween. That night there was no need to. Eventually, I threw them away.

Interpreter of Maladies

A T THE tea stall Mr. and Mrs. Das bickered about who should take Tina to the toilet. Eventually Mrs. Das relented when Mr. Das pointed out that he had given the girl her bath the night before. In the rearview mirror Mr. Kapasi watched as Mrs. Das emerged slowly from his bulky white Ambassador, dragging her shaved, largely bare legs across the back seat. She did not hold the little girl's hand as they walked to the rest room.

They were on their way to see the Sun Temple at Konarak. It was a dry, bright Saturday, the mid-July heat tempered by a steady ocean breeze, ideal weather for sightseeing. Ordinarily Mr. Kapasi would not have stopped so soon along the way, but less than five minutes after he'd picked up the family that morning in front of Hotel Sandy Villa, the little girl had complained. The first thing Mr. Kapasi had noticed when he saw Mr. and Mrs. Das, standing with their children under the portico of the hotel, was that they were very young, perhaps not even thirty. In addition to Tina they had two boys, Ronny and Bobby, who appeared very close in age and had teeth covered in a network of flashing silver wires. The family looked Indian but dressed as foreigners did, the children in stiff, brightly colored clothing and caps with translucent visors. Mr. Kapasi was accustomed to foreign tourists; he was assigned to them regularly because he could speak English. Yesterday he had driven an elderly couple from Scotland, both with spotted faces and fluffy white hair so thin it exposed their sunburnt scalps. In comparison, the tanned, youthful faces of Mr. and Mrs. Das were all the more striking. When he'd introduced himself, Mr. Kapasi had pressed his palms together in greeting, but Mr. Das squeezed hands like an American so that Mr. Kapasi felt it in his elbow. Mrs. Das, for her part, had flexed one side of her mouth, smiling dutifully at Mr. Kapasi, without displaying any interest in him.

As they waited at the tea stall, Ronny, who looked like the older of the two boys, clambered suddenly out of the back seat, intrigued by a goat tied to a stake in the ground.

"Don't touch it," Mr. Das said. He glanced up from his paperback tour book, which said "INDIA" in yellow letters and looked as if it had been published abroad. His voice, somehow tentative and a little shrill, sounded as though it had not yet settled into maturity.

"I want to give it a piece of gum," the boy called back as he trotted ahead.

Mr. Das stepped out of the car and stretched his legs by squatting briefly to the ground. A clean-shaven man, he looked exactly like a magnified version of Ronny. He had a sapphire blue visor, and was dressed in shorts, sneakers, and a T-shirt. The camera slung around his neck, with an impressive telephoto lens and numerous buttons and markings, was the only complicated thing he wore. He frowned, watching as Ronny rushed toward the goat, but appeared to have no intention of intervening. "Bobby, make sure that your brother doesn't do anything stupid."

"I don't feel like it," Bobby said, not moving. He was sitting in the front seat beside Mr. Kapasi, studying a picture of the elephant god taped to the glove compartment.

"No need to worry," Mr. Kapasi said. "They are quite tame." Mr. Kapasi was forty-six years old, with receding hair that had gone completely silver, but his butterscotch complexion and his unlined brow, which he treated in spare moments to dabs of lotus-oil balm, made it easy to imagine what he must have looked like at an earlier age. He wore gray trousers and a matching jacket-style shirt, tapered at the waist, with short sleeves and a large pointed collar, made of a thin but durable synthetic material. He had specified both the cut and the fabric to his tailor — it was his preferred uniform for giving tours because it did not get crushed during his long hours behind the wheel. Through the windshield he watched as Ronny circled around the goat, touched it quickly on its side, then trotted back to the car.

"You left India as a child?" Mr. Kapasi asked when Mr. Das had settled once again into the passenger seat.

"Oh, Mina and I were both born in America," Mr. Das announced with an air of sudden confidence. "Born and raised. Our parents live here now. They retired. We visit them every couple years." He turned to watch as the little girl ran toward the car, the wide purple bows of her sundress flopping on her narrow brown shoulders. She was holding to her chest a doll with yellow hair that looked as if it had been chopped, as a punitive measure, with a pair of dull scissors. "This is Tina's first trip to India, isn't it, Tina?"

"I don't have to go to the bathroom anymore," Tina announced.

"Where's Mina?" Mr. Das asked.

Mr. Kapasi found it strange that Mr. Das should refer to his wife by her first name when speaking to the little girl. Tina pointed to where Mrs. Das was purchasing something from one of the shirtless men who worked at the tea stall. Mr. Kapasi heard one of the shirtless men sing a phrase from a popular Hindi love song as Mrs. Das walked back to the car, but she did not appear to understand the words of the song, for she did not express irritation, or embarrassment, or react in any other way to the man's declarations.

He observed her. She wore a red-and-white-checkered skirt that stopped above her knees, slip-on shoes with a square wooden heel, and a close-fitting blouse styled like a man's undershirt. The blouse was decorated at chest-level with a calico appliqué in the shape of a strawberry. She was a short woman, with small hands like paws, her frosty pink fingernails painted to match her lips, and was slightly plump in her figure. Her hair, shorn only a little longer than her husband's, was parted far to one side. She was wearing large dark brown sunglasses with a pinkish tint to them, and carried a big straw bag, almost as big as her torso, shaped like a bowl, with a water bottle poking out of it. She walked slowly, carrying some puffed rice tossed with peanuts and chili peppers in a large packet made from newspapers. Mr. Kapasi turned to Mr. Das.

"Where in America do you live?"

"New Brunswick, New Jersey."

"Next to New York?"

"Exactly. I teach middle school there."

"What subject?"

"Science. In fact, every year I take my students on a trip to the Museum of Natural History in New York City. In a way we have a lot in common, you could say, you and I. How long have you been a tour guide, Mr. Kapasi?"

"Five years."

Mrs. Das reached the car. "How long's the trip?" she asked, shutting the door.

"About two and a half hours," Mr. Kapasi replied.

At this Mrs. Das gave an impatient sigh, as if she had been

traveling her whole life without pause. She fanned herself with a folded Bombay film magazine written in English.

"I thought that the Sun Temple is only eighteen miles north of Puri," Mr. Das said, tapping on the tour book.

"The roads to Konarak are poor. Actually it is a distance of fifty-two miles," Mr. Kapasi explained.

Mr. Das nodded, readjusting the camera strap where it had begun to chafe the back of his neck.

Before starting the ignition, Mr. Kapasi reached back to make sure the cranklike locks on the inside of each of the back doors were secured. As soon as the car began to move the little girl began to play with the lock on her side, clicking it with some effort forward and backward, but Mrs. Das said nothing to stop her. She sat a bit slouched at one end of the back seat, not offering her puffed rice to anyone. Ronny and Tina sat on either side of her, both snapping bright green gum.

"Look," Bobby said as the car began to gather speed. He pointed with his finger to the tall trees that lined the road. "Look."

"Monkeys!" Ronny shrieked. "Wow!"

They were seated in groups along the branches, with shining black faces, silver bodies, horizontal eyebrows, and crested heads. Their long gray tails dangled like a series of ropes among the leaves. A few scratched themselves with black leathery hands, or swung their feet, staring as the car passed.

"We call them the hanuman," Mr. Kapasi said. "They are quite common in the area."

As soon as he spoke, one of the monkeys leaped into the middle of the road, causing Mr. Kapasi to brake suddenly. Another bounced onto the hood of the car, then sprang away. Mr. Kapasi beeped his horn. The children began to get excited, sucking in their breath and covering their faces partly with their hands. They had never seen monkeys outside of a zoo,

Mr. Das explained. He asked Mr. Kapasi to stop the car so that he could take a picture.

While Mr. Das adjusted his telephoto lens, Mrs. Das reached into her straw bag and pulled out a bottle of colorless nail polish, which she proceeded to stroke on the tip of her index finger.

The little girl stuck out a hand. "Mine too. Mommy, do mine too."

"Leave me alone," Mrs. Das said, blowing on her nail and turning her body slightly. "You're making me mess up."

The little girl occupied herself by buttoning and unbuttoning a pinafore on the doll's plastic body.

"All set," Mr. Das said, replacing the lens cap.

The car rattled considerably as it raced along the dusty road, causing them all to pop up from their seats every now and then, but Mrs. Das continued to polish her nails. Mr. Kapasi eased up on the accelerator, hoping to produce a smoother ride. When he reached for the gearshift the boy in front accommodated him by swinging his hairless knees out of the way. Mr. Kapasi noted that this boy was slightly paler than the other children. "Daddy, why is the driver sitting on the wrong side in this car, too?" the boy asked.

"They all do that here, dummy," Ronny said.

"Don't call your brother a dummy," Mr. Das said. He turned to Mr. Kapasi. "In America, you know . . . it confuses them."

"Oh yes, I am well aware," Mr. Kapasi said. As delicately as he could, he shifted gears again, accelerating as they approached a hill in the road. "I see it on *Dallas*, the steering wheels are on the left-hand side."

"What's *Dallas*?" Tina asked, banging her now naked doll on the seat behind Mr. Kapasi.

"It went off the air," Mr. Das explained. "It's a television show."

They were all like siblings, Mr. Kapasi thought as they

passed a row of date trees. Mr. and Mrs. Das behaved like an older brother and sister, not parents. It seemed that they were in charge of the children only for the day; it was hard to believe they were regularly responsible for anything other than themselves. Mr. Das tapped on his lens cap, and his tour book, dragging his thumbnail occasionally across the pages so that they made a scraping sound. Mrs. Das continued to polish her nails. She had still not removed her sunglasses. Every now and then Tina renewed her plea that she wanted her nails done, too, and so at one point Mrs. Das flicked a drop of polish on the little girl's finger before depositing the bottle back inside her straw bag.

"Isn't this an air-conditioned car?" she asked, still blowing on her hand. The window on Tina's side was broken and could not be rolled down.

"Quit complaining," Mr. Das said. "It isn't so hot."

"I told you to get a car with air-conditioning," Mrs. Das continued. "Why do you do this, Raj, just to save a few stupid rupees. What are you saving us, fifty cents?"

Their accents sounded just like the ones Mr. Kapasi heard on American television programs, though not like the ones on *Dallas*.

"Doesn't it get tiresome, Mr. Kapasi, showing people the same thing every day?" Mr. Das asked, rolling down his own window all the way. "Hey, do you mind stopping the car. I just want to get a shot of this guy."

Mr. Kapasi pulled over to the side of the road as Mr. Das took a picture of a barefoot man, his head wrapped in a dirty turban, seated on top of a cart of grain sacks pulled by a pair of bullocks. Both the man and the bullocks were emaciated. In the back seat Mrs. Das gazed out another window, at the sky, where nearly transparent clouds passed quickly in front of one another.

"I look forward to it, actually," Mr. Kapasi said as they continued on their way. "The Sun Temple is one of my favorite places. In that way it is a reward for me. I give tours on Fridays and Saturdays only. I have another job during the week."

"Oh? Where?" Mr. Das asked.

"I work in a doctor's office."

"You're a doctor?"

"I am not a doctor. I work with one. As an interpreter."

"What does a doctor need an interpreter for?"

"He has a number of Gujarati patients. My father was Gujarati, but many people do not speak Gujarati in this area, including the doctor. And so the doctor asked me to work in his office, interpreting what the patients say."

"Interesting. I've never heard of anything like that," Mr. Das said.

Mr. Kapasi shrugged. "It is a job like any other."

"But so romantic," Mrs. Das said dreamily, breaking her extended silence. She lifted her pinkish brown sunglasses and arranged them on top of her head like a tiara. For the first time, her eyes met Mr. Kapasi's in the rearview mirror: pale, a bit small, their gaze fixed but drowsy.

Mr. Das craned to look at her. "What's so romantic about it?"

"I don't know. Something." She shrugged, knitting her brows together for an instant. "Would you like a piece of gum, Mr. Kapasi?" she asked brightly. She reached into her straw bag and handed him a small square wrapped in green-and-white-striped paper. As soon as Mr. Kapasi put the gum in his mouth a thick sweet liquid burst onto his tongue.

"Tell us more about your job, Mr. Kapasi," Mrs. Das said.

"What would you like to know, madame?"

"I don't know," again she shrugged, munching on some puffed rice and licking the mustard oil from the corners of her mouth. "Tell us a typical situation." She settled back in her seat, her head tilted in a patch of sun, and closed her eyes. "I want to picture what happens."

"Very well. The other day a man came in with a pain in his throat."

"Did he smoke cigarettes?"

"No. It was very curious. He complained that he felt as if there were long pieces of straw stuck in his throat. When I told the doctor he was able to prescribe the proper medication."

"That's so neat."

"Yes," Mr. Kapasi agreed after some hesitation.

"So these patients are totally dependent on you," Mrs. Das said. She spoke slowly, as if she were thinking aloud. "In a way, more dependent on you than the doctor."

"How do you mean? How could it be?"

"Well, for example, you could tell the doctor that the pain felt like a burning, not straw. The patient would never know what you had told the doctor, and the doctor wouldn't know that you had told the wrong thing. It's a big responsibility."

"Yes, a big responsibility you have there, Mr. Kapasi," Mr. Das agreed.

Mr. Kapasi had never thought of his job in such complimentary terms. To him it was a thankless occupation. He found nothing noble in interpreting people's maladies, assiduously translating the symptoms of so many swollen bones, countless cramps of bellies and bowels, spots on people's palms that changed color, shape, or size. The doctor, nearly half his age, had an affinity for bell-bottom trousers and made humorless jokes about the Congress party. Together they worked in a stale little infirmary where Mr. Kapasi's smartly tailored clothes clung to him in the heat, in spite of the blackened blades of a ceiling fan churning over their heads.

The job was a sign of his failings. In his youth he'd been a devoted scholar of foreign languages, the owner of an impressive collection of dictionaries. He had dreamed of being an interpreter for diplomats and dignitaries, resolving conflicts between people and nations, settling disputes of which he alone could understand both sides. He was a self-educated man. In a series of notebooks, in the evenings before his parents settled his marriage, he had listed the common etymologies of words, and at one point in his life he was confident that he could converse, if given the opportunity, in English, French, Russian, Portuguese, and Italian, not to mention Hindi, Bengali, Oriya, and Gujarati. Now only a handful of European phrases remained in his memory, scattered words for things like saucers and chairs. English was the only non-Indian language he spoke fluently anymore. Mr. Kapasi knew it was not a remarkable talent. Sometimes he feared that his children knew better English than he did, just from watching television. Still, it came in handy for the tours.

He had taken the job as an interpreter after his first son, at the age of seven, contracted typhoid—that was how he had first made the acquaintance of the doctor. At the time Mr. Kapasi had been teaching English in a grammar school, and he bartered his skills as an interpreter to pay the increasingly exorbitant medical bills. In the end the boy had died one evening in his mother's arms, his limbs burning with fever, but then there was the funeral to pay for, and the other children who were born soon enough, and the newer, bigger house, and the good schools and tutors, and the fine shoes and the television, and the countless other ways he tried to console his wife and to keep her from crying in her sleep, and so when the doctor offered to pay him twice as much as he earned at the grammar school, he accepted. Mr. Kapasi knew that his wife had little regard for his career as an interpreter. He knew it reminded her of the son she'd lost, and that she resented the other lives he helped, in his own small way, to save. If ever she referred to his position, she used the phrase "doctor's assistant," as if the process of interpretation were equal to taking someone's temperature, or changing a bedpan. She never asked him about the patients who came to the doctor's office, or said that his job was a big responsibility.

For this reason it flattered Mr. Kapasi that Mrs. Das was so intrigued by his job. Unlike his wife, she had reminded him of its intellectual challenges. She had also used the word "romantic." She did not behave in a romantic way toward her husband, and yet she had used the word to describe him. He wondered if Mr. and Mrs. Das were a bad match, just as he and his wife were. Perhaps they, too, had little in common apart from three children and a decade of their lives. The signs he recognized from his own marriage were there—the bickering, the indifference, the protracted silences. Her sudden interest in him, an interest she did not express in either her husband or her children, was mildly intoxicating. When Mr. Kapasi thought once again about how she had said "romantic," the feeling of intoxication grew.

He began to check his reflection in the rearview mirror as he drove, feeling grateful that he had chosen the gray suit that morning and not the brown one, which tended to sag a little in the knees. From time to time he glanced through the mirror at Mrs. Das. In addition to glancing at her face he glanced at the strawberry between her breasts, and the golden brown hollow in her throat. He decided to tell Mrs. Das about another patient, and another: the young woman who had complained of a sensation of raindrops in her spine, the gentleman whose birthmark had begun to sprout hairs. Mrs. Das listened attentively, stroking her hair with a small plastic brush that resembled an oval bed of nails, asking more questions, for yet another example. The children were quiet, intent on spotting more monkeys in the trees, and Mr. Das was absorbed by his tour book, so it seemed like a private conversation between Mr.

Kapasi and Mrs. Das. In this manner the next half hour passed, and when they stopped for lunch at a roadside restaurant that sold fritters and omelette sandwiches, usually something Mr. Kapasi looked forward to on his tours so that he could sit in peace and enjoy some hot tea, he was disappointed. As the Das family settled together under a magenta umbrella fringed with white and orange tassels, and placed their orders with one of the waiters who marched about in tricornered caps, Mr. Kapasi reluctantly headed toward a neighboring table.

"Mr. Kapasi, wait. There's room here," Mrs. Das called out. She gathered Tina onto her lap, insisting that he accompany them. And so, together, they had bottled mango juice and sandwiches and plates of onions and potatoes deep-fried in graham-flour batter. After finishing two omelette sandwiches Mr. Das took more pictures of the group as they ate.

"How much longer?" he asked Mr. Kapasi as he paused to load a new roll of film in the camera.

"About half an hour more."

By now the children had gotten up from the table to look at more monkeys perched in a nearby tree, so there was a considerable space between Mrs. Das and Mr. Kapasi. Mr. Das placed the camera to his face and squeezed one eye shut, his tongue exposed at one corner of his mouth. "This looks funny. Mina, you need to lean in closer to Mr. Kapasi."

She did. He could smell a scent on her skin, like a mixture of whiskey and rosewater. He worried suddenly that she could smell his perspiration, which he knew had collected beneath the synthetic material of his shirt. He polished off his mango juice in one gulp and smoothed his silver hair with his hands. A bit of the juice dripped onto his chin. He wondered if Mrs. Das had noticed.

She had not. "What's your address, Mr. Kapasi?" she inquired, fishing for something inside her straw bag.

"You would like my address?"

"So we can send you copies," she said. "Of the pictures." She handed him a scrap of paper which she had hastily ripped from a page of her film magazine. The blank portion was limited, for the narrow strip was crowded by lines of text and a tiny picture of a hero and heroine embracing under a eucalyptus tree.

The paper curled as Mr. Kapasi wrote his address in clear, careful letters. She would write to him, asking about his days interpreting at the doctor's office, and he would respond eloquently, choosing only the most entertaining anecdotes, ones that would make her laugh out loud as she read them in her house in New Jersey. In time she would reveal the disappointment of her marriage, and he his. In this way their friendship would grow, and flourish. He would possess a picture of the two of them, eating fried onions under a magenta umbrella, which he would keep, he decided, safely tucked between the pages of his Russian grammar. As his mind raced, Mr. Kapasi experienced a mild and pleasant shock. It was similar to a feeling he used to experience long ago when, after months of translating with the aid of a dictionary, he would finally read a passage from a French novel, or an Italian sonnet, and understand the words, one after another, unencumbered by his own efforts. In those moments Mr. Kapasi used to believe that all was right with the world, that all struggles were rewarded, that all of life's mistakes made sense in the end. The promise that he would hear from Mrs. Das now filled him with the same belief.

When he finished writing his address Mr. Kapasi handed her the paper, but as soon as he did so he worried that he had either misspelled his name, or accidentally reversed the numbers of his postal code. He dreaded the possibility of a lost letter, the photograph never reaching him, hovering somewhere in Orissa, close but ultimately unattainable. He thought of asking for the slip of paper again, just to make sure he had written his address accurately, but Mrs. Das had already dropped it into the jumble of her bag.

They reached Konarak at two-thirty. The temple, made of sandstone, was a massive pyramid-like structure in the shape of a chariot. It was dedicated to the great master of life, the sun, which struck three sides of the edifice as it made its journey each day across the sky. Twenty-four giant wheels were carved on the north and south sides of the plinth. The whole thing was drawn by a team of seven horses, speeding as if through the heavens. As they approached, Mr. Kapasi explained that the temple had been built between A.D. 1243 and 1255, with the efforts of twelve hundred artisans, by the great ruler of the Ganga dynasty, King Narasimhadeva the First, to commemorate his victory against the Muslim army.

"It says the temple occupies about a hundred and seventy acres of land," Mr. Das said, reading from his book.

"It's like a desert," Ronny said, his eyes wandering across the sand that stretched on all sides beyond the temple.

"The Chandrabhaga River once flowed one mile north of here. It is dry now," Mr. Kapasi said, turning off the engine.

They got out and walked toward the temple, posing first for pictures by the pair of lions that flanked the steps. Mr. Kapasi led them next to one of the wheels of the chariot, higher than any human being, nine feet in diameter.

"'The wheels are supposed to symbolize the wheel of life,'" Mr. Das read. "'They depict the cycle of creation, preservation, and achievement of realization.' Cool." He turned the page of his book. "'Each wheel is divided into eight thick and thin spokes, dividing the day into eight equal parts. The rims are carved with designs of birds and animals, whereas the medallions in the spokes are carved with women in luxurious poses, largely erotic in nature.'"

What he referred to were the countless friezes of entwined naked bodies, making love in various positions, women clinging to the necks of men, their knees wrapped eternally around their lovers' thighs. In addition to these were assorted scenes from daily life, of hunting and trading, of deer being killed with bows and arrows and marching warriors holding swords in their hands.

It was no longer possible to enter the temple, for it had filled with rubble years ago, but they admired the exterior, as did all the tourists Mr. Kapasi brought there, slowly strolling along each of its sides. Mr. Das trailed behind, taking pictures. The children ran ahead, pointing to figures of naked people, intrigued in particular by the Nagamithunas, the half-human, half-serpentine couples who were said, Mr. Kapasi told them, to live in the deepest waters of the sea. Mr. Kapasi was pleased that they liked the temple, pleased especially that it appealed to Mrs. Das. She stopped every three or four paces, staring silently at the carved lovers, and the processions of elephants, and the topless female musicians beating on two-sided drums.

Though Mr. Kapasi had been to the temple countless times, it occurred to him, as he, too, gazed at the topless women, that he had never seen his own wife fully naked. Even when they had made love she kept the panels of her blouse hooked together, the string of her petticoat knotted around her waist. He had never admired the backs of his wife's legs the way he now admired those of Mrs. Das, walking as if for his benefit alone. He had, of course, seen plenty of bare limbs before, belonging to the American and European ladies who took his tours. But Mrs. Das was different. Unlike the other women, who had an interest only in the temple, and kept their noses buried in a guidebook, or their eyes behind the lens of a camera, Mrs. Das had taken an interest in him.

Mr. Kapasi was anxious to be alone with her, to continue their private conversation, yet he felt nervous to walk at her side. She was lost behind her sunglasses, ignoring her husband's requests that she pose for another picture, walking past her children as if they were strangers. Worried that he might disturb her, Mr. Kapasi walked ahead, to admire, as he always did, the three life-sized bronze avatars of Surya, the sun god, each emerging from its own niche on the temple facade to greet the sun at dawn, noon, and evening. They wore elaborate headdresses, their languid, elongated eyes closed, their bare chests draped with carved chains and amulets. Hibiscus petals, offerings from previous visitors, were strewn at their gray-green feet. The last statue, on the northern wall of the temple, was Mr. Kapasi's favorite. This Surya had a tired expression, weary after a hard day of work, sitting astride a horse with folded legs. Even his horse's eyes were drowsy. Around his body were smaller sculptures of women in pairs, their hips thrust to one side.

"Who's that?" Mrs. Das asked. He was startled to see that she was standing beside him.

"He is the Astachala-Surya," Mr. Kapasi said. "The setting sun."

"So in a couple of hours the sun will set right here?" She slipped a foot out of one of her square-heeled shoes, rubbed her toes on the back of her other leg.

"That is correct."

She raised her sunglasses for a moment, then put them back on again. "Neat."

Mr. Kapasi was not certain exactly what the word suggested, but he had a feeling it was a favorable response. He hoped that Mrs. Das had understood Surya's beauty, his power. Perhaps they would discuss it further in their letters. He would explain things to her, things about India, and she would explain things to him about America. In its own way this correspondence would fulfill his dream, of serving as an interpreter between nations. He looked at her straw bag, delighted that his address lay nestled among its contents. When he pictured her so many thousands of miles away he plummeted, so much so that he had an overwhelming urge to wrap his arms around her, to freeze with her, even for an instant, in an embrace witnessed by his favorite Surya. But Mrs. Das had already started walking.

"When do you return to America?" he asked, trying to sound placid.

"In ten days."

He calculated: A week to settle in, a week to develop the pictures, a few days to compose her letter, two weeks to get to India by air. According to his schedule, allowing room for delays, he would hear from Mrs. Das in approximately six weeks' time.

The family was silent as Mr. Kapasi drove them back, a little past four-thirty, to Hotel Sandy Villa. The children had bought miniature granite versions of the chariot's wheels at a souvenir stand, and they turned them round in their hands. Mr. Das continued to read his book. Mrs. Das untangled Tina's hair with her brush and divided it into two little ponytails.

Mr. Kapasi was beginning to dread the thought of dropping them off. He was not prepared to begin his six-week wait to hear from Mrs. Das. As he stole glances at her in the rearview mirror, wrapping elastic bands around Tina's hair, he wondered how he might make the tour last a little longer. Ordinarily he sped back to Puri using a shortcut, eager to return home, scrub his feet and hands with sandalwood soap, and enjoy the evening newspaper and a cup of tea that his wife would serve him in silence. The thought of that silence, something to which he'd long been resigned, now oppressed him. It was then that he suggested visiting the hills at Udayagiri and Khandagiri, where a number of monastic dwellings were hewn out of the ground, facing one another across a defile. It was some miles away, but well worth seeing, Mr. Kapasi told them.

"Oh yeah, there's something mentioned about it in this book," Mr. Das said. "Built by a Jain king or something."

"Shall we go then?" Mr. Kapasi asked. He paused at a turn in the road. "It's to the left."

Mr. Das turned to look at Mrs. Das. Both of them shrugged.

"Left, left," the children chanted.

Mr. Kapasi turned the wheel, almost delirious with relief. He did not know what he would do or say to Mrs. Das once they arrived at the hills. Perhaps he would tell her what a pleasing smile she had. Perhaps he would compliment her strawberry shirt, which he found irresistibly becoming. Perhaps, when Mr. Das was busy taking a picture, he would take her hand.

He did not have to worry. When they got to the hills, divided by a steep path thick with trees, Mrs. Das refused to get out of the car. All along the path, dozens of monkeys were seated on stones, as well as on the branches of the trees. Their hind legs were stretched out in front and raised to shoulder level, their arms resting on their knees.

"My legs are tired," she said, sinking low in her seat. "I'll stay here."

"Why did you have to wear those stupid shoes?" Mr. Das said. "You won't be in the pictures."

"Pretend I'm there."

"But we could use one of these pictures for our Christmas card this year. We didn't get one of all five of us at the Sun Temple. Mr. Kapasi could take it."

"I'm not coming. Anyway, those monkeys give me the creeps."

"But they're harmless," Mr. Das said. He turned to Mr. Kapasi. "Aren't they?"

"They are more hungry than dangerous," Mr. Kapasi said.

"Do not provoke them with food, and they will not bother you."

Mr. Das headed up the defile with the children, the boys at his side, the little girl on his shoulders. Mr. Kapasi watched as they crossed paths with a Japanese man and woman, the only other tourists there, who paused for a final photograph, then stepped into a nearby car and drove away. As the car disappeared out of view some of the monkeys called out, emitting soft whooping sounds, and then walked on their flat black hands and feet up the path. At one point a group of them formed a little ring around Mr. Das and the children. Tina screamed in delight. Ronny ran in circles around his father. Bobby bent down and picked up a fat stick on the ground. When he extended it, one of the monkeys approached him and snatched it, then briefly beat the ground.

"I'll join them," Mr. Kapasi said, unlocking the door on his side. "There is much to explain about the caves."

"No. Stay a minute," Mrs. Das said. She got out of the back seat and slipped in beside Mr. Kapasi. "Raj has his dumb book anyway." Together, through the windshield, Mrs. Das and Mr. Kapasi watched as Bobby and the monkey passed the stick back and forth between them.

"A brave little boy," Mr. Kapasi commented.

"It's not so surprising," Mrs. Das said.

"No?"

"He's not his."

"I beg your pardon?"

"Raj's. He's not Raj's son."

Mr. Kapasi felt a prickle on his skin. He reached into his shirt pocket for the small tin of lotus-oil balm he carried with him at all times, and applied it to three spots on his forehead. He knew that Mrs. Das was watching him, but he did not turn to face her. Instead he watched as the figures of Mr. Das and

the children grew smaller, climbing up the steep path, pausing every now and then for a picture, surrounded by a growing
number of monkeys.

"Are you surprised?" The way she put it made him choose
his words with care.

"It's not the type of thing one assumes," Mr. Kapasi replied
slowly. He put the tin of lotus-oil balm back in his pocket.

"No, of course not. And no one knows, of course. No one at
all. I've kept it a secret for eight whole years." She looked at Mr.
Kapasi, tilting her chin as if to gain a fresh perspective. "But
now I've told you."

Mr. Kapasi nodded. He felt suddenly parched, and his forehead was warm and slightly numb from the balm. He considered asking Mrs. Das for a sip of water, then decided against it.

"We met when we were very young," she said. She reached
into her straw bag in search of something, then pulled out a
packet of puffed rice. "Want some?"

"No, thank you."

She put a fistful in her mouth, sank into the seat a little, and
looked away from Mr. Kapasi, out the window on her side of
the car. "We married when we were still in college. We were in
high school when he proposed. We went to the same college, of
course. Back then we couldn't stand the thought of being separated, not for a day, not for a minute. Our parents were best
friends who lived in the same town. My entire life I saw him
every weekend, either at our house or theirs. We were sent upstairs to play together while our parents joked about our marriage. Imagine! They never caught us at anything, though in a
way I think it was all more or less a setup. The things we did
those Friday and Saturday nights, while our parents sat downstairs drinking tea . . . I could tell you stories, Mr. Kapasi."

As a result of spending all her time in college with Raj, she
continued, she did not make many close friends. There was no

one to confide in about him at the end of a difficult day, or to
share a passing thought or a worry. Her parents now lived on
the other side of the world, but she had never been very close to
them, anyway. After marrying so young she was overwhelmed
by it all, having a child so quickly, and nursing, and warming
up bottles of milk and testing their temperature against her
wrist while Raj was at work, dressed in sweaters and corduroy pants, teaching his students about rocks and dinosaurs. Raj
never looked cross or harried, or plump as she had become after the first baby.

Always tired, she declined invitations from her one or two
college girlfriends, to have lunch or shop in Manhattan. Eventually the friends stopped calling her, so that she was left at
home all day with the baby, surrounded by toys that made her
trip when she walked or wince when she sat, always cross and
tired. Only occasionally did they go out after Ronny was born,
and even more rarely did they entertain. Raj didn't mind; he
looked forward to coming home from teaching and watching
television and bouncing Ronny on his knee. She had been outraged when Raj told her that a Punjabi friend, someone whom
she had once met but did not remember, would be staying with
them for a week for some job interviews in the New Brunswick
area.

Bobby was conceived in the afternoon, on a sofa littered with
rubber teething toys, after the friend learned that a London
pharmaceutical company had hired him, while Ronny cried
to be freed from his playpen. She made no protest when the
friend touched the small of her back as she was about to make
a pot of coffee, then pulled her against his crisp navy suit. He
made love to her swiftly, in silence, with an expertise she had
never known, without the meaningful expressions and smiles
Raj always insisted on afterward. The next day Raj drove the
friend to JFK. He was married now, to a Punjabi girl, and they

lived in London still, and every year they exchanged Christmas cards with Raj and Mina, each couple tucking photos of their families into the envelopes. He did not know that he was Bobby's father. He never would.

"I beg your pardon, Mrs. Das, but why have you told me this information?" Mr. Kapasi asked when she had finally finished speaking, and had turned to face him once again.

"For God's sake, stop calling me Mrs. Das. I'm twenty-eight. You probably have children my age."

"Not quite." It disturbed Mr. Kapasi to learn that she thought of him as a parent. The feeling he had had toward her, that had made him check his reflection in the rearview mirror as they drove, evaporated a little.

"I told you because of your talents." She put the packet of puffed rice back into her bag without folding over the top.

"I don't understand," Mr. Kapasi said.

"Don't you see? For eight years I haven't been able to express this to anybody, not to friends, certainly not to Raj. He doesn't even suspect it. He thinks I'm still in love with him. Well, don't you have anything to say?"

"About what?"

"About what I've just told you. About my secret, and about how terrible it makes me feel. I feel terrible looking at my children, and at Raj, always terrible. I have terrible urges, Mr. Kapasi, to throw things away. One day I had the urge to throw everything I own out the window, the television, the children, everything. Don't you think it's unhealthy?"

He was silent.

"Mr. Kapasi, don't you have anything to say? I thought that was your job."

"My job is to give tours, Mrs. Das."

"Not that. Your other job. As an interpreter."

"But we do not face a language barrier. What need is there for an interpreter?"

"That's not what I mean. I would never have told you other-wise. Don't you realize what it means for me to tell you?"

"What does it mean?"

"It means that I'm tired of feeling so terrible all the time. Eight years, Mr. Kapasi, I've been in pain eight years. I was hoping you could help me feel better, say the right thing. Suggest some kind of remedy."

He looked at her, in her red plaid skirt and strawberry T-shirt, a woman not yet thirty, who loved neither her husband nor her children, who had already fallen out of love with life. Her confession depressed him, depressed him all the more when he thought of Mr. Das at the top of the path, Tina clinging to his shoulders, taking pictures of ancient monastic cells cut into the hills to show his students in America, unsuspecting and unaware that one of his sons was not his own. Mr. Kapasi felt insulted that Mrs. Das should ask him to interpret her common, trivial little secret. She did not resemble the patients in the doctor's office, those who came glassy-eyed and desperate, unable to sleep or breathe or urinate with ease, unable, above all, to give words to their pains. Still, Mr. Kapasi believed it was his duty to assist Mrs. Das. Perhaps he ought to tell her to confess the truth to Mr. Das. He would explain that honesty was the best policy. Honesty, surely, would help her feel better, as she'd put it. Perhaps he would offer to preside over the discussion, as a mediator. He decided to begin with the most obvious question, to get to the heart of the matter, and so he asked, "Is it really pain you feel, Mrs. Das, or is it guilt?"

She turned to him and glared, mustard oil thick on her frosty pink lips. She opened her mouth to say something, but as she glared at Mr. Kapasi some certain knowledge seemed to pass before her eyes, and she stopped. It crushed him; he knew at that moment that he was not even important enough to be properly insulted. She opened the car door and began walking up the path, wobbling a little on her square wooden heels, reaching into her straw bag to eat handfuls of puffed rice. It fell through her fingers, leaving a zigzagging trail, causing a monkey to leap down from a tree and devour the little white grains. In search of more, the monkey began to follow Mrs. Das. Others joined him, so that she was soon being followed by about half a dozen of them, their velvety tails dragging behind.

Mr. Kapasi stepped out of the car. He wanted to holler, to alert her in some way, but he worried that if she knew they were behind her, she would grow nervous. Perhaps she would lose her balance. Perhaps they would pull at her bag or her hair. He began to jog up the path, taking a fallen branch in his hand to scare away the monkeys. Mrs. Das continued walking, oblivious, trailing grains of puffed rice. Near the top of the incline, before a group of cells fronted by a row of squat stone pillars, Mr. Das was kneeling on the ground, focusing the lens of his camera. The children stood under the arcade, now hiding, now emerging from view.

"Wait for me," Mrs. Das called out. "I'm coming."

Tina jumped up and down. "Here comes Mommy!"

"Great," Mr. Das said without looking up. "Just in time. We'll get Mr. Kapasi to take a picture of the five of us."

Mr. Kapasi quickened his pace, waving his branch so that the monkeys scampered away, distracted, in another direction.

"Where's Bobby?" Mrs. Das asked when she stopped.

Mr. Das looked up from the camera. "I don't know. Ronny, where's Bobby?"

Ronny shrugged. "I thought he was right here."

"Where is he?" Mrs. Das repeated sharply. "What's wrong with all of you?"

They began calling his name, wandering up and down the path a bit. Because they were calling, they did not initially hear the boy's screams. When they found him, a little farther down the path under a tree, he was surrounded by a group of monkeys, over a dozen of them, pulling at his T-shirt with their long black fingers. The puffed rice Mrs. Das had spilled was scattered at his feet, raked over by the monkeys' hands. The boy was silent, his body frozen, swift tears running down his startled face. His bare legs were dusty and red with welts from where one of the monkeys struck him repeatedly with the stick he had given to it earlier.

"Daddy, the monkey's hurting Bobby," Tina said.

Mr. Das wiped his palms on the front of his shorts. In his nervousness he accidentally pressed the shutter on his camera; the whirring noise of the advancing film excited the monkeys, and the one with the stick began to beat Bobby more intently. "What are we supposed to do? What if they start attacking?"

"Mr. Kapasi," Mrs. Das shrieked, noticing him standing to one side. "Do something, for God's sake, do something!"

Mr. Kapasi took his branch and shooed them away, hissing at the ones that remained, stomping his feet to scare them. The animals retreated slowly, with a measured gait, obedient but unintimidated. Mr. Kapasi gathered Bobby in his arms and brought him back to where his parents and siblings were standing. As he carried him he was tempted to whisper a secret into the boy's ear. But Bobby was stunned, and shivering with fright, his legs bleeding slightly where the stick had broken the skin. When Mr. Kapasi delivered him to his parents, Mr. Das brushed some dirt off the boy's T-shirt and put the visor on him the right way. Mrs. Das reached into her straw bag to find a bandage which she taped over the cut on his knee. Ronny offered his brother a fresh piece of gum. "He's fine. Just a little scared, right, Bobby?" Mr. Das said, patting the top of his head.

"God, let's get out of here," Mrs. Das said. She folded her arms across the strawberry on her chest. "This place gives me the creeps."

"Yeah. Back to the hotel, definitely," Mr. Das agreed.

"Poor Bobby," Mrs. Das said. "Come here a second. Let Mommy fix your hair." Again she reached into her straw bag, this time for her hairbrush, and began to run it around the edges of the translucent visor. When she whipped out the hairbrush, the slip of paper with Mr. Kapasi's address on it fluttered away in the wind. No one but Mr. Kapasi noticed. He watched as it rose, carried higher and higher by the breeze, into the trees where the monkeys now sat, solemnly observing the scene below. Mr. Kapasi observed it too, knowing that this was the picture of the Das family he would preserve forever in his mind.

A Real Durwan

BOORI Ma, sweeper of the stairwell, had not slept in two nights. So the morning before the third night she shook the mites out of her bedding. She shook the quilts once underneath the letter boxes where she lived, then once again at the mouth of the alley, causing the crows who were feeding on vegetable peels to scatter in several directions.

As she started up the four flights to the roof, Boori Ma kept one hand placed over the knee that swelled at the start of every rainy season. That meant that her bucket, quilts, and the bundle of reeds which served as her broom all had to be braced under one arm. Lately Boori Ma had been thinking that the stairs were getting steeper; climbing them felt more like climbing a ladder than a staircase. She was sixty-four years old, with hair in a knot no larger than a walnut, and she looked almost as narrow from the front as she did from the side.

In fact, the only thing that appeared three-dimensional about Boori Ma was her voice: brittle with sorrows, as tart as curds, and shrill enough to grate meat from a coconut. It was with this voice that she enumerated, twice a day as she swept the stairwell, the details of her plight and losses suffered since her deportation to Calcutta after Partition. At that time, she maintained, the turmoil had separated her from a husband, four daughters, a two-story brick house, a rosewood *almari*, and a number of coffer boxes whose skeleton keys she still wore, along with her life savings, tied to the free end of her sari.

Aside from her hardships, the other thing Boori Ma liked to chronicle was easier times. And so, by the time she reached the second-floor landing, she had already drawn to the whole building's attention the menu of her third daughter's wedding night. "We married her to a school principal. The rice was cooked in rosewater. The mayor was invited. Everybody washed their fingers in pewter bowls." Here she paused, evened out her breath, and readjusted the supplies under her arm. She took the opportunity also to chase a cockroach out of the banister poles, then continued: "Mustard prawns were steamed in banana leaves. Not a delicacy was spared. Not that this was an extravagance for us. At our house, we ate goat twice a week. We had a pond on our property, full of fish."

By now Boori Ma could see some light from the roof spilling into the stairwell. And though it was only eight o'clock, the sun was already strong enough to warm the last of the cement steps under her feet. It was a very old building, the kind with bathwater that still had to be stored in drums, windows without glass, and privy scaffolds made of bricks.

"A man came to pick our dates and guavas. Another clipped hibiscus. Yes, there I tasted life. Here I eat my dinner from a rice pot." At this point in the recital Boori Ma's ears started to burn; a pain chewed through her swollen knee. "Have I mentioned that I crossed the border with just two bracelets on my wrist? Yet there was a day when my feet touched nothing but marble. Believe me, don't believe me, such comforts you cannot even dream them."

Whether there was any truth to Boori Ma's litanies no one could be sure. For one thing, every day, the perimeters of her former estate seemed to double, as did the contents of her *al-mari* and coffer boxes. No one doubted she was a refugee; the accent in her Bengali made that clear. Still, the residents of this particular flat-building could not reconcile Boori Ma's claims to prior wealth alongside the more likely account of how she had crossed the East Bengal border, with the thousands of others, on the back of a truck, between sacks of hemp. And yet there were days when Boori Ma insisted that she had come to Calcutta on a bullock cart.

"Which was it, by truck or by cart?" the children sometimes asked her on their way to play cops and robbers in the alley. To which Boori Ma would reply, shaking the free end of her sari so that the skeleton keys rattled, "Why demand specifics? Why scrape lime from a betel leaf? Believe me, don't believe me. My life is composed of such griefs you cannot even dream them."

So she garbled facts. She contradicted herself. She embellished almost everything. But her rants were so persuasive, her fretting so vivid, that it was not so easy to dismiss her.

What kind of landowner ended up sweeping stairs? That was what Mr. Dalal of the third floor always wondered as he passed Boori Ma on his way to and from the office, where he filed receipts for a wholesale distributor of rubber tubes, pipes, and valve fittings in the plumbing district of College Street.

Bechareh, she probably constructs tales as a way of mourning the loss of her family, was the collective surmise of most of the wives.

And "Boori Ma's mouth is full of ashes, but she is the victim of changing times" was the refrain of old Mr. Chatterjee. He had neither strayed from his balcony nor opened a newspaper since Independence, but in spite of this fact, or maybe because of it, his opinions were always highly esteemed.

The theory eventually circulated that Boori Ma had once worked as hired help for a prosperous *zamindar* back east, and was therefore capable of exaggerating her past at such elaborate lengths and heights. Her throaty impostures hurt no one. All agreed that she was a superb entertainer. In exchange for her lodging below the letter boxes, Boori Ma kept their crooked stairwell spotlessly clean. Most of all, the residents liked that Boori Ma, who slept each night behind the collapsible gate, stood guard between them and the outside world.

No one in this particular flat-building owned much worth stealing. The second-floor widow, Mrs. Misra, was the only one with a telephone. Still, the residents were thankful that Boori Ma patrolled activities in the alley, screened the itinerant peddlers who came to sell combs and shawls from door to door, was able to summon a rickshaw at a moment's calling, and could, with a few slaps of her broom, rout any suspicious character who strayed into the area in order to spit, urinate, or cause some other trouble.

In short, over the years, Boori Ma's services came to resemble those of a real *durwan*. Though under normal circumstances this was no job for a woman, she honored the responsibility, and maintained a vigil no less punctilious than if she were the gatekeeper of a house on Lower Circular Road, or Jodhpur Park, or any other fancy neighborhood.

On the rooftop Boori Ma hung her quilts over the clothesline. The wire, strung diagonally from one corner of the parapet to the other, stretched across her view of television antennas, billboards, and the distant arches of Howrah Bridge. Boori Ma consulted the horizon on all four sides. Then she ran the tap at the base of the cistern. She washed her face, rinsed her feet, and rubbed two fingers over her teeth. After this she started to beat the quilts on each side with her broom. Every now and then she stopped and squinted at the cement, hoping to identify the culprit of her sleepless nights. She was so absorbed in this process that it was some moments before she noticed Mrs. Dalal of the third floor, who had come to set a tray of salted lemon peels out to dry in the sun.

"Whatever is inside this quilt is keeping me awake at night," Boori Ma said. "Tell me, where do you see them?"

Mrs. Dalal had a soft spot for Boori Ma; occasionally she gave the old woman some ginger paste with which to flavor her stews. "I don't see anything," Mrs. Dalal said after a while. She had diaphanous eyelids and very slender toes with rings on them.

"Then they must have wings," Boori Ma concluded. She put down her broom and observed one cloud passing behind another. "They fly away before I can squash them. But just see my back. I must be purple from their bites."

Mrs. Dalal lifted the drape of Boori Ma's sari, a cheap white weave with a border the color of a dirty pond. She examined the skin above and below her blouse, cut in a style no longer sold in shops. Then she said, "Boori Ma, you are imagining things."

"I tell you, these mites are eating me alive."

"It could be a case of prickly heat," Mrs. Dalal suggested.

At this Boori Ma shook the free end of her sari and made her skeleton keys rattle. She said, "I know prickly heat. This is not prickly heat. I haven't slept in three, perhaps four days. Who can count? I used to keep a clean bed. Our linens were muslin. Believe me, don't believe me, our mosquito nets were as soft as silk. Such comforts you cannot even dream them."

"I cannot dream them," Mrs. Dalal echoed. She lowered her diaphanous eyelids and sighed. "I cannot dream them, Boori Ma. I live in two broken rooms, married to a man who sells toilet parts." Mrs. Dalal turned away and looked at one of the quilts. She ran a finger over part of the stitching. Then she asked:

"Boori Ma, how long have you slept on this bedding?"

Boori Ma put a finger to her lips before replying that she could not remember.

"Then why no mention of it until today? Do you think it's beyond us to provide you with clean quilts? An oilcloth, for that matter?" She looked insulted.

"There is no need," Boori Ma said. "They are clean now. I beat them with my broom."

"I am hearing no arguments," Mrs. Dalal said. "You need a new bed. Quilts, a pillow. A blanket when winter comes." As she spoke Mrs. Dalal kept track of the necessary items by touching her thumb to the pads of her fingers.

"On festival days the poor came to our house to be fed," Boori Ma said. She was filling her bucket from the coal heap on the other side of the roof.

"I will have a word with Mr. Dalal when he returns from the office," Mrs. Dalal called back as she headed down the stairs. "Come in the afternoon. I will give you some pickles and some powder for your back."

"It's not prickly heat," Boori Ma said.

It was true that prickly heat was common during the rainy season. But Boori Ma preferred to think that what irritated her bed, what stole her sleep, what burned like peppers across her thinning scalp and skin, was of a less mundane origin.

She was ruminating on these things as she swept the stairwell — she always worked from top to bottom — when it started to rain. It came slapping across the roof like a boy in slippers too big for him and washed Mrs. Dalal's lemon peels into the gutter. Before pedestrians could open their umbrellas, it rushed down collars, pockets, and shoes. In that particular flat-building and all the neighboring buildings, creaky shutters were closed and tied with petticoat strings to the window bars.

At the time, Boori Ma was working all the way down on the

second-floor landing. She looked up the ladderlike stairs, and as the sound of falling water tightened around her she knew her quilts were turning into yogurt.

But then she recalled her conversation with Mrs. Dalal. And so she continued, at the same pace, to sweep the dust, cigarette ends, and lozenge wrappers from the rest of the steps, until she reached the letter boxes at the bottom. To keep out the wind, she rummaged through her baskets for some newspapers and crammed them into the diamond-shaped openings of the collapsible gate. Then on her bucket of coals she set her lunch to boil, and monitored the flame with a plaited palm fan.

That afternoon, as was her habit, Boori Ma reknotted her hair, untied the loose end of her sari, and counted out her life savings. She had just woken from a nap of twenty minutes, which she had taken on a temporary bed made from newspapers. The rain had stopped and now the sour smell that rises from wet mango leaves was hanging low over the alley.

On certain afternoons Boori Ma visited her fellow residents. She enjoyed drifting in and out of the various households. The residents, for their part, assured Boori Ma that she was always welcome; they never drew the latch bars across their doors except at night. They went about their business, scolding children or adding up expenses or picking stones out of the evening rice. From time to time she was handed a glass of tea, the cracker tin was passed in her direction, and she helped children shoot chips across the carom board. Knowing not to sit on the furniture, she crouched, instead, in doorways and hallways, and observed gestures and manners in the same way a person tends to watch traffic in a foreign city.

On this particular afternoon Boori Ma decided to accept Mrs. Dalal's invitation. Her back still itched, even after napping on the newspapers, and she was beginning to want some prickly-heat powder after all. She picked up her broom—she never felt quite herself without it—and was about to climb upstairs, when a rickshaw pulled up to the collapsible gate.

It was Mr. Dalal. The years he had spent filing receipts had left him with purple crescents under his eyes. But today his gaze was bright. The tip of his tongue played between his teeth, and in the clamp of his thighs he held two small ceramic basins.

"Boori Ma, I have a job for you. Help me carry these basins upstairs." He pressed a folded handkerchief to his forehead and throat and gave the rickshaw driver a coin. Then he and Boori Ma carried the basins all the way up to the third floor. It wasn't until they were inside the flat that he finally announced, to Mrs. Dalal, to Boori Ma, and to a few other residents who had followed them out of curiosity, the following things: That his hours filing receipts for a distributor of rubber tubes, pipes, and valve fittings had ended. That the distributor himself, who craved fresher air, and whose profits had doubled, was opening a second branch in Burdwan. And that, following an assessment of his sedulous performance over the years, the distributor was promoting Mr. Dalal to manage the College Street branch. In his excitement on his way home through the plumbing district, Mr. Dalal had bought two basins.

"What are we supposed to do with two basins in a two-room flat?" Mrs. Dalal demanded. She had already been sulking over her lemon peels. "Who ever heard of it? I still cook on kerosene. You refuse to apply for a phone. And I have yet to see the fridge you promised when we married. You expect two basins to make up for all that?"

The argument that followed was loud enough to be heard all the way down to the letter boxes. It was loud enough, and long enough, to rise above a second spell of rain that fell after dark. It was loud enough even to distract Boori Ma as she swept the stairwell from top to bottom for the second time that day, and for this reason she spoke neither of her hardships, nor of easier times. She spent the night on a bed of newspapers.

The argument between Mr. and Mrs. Dalal was still more or less in effect early the next morning, when a barefoot team of workmen came to install the basins. After a night of tossing and pacing, Mr. Dalal had decided to install one basin in the sitting room of their flat, and the other one in the stairwell of the building, on the first-floor landing. "This way everyone can use it," he explained from door to door. The residents were delighted; for years they had all brushed their teeth with stored water poured from mugs.

Mr. Dalal, meanwhile, was thinking: A sink in the stairwell is sure to impress visitors. Now that he was a company manager, who could say who might visit the building?

The workmen toiled for several hours. They ran up and down the stairs and ate their lunches squatting against the banister poles. They hammered, shouted, spat, and cursed. They wiped their sweat with the ends of their turbans. In general, they made it impossible for Boori Ma to sweep the stairwell that day.

To occupy the time, Boori Ma retired to the rooftop. She shuffled along the parapets, but her hips were sore from sleeping on newspapers. After consulting the horizon on all four sides, she tore what was left of her quilts into several strips and resolved to polish the banister poles at a later time.

By early evening the residents gathered to admire the day's labors. Even Boori Ma was urged to rinse her hands under the clear running water. She sniffed. "Our bathwater was scented with petals and attars. Believe me, don't believe me, it was a luxury you cannot dream."

Mr. Dalal proceeded to demonstrate the basin's various features. He turned each faucet completely on and completely off. Then he turned on both faucets at the same time, to illustrate the difference in water pressure. Lifting a small lever between the faucets allowed water to collect in the basin, if desired.

"The last word in elegance," Mr. Dalal concluded.

"A sure sign of changing times," Mr. Chatterjee reputedly admitted from his balcony.

Among the wives, however, resentment quickly brewed. Standing in line to brush their teeth in the mornings, each grew frustrated with having to wait her turn, for having to wipe the faucets after every use, and for not being able to leave her own soap and toothpaste tube on the basin's narrow periphery. The Dalals had their own sink; why did the rest of them have to share?

"Is it beyond us to buy sinks of our own?" one of them finally burst out one morning.

"Are the Dalals the only ones who can improve the conditions of this building?" asked another.

Rumors began spreading: that, following their argument, Mr. Dalal had consoled his wife by buying her two kilos of mustard oil, a Kashmiri shawl, a dozen cakes of sandalwood soap; that Mr. Dalal had filed an application for a telephone line; that Mrs. Dalal did nothing but wash her hands in her basin all day. As if this weren't enough, the next morning, a taxi bound for Howrah Station crammed its wheels into the alley; the Dalals were going to Simla for ten days.

"Boori Ma, I haven't forgotten. We will bring you back a sheep's-hair blanket made in the mountains," Mrs. Dalal said through the open window of the taxi. She was holding a leather purse in her lap which matched the turquoise border of her sari.

"We will bring two!" cried Mr. Dalal, who was sitting beside his wife, checking his pockets to make sure his wallet was in place.

Of all the people who lived in that particular flat-building,

Boori Ma was the only one who stood by the collapsible gate and wished them a safe journey.

As soon as the Dalals were gone, the other wives began planning renovations of their own. One decided to barter a stack of her wedding bracelets and commissioned a whitewasher to freshen the walls of the stairwell. Another pawned her sewing machine and summoned an exterminator. A third went to the silversmith and sold back a set of pudding bowls; she intended to have the shutters painted yellow.

Workers began to occupy this particular flat-building night and day. To avoid the traffic, Boori Ma took to sleeping on the rooftop. So many people passed in and out of the collapsible gate, so many others clogged the alley at all times, that there was no point in keeping track of them.

After a few days Boori Ma moved her baskets and her cooking bucket to the rooftop as well. There was no need to use the basin downstairs, for she could just as easily wash, as she always had, from the cistern tap. She still planned to polish the banister poles with the strips she had torn from her quilts. She continued to sleep on her newspapers.

More rains came. Below the dripping awning, a newspaper pressed over her head, Boori Ma squatted and watched the monsoon ants as they marched along the clothesline, carrying eggs in their mouths. Damper winds soothed her back. Her newspapers were running low.

Her mornings were long, her afternoons longer. She could not remember her last glass of tea. Thinking neither of her hardships nor of earlier times, she wondered when the Dalals would return with her new bedding.

She grew restless on the roof, and so for some exercise, Boori Ma started circling the neighborhood in the afternoons. Reed broom in hand, sari smeared with newsprint ink, she wandered through markets and began spending her life savings on small treats: today a packet of puffed rice, tomorrow some cashews, the day after that, a cup of sugarcane juice. One day she walked as far as the bookstalls on College Street. The next day she walked even farther, to the produce markets in Bow Bazaar. It was there, while she was standing in a shopping arcade survey-ing jackfruits and persimmons, that she felt something tugging on the free end of her sari. When she looked, the rest of her life savings and her skeleton keys were gone.

The residents were waiting for Boori Ma when she returned that afternoon at the collapsible gate. Baleful cries rang up and down the stairwell, all echoing the same news: the basin on the stairwell had been stolen. There was a big hole in the recently whitewashed wall, and a tangle of rubber tubes and pipes was sticking out of it. Chunks of plaster littered the landing. Boori Ma gripped her reed broom and said nothing.

In their haste the residents practically carried Boori Ma up the stairs to the roof, where they planted her on one side of the clothesline and started screaming at her from the other.

"This is all her doing," one of them hollered, pointing at Boori Ma. "She informed the robbers. Where was she when she was supposed to guard the gate?"

"For days she has been wandering the streets, speaking to strangers," another reported.

"We shared our coal, gave her a place to sleep. How could she betray us this way?" a third wanted to know.

Though none of them spoke directly to Boori Ma, she re-plied, "Believe me, believe me. I did not inform the robbers."

"For years we have put up with your lies," they retorted. "You expect us, now, to believe you?"

Their recriminations persisted. How would they explain it to the Dalals? Eventually they sought the advice of Mr. Chat-terjee. They found him sitting on his balcony, watching a traffic jam.

One of the second-floor residents said, "Boori Ma has endangered the security of this building. We have valuables. The widow Mrs. Misra lives alone with her phone. What should we do?"

Mr. Chatterjee considered their arguments. As he thought things over, he adjusted the shawl that was wrapped around his shoulders and gazed at the bamboo scaffolding that now surrounded his balcony. The shutters behind him, colorless for as long as he could remember, had been painted yellow. Finally he said:

"Boori Ma's mouth is full of ashes. But that is nothing new. What is new is the face of this building. What a building like this needs is a real *durwan*."

So the residents tossed her bucket and rags, her baskets and reed broom, down the stairwell, past the letter boxes, through the collapsible gate, and into the alley. Then they tossed out Boori Ma. All were eager to begin their search for a real *durwan*.

From the pile of belongings Boori Ma kept only her broom. "Believe me, believe me," she said once more as her figure began to recede. She shook the free end of her sari, but nothing rattled.

Sexy

I T WAS a wife's worst nightmare. After nine years of marriage, Laxmi told Miranda, her cousin's husband had fallen in love with another woman. He sat next to her on a plane, on a flight from Delhi to Montreal, and instead of flying home to his wife and son, he got off with the woman at Heathrow. He called his wife, and told her he'd had a conversation that had changed his life, and that he needed time to figure things out. Laxmi's cousin had taken to her bed.

"Not that I blame her," Laxmi said. She reached for the Hot Mix she munched throughout the day, which looked to Miranda like dusty orange cereal. "Imagine. An English girl, half his age." Laxmi was only a few years older than Miranda, but she was already married, and kept a photo of herself and her husband, seated on a white stone bench in front of the Taj Mahal, tacked to the inside of her cubicle, which was next to Miranda's. Laxmi had been on the phone for at least an hour, trying to calm her cousin down. No one noticed; they worked for a public radio station, in the fund-raising department, and were surrounded by people who spent all day on the phone, soliciting pledges.

"I feel worst for the boy," Laxmi added. "He's been at home for days. My cousin said she can't even take him to school."

"It sounds awful," Miranda said. Normally Laxmi's phone conversations—mainly to her husband, about what to cook for dinner—distracted Miranda as she typed letters, asking members of the radio station to increase their annual pledge in exchange for a tote bag or an umbrella. She could hear Laxmi clearly, her sentences peppered every now and then with an Indian word, through the laminated wall between their desks. But that afternoon Miranda hadn't been listening. She'd been on the phone herself, with Dev, deciding where to meet later that evening.

"Then again, a few days at home won't hurt him." Laxmi ate some more Hot Mix, then put it away in a drawer. "He's something of a genius. He has a Punjabi mother and a Bengali father, and because he learns French and English at school he already speaks four languages. I think he skipped two grades."

Dev was Bengali, too. At first Miranda thought it was a religion. But then he pointed it out to her, a place in India called Bengal, in a map printed in an issue of *The Economist*. He had brought the magazine specially to her apartment, for she did not own an atlas, or any other books with maps in them. He'd pointed to the city where he'd been born, and another city where his father had been born. One of the cities had a box around it, intended to attract the reader's eye. When Miranda asked what the box indicated, Dev rolled up the magazine, and said, "Nothing you'll ever need to worry about," and he tapped her playfully on the head.

Before leaving her apartment he'd tossed the magazine in the garbage, along with the ends of the three cigarettes he always smoked in the course of his visits. But after she watched his car disappear down Commonwealth Avenue, back to his house in the suburbs, where he lived with his wife, Miranda retrieved it, and brushed the ashes off the cover, and rolled it in the opposite direction to get it to lie flat. She got into bed, still rumpled from their lovemaking, and studied the borders of Bengal. There was a bay below and mountains above. The map was connected to an article about something called the Gramin Bank. She turned the page, hoping for a photograph of the city where Dev was born, but all she found were graphs and grids. Still, she stared at them, thinking the whole while about Dev, about how only fifteen minutes ago he'd propped her feet on top of his shoulders, and pressed her knees to her chest, and told her that he couldn't get enough of her.

She'd met him a week ago, at Filene's. She was there on her lunch break, buying discounted pantyhose in the Basement. Afterward she took the escalator to the main part of the store, to the cosmetics department, where soaps and creams were displayed like jewels, and eye shadows and powders shimmered like butterflies pinned behind protective glass. Though Miranda had never bought anything other than a lipstick, she liked walking through the cramped, confined maze, which was familiar to her in a way the rest of Boston still was not. She liked negotiating her way past the women planted at every turn, who sprayed cards with perfume and waved them in the air; sometimes she would find a card days afterward, folded in her coat pocket, and the rich aroma, still faintly preserved, would warm her as she waited on cold mornings for the T.

That day, stopping to smell one of the more pleasing cards, Miranda noticed a man standing at one of the counters. He held a slip of paper covered in a precise, feminine hand. A saleswoman took one look at the paper and began to open drawers. She produced an oblong cake of soap in a black case, a hydrating mask, a vial of cell renewal drops, and two tubes of face cream. The man was tanned, with black hair that was visible on his knuckles. He wore a flamingo pink shirt, a navy blue suit, a camel overcoat with gleaming leather buttons. In order to pay he had taken off pigskin gloves. Crisp bills emerged from a burgundy wallet. He didn't wear a wedding ring.

"What can I get you, honey?" the saleswoman asked Miranda. She looked over the tops of her tortoiseshell glasses, assessing Miranda's complexion.

Miranda didn't know what she wanted. All she knew was that she didn't want the man to walk away. He seemed to be lingering, waiting, along with the saleswoman, for her to say something. She stared at some bottles, some short, others tall, arranged on an oval tray, like a family posing for a photograph.

"A cream," Miranda said eventually.

"How old are you?"

"Twenty-two."

The saleswoman nodded, opening a frosted bottle. "This may seem a bit heavier than what you're used to, but I'd start now. All your wrinkles are going to form by twenty-five. After that they just start showing."

While the saleswoman dabbed the cream on Miranda's face, the man stood and watched. While Miranda was told the proper way to apply it, in swift upward strokes beginning at the base of her throat, he spun the lipstick carousel. He pressed a pump that dispensed cellulite gel and massaged it into the back of his ungloved hand. He opened a jar, leaned over, and drew so close that a drop of cream flecked his nose.

Miranda smiled, but her mouth was obscured by a large brush that the saleswoman was sweeping over her face. "This is blusher Number Two," the woman said. "Gives you some color."

Miranda nodded, glancing at her reflection in one of the angled mirrors that lined the counter. She had silver eyes and skin as pale as paper, and the contrast with her hair, as dark and glossy as an espresso bean, caused people to describe her as striking, if not pretty. She had a narrow, egg-shaped head that rose to a prominent point. Her features, too, were narrow, with nostrils so slim that they appeared to have been pinched with a clothespin. Now her face glowed, rosy at the cheeks, smoky below the brow bone. Her lips glistened.

The man was glancing in a mirror, too, quickly wiping the cream from his nose. Miranda wondered where he was from. She thought he might be Spanish, or Lebanese. When he opened another jar, and said, to no one in particular, "This one smells like pineapple," she detected only the hint of an accent.

"Anything else for you today?" the saleswoman asked, accepting Miranda's credit card.

"No thanks."

The woman wrapped the cream in several layers of red tissue. "You'll be very happy with this product." Miranda's hand was unsteady as she signed the receipt. The man hadn't budged.

"I threw in a sample of our new eye gel," the saleswoman added, handing Miranda a small shopping bag. She looked at Miranda's credit card before sliding it across the counter. "Bye-bye, Miranda."

Miranda began walking. At first she sped up. Then, noticing the doors that led to Downtown Crossing, she slowed down.

"Part of your name is Indian," the man said, pacing his steps with hers.

She stopped, as did he, at a circular table piled with sweaters, flanked with pinecones and velvet bows. "Miranda?"

"Mira. I have an aunt named Mira."

His name was Dev. He worked in an investment bank back that way, he said, tilting his head in the direction of South Station. He was the first man with a mustache, Miranda decided, she found handsome.

They walked together toward Park Street station, past the kiosks that sold cheap belts and handbags. A fierce January wind spoiled the part in her hair. As she fished for a token in her coat pocket, her eyes fell to his shopping bag. "And those are for her?"

"Who?"

"Your Aunt Mira."

"They're for my wife." He uttered the words slowly, holding Miranda's gaze. "She's going to India for a few weeks." He rolled his eyes. "She's addicted to this stuff."

Somehow, without the wife there, it didn't seem so wrong. At first Miranda and Dev spent every night together, almost. He explained that he couldn't spend the whole night at her place, because his wife called every day at six in the morning, from India, where it was four in the afternoon. And so he left her apartment at two, three, often as late as four in the morning, driving back to his house in the suburbs. During the day he called her every hour, it seemed, from work, or from his cell phone. Once he learned Miranda's schedule he left her a message each evening at five-thirty, when she was on the T coming back to her apartment, just so, he said, she could hear his voice as soon as she walked through the door. "I'm thinking about you," he'd say on the tape. "I can't wait to see you." He told her he liked spending time in her apartment, with its kitchen counter no wider than a breadbox, and scratchy floors that sloped, and a buzzer in the lobby that always made a slightly embarrassing sound when he pressed it. He said he admired her for moving to Boston, where she knew no one, instead of remaining in Michigan, where she'd grown up and gone to college. When Miranda told him it was nothing to admire, that she'd moved to Boston precisely for that reason, he shook his head. "I know what it's like to be lonely," he said, suddenly serious, and at that moment Miranda felt that he understood her—understood how she felt some nights on the T, after seeing a movie on her own, or going to a bookstore to read magazines, or having drinks with Laxmi, who always had to meet her husband at Alewife station in an hour or two. In less serious moments Dev said he liked that her legs were longer than her torso, something he'd observed the first time she walked across a room naked. "You're the first," he told her, admiring her from the bed. "The first woman I've known with legs this long."

Dev was the first to tell her that. Unlike the boys she dated in college, who were simply taller, heavier versions of the ones she dated in high school, Dev was the first always to pay for things, and hold doors open, and reach across a table in a restaurant to kiss her hand. He was the first to bring her a bouquet of flowers so immense she'd had to split it up into all six of her drinking glasses, and the first to whisper her name again and again when they made love. Within days of meeting him, when she was at work, Miranda began to wish that there were a picture of her and Dev tacked to the inside of her cubicle, like the one of Laxmi and her husband in front of the Taj Mahal. She didn't tell Laxmi about Dev. She didn't tell anyone. Part of her wanted to tell Laxmi, if only because Laxmi was Indian, too. But Laxmi was always on the phone with her cousin these days, who was still in bed, whose husband was still in London, and whose son still wasn't going to school. "You must eat something," Laxmi would urge. "You mustn't lose your health." When she wasn't speaking to her cousin, she spoke to her husband, shorter conversations, in which she ended up arguing about whether to have chicken or lamb for dinner. "I'm sorry," Miranda heard her apologize at one point. "This whole thing just makes me a little paranoid."

Miranda and Dev didn't argue. They went to movies at the Nickelodeon and kissed the whole time. They ate pulled pork and cornbread in Davis Square, a paper napkin tucked like a cravat into the collar of Dev's shirt. They sipped sangria at the bar of a Spanish restaurant, a grinning pig's head presiding over their conversation. They went to the MFA and picked out a poster of water lilies for her bedroom. One Saturday, following an afternoon concert at Symphony Hall, he showed her his favorite place in the city, the Mapparium at the Christian

Science center, where they stood inside a room made of glowing stained-glass panels, which was shaped like the inside of a globe, but looked like the outside of one. In the middle of the room was a transparent bridge, so that they felt as if they were standing in the center of the world. Dev pointed to India, which was red, and far more detailed than the map in *The Economist*. He explained that many of the countries, like Siam and Italian Somaliland, no longer existed in the same way; the names had changed by now. The ocean, as blue as a peacock's breast, appeared in two shades, depending on the depth of the water. He showed her the deepest spot on earth, seven miles deep, above the Mariana Islands. They peered over the bridge and saw the Antarctic archipelago at their feet, craned their necks and saw a giant metal star overhead. As Dev spoke, his voice bounced wildly off the glass, sometimes loud, sometimes soft, sometimes seeming to land in Miranda's chest, sometimes eluding her ear altogether. When a group of tourists walked onto the bridge, she could hear them clearing their throats, as if through microphones. Dev explained that it was because of the acoustics.

Miranda found London, where Laxmi's cousin's husband was, with the woman he'd met on the plane. She wondered which of the cities in India Dev's wife was in. The farthest Miranda had ever been was to the Bahamas once when she was a child. She searched but couldn't find it on the glass panels. When the tourists left and she and Dev were alone again, he told her to stand at one end of the bridge. Even though they were thirty feet apart, Dev said, they'd be able to hear each other whisper.

"I don't believe you," Miranda said. It was the first time she'd spoken since they'd entered. She felt as if speakers were embedded in her ears.

"Go ahead," he urged, walking backward to his end of the bridge. His voice dropped to a whisper. "Say something." She watched his lips forming the words; at the same time she heard them so clearly that she felt them under her skin, under her winter coat, so near and full of warmth that she felt herself go hot.

"Hi," she whispered, unsure of what else to say.

"You're sexy," he whispered back.

At work the following week, Laxmi told Miranda that it wasn't the first time her cousin's husband had had an affair. "She's decided to let him come to his senses," Laxmi said one evening as they were getting ready to leave the office. "She says it's for the boy. She's willing to forgive him for the boy." Miranda waited as Laxmi shut off her computer. "He'll come crawling back, and she'll let him," Laxmi said, shaking her head. "Not me. If my husband so much as looked at another woman I'd change the locks." She studied the picture tacked to her cubicle. Laxmi's husband had his arm draped over her shoulder, his knees leaning in toward her on the bench. She turned to Miranda. "Wouldn't you?"

She nodded. Dev's wife was coming back from India the next day. That afternoon he'd called Miranda at work, to say he had to go to the airport to pick her up. He promised he'd call as soon as he could.

"What's the Taj Mahal like?" she asked Laxmi.

"The most romantic spot on earth." Laxmi's face brightened at the memory. "An everlasting monument to love."

While Dev was at the airport, Miranda went to Filene's Basement to buy herself things she thought a mistress should have. She found a pair of black high heels with buckles smaller than a baby's teeth. She found a satin slip with scalloped edges and a knee-length silk robe. Instead of the pantyhose she normally wore to work, she found sheer stockings with a seam.

She searched through piles and wandered through racks, pressing back hanger after hanger, until she found a cocktail dress made of a slinky silvery material that matched her eyes, with little chains for straps. As she shopped she thought about Dev, and about what he'd told her in the Mapparium. It was the first time a man had called her sexy, and when she closed her eyes she could still feel his whisper drifting through her body, under her skin. In the fitting room, which was just one big room with mirrors on the walls, she found a spot next to an older woman with a shiny face and coarse frosted hair. The woman stood barefoot in her underwear, pulling the black net of a body stocking taut between her fingers.

"Always check for snags," the woman advised.

Miranda pulled out the satin slip with scalloped edges. She held it to her chest.

The woman nodded with approval. "Oh yes."

"And this?" She held up the silver cocktail dress.

"Absolutely," the woman said. "He'll want to rip it right off you."

Miranda pictured the two of them at a restaurant in the South End they'd been to, where Dev had ordered foie gras and a soup made with champagne and raspberries. She pictured herself in the cocktail dress, and Dev in one of his suits, kissing her hand across the table. Only the next time Dev came to visit her, on a Sunday afternoon several days since the last time they'd seen each other, he was in gym clothes. After his wife came back, that was his excuse: on Sundays he drove into Boston and went running along the Charles. The first Sunday she opened the door in the knee-length robe, but Dev didn't even notice it; he carried her over to the bed, wearing sweatpants and sneakers, and entered her without a word. Later, she slipped on the robe when she walked across the room to get him a saucer for his cigarette ashes, but he complained that she was depriving him of the sight of her long legs, and demanded that she remove it. So the next Sunday she didn't bother. She wore jeans. She kept the lingerie at the back of a drawer, behind her socks and everyday underwear. The silver cocktail dress hung in her closet, the tag dangling from the seam. Often, in the morning, the dress would be in a heap on the floor; the chain straps always slipped off the metal hanger.

Still, Miranda looked forward to Sundays. In the mornings she went to a deli and bought a baguette and little containers of things Dev liked to eat, like pickled herring, and potato salad, and tortes of pesto and mascarpone cheese. They ate in bed, picking up the herring with their fingers and ripping the baguette with their hands. Dev told her stories about his childhood, when he would come home from school and drink mango juice served to him on a tray, and then play cricket by a lake, dressed all in white. He told her about how, at eighteen, he'd been sent to a college in upstate New York during something called the Emergency, and about how it took him years to be able to follow American accents in movies, in spite of the fact that he'd had an English-medium education. As he talked he smoked three cigarettes, crushing them in a saucer by the side of her bed. Sometimes he asked her questions, like how many lovers she'd had (three) and how old she'd been the first time (nineteen). After lunch they made love, on sheets covered with crumbs, and then Dev took a nap for twelve minutes. Miranda had never known an adult who took naps, but Dev said it was something he'd grown up doing in India, where it was so hot that people didn't leave their homes until the sun went down. "Plus it allows us to sleep together," he murmured mischievously, curving his arm like a big bracelet around her body.

Only Miranda never slept. She watched the clock on her bedside table, or pressed her face against Dev's fingers, intertwined with hers, each with its half-dozen hairs at the knuckle. After six minutes she turned to face him, sighing and stretching, to test if he was really sleeping. He always was. His ribs were visible through his skin as he breathed, and yet he was beginning to develop a paunch. He complained about the hair on his shoulders, but Miranda thought him perfect, and refused to imagine him any other way.

At the end of twelve minutes Dev would open his eyes as if he'd been awake all along, smiling at her, full of a contentment she wished she felt herself. "The best twelve minutes of the week." He'd sigh, running a hand along the backs of her calves. Then he'd spring out of bed, pulling on his sweatpants and lacing up his sneakers. He would go to the bathroom and brush his teeth with his index finger, something he told her all Indians knew how to do, to get rid of the smoke in his mouth. When she kissed him good-bye she smelled herself sometimes in his hair. But she knew that his excuse, that he'd spent the afternoon jogging, allowed him to take a shower when he got home, first thing.

Apart from Laxmi and Dev, the only Indians whom Miranda had known were a family in the neighborhood where she'd grown up, named the Dixits. Much to the amusement of the neighborhood children, including Miranda, but not including the Dixit children, Mr. Dixit would jog each evening along the flat winding streets of their development in his everyday shirt and trousers, his only concession to athletic apparel a pair of cheap Keds. Every weekend, the family—mother, father, two boys, and a girl—piled into their car and went away, to where nobody knew. The fathers complained that Mr. Dixit did not fertilize his lawn properly, did not rake his leaves on time, and agreed that the Dixits' house, the only one with vinyl siding, detracted from the neighborhood's charm. The mothers never invited Mrs. Dixit to join them around the Armstrongs' swimming pool. Waiting for the school bus with the Dixit children standing to one side, the other children would say "The Dixits dig shit," under their breath, and then burst into laughter.

One year, all the neighborhood children were invited to the birthday party of the Dixit girl. Miranda remembered a heavy aroma of incense and onions in the house, and a pile of shoes heaped by the front door. But most of all she remembered a piece of fabric, about the size of a pillowcase, which hung from a wooden dowel at the bottom of the stairs. It was a painting of a naked woman with a red face shaped like a knight's shield. She had enormous white eyes that tilted toward her temples, and mere dots for pupils. Two circles, with the same dots at their centers, indicated her breasts. In one hand she brandished a dagger. With one foot she crushed a struggling man on the ground. Around her body was a necklace composed of bleeding heads, strung together like a popcorn chain. She stuck her tongue out at Miranda.

"It is the goddess Kali," Mrs. Dixit explained brightly, shifting the dowel slightly in order to straighten the image. Mrs. Dixit's hands were painted with henna, an intricate pattern of zigzags and stars. "Come please, time for cake."

Miranda, then nine years old, had been too frightened to eat the cake. For months afterward she'd been too frightened even to walk on the same side of the street as the Dixits' house, which she had to pass twice daily, once to get to the bus stop, and once again to come home. For a while she even held her breath until she reached the next lawn, just as she did when the school bus passed a cemetery.

It shamed her now. Now, when she and Dev made love, Miranda closed her eyes and saw deserts and elephants, and marble pavilions floating on lakes beneath a full moon. One Saturday, having nothing else to do, she walked all the way to

Central Square, to an Indian restaurant, and ordered a plate of tandoori chicken. As she ate she tried to memorize phrases printed at the bottom of the menu, for things like "delicious" and "water" and "check, please." The phrases didn't stick in her mind, and so she began to stop from time to time in the foreign-language section of a bookstore in Kenmore Square, where she studied the Bengali alphabet in the Teach Yourself series. Once she went so far as to try to transcribe the Indian part of her name, "Mira," into her Filofax, her hand moving in unfamiliar directions, stopping and turning and picking up her pen when she least expected to. Following the arrows in the book, she drew a bar from left to right from which the letters hung; one looked more like a number than a letter, another looked like a triangle on its side. It had taken her several tries to get the letters of her name to resemble the sample letters in the book, and even then she wasn't sure if she'd written Mira or Mara. It was a scribble to her, but somewhere in the world, she realized with a shock, it meant something.

During the week it wasn't so bad. Work kept her busy, and she and Laxmi had begun having lunch together at a new Indian restaurant around the corner, during which Laxmi reported the latest status of her cousin's marriage. Sometimes Miranda tried to change the topic; it made her feel the way she once felt in college, when she and her boyfriend at the time had walked away from a crowded house of pancakes without paying for their food, just to see if they could get away with it. But Laxmi spoke of nothing else. "If I were her I'd fly straight to London and shoot them both," she announced one day. She snapped a papadum in half and dipped it into chutney. "I don't know how she can just wait this way."

Miranda knew how to wait. In the evenings she sat at her dining table and coated her nails with clear nail polish, and ate salad straight from the salad bowl, and watched television, and waited for Sunday. Saturdays were the worst because by Saturday it seemed that Sunday would never come. One Saturday when Dev called, late at night, she heard people laughing and talking in the background, so many that she asked him if he was at a concert hall. But he was only calling from his house in the suburbs. "I can't hear you that well," he said. "We have guests. Miss me?" She looked at the television screen, a sitcom that she'd muted with the remote control when the phone rang. She pictured him whispering into his cell phone, in a room upstairs, a hand on the doorknob, the hallway filled with guests. "Miranda, do you miss me?" he asked again. She told him that she did.

The next day, when Dev came to visit, Miranda asked him what his wife looked like. She was nervous to ask, waiting until he'd smoked the last of his cigarettes, crushing it with a firm twist into the saucer. She wondered if they'd quarrel. But Dev wasn't surprised by the question. He told her, spreading some smoked whitefish on a cracker, that his wife resembled an actress in Bombay named Madhuri Dixit.

For an instant Miranda's heart stopped. But no, the Dixit girl had been named something else, something that began with P. Still, she wondered if the actress and the Dixit girl were related. She'd been plain, wearing her hair in two braids all through high school.

A few days later Miranda went to an Indian grocery in Central Square which also rented videos. The door opened to a complicated tinkling of bells. It was dinnertime, and she was the only customer. A video was playing on a television hooked up in a corner of the store: a row of young women in harem pants were thrusting their hips in synchrony on a beach.

"Can I help you?" the man standing at the cash register asked. He was eating a samosa, dipping it into some dark brown sauce on a paper plate. Below the glass counter at his waist were trays of more plump samosas, and what looked like pale, diamond-shaped pieces of fudge covered with foil, and some bright orange pastries floating in syrup. "You like some video?"

Miranda opened up her Filofax, where she had written "Mottery Dixit." She looked up at the videos on the shelves behind the counter. She saw women wearing skirts that sat low on the hips and tops that tied like bandannas between their breasts. Some leaned back against a stone wall, or a tree. They were beautiful, the way the women dancing on the beach were beautiful, with kohl-rimmed eyes and long black hair. She knew then that Madhuri Dixit was beautiful, too.

"We have subtitled versions, miss," the man continued. He wiped his fingertips quickly on his shirt and pulled out three titles.

"No," Miranda said. "Thank you, no." She wandered through the store, studying shelves lined with unlabeled packets and tins. The freezer case was stuffed with bags of pita bread and vegetables she didn't recognize. The only thing she recognized was a rack lined with bags and bags of the Hot Mix that Laxmi was always eating. She thought about buying some for Laxmi, then hesitated, wondering how to explain what she'd been doing in an Indian grocery.

"Very spicy," the man said, shaking his head, his eyes traveling across Miranda's body. "Too spicy for you."

By February, Laxmi's cousin's husband still hadn't come to his senses. He had returned to Montreal, argued bitterly with his wife for two weeks, packed two suitcases, and flown back to London. He wanted a divorce.

Miranda sat in her cubicle and listened as Laxmi kept telling her cousin that there were better men in the world, just waiting to come out of the woodwork. The next day the cousin said she and her son were going to her parents' house in California, to try to recuperate. Laxmi convinced her to arrange a weekend layover in Boston. "A quick change of place will do you good," Laxmi insisted gently, "besides which, I haven't seen you in years."

Miranda stared at her own phone, wishing Dev would call. It had been four days since their last conversation. She heard Laxmi dialing directory assistance, asking for the number of a beauty salon. "Something soothing," Laxmi requested. She scheduled massages, facials, manicures, and pedicures. Then she reserved a table for lunch at the Four Seasons. In her determination to cheer up her cousin, Laxmi had forgotten about the boy. She rapped her knuckles on the laminated wall.

"Are you busy Saturday?"

The boy was thin. He wore a yellow knapsack strapped across his back, gray herringbone trousers, a red V-necked sweater, and black leather shoes. His hair was cut in a thick fringe over his eyes, which had dark circles under them. They were the first thing Miranda noticed. They made him look haggard, as if he smoked a great deal and slept very little, in spite of the fact that he was only seven years old. He clasped a large sketch pad with a spiral binding. His name was Rohin.

"Ask me a capital," he said, staring up at Miranda.

She stared back at him. It was eight-thirty on a Saturday morning. She took a sip of coffee. "A what?"

"It's a game he's been playing," Laxmi's cousin explained. She was thin like her son, with a long face and the same dark circles under her eyes. A rust-colored coat hung heavy on her shoulders. Her black hair, with a few strands of gray at the temples, was pulled back like a ballerina's. "You ask him a country and he tells you the capital."

"You should have heard him in the car," Laxmi said. "He's already memorized all of Europe."

"It's not a game," Rohin said. "I'm having a competition with a boy at school. We're competing to memorize all the capitals. I'm going to beat him."

Miranda nodded. "Okay. What's the capital of India?"

"That's no good." He marched away, his arms swinging like a toy soldier. Then he marched back to Laxmi's cousin and tugged at a pocket of her overcoat. "Ask me a hard one."

"Senegal," she said.

"Dakar!" Rohin exclaimed triumphantly, and began running in larger and larger circles. Eventually he ran into the kitchen. Miranda could hear him opening and closing the fridge.

"Rohin, don't touch without asking," Laxmi's cousin called out wearily. She managed a smile for Miranda. "Don't worry, he'll fall asleep in a few hours. And thanks for watching him."

"Back at three," Laxmi said, disappearing with her cousin down the hallway. "We're double-parked."

Miranda fastened the chain on the door. She went to the kitchen to find Rohin, but he was now in the living room, at the dining table, kneeling on one of the director's chairs. He unzipped his knapsack, pushed Miranda's basket of manicure supplies to one side of the table, and spread his crayons over the surface. Miranda stood over his shoulder. She watched as he gripped a blue crayon and drew the outline of an airplane.

"It's lovely," she said. When he didn't reply, she went to the kitchen to pour herself more coffee.

"Some for me, please," Rohin called out.

She returned to the living room. "Some what?"

"Some coffee. There's enough in the pot. I saw."

She walked over to the table and sat opposite him. At times he nearly stood up to reach for a new crayon. He barely made a dent in the director's chair.

"You're too young for coffee."

Rohin leaned over the sketch pad, so that his tiny chest and shoulders almost touched it, his head tilted to one side. "The stewardess let me have coffee," he said. "She made it with milk and lots of sugar." He straightened, revealing a woman's face beside the plane, with long wavy hair and eyes like asterisks. "Her hair was more shiny," he decided, adding, "My father met a pretty woman on a plane, too." He looked at Miranda. His face darkened as he watched her sip. "Can't I have just a little coffee? Please?"

She wondered, in spite of his composed, brooding expression, if he were the type to throw a tantrum. She imagined his kicking her with his leather shoes, screaming for coffee, screaming and crying until his mother and Laxmi came back to fetch him. She went to the kitchen and prepared a cup for him as he'd requested. She selected a mug she didn't care for, in case he dropped it.

"Thank you," he said when she put it on the table. He took short sips, holding the mug securely with both hands.

Miranda sat with him while he drew, but when she attempted to put a coat of clear polish on her nails he protested. Instead he pulled out a paperback world almanac from his knapsack and asked her to quiz him. The countries were arranged by continent, six to a page, with the capitals in boldface, followed by a short entry on the population, government, and other statistics. Miranda turned to a page in the Africa section and went down the list.

"Mali," she asked him.

"Bamako," he replied instantly.

"Malawi."

"Lilongwe."

She remembered looking at Africa in the Mapparium. She remembered the fat part of it was green.

"Go on," Rohin said.

"Mauritania."

"Nouakchott."

"Mauritius."

He paused, squeezed his eyes shut, then opened them, defeated. "I can't remember."

"Port Louis," she told him.

"Port Louis." He began to say it again and again, like a chant under his breath.

When they reached the last of the countries in Africa, Rohin said he wanted to watch cartoons, telling Miranda to watch them with him. When the cartoons ended, he followed her to the kitchen, and stood by her side as she made more coffee. He didn't follow her when she went to the bathroom a few minutes later, but when she opened the door she was startled to find him standing outside.

"Do you need to go?"

He shook his head but walked into the bathroom anyway. He put the cover of the toilet down, climbed on top of it, and surveyed the narrow glass shelf over the sink which held Miranda's toothbrush and makeup.

"What's this for?" he asked, picking up the sample of eye gel she'd gotten the day she met Dev.

"Puffiness."

"What's puffiness?"

"Here," she explained, pointing.

"After you've been crying?"

"I guess so."

Rohin opened the tube and smelled it. He squeezed a drop of it onto a finger, then rubbed it on his hand. "It stings." He inspected the back of his hand closely, as if expecting it to change color. "My mother has puffiness. She says it's a cold, but really she cries, sometimes for hours. Sometimes straight through dinner. Sometimes she cries so hard her eyes puff up like bullfrogs."

Miranda wondered if she ought to feed him. In the kitchen

she discovered a bag of rice cakes and some lettuce. She offered to go out, to buy something from the deli, but Rohin said he wasn't very hungry, and accepted one of the rice cakes. "You eat one too," he said. They sat at the table, the rice cakes between them. He turned to a fresh page in his sketch pad. "You draw."

She selected a blue crayon. "What should I draw?"

He thought for a moment. "I know," he said. He asked her to draw things in the living room: the sofa, the director's chairs, the television, the telephone. "This way I can memorize it."

"Memorize what?"

"Our day together." He reached for another rice cake.

"Why do you want to memorize it?"

"Because we're never going to see each other, ever again."

The precision of the phrase startled her. She looked at him, feeling slightly depressed. Rohin didn't look depressed. He tapped the page. "Go on."

And so she drew the items as best as she could—the sofa, the director's chairs, the television, the telephone. He sidled up to her, so close that it was sometimes difficult to see what she was doing. He put his small brown hand over hers. "Now me."

She handed him the crayon.

He shook his head. "No, now draw me."

"I can't," she said. "It won't look like you."

The brooding look began to spread across Rohin's face again, just as it had when she'd refused him coffee. "Please?"

She drew his face, outlining his head and the thick fringe of hair. He sat perfectly still, with a formal, melancholy expression, his gaze fixed to one side. Miranda wished she could draw a good likeness. Her hand moved in conjunction with her eyes, in unknown ways, just as it had that day in the bookstore when she'd transcribed her name in Bengali letters. It looked nothing like him. She was in the middle of drawing his nose when he wriggled away from the table.

"I'm bored," he announced, heading toward her bedroom. She heard him opening the door, opening the drawers of her bureau and closing them.

When she joined him he was inside the closet. After a moment he emerged, his hair disheveled, holding the silver cocktail dress. "This was on the floor."

"It falls off the hanger."

Rohin looked at the dress and then at Miranda's body. "Put it on."

"Excuse me?"

"Put it on."

There was no reason to put it on. Apart from in the fitting room at Filene's she had never worn it, and as long as she was with Dev she knew she never would. She knew they would never go to restaurants, where he would reach across a table and kiss her hand. They would meet in her apartment, on Sundays, he in his sweatpants, she in her jeans. She took the dress from Rohin and shook it out, even though the slinky fabric never wrinkled. She reached into the closet for a free hanger.

"Please put it on," Rohin asked, suddenly standing behind her. He pressed his face against her, clasping her waist with both his thin arms. "Please?"

"All right," she said, surprised by the strength of his grip.

He smiled, satisfied, and sat on the edge of her bed.

"You have to wait out there," she said, pointing to the door. "I'll come out when I'm ready."

"But my mother always takes her clothes off in front of me."

"She does?"

Rohin nodded. "She doesn't even pick them up afterward. She leaves them all on the floor by the bed, all tangled.

"One day she slept in my room," he continued. "She said it felt better than her bed, now that my father's gone."

"I'm not your mother," Miranda said, lifting him by the armpits off her bed. When he refused to stand, she picked him up. He was heavier than she expected, and he clung to her, his legs wrapped firmly around her hips, his head resting against her chest. She set him down in the hallway and shut the door. As an extra precaution she fastened the latch. She changed into the dress, glancing into the full-length mirror nailed to the back of the door. Her ankle socks looked silly, and so she opened a drawer and found the stockings. She searched through the back of the closet and slipped on the high heels with the tiny buckles. The chain straps of the dress were as light as paper clips against her collarbone. It was a bit loose on her. She could not zip it herself.

Rohin began knocking. "May I come in now?"

She opened the door. Rohin was holding his almanac in his hands, muttering something under his breath. His eyes opened wide at the sight of her. "I need help with the zipper," she said. She sat on the edge of the bed.

Rohin fastened the zipper to the top, and then Miranda stood up and twirled. Rohin put down the almanac. "You're sexy," he declared.

"What did you say?"

"You're sexy."

Miranda sat down again. Though she knew it meant nothing, her heart skipped a beat. Rohin probably referred to all women as sexy. He'd probably heard the word on television, or seen it on the cover of a magazine. She remembered the day in the Mapparium, standing across the bridge from Dev. At the time she thought she knew what his words meant. At the time they'd made sense.

Miranda folded her arms across her chest and looked Rohin in the eyes. "Tell me something."

He was silent.

"What does it mean?"

"What?"

"That word. 'Sexy.' What does it mean?"

He looked down, suddenly shy. "I can't tell you."

"Why not?"

"It's a secret." He pressed his lips together, so hard that a bit of them went white.

"Tell me the secret. I want to know."

Rohin sat on the bed beside Miranda and began to kick the edge of the mattress with the backs of his shoes. He giggled nervously, his thin body flinching as if it were being tickled.

"Tell me," Miranda demanded. She leaned over and gripped his ankles, holding his feet still.

Rohin looked at her, his eyes like slits. He struggled to kick the mattress again, but Miranda pressed against him. He fell back on the bed, his back straight as a board. He cupped his hands around his mouth, and then he whispered, "It means loving someone you don't know."

Miranda felt Rohin's words under her skin, the same way she'd felt Dev's. But instead of going hot she felt numb. It reminded her of the way she'd felt at the Indian grocery, the moment she knew, without even looking at a picture, that Madhuri Dixit, whom Dev's wife resembled, was beautiful.

"That's what my father did," Rohin continued. "He sat next to someone he didn't know, someone sexy, and now he loves her instead of my mother."

He took off his shoes and placed them side by side on the floor. Then he peeled back the comforter and crawled into Miranda's bed with the almanac. A minute later the book dropped from his hands, and he closed his eyes. Miranda watched him sleep, the comforter rising and falling as he breathed. He didn't wake up after twelve minutes like Dev, or even twenty. He didn't open his eyes as she stepped out of the silver cocktail dress and back into her jeans, and put the high-heeled shoes in the back of the closet, and rolled up the stockings and put them back in her drawer.

When she had put everything away she sat on the bed. She leaned toward him, close enough to see some white powder from the rice cakes stuck to the corners of his mouth, and picked up the almanac. As she turned the pages she imagined the quarrels Rohin had overheard in his house in Montreal. "Is she pretty?" his mother would have asked his father, wearing the same bathrobe she'd worn for weeks, her own pretty face turning spiteful. "Is she sexy?" His father would deny it at first, try to change the subject. "Tell me," Rohin's mother would shriek, "tell me if she's sexy." In the end his father would admit that she was, and his mother would cry and cry, in a bed surrounded by a tangle of clothes, her eyes puffing up like bullfrogs. "How could you," she'd ask, sobbing, "how could you love a woman you don't even know?"

As Miranda imagined the scene she began to cry a little herself. In the Mapparium that day, all the countries had seemed close enough to touch, and Dev's voice had bounced wildly off the glass. From across the bridge, thirty feet away, his words had reached her ears, so near and full of warmth that they'd drifted for days under her skin. Miranda cried harder, unable to stop. But Rohin still slept. She guessed that he was used to it now, to the sound of a woman crying.

On Sunday, Dev called to tell Miranda he was on his way. "I'm almost ready. I'll be there at two."

She was watching a cooking show on television. A woman pointed to a row of apples, explaining which were best for baking. "You shouldn't come today."

"Why not?"

"I have a cold," she lied. It wasn't far from the truth; crying had left her congested. "I've been in bed all morning."

"You do sound stuffed up." There was a pause. "Do you need anything?"

"I'm all set."

"Drink lots of fluids."

"Dev?"

"Yes, Miranda?"

"Do you remember that day we went to the Mapparium?"

"Of course."

"Do you remember how we whispered to each other?"

"I remember," Dev whispered playfully.

"Do you remember what you said?"

There was a pause. "'Let's go back to your place.'" He laughed quietly. "Next Sunday, then?"

The day before, as she'd cried, Miranda had believed she would never forget anything—not even the way her name looked written in Bengali. She'd fallen asleep beside Rohin and when she woke up he was drawing an airplane on the copy of *The Economist* she'd saved, hidden under the bed. "Who's Devajit Mitra?" he had asked, looking at the address label.

Miranda pictured Dev, in his sweatpants and sneakers, laughing into the phone. In a moment he'd join his wife downstairs, and tell her he wasn't going jogging. He'd pulled a muscle while stretching, he'd say, settling down to read the paper. In spite of herself, she longed for him. She would see him one more Sunday, she decided, perhaps two. Then she would tell him the things she had known all along: that it wasn't fair to her, or to his wife, that they both deserved better, that there was no point in it dragging on.

But the next Sunday it snowed, so much so that Dev couldn't tell his wife he was going running along the Charles. The Sunday after that, the snow had melted, but Miranda made plans to go to the movies with Laxmi, and when she told Dev this over the phone, he didn't ask her to cancel them. The third Sunday she got up early and went out for a walk. It was cold but sunny, and so she walked all the way down Commonwealth Avenue, past the restaurants where Dev had kissed her, and then she walked all the way to the Christian Science center. The Mapparium was closed, but she bought a cup of coffee nearby and sat on one of the benches in the plaza outside the church, gazing at its giant pillars and its massive dome, and at the clear-blue sky spread over the city.

Mrs. Sen's

LIOT had been going to Mrs. Sen's for nearly a month, ever since school started in September. The year before he was looked after by a university student named Abby, a slim, freckled girl who read books without pictures on their covers, and refused to prepare any food for Eliot containing meat. Before that an older woman, Mrs. Linden, greeted him when he came home each afternoon, sipping coffee from a thermos and working on crossword puzzles while Eliot played on his own. Abby received her degree and moved off to another university, while Mrs. Linden was, in the end, fired when Eliot's mother discovered that Mrs. Linden's thermos contained more whiskey than coffee. Mrs. Sen came to them in tidy ballpoint script, posted on an index card outside the supermarket: "Professor's wife, responsible and kind, I will care for your child in my home." On the telephone Eliot's mother told Mrs. Sen that the previous babysitters had come to their house. "Eliot is eleven. He can feed and entertain himself; I just want an adult in the house, in case of an emergency." But Mrs. Sen did not know how to drive.

"As you can see, our home is quite clean, quite safe for a child," Mrs. Sen had said at their first meeting. It was a university apartment located on the fringes of the campus. The lobby was tiled in unattractive squares of tan, with a row of mailboxes marked with masking tape or white labels. Inside, intersecting shadows left by a vacuum cleaner were frozen on the surface of a plush pear-colored carpet. Mismatched remnants of other carpets were positioned in front of the sofa and chairs, like individual welcome mats anticipating where a person's feet would contact the floor. White drum-shaped lampshades flanking the sofa were still wrapped in the manufacturer's plastic. The TV and the telephone were covered by pieces of yellow fabric with scalloped edges. There was tea in a tall gray pot, along with mugs, and butter biscuits on a tray. Mr. Sen, a short, stocky man with slightly protuberant eyes and glasses with black rectangular frames, had been there, too. He crossed his legs with some effort, and held his mug with both hands very close to his mouth, even when he wasn't drinking. Neither Mr. nor Mrs. Sen wore shoes; Eliot noticed several pairs lined on the shelves of a small bookcase by the front door. They wore flip-flops. "Mr. Sen teaches mathematics at the university," Mrs. Sen had said by way of introduction, as if they were only distantly acquainted.

She was about thirty. She had a small gap between her teeth and faded pockmarks on her chin, yet her eyes were beautiful, with thick, flaring brows and liquid flourishes that extended beyond the natural width of the lids. She wore a shimmering white sari patterned with orange paisleys, more suitable for an evening affair than for that quiet, faintly drizzling August afternoon. Her lips were coated in a complementary coral gloss, and a bit of the color had strayed beyond the borders.

Yet it was his mother, Eliot had thought, in her cuffed, beige shorts and her rope-soled shoes, who looked odd. Her cropped hair, a shade similar to her shorts, seemed too lank and sensible, and in that room where all things were so carefully covered, her shaved knees and thighs too exposed. She refused a biscuit each time Mrs. Sen extended the plate in her direction, and asked a long series of questions, the answers to which she recorded on a steno pad. Would there be other children in the apartment? Had Mrs. Sen cared for children before? How long had she lived in this country? Most of all she was concerned that Mrs. Sen did not know how to drive. Eliot's mother worked in an office fifty miles north, and his father, the last she had heard, lived two thousand miles west.

"I have been giving her lessons, actually," Mr. Sen said, setting his mug on the coffee table. It was the first time he had spoken. "By my estimate Mrs. Sen should have her driver's license by December."

"Is that so?" Eliot's mother noted the information on her pad.

"Yes, I am learning," Mrs. Sen said. "But I am a slow student. At home, you know, we have a driver."

"You mean a chauffeur?"

Mrs. Sen glanced at Mr. Sen, who nodded.

Eliot's mother nodded, too, looking around the room. "And that's all . . . in India?"

"Yes," Mrs. Sen replied. The mention of the word seemed to release something in her. She neatened the border of her sari where it rose diagonally across her chest. She, too, looked around the room, as if she noticed in the lampshades, in the teapot, in the shadows frozen on the carpet, something the rest of them could not. "Everything is there."

Eliot didn't mind going to Mrs. Sen's after school. By September the tiny beach house where he and his mother lived year-round was already cold; Eliot and his mother had to bring a portable heater along whenever they moved from one room to another, and to seal the windows with plastic sheets and a hair drier. The beach was barren and dull to play on alone; the only neighbors who stayed on past Labor Day, a young married couple, had no children, and Eliot no longer found it interesting to gather broken mussel shells in his bucket, or to stroke the seaweed, strewn like strips of emerald lasagna on the sand. Mrs. Sen's apartment was warm, sometimes too warm; the radiators continuously hissed like a pressure cooker. Eliot learned to remove his sneakers first thing in Mrs. Sen's doorway, and to place them on the bookcase next to a row of Mrs. Sen's slippers, each a different color, with soles as flat as cardboard and a ring of leather to hold her big toe.

He especially enjoyed watching Mrs. Sen as she chopped things, seated on newspapers on the living room floor. Instead of a knife she used a blade that curved like the prow of a Viking ship, sailing to battle in distant seas. The blade was hinged at one end to a narrow wooden base. The steel, more black than silver, lacked a uniform polish, and had a serrated crest, she told Eliot, for grating. Each afternoon Mrs. Sen lifted the blade and locked it into place, so that it met the base at an angle. Facing the sharp edge without ever touching it, she took whole vegetables between her hands and hacked them apart: cauliflower, cabbage, butternut squash. She split things in half, then quarters, speedily producing florets, cubes, slices, and shreds. She could peel a potato in seconds. At times she sat cross-legged, at times with legs splayed, surrounded by an array of colanders and shallow bowls of water in which she immersed her chopped ingredients.

While she worked she kept an eye on the television and an eye on Eliot, but she never seemed to keep an eye on the blade. Nevertheless she refused to let Eliot walk around when she was chopping. "Just sit, sit please, it will take just two more minutes," she said, pointing to the sofa, which was draped at all times with a green and black bedcover printed with rows of elephants bearing palanquins on their backs. The daily procedure took about an hour. In order to occupy Eliot she supplied him with the comics section of the newspaper, and crackers spread with peanut butter, and sometimes a Popsicle, or carrot sticks sculpted with her blade. She would have roped off the area if she could. Once, though, she broke her own rule; in need of additional supplies, and reluctant to rise from the catastrophic mess that barricaded her, she asked Eliot to fetch something from the kitchen. "If you don't mind, there is a plastic bowl, large enough to hold this spinach, in the cabinet next to the fridge. Careful, oh dear, be careful," she cautioned as he approached. "Just leave it, thank you, on the coffee table, I can reach."

She had brought the blade from India, where apparently there was at least one in every household. "Whenever there is a wedding in the family," she told Eliot one day, "or a large celebration of any kind, my mother sends out word in the evening for all the neighborhood women to bring blades just like this one, and then they sit in an enormous circle on the roof of our building, laughing and gossiping and slicing fifty kilos of vegetables through the night." Her profile hovered protectively over her work, a confetti of cucumber, eggplant, and onion skins heaped around her. "It is impossible to fall asleep those nights, listening to their chatter." She paused to look at a pine tree framed by the living room window. "Here, in this place where Mr. Sen has brought me, I cannot sometimes sleep in so much silence."

Another day she sat prying the pimpled yellow fat off chicken parts, then dividing them between thigh and leg. As the bones cracked apart over the blade her golden bangles jostled, her forearms glowed, and she exhaled audibly through her nose. At one point she paused, gripping the chicken with both hands, and stared out the window. Fat and sinew clung to her fingers.

"Eliot, if I began to scream right now at the top of my lungs, would someone come?"

"Mrs. Sen, what's wrong?"

"Nothing. I am only asking if someone would come."

Eliot shrugged. "Maybe."

"At home that is all you have to do. Not everybody has a telephone. But just raise your voice a bit, or express grief or joy of any kind, and one whole neighborhood and half of another has come to share the news, to help with arrangements."

By then Eliot understood that when Mrs. Sen said home, she meant India, not the apartment where she sat chopping vegetables. He thought of his own home, just five miles away, and the young married couple who waved from time to time as they jogged at sunset along the shore. On Labor Day they'd had a party. People were piled on the deck, eating, drinking, the sound of their laughter rising above the weary sigh of the waves. Eliot and his mother weren't invited. It was one of the rare days his mother had off, but they didn't go anywhere. She did the laundry, and balanced the checkbook, and, with Eliot's help, vacuumed the inside of the car. Eliot had suggested that they go through the car wash a few miles down the road as they did every now and then, so that they could sit inside, safe and dry, as soap and water and a circle of giant canvas ribbons slapped the windshield, but his mother said she was too tired, and sprayed the car with a hose. When, by evening, the crowd on the neighbors' deck began dancing, she looked up their number in the phone book and asked them to keep it down.

"They might call you," Eliot said eventually to Mrs. Sen. "But they might complain that you were making too much noise."

From where Eliot sat on the sofa he could detect her curious scent of mothballs and cumin, and he could see the perfectly centered part in her braided hair, which was shaded with crushed vermilion and therefore appeared to be blushing. At first Eliot had wondered if she had cut her scalp, or if something had bitten her there. But then one day he saw her standing before the bathroom mirror, solemnly applying, with the head of a thumbtack, a fresh stroke of scarlet powder, which she stored in a small jam jar. A few grains of the powder fell onto the bridge of her nose as she used the thumbtack to stamp a dot above her eyebrows. "I must wear the powder every day," she explained when Eliot asked her what it was for, "for the rest of the days that I am married."

"Like a wedding ring, you mean?"

"Exactly, Eliot, exactly like a wedding ring. Only with no fear of losing it in the dishwater."

By the time Eliot's mother arrived at twenty past six, Mrs. Sen always made sure all evidence of her chopping was disposed of. The blade was scrubbed, rinsed, dried, folded, and stowed away in a cupboard with the aid of a stepladder. With Eliot's help the newspapers were crushed with all the peels and seeds and skins inside them. Brimming bowls and colanders lined the countertop, spices and pastes were measured and blended, and eventually a collection of broths simmered over periwinkle flames on the stove. It was never a special occasion, nor was she ever expecting company. It was merely dinner for herself and Mr. Sen, as indicated by the two plates and two glasses she set, without napkins or silverware, on the square Formica table at one end of the living room.

As he pressed the newspapers deeper into the garbage pail, Eliot felt that he and Mrs. Sen were disobeying some unspoken rule. Perhaps it was because of the urgency with which Mrs. Sen accomplished everything, pinching salt and sugar between her fingernails, running water through lentils, sponging all imaginable surfaces, shutting cupboard doors with a series of successive clicks. It gave him a little shock to see his mother all of a sudden, in the transparent stockings and shoulder-padded suits she wore to her job, peering into the corners of Mrs. Sen's apartment. She tended to hover on the far side of the door frame, calling to Eliot to put on his sneakers and gather his things, but Mrs. Sen would not allow it. Each evening she insisted that his mother sit on the sofa, where she was served something to eat: a glass of bright pink yogurt with rose syrup, breaded mincemeat with raisins, a bowl of semolina halvah.

"Really, Mrs. Sen. I take a late lunch. You shouldn't go to so much trouble."

"It is no trouble. Just like Eliot. No trouble at all."

His mother nibbled Mrs. Sen's concoctions with eyes cast upward, in search of an opinion. She kept her knees pressed together, the high heels she never removed pressed into the pear-colored carpet. "It's delicious," she would conclude, setting down the plate after a bite or two. Eliot knew she didn't like the tastes; she'd told him so once in the car. He also knew she didn't eat lunch at work, because the first thing she did when they were back at the beach house was pour herself a glass of wine and eat bread and cheese, sometimes so much of it that she wasn't hungry for the pizza they normally ordered for dinner. She sat at the table as he ate, drinking more wine and asking how his day was, but eventually she went to the deck to smoke a cigarette, leaving Eliot to wrap up the leftovers.

Each afternoon Mrs. Sen stood in a grove of pine trees by the main road where the school bus dropped off Eliot along with two or three other children who lived nearby. Eliot always sensed that Mrs. Sen had been waiting for some time, as if eager to greet a person she hadn't seen in years. The hair at her temples blew about in the breeze, the column of vermilion fresh in her part. She wore navy blue sunglasses a little too big for her face. Her sari, a different pattern each day, fluttered below the hem of a checkered all-weather coat. Acorns and caterpillars dotted the asphalt loop that framed the complex of about a dozen brick buildings, all identical, embedded in a communal expanse of log chips. As they walked back from the bus stop she produced a sandwich bag from her pocket, and offered Eliot the peeled wedges of an orange, or lightly salted peanuts, which she had already shelled.

They proceeded directly to the car, and for twenty minutes Mrs. Sen practiced driving. It was a toffee-colored sedan with vinyl seats. There was an AM radio with chrome buttons, and on the ledge over the back seat, a box of Kleenex and an ice scraper. Mrs. Sen told Eliot she didn't feel right leaving him alone in the apartment, but Eliot knew she wanted him sitting beside her because she was afraid. She dreaded the roar of the ignition, and placed her hands over her ears to block out the sound as she pressed her slippered feet to the gas, revving the engine.

"Mr. Sen says that once I receive my license, everything will improve. What do you think, Eliot? Will things improve?"

"You could go places," Eliot suggested. "You could go anywhere."

"Could I drive all the way to Calcutta? How long would that take, Eliot? Ten thousand miles, at fifty miles per hour?"

Eliot could not do the math in his head. He watched Mrs. Sen adjust the driver's seat, the rearview mirror, the sunglasses on top of her head. She tuned the radio to a station that played symphonies. "Is it Beethoven?" she asked once, pronouncing the first part of the composer's name not "bay," but "bee," like the insect. She rolled down the window on her side, and asked Eliot to do the same. Eventually she pressed her foot to the brake pedal, manipulated the automatic gear shift as if it were an enormous, leaky pen, and backed inch by inch out of the parking space. She circled the apartment complex once, then once again.

"How am I doing, Eliot? Am I going to pass?"

She was continuously distracted. She stopped the car without warning to listen to something on the radio, or to stare at something, anything, in the road. If she passed a person, she waved. If she saw a bird twenty feet in front of her, she beeped the horn with her index finger and waited for it to fly away. In India, she said, the driver sat on the right side, not the left. Slowly they crept past the swing set, the laundry building, the dark green trash bins, the rows of parked cars. Each time they approached the grove of pine trees where the asphalt loop met the main road, she leaned forward, pinning all her weight against the brake as cars hurtled past. It was a narrow road painted with a solid yellow stripe, with one lane of traffic in either direction.

"Impossible, Eliot. How can I go there?"

"You need to wait until no one's coming."

"Why will not anybody slow down?"

"No one's coming now."

"But what about the car from the right, do you see? And look, a truck is behind it. Anyway, I am not allowed on the main road without Mr. Sen."

"You have to turn and speed up fast," Eliot said. That was the way his mother did it, as if without thinking. It seemed so simple when he sat beside his mother, gliding in the evenings back to the beach house. Then the road was just a road, the other cars merely part of the scenery. But when he sat with Mrs. Sen, under an autumn sun that glowed without warmth through the trees, he saw how that same stream of cars made her knuckles pale, her wrists tremble, and her English falter.

"Everyone, this people, too much in their world."

• • •

Two things, Eliot learned, made Mrs. Sen happy. One was the arrival of a letter from her family. It was her custom to check the mailbox after driving practice. She would unlock the box, but she would ask Eliot to reach inside, telling him what to look for, and then she would shut her eyes and shield them with her hands while he shuffled through the bills and magazines that came in Mr. Sen's name. At first Eliot found Mrs. Sen's anxiety incomprehensible; his mother had a p.o. box in town, and she collected mail so infrequently that once their electricity was cut off for three days. Weeks passed at Mrs. Sen's before he found a blue aerogram, grainy to the touch, crammed with stamps showing a bald man at a spinning wheel, and blackened by postmarks.

"Is this it, Mrs. Sen?"

For the first time she embraced him, clasping his face to her sari, surrounding him with her odor of mothballs and cumin. She seized the letter from his hands.

As soon as they were inside the apartment she kicked off her slippers this way and that, drew a wire pin from her hair, and slit the top and sides of the aerogram in three strokes. Her eyes darted back and forth as she read. As soon as she was finished, she cast aside the embroidery that covered the telephone, dialed, and asked, "Yes, is Mr. Sen there, please? It is Mrs. Sen and it is very important."

Subsequently she spoke in her own language, rapid and riotous to Eliot's ears; it was clear that she was reading the contents of the letter, word by word. As she read her voice was louder and seemed to shift in key. Though she stood plainly before him, Eliot had the sensation that Mrs. Sen was no longer present in the room with the pear-colored carpet.

Afterward the apartment was suddenly too small to contain her. They crossed the main road and walked a short distance to the university quadrangle, where bells in a stone tower chimed on the hour. They wandered through the student union, and dragged a tray together along the cafeteria ledge, and ate french fries heaped in a cardboard boat among students chatting at circular tables. Eliot drank soda from a paper cup, Mrs. Sen steeped a tea bag with sugar and cream. After eating they explored the art building, looking at sculptures and silk screens in cool corridors thick with the fragrance of wet paint and clay. They walked past the mathematics building, where Mr. Sen taught his classes.

They ended up in the noisy, chlorine-scented wing of the athletic building where, through a wide window on the fourth floor, they watched swimmers crossing from end to end in glaring turquoise pools. Mrs. Sen took the aerogram from India out of her purse and studied the front and back. She unfolded it and reread to herself, sighing every now and then. When she had finished she gazed for some time at the swimmers.

"My sister has had a baby girl. By the time I see her, depending if Mr. Sen gets his tenure, she will be three years old. Her own aunt will be a stranger. If we sit side by side on a train she will not know my face." She put away the letter, then placed a hand on Eliot's head. "Do you miss your mother, Eliot, these afternoons with me?"

The thought had never occurred to him.

"You must miss her. When I think of you, only a boy, separated from your mother for so much of the day, I am ashamed."

"I see her at night."

"When I was your age I was without knowing that one day I would be so far. You are wiser than that, Eliot. You already taste the way things must be."

The other thing that made Mrs. Sen happy was fish from the seaside. It was always a whole fish she desired, not shellfish, or the fillets Eliot's mother had broiled one night a few months ago when she'd invited a man from her office to dinner—a man who'd spent the night in his mother's bedroom, but whom Eliot never saw again. One evening when Eliot's mother came to pick him up, Mrs. Sen served her a tuna croquette, explaining that it was really supposed to be made with a fish called bhetki. "It is very frustrating," Mrs. Sen apologized, with an emphasis on the second syllable of the word. "To live so close to the ocean and not to have so much fish." In the summer, she said, she liked to go to a market by the beach. She added that while the fish there tasted nothing like the fish in India, at least it was fresh. Now that it was getting colder, the boats were no longer going out regularly, and sometimes there was no whole fish available for weeks at a time.

"Try the supermarket," his mother suggested.

Mrs. Sen shook her head. "In the supermarket I can feed a cat thirty-two dinners from one of thirty-two tins, but I can never find a single fish I like, never a single." Mrs. Sen said she had grown up eating fish twice a day. She added that in Calcutta people ate fish first thing in the morning, last thing before bed, as a snack after school if they were lucky. They ate the tail, the eggs, even the head. It was available in any market, at any hour, from dawn until midnight. "All you have to do is leave the house and walk a bit, and there you are."

Every few days Mrs. Sen would open up the yellow pages, dial a number that she had ticked in the margin, and ask if there was any whole fish available. If so, she would ask the market to hold it. "Under Sen, yes, S as in Sam, N as in New York. Mr. Sen will be there to pick it up." Then she would call Mr. Sen at the university. A few minutes later Mr. Sen would arrive, patting Eliot on the head but not kissing Mrs. Sen. He read his mail at the Formica table and drank a cup of tea before heading out; half an hour later he would return, carrying a paper bag with a smiling lobster drawn on the front of it, and hand it

to Mrs. Sen, and head back to the university to teach his evening class. One day, when he handed Mrs. Sen the paper bag,
he said, "No more fish for a while. Cook the chicken in the
freezer. I need to start holding office hours."

For the next few days, instead of calling the fish market, Mrs.
Sen thawed chicken legs in the kitchen sink and chopped them
with her blade. One day she made a stew with green beans and
tinned sardines. But the following week the man who ran the
fish market called Mrs. Sen; he assumed she wanted the fish,
and said he would hold it until the end of the day under her
name. She was flattered. "Isn't that nice of him, Eliot? The man
said he looked up my name in the telephone book. He said
there is only one Sen. Do you know how many Sens are in the
Calcutta telephone book?"

She told Eliot to put on his shoes and his jacket, and then
she called Mr. Sen at the university. Eliot tied his sneakers by
the bookcase and waited for her to join him, to choose from
her row of slippers. After a few minutes he called out her name.
When Mrs. Sen did not reply, he untied his sneakers and returned to the living room, where he found her on the sofa,
weeping. Her face was in her hands and tears dripped through
her fingers. Through them she murmured something about a
meeting Mr. Sen was required to attend. Slowly she stood up
and rearranged the cloth over the telephone. Eliot followed
her, walking for the first time in his sneakers across the pear-
colored carpet. She stared at him. Her lower eyelids were
swollen into thin pink crests. "Tell me, Eliot. Is it too much to
ask?"

Before he could answer, she took him by the hand and led
him to the bedroom, whose door was normally kept shut. Apart
from the bed, which lacked a headboard, the only other things
in the room were a side table with a telephone on it, an ironing
board, and a bureau. She flung open the drawers of the bureau

and the door of the closet, filled with saris of every imaginable texture and shade, brocaded with gold and silver threads. Some were transparent, tissue thin, others as thick as drapes, with tassels knotted along the edges. In the closet they were on hangers; in the drawers they were folded flat, or wound tightly like thick scrolls. She sifted through the drawers, letting saris spill over the edges. "When have I ever worn this one? And this? And this?" She tossed the saris one by one from the drawers, then pried several from their hangers. They landed like a pile of tangled sheets on the bed. The room was filled with an intense smell of mothballs.

"'Send pictures,' they write. 'Send pictures of your new life.' What picture can I send?" She sat, exhausted, on the edge of the bed, where there was now barely room for her. "They think I live the life of a queen, Eliot." She looked around the blank walls of the room. "They think I press buttons and the house is clean. They think I live in a palace."

The phone rang. Mrs. Sen let it ring several times before picking up the extension by the bed. During the conversation she seemed only to be replying to things, and wiping her face with the ends of one of the saris. When she got off the phone she stuffed the saris without folding them back into the drawers, and then she and Eliot put on their shoes and went to the car, where they waited for Mr. Sen to meet them.

"Why don't you drive today?" Mr. Sen asked when he appeared, rapping on the hood of the car with his knuckles. They always spoke to each other in English when Eliot was present.

"Not today. Another day."

"How do you expect to pass the test if you refuse to drive on a road with other cars?"

"Eliot is here today."

"He is here every day. It's for your own good. Eliot, tell Mrs. Sen it's for her own good."

She refused.

They drove in silence, along the same roads that Eliot and his mother took back to the beach house each evening. But in the back seat of Mr. and Mrs. Sen's car the ride seemed unfamiliar, and took longer than usual. The gulls whose tedious cries woke him each morning now thrilled him as they dipped and flapped across the sky. They passed one beach after another, and the shacks, now locked up, that sold frozen lemonade and quahogs in summer. Only one of the shacks was open. It was the fish market.

Mrs. Sen unlocked her door and turned toward Mr. Sen, who had not yet unfastened his seat belt. "Are you coming?"

Mr. Sen handed her some bills from his wallet. "I have a meeting in twenty minutes," he said, staring at the dashboard as he spoke. "Please don't waste time."

Eliot accompanied her into the dank little shop, whose walls were festooned with nets and starfish and buoys. A group of tourists with cameras around their necks huddled by the counter, some sampling stuffed clams, others pointing to a large chart illustrating fifty different varieties of North Atlantic fish. Mrs. Sen took a ticket from the machine at the counter and waited in line. Eliot stood by the lobsters, which stirred one on top of another in their murky tank, their claws bound by yellow rubber bands. He watched as Mrs. Sen laughed and chatted, when it was her turn in line, with a man with a bright red face and yellow teeth, dressed in a black rubber apron. In either hand he held a mackerel by the tail.

"You are sure what you sell me is very fresh?"

"Any fresher and they'd answer that question themselves."

The dial shivered toward its verdict on the scale.

"You want this cleaned, Mrs. Sen?"

She nodded. "Leave the heads on, please."

"You got cats at home?"

"No cats. Only a husband."

Later, in the apartment, she pulled the blade out of the cupboard, spread newspapers across the carpet, and inspected her treasures. One by one she drew them from the paper wrapping, wrinkled and tinged with blood. She stroked the tails, prodded the bellies, pried apart the gutted flesh. With a pair of scissors she clipped the fins. She tucked a finger under the gills, a red so bright they made her vermilion seem pale. She grasped the body, lined with inky streaks, at either end, and notched it at intervals against the blade.

"Why do you do that?" Eliot asked.

"To see how many pieces. If I cut properly, from this fish I will get three meals." She sawed off the head and set it on a pie plate.

In November came a series of days when Mrs. Sen refused to practice driving. The blade never emerged from the cupboard, newspapers were not spread on the floor. She did not call the fish store, nor did she thaw chicken. In silence she prepared crackers with peanut butter for Eliot, then sat reading old aerograms from a shoebox. When it was time for Eliot to leave she gathered together his things without inviting his mother to sit on the sofa and eat something first. When, eventually, his mother asked him in the car if he'd noticed a change in Mrs. Sen's behavior, he said he hadn't. He didn't tell her that Mrs. Sen paced the apartment, staring at the plastic-covered lampshades as if noticing them for the first time. He didn't tell her she switched on the television but never watched it, or that she made herself tea but let it grow cold on the coffee table. One day she played a tape of something she called a raga; it sounded a little bit like someone plucking very slowly and then very quickly on a violin, and Mrs. Sen said it was supposed to be heard only in the late afternoon, as the sun was setting. As the music played, for nearly an hour, she sat on the sofa with her eyes closed. Afterward she said, "It is more sad even than your Beethoven, isn't it?" Another day she played a cassette of people talking in her language—a farewell present, she told Eliot, that her family had made for her. As the succession of voices laughed and said their bit, Mrs. Sen identified each speaker. "My third uncle, my cousin, my father, my grandfather." One speaker sang a song. Another recited a poem. The final voice on the tape belonged to Mrs. Sen's mother. It was quieter and sounded more serious than the others. There was a pause between each sentence, and during this pause Mrs. Sen translated for Eliot: "The price of goat rose two rupees. The mangoes at the market are not very sweet. College Street is flooded." She turned off the tape. "These are things that happened the day I left India." The next day she played the same cassette all over again. This time, when her grandfather was speaking, she stopped the tape. She told Eliot she'd received a letter over the weekend. Her grandfather was dead.

A week later Mrs. Sen began cooking again. One day as she sat slicing cabbage on the living room floor, Mr. Sen called. He wanted to take Eliot and Mrs. Sen to the seaside. For the occasion Mrs. Sen put on a red sari and red lipstick; she freshened the vermilion in her part and rebraided her hair. She knotted a scarf under her chin, arranged her sunglasses on top of her head, and put a pocket camera in her purse. As Mr. Sen backed out of the parking lot, he put his arm across the top of the front seat, so that it looked as if he had his arm around Mrs. Sen. "It's getting too cold for that top coat," he said to her at one point. "We should get you something warmer." At the shop they bought mackerel, and butterfish, and sea bass. This time Mr. Sen came into the shop with them. It was Mr. Sen who asked whether the fish was fresh and to cut it this way or that way. They bought so much fish that Eliot had to hold one of the bags. After they put the bags in the trunk, Mr. Sen announced that he was hungry, and Mrs. Sen agreed, so they crossed the street to a restaurant where the take-out window was still open. They sat at a picnic table and ate two baskets of clam cakes. Mrs. Sen put a good deal of Tabasco sauce and black pepper on hers. "Like pakoras, no?" Her face was flushed, her lipstick faded, and she laughed at everything Mr. Sen said.

Behind the restaurant was a small beach, and when they were done eating they walked for a while along the shore, into a wind so strong that they had to walk backward. Mrs. Sen pointed to the water, and said that at a certain moment, each wave resembled a sari drying on a clothesline. "Impossible!" she shouted eventually, laughing as she turned back, her eyes teary. "I cannot move." Instead she took a picture of Eliot and Mr. Sen standing on the sand. "Now one of us," she said, pressing Eliot against her checkered coat and giving the camera to Mr. Sen. Finally the camera was given to Eliot. "Hold it steady," said Mr. Sen. Eliot looked through the tiny window in the camera and waited for Mr. and Mrs. Sen to move closer together, but they didn't. They didn't hold hands or put their arms around each other's waists. Both smiled with their mouths closed, squinting into the wind, Mrs. Sen's red sari leaping like flames under her coat.

In the car, warm at last and exhausted from the wind and the clam cakes, they admired the dunes, the ships they could see in the distance, the view of the lighthouse, the peach and purple sky. After a while Mr. Sen slowed down and stopped by the side of the road.

"What's wrong?" Mrs. Sen asked.

"You are going to drive home today."

"Not today."

"Yes, today." Mr. Sen stepped out of the car and opened the

door on Mrs. Sen's side. A fierce wind blew into the car, accompanied by the sound of waves crashing on the shore. Finally she slid over to the driver's side, but spent a long time adjusting her sari and her sunglasses. Eliot turned and looked through the back window. The road was empty. Mrs. Sen turned on the radio, filling up the car with violin music.

"There's no need," Mr. Sen said, clicking it off.

"It helps me to concentrate," Mrs. Sen said, and turned the radio on again.

"Put on your signal," Mr. Sen directed.

"I know what to do."

For about a mile she was fine, though far slower than the other cars that passed her. But when the town approached, and traffic lights loomed on wires in the distance, she went even slower.

"Switch lanes," Mr. Sen said. "You will have to bear left at the rotary."

Mrs. Sen did not.

"Switch lanes, I tell you." He shut off the radio. "Are you listening to me?"

A car beeped its horn, then another. She beeped defiantly in response, stopped, then pulled without signaling to the side of the road. "No more," she said, her forehead resting against the top of the steering wheel. "I hate it. I hate driving. I won't go on."

She stopped driving after that. The next time the fish store called she did not call Mr. Sen at his office. She had decided to try something new. There was a town bus that ran on an hourly schedule between the university and the seaside. After the university it made two stops, first at a nursing home, then at a shopping plaza without a name, which consisted of a bookstore, a shoe store, a drugstore, a pet store, and a record store.

On benches under the portico, elderly women from the nursing home sat in pairs, in knee-length overcoats with oversized
buttons, eating lozenges.

"Eliot," Mrs. Sen asked him while they were sitting on the
bus, "will you put your mother in a nursing home when she is
old?"

"Maybe," he said. "But I would visit every day."

"You say that now, but you will see, when you are a man
your life will be in places you cannot know now." She counted
on her fingers: "You will have a wife, and children of your own,
and they will want to be driven to different places at the same
time. No matter how kind they are, one day they will complain about visiting your mother, and you will get tired of it
too, Eliot. You will miss one day, and another, and then she
will have to drag herself onto a bus just to get herself a bag of
lozenges."

At the fish shop the ice beds were nearly empty, as were the
lobster tanks, where rust-colored stains were visible through
the water. A sign said the shop would be closing for winter at
the end of the month. There was only one person working behind the counter, a young boy who did not recognize Mrs. Sen
as he handed her a bag reserved under her name.

"Has it been cleaned and scaled?" Mrs. Sen asked.

The boy shrugged. "My boss left early. He just said to give
you this bag."

In the parking lot Mrs. Sen consulted the bus schedule. They
would have to wait forty-five minutes for the next one, and so
they crossed the street and bought clam cakes at the take-out
window they had been to before. There was no place to sit. The
picnic tables were no longer in use, their benches chained upside down on top of them.

On the way home an old woman on the bus kept watching
them, her eyes shifting from Mrs. Sen to Eliot to the blood-

lined bag between their feet. She wore a black overcoat, and in her lap she held, with gnarled, colorless hands, a crisp white bag from the drugstore. The only other passengers were two college students, boyfriend and girlfriend, wearing matching sweatshirts, their fingers linked, slouched in the back seat. In silence Eliot and Mrs. Sen ate the last few clam cakes in the bag. Mrs. Sen had forgotten napkins, and traces of fried batter dotted the corners of her mouth. When they reached the nursing home the woman in the overcoat stood up, said something to the driver, then stepped off the bus. The driver turned his head and glanced back at Mrs. Sen. "What's in the bag?"

Mrs. Sen looked up, startled.

"Speak English?" The bus began to move again, causing the driver to look at Mrs. Sen and Eliot in his enormous rearview mirror.

"Yes, I can speak."

"Then what's in the bag?"

"A fish," Mrs. Sen replied.

"The smell seems to be bothering the other passengers. Kid, maybe you should open her window or something."

One afternoon a few days later the phone rang. Some very tasty halibut had arrived on the boats. Would Mrs. Sen like to pick one up? She called Mr. Sen, but he was not at his desk. A second time she tried calling, then a third. Eventually she went to the kitchen and returned to the living room with the blade, an eggplant, and some newspapers. Without having to be told Eliot took his place on the sofa and watched as she sliced the stems off the eggplant. She divided it into long, slender strips, then into small squares, smaller and smaller, as small as sugar cubes.

"I am going to put these in a very tasty stew with fish and green bananas," she announced. "Only I will have to do without the green bananas."

"Are we going to get the fish?"

"We are going to get the fish."

"Is Mr. Sen going to take us?"

"Put on your shoes."

They left the apartment without cleaning up. Outside it was so cold that Eliot could feel the chill on his teeth. They got in the car, and Mrs. Sen drove around the asphalt loop several times. Each time she paused by the grove of pine trees to observe the traffic on the main road. Eliot thought she was just practicing while they waited for Mr. Sen. But then she gave a signal and turned.

The accident occurred quickly. After about a mile Mrs. Sen took a left before she should have, and though the oncoming car managed to swerve out of her way, she was so startled by the horn that she lost control of the wheel and hit a telephone pole on the opposite corner. A policeman arrived and asked to see her license, but she did not have one to show him. "Mr. Sen teaches mathematics at the university" was all she said by way of explanation.

The damage was slight. Mrs. Sen cut her lip, Eliot complained briefly of a pain in his ribs, and the car's fender would have to be straightened. The policeman thought Mrs. Sen had also cut her scalp, but it was only the vermilion. When Mr. Sen arrived, driven by one of his colleagues, he spoke at length with the policeman as he filled out some forms, but he said nothing to Mrs. Sen as he drove them back to the apartment. When they got out of the car, Mr. Sen patted Eliot's head. "The policeman said you were lucky. Very lucky to come out without a scratch."

After taking off her slippers and putting them on the bookcase, Mrs. Sen put away the blade that was still on the living room floor and threw the eggplant pieces and the newspapers into the garbage pail. She prepared a plate of crackers with peanut butter, placed them on the coffee table, and turned on the television for Eliot's benefit. "If he is still hungry give him a Popsicle from the box in the freezer," she said to Mr. Sen, who sat at the Formica table sorting through the mail. Then she went into her bedroom and shut the door. When Eliot's mother arrived at quarter to six, Mr. Sen told her the details of the accident and offered a check reimbursing November's payment. As he wrote out the check he apologized on behalf of Mrs. Sen. He said she was resting, though when Eliot had gone to the bathroom he'd heard her crying. His mother was satisfied with the arrangement, and in a sense, she confessed to Eliot as they drove home, she was relieved. It was the last afternoon Eliot spent with Mrs. Sen, or with any baby-sitter. From then on his mother gave him a key, which he wore on a string around his neck. He was to call the neighbors in case of an emergency, and to let himself into the beach house after school. The first day, just as he was taking off his coat, the phone rang. It was his mother calling from her office. "You're a big boy now, Eliot," she told him. "You okay?" Eliot looked out the kitchen window, at gray waves receding from the shore, and said that he was fine.

This Blessed House

THEY discovered the first one in a cupboard above the stove, beside an unopened bottle of malt vinegar.

"Guess what I found." Twinkle walked into the living room, lined from end to end with taped-up packing boxes, waving the vinegar in one hand and a white porcelain effigy of Christ, roughly the same size as the vinegar bottle, in the other.

Sanjeev looked up. He was kneeling on the floor, marking, with ripped bits of a Post-it, patches on the baseboard that needed to be retouched with paint. "Throw it away."

"Which?"

"Both."

"But I can cook something with the vinegar. It's brand-new."

"You've never cooked anything with vinegar."

"I'll look something up. In one of those books we got for our wedding."

Sanjeev turned back to the baseboard, to replace a Post-it scrap that had fallen to the floor. "Check the expiration. And at the very least get rid of that idiotic statue."

"But it could be worth something. Who knows?" She turned it upside down, then stroked, with her index finger, the minuscule frozen folds of its robes. "It's pretty."

"We're not Christian," Sanjeev said. Lately he had begun noticing the need to state the obvious to Twinkle. The day before he had to tell her that if she dragged her end of the bureau instead of lifting it, the parquet floor would scratch.

She shrugged. "No, we're not Christian. We're good little Hindus." She planted a kiss on top of Christ's head, then placed the statue on top of the fireplace mantel, which needed, Sanjeev observed, to be dusted.

By the end of the week the mantel had still not been dusted; it had, however, come to serve as the display shelf for a sizable collection of Christian paraphernalia. There was a 3-D postcard of Saint Francis done in four colors, which Twinkle had found taped to the back of the medicine cabinet, and a wooden cross key chain, which Sanjeev had stepped on with bare feet as he was installing extra shelving in Twinkle's study. There was a framed paint-by-number of the three wise men, against a black velvet background, tucked in the linen closet. There was also a tile trivet depicting a blond, unbearded Jesus, delivering a sermon on a mountaintop, left in one of the drawers of the built-in china cabinet in the dining room.

"Do you think the previous owners were born-agains?" asked Twinkle, making room the next day for a small plastic snow-filled dome containing a miniature Nativity scene, found behind the pipes of the kitchen sink.

Sanjeev was organizing his engineering texts from MIT in alphabetical order on a bookshelf, though it had been several years since he had needed to consult any of them. After graduating, he moved from Boston to Connecticut, to work for a firm near Hartford, and he had recently learned that he was being considered for the position of vice president. At thirty-three he had a secretary of his own and a dozen people working under his supervision who gladly supplied him with any information he needed. Still, the presence of his college books in the room reminded him of a time in his life he recalled with fondness, when he would walk each evening across the Mass. Avenue bridge to order Mughlai chicken with spinach from his favorite Indian restaurant on the other side of the Charles, and return to his dorm to write out clean copies of his problem sets.

"Or perhaps it's an attempt to convert people," Twinkle mused.

"Clearly the scheme has succeeded in your case."

She disregarded him, shaking the little plastic dome so that the snow swirled over the manger.

He studied the items on the mantel. It puzzled him that each was in its own way so silly. Clearly they lacked a sense of sacredness. He was further puzzled that Twinkle, who normally displayed good taste, was so charmed. These objects meant something to Twinkle, but they meant nothing to him. They irritated him. "We should call the Realtor. Tell him there's all this nonsense left behind. Tell him to take it away."

"Oh, Sanj." Twinkle groaned. "Please. I would feel terrible throwing them away. Obviously they were important to the people who used to live here. It would feel, I don't know, sacrilegious or something."

"If they're so precious, then why are they hidden all over the house? Why didn't they take them with them?

"There must be others," Twinkle said. Her eyes roamed the bare off-white walls of the room, as if there were other things concealed behind the plaster. "What else do you think we'll find?"

But as they unpacked their boxes and hung up their winter clothes and the silk paintings of elephant processions bought on their honeymoon in Jaipur, Twinkle, much to her dismay, could not find a thing. Nearly a week had passed before they discovered, one Saturday afternoon, a larger-than-life-sized watercolor poster of Christ, weeping translucent tears the size of peanut shells and sporting a crown of thorns, rolled up behind a radiator in the guest bedroom. Sanjeev had mistaken it for a window shade.

"Oh, we must, we simply must put it up. It's too spectacular." Twinkle lit a cigarette and began to smoke it with relish, waving it around Sanjeev's head as if it were a conductor's baton as Mahler's Fifth Symphony roared from the stereo downstairs.

"Now, look. I will tolerate, for now, your little biblical menagerie in the living room. But I refuse to have this," he said, flicking at one of the painted peanut-tears, "displayed in our home."

Twinkle stared at him, placidly exhaling, the smoke emerging in two thin blue streams from her nostrils. She rolled up the poster slowly, securing it with one of the elastic bands she always wore around her wrist for tying back her thick, unruly hair, streaked here and there with henna. "I'm going to put it in my study," she informed him. "That way you don't have to look at it."

"What about the housewarming? They'll want to see all the rooms. I've invited people from the office."

She rolled her eyes. Sanjeev noted that the symphony, now in its third movement, had reached a crescendo, for it pulsed with the telltale clashing of cymbals.

"I'll put it behind the door," she offered. "That way, when they peek in, they won't see. Happy?"

He stood watching her as she left the room, with her poster and her cigarette; a few ashes had fallen to the floor where she'd been standing. He bent down, pinched them between his fingers, and deposited them in his cupped palm. The tender fourth movement, the *adagietto*, began. During breakfast, Sanjeev had read in the liner notes that Mahler had proposed to his wife by sending her the manuscript of this portion of the score. Although there were elements of tragedy and struggle in the Fifth Symphony, he had read, it was principally music of love and happiness.

He heard the toilet flush. "By the way," Twinkle hollered, "if you want to impress people, I wouldn't play this music. It's putting me to sleep."

Sanjeev went to the bathroom to throw away the ashes. The cigarette butt still bobbed in the toilet bowl, but the tank was refilling, so he had to wait a moment before he could flush it again. In the mirror of the medicine cabinet he inspected his long eyelashes—like a girl's, Twinkle liked to tease. Though he was of average build, his cheeks had a plumpness to them; this, along with the eyelashes, detracted, he feared, from what he hoped was a distinguished profile. He was of average height as well, and had wished ever since he had stopped growing that he were just one inch taller. For this reason it irritated him when Twinkle insisted on wearing high heels, as she had done the other night when they ate dinner in Manhattan. This was the first weekend after they'd moved into the house; by then the mantel had already filled up considerably, and they had bickered about it in the car on the way down. But then Twinkle had drunk four glasses of whiskey in a nameless bar in Alphabet City, and forgot all about it. She dragged him to a tiny bookshop on St. Mark's Place, where she browsed for nearly an hour, and when they left she insisted that they dance a tango on the sidewalk in front of strangers.

Afterward, she tottered on his arm, rising faintly over his line of vision, in a pair of suede three-inch leopard-print pumps. In this manner they walked the endless blocks back to a parking garage on Washington Square, for Sanjeev had heard far too many stories about the terrible things that happened to cars in Manhattan. "But I do nothing all day except sit at my desk," she fretted when they were driving home, after he had mentioned that her shoes looked uncomfortable and suggested that perhaps she should not wear them. "I can't exactly wear heels when I'm typing." Though he abandoned the argument, he knew for a fact that she didn't spend all day at her desk; just that afternoon, when he got back from a run, he found her inexplicably in bed, reading. When he asked why she was in bed in the middle of the day she told him she was bored. He had wanted to say to her then, You could unpack some boxes. You could sweep the attic. You could retouch the paint on the bathroom windowsill, and after you do it you could warn me so that I don't put my watch on it. They didn't bother her, these scattered, unsettled matters. She seemed content with whatever clothes she found at the front of the closet, with whatever magazine was lying around, with whatever song was on the radio—content yet curious. And now all of her curiosity centered around discovering the next treasure.

A few days later when Sanjeev returned from the office, he found Twinkle on the telephone, smoking and talking to one of her girlfriends in California even though it was before five o'clock and the long-distance rates were at their peak. "Highly devout people," she was saying, pausing every now and then to exhale. "Each day is like a treasure hunt. I'm serious. This you won't believe. The switch plates in the bedrooms were decorated with scenes from the Bible. You know, Noah's Ark and all that. Three bedrooms, but one is my study. Sanjeev went to the hardware store right away and replaced them, can you imagine, he replaced every single one."

Now it was the friend's turn to talk. Twinkle nodded, slouched on the floor in front of the fridge, wearing black stirrup pants and a yellow chenille sweater, groping for her lighter. Sanjeev could smell something aromatic on the stove, and he picked his way carefully across the extra-long phone cord tangled on the Mexican terra-cotta tiles. He opened the lid of a pot with some sort of reddish brown sauce dripping over the sides, boiling furiously.

"It's a stew made with fish. I put the vinegar in it," she said to him, interrupting her friend, crossing her fingers. "Sorry, you were saying?" She was like that, excited and delighted by little things, crossing her fingers before any remotely unpredictable event, like tasting a new flavor of ice cream, or dropping a letter in a mailbox. It was a quality he did not understand. It made him feel stupid, as if the world contained hidden wonders he could not anticipate, or see. He looked at her face, which, it occurred to him, had not grown out of its girlhood, the eyes untroubled, the pleasing features unfirm, as if they still had to settle into some sort of permanent expression. Nicknamed after a nursery rhyme, she had yet to shed a childhood endearment. Now, in the second month of their marriage, certain things nettled him—the way she sometimes spat a little when she spoke, or left her undergarments after removing them at night at the foot of their bed rather than depositing them in the laundry hamper.

They had met only four months before. Her parents, who lived in California, and his, who still lived in Calcutta, were old friends, and across continents they had arranged the occasion at which Twinkle and Sanjeev were introduced—a sixteenth birthday party for a daughter in their circle—when Sanjeev was in Palo Alto on business. At the restaurant they were seated side by side at a round table with a revolving platter of spareribs and egg rolls and chicken wings, which, they concurred, all tasted the same. They had concurred too on their adolescent but still persistent fondness for Wodehouse novels, and their dislike for the sitar, and later Twinkle confessed that she was charmed by the way Sanjeev had dutifully refilled her teacup during their conversation.

And so the phone calls began, and grew longer, and then the visits, first he to Stanford, then she to Connecticut, after which Sanjeev would save in an ashtray left on the balcony the crushed cigarettes she had smoked during the weekend—saved them, that is, until the next time she came to visit him, and then he vacuumed the apartment, washed the sheets, even dusted the plant leaves in her honor. She was twenty-seven and recently abandoned, he had gathered, by an American who had tried and failed to be an actor; Sanjeev was lonely, with an excessively generous income for a single man, and had never been in love. At the urging of their matchmakers, they married in India, amid hundreds of well-wishers whom he barely remembered from his childhood, in incessant August rains, under a red and orange tent strung with Christmas tree lights on Mandeville Road.

"Did you sweep the attic?" he asked Twinkle later as she was folding paper napkins and wedging them by their plates. The attic was the only part of the house they had not yet given an initial cleaning.

"Not yet. I will, I promise. I hope this tastes good," she said, planting the steaming pot on top of the Jesus trivet. There was a loaf of Italian bread in a little basket, and iceberg lettuce and grated carrots tossed with bottled dressing and croutons, and glasses of red wine. She was not terribly ambitious in the kitchen. She bought preroasted chickens from the supermarket and served them with potato salad prepared who knew when, sold in little plastic containers. Indian food, she complained, was a bother; she detested chopping garlic, and peeling ginger, and could not operate a blender, and so it was Sanjeev who, on weekends, seasoned mustard oil with cinnamon sticks and cloves in order to produce a proper curry.

He had to admit, though, that whatever it was that she had cooked today, it was unusually tasty, attractive even, with bright white cubes of fish, and flecks of parsley, and fresh tomatoes gleaming in the dark brown-red broth.

"How did you make it?"

"I made it up."

"What did you do?"

"I just put some things into the pot and added the malt vinegar at the end."

"How much vinegar?"

She shrugged, ripping off some bread and plunging it into her bowl.

"What do you mean you don't know? You should write it down. What if you need to make it again, for a party or something?"

"I'll remember," she said. She covered the bread basket with a dishtowel that had, he suddenly noticed, the Ten Commandments printed on it. She flashed him a smile, giving his knee a little squeeze under the table. "Face it. This house is blessed."

The housewarming party was scheduled for the last Saturday in October, and they had invited about thirty people. All were Sanjeev's acquaintances, people from the office, and a number of Indian couples in the Connecticut area, many of whom he barely knew, but who had regularly invited him, in his bachelor days, to supper on Saturdays. He often wondered why they included him in their circle. He had little in common with any of them, but he always attended their gatherings, to eat spiced chickpeas and shrimp cutlets, and gossip and discuss politics, for he seldom had other plans. So far, no one had met Twinkle; back when they were still dating, Sanjeev didn't want to waste their brief weekends together with people he associated with being alone. Other than Sanjeev and an ex-boyfriend who she believed worked in a pottery studio in Brookfield, she knew no one in the state of Connecticut. She was completing her master's thesis at Stanford, a study of an Irish poet whom Sanjeev had never heard of.

Sanjeev had found the house on his own before leaving for the wedding, for a good price, in a neighborhood with a fine school system. He was impressed by the elegant curved staircase with its wrought-iron banister, and the dark wooden wainscoting, and the solarium overlooking rhododendron bushes, and the solid brass 22, which also happened to be the date of his birth, nailed impressively to the vaguely Tudor facade. There were two working fireplaces, a two-car garage, and an attic suitable for converting into extra bedrooms if, the Realtor mentioned, the need should arise. By then Sanjeev had already made up his mind, was determined that he and Twinkle should live there together, forever, and so he had not bothered to notice the switch plates covered with biblical stickers, or the transparent decal of the Virgin on the half shell, as Twinkle liked to call it, adhered to the window in the master bedroom. When, after moving in, he tried to scrape it off, he scratched the glass.

The weekend before the party they were raking the lawn when he heard Twinkle shriek. He ran to her, clutching his rake, worried that she had discovered a dead animal, or a snake. A brisk October breeze stung the tops of his ears as his sneakers crunched over brown and yellow leaves. When he reached her, she had collapsed on the grass, dissolved in nearly silent laughter. Behind an overgrown forsythia bush was a plaster Virgin Mary as tall as their waists, with a blue painted hood draped over her head in the manner of an Indian bride. Twinkle grabbed the hem of her T-shirt and began wiping away the dirt staining the statue's brow.

"I suppose you want to put her by the foot of our bed," Sanjeev said.

She looked at him, astonished. Her belly was exposed, and he saw that there were goose bumps around her navel. "What do you think? Of course we can't put this in our bedroom."

"We can't?"

"No, silly Sanj. This is meant for outside. For the lawn."

"Oh God, no. Twinkle, no."

"But we must. It would be bad luck not to."

"All the neighbors will see. They'll think we're insane."

"Why, for having a statue of the Virgin Mary on our lawn? Every other person in this neighborhood has a statue of Mary on the lawn. We'll fit right in."

"We're not Christian."

"So you keep reminding me." She spat onto the tip of her finger and started to rub intently at a particularly stubborn stain on Mary's chin. "Do you think this is dirt, or some kind of fungus?"

He was getting nowhere with her, with this woman whom he had known for only four months and whom he had married, this woman with whom he now shared his life. He thought with a flicker of regret of the snapshots his mother used to send him from Calcutta, of prospective brides who could sing and sew and season lentils without consulting a cookbook. Sanjeev had considered these women, had even ranked them in order of preference, but then he had met Twinkle. "Twinkle, I can't have the people I work with see this statue on my lawn."

"They can't fire you for being a believer. It would be discrimination."

"That's not the point."

"Why does it matter to you so much what other people think?"

"Twinkle, please." He was tired. He let his weight rest against his rake as she began dragging the statue toward an oval bed of myrtle, beside the lamppost that flanked the brick pathway. "Look, Sanj. She's so lovely."

He returned to his pile of leaves and began to deposit them by handfuls into a plastic garbage bag. Over his head the blue sky was cloudless. One tree on the lawn was still full of leaves, red and orange, like the tent in which he had married Twinkle.

He did not know if he loved her. He said he did when she had first asked him, one afternoon in Palo Alto as they sat side by side in a darkened, nearly empty movie theater. Before the film, one of her favorites, something in German that he found extremely depressing, she had pressed the tip of her nose to his so that he could feel the flutter of her mascara-coated eyelashes. That afternoon he had replied, yes, he loved her, and she was delighted, and fed him a piece of popcorn, letting her finger linger an instant between his lips, as if it were his reward for coming up with the right answer.

Though she did not say it herself, he assumed then that she loved him too, but now he was no longer sure. In truth, Sanjeev did not know what love was, only what he thought it was not. It was not, he had decided, returning to an empty carpeted condominium each night, and using only the top fork in his cutlery drawer, and turning away politely at those weekend dinner parties when the other men eventually put their arms around the waists of their wives and girlfriends, leaning over every now and again to kiss their shoulders or necks. It was not sending away for classical music CDs by mail, working his way methodically through the major composers that the catalogue recommended, and always sending his payments in on time. In the months before meeting Twinkle, Sanjeev had begun to realize this. "You have enough money in the bank to raise three families," his mother reminded him when they spoke at the start of each month on the phone. "You need a wife to look after and love." Now he had one, a pretty one, from a suitably high caste, who would soon have a master's degree. What was there not to love?

That evening Sanjeev poured himself a gin and tonic, drank it and most of another during one segment of the news, and then approached Twinkle, who was taking a bubble bath, for she announced that her limbs ached from raking the lawn, something she had never done before. He didn't knock. She had applied a bright blue mask to her face, was smoking and sipping some bourbon with ice and leafing through a fat paperback book whose pages had buckled and turned gray from the water. He glanced at the cover; the only thing written on it was the word "Sonnets" in dark red letters. He took a breath, and then he informed her very calmly that after finishing his drink he was going to put on his shoes and go outside and remove the Virgin from the front lawn.

"Where are you going to put it?" she asked him dreamily, her eyes closed. One of her legs emerged, unfolding gracefully, from the layer of suds. She flexed and pointed her toes.

"For now I am going to put it in the garage. Then tomorrow morning on my way to work I am going to take it to the dump."

"Don't you dare." She stood up, letting the book fall into the water, bubbles dripping down her thighs. "I hate you," she informed him, her eyes narrowing at the word "hate." She reached for her bathrobe, tied it tightly about her waist, and padded down the winding staircase, leaving sloppy wet footprints along the parquet floor. When she reached the foyer, Sanjeev said, "Are you planning on leaving the house that way?" He felt a throbbing in his temples, and his voice revealed an unfamiliar snarl when he spoke.

"Who cares? Who cares what way I leave this house?"

"Where are you planning on going at this hour?"

"You can't throw away that statue. I won't let you." Her mask, now dry, had assumed an ashen quality, and water from her hair dripped onto the caked contours of her face.

"Yes I can. I will."

"No," Twinkle said, her voice suddenly small. "This is our house. We own it together. The statue is a part of our property." She had begun to shiver. A small pool of bathwater had collected around her ankles. He went to shut a window, fearing that she would catch cold. Then he noticed that some of the water dripping down her hard blue face was tears.

"Oh God, Twinkle, please, I didn't mean it." He had never seen her cry before, had never seen such sadness in her eyes. She didn't turn away or try to stop the tears; instead she looked strangely at peace. For a moment she closed her lids, pale and unprotected compared to the blue that caked the rest of her face. Sanjeev felt ill, as if he had eaten either too much or too little.

She went to him, placing her damp toweled arms about his neck, sobbing into his chest, soaking his shirt. The mask flaked onto his shoulders.

In the end they settled on a compromise: the statue would be placed in a recess at the side of the house, so that it wasn't obvious to passersby, but was still clearly visible to all who came.

The menu for the party was fairly simple: there would be a case of champagne, and samosas from an Indian restaurant in Hartford, and big trays of rice with chicken and almonds and orange peels, which Sanjeev had spent the greater part of the morning and afternoon preparing. He had never entertained on such a large scale before and, worried that there would not be enough to drink, ran out at one point to buy another case of champagne just in case. For this reason he burned one of the rice trays and had to start it over again. Twinkle swept the floors and volunteered to pick up the samosas; she had an appointment for a manicure and a pedicure in that direction, anyway. Sanjeev had planned to ask if she would consider clearing the menagerie off the mantel, if only for the party, but she left while he was in the shower. She was gone for a good three hours, and so it was Sanjeev who did the rest of the cleaning. By five-thirty the entire house sparkled, with scented candles that Twinkle had picked up in Hartford illuminating the items on the mantel, and slender stalks of burning incense planted into the soil of potted plants. Each time he passed the mantel he winced, dreading the raised eyebrows of his guests as they viewed the flickering ceramic saints, the salt and pepper shakers designed to resemble Mary and Joseph. Still, they would be impressed, he hoped, by the lovely bay windows, the shining parquet floors, the impressive winding staircase, the wooden wainscoting, as they sipped champagne and dipped samosas in chutney.

Douglas, one of the new consultants at the firm, and his girlfriend Nora were the first to arrive. Both were tall and blond, wearing matching wire-rimmed glasses and long black overcoats. Nora wore a black hat full of sharp thin feathers that corresponded to the sharp thin angles of her face. Her left hand was joined with Douglas's. In her right hand was a bottle of cognac with a red ribbon wrapped around its neck, which she gave to Twinkle.

"Great lawn, Sanjeev," Douglas remarked. "We've got to get that rake out ourselves, sweetie. And this must be . . ."

"My wife. Tanima."

"Call me Twinkle."

"What an unusual name," Nora remarked.

Twinkle shrugged. "Not really. There's an actress in Bombay named Dimple Kapadia. She even has a sister named Simple."

Douglas and Nora raised their eyebrows simultaneously, nodding slowly, as if to let the absurdity of the names settle in. "Pleased to meet you, Twinkle."

"Help yourself to champagne. There's gallons."

"I hope you don't mind my asking," Douglas said, "but I noticed the statue outside, and are you guys Christian? I thought you were Indian."

"There are Christians in India," Sanjeev replied, "but we're not."

"I love your outfit," Nora told Twinkle.

"And I adore your hat. Would you like the grand tour?"

The bell rang again, and again and again. Within minutes, it seemed, the house had filled with bodies and conversations and unfamiliar fragrances. The women wore heels and sheer stockings, and short black dresses made of crepe and chiffon. They handed their wraps and coats to Sanjeev, who draped them carefully on hangers in the spacious coat closet, though Twinkle told people to throw their things on the ottomans in the solarium. Some of the Indian women wore their finest saris, made with gold filigree that draped in elegant pleats over their shoulders. The men wore jackets and ties and citrus-scented aftershaves. As people filtered from one room to the next, presents piled onto the long cherry-wood table that ran from one end of the downstairs hall to the other.

It bewildered Sanjeev that it was for him, and his house, and his wife, that they had all gone to so much care. The only other time in his life that something similar had happened was his wedding day, but somehow this was different, for these were not his family, but people who knew him only casually, and in a sense owed him nothing. Everyone congratulated him. Lester, another coworker, predicted that Sanjeev would be promoted to vice president in two months maximum. People devoured the samosas, and dutifully admired the freshly painted ceilings and walls, the hanging plants, the bay windows, the silk paintings from Jaipur. But most of all they admired Twinkle, and her brocaded *salwar-kameez*, which was the shade of a persimmon with a low scoop in the back, and the little string of white rose petals she had coiled cleverly around her head, and the pearl choker with a sapphire at its center that adorned her throat. Over hectic jazz records, played under Twinkle's supervision, they laughed at her anecdotes and observations, forming a widening circle around her, while Sanjeev replenished the samosas that he kept warming evenly in the oven, and getting ice for people's drinks, and opening more bottles of champagne with some difficulty, and explaining for the fortieth time that he wasn't Christian. It was Twinkle who led them in separate groups up and down the winding stairs, to gaze at the back lawn, to peer down the cellar steps. "Your friends adore the poster in my study," she mentioned to him triumphantly, placing her hand on the small of his back as they, at one point, brushed past each other.

Sanjeev went to the kitchen, which was empty, and ate a piece of chicken out of the tray on the counter with his fingers because he thought no one was looking. He ate a second piece, then washed it down with a gulp of gin straight from the bottle.

"Great house. Great rice." Sunil, an anesthesiologist, walked in, spooning food from his paper plate into his mouth. "Do you have more champagne?"

"Your wife's wow," added Prabal, following behind. He was an unmarried professor of physics at Yale. For a moment Sanjeev stared at him blankly, then blushed; once at a dinner party Prabal had pronounced that Sophia Loren was wow, as was Audrey Hepburn. "Does she have a sister?"

Sunil picked a raisin out of the rice tray. "Is her last name Little Star?"

The two men laughed and started eating more rice from the tray, plowing through it with their plastic spoons. Sanjeev went down to the cellar for more liquor. For a few minutes he paused on the steps, in the damp, cool silence, hugging the second crate of champagne to his chest as the party drifted above the rafters. Then he set the reinforcements on the dining table.

"Yes, everything, we found them all in the house, in the most unusual places," he heard Twinkle saying in the living room. "In fact we keep finding them."

"No!"

"Yes! Every day is like a treasure hunt. It's too good. God only knows what else we'll find, no pun intended."

That was what started it. As if by some unspoken pact, the whole party joined forces and began combing through each of the rooms, opening closets on their own, peering under chairs and cushions, feeling behind curtains, removing books from bookcases. Groups scampered, giggling and swaying, up and down the winding staircase.

"We've never explored the attic," Twinkle announced suddenly, and so everybody followed.

"How do we get up there?"

"There's a ladder in the hallway, somewhere in the ceiling."

Wearily Sanjeev followed at the back of the crowd, to point out the location of the ladder, but Twinkle had already found it on her own. "Eureka!" she hollered.

Douglas pulled the chain that released the steps. His face was flushed and he was wearing Nora's feather hat on his head. One by one the guests disappeared, men helping women as they placed their strappy high heels on the narrow slats of the ladder, the Indian women wrapping the free ends of their expensive saris into their waistbands. The men followed behind, all quickly disappearing, until Sanjeev alone remained at the top of the winding staircase. Footsteps thundered over his head. He had no desire to join them. He wondered if the ceiling would collapse, imagined, for a split second, the sight of all the tumbling drunk perfumed bodies crashing, tangled, around him. He heard a shriek, and then rising, spreading waves of laughter in discordant tones. Something fell, something else shattered. He could hear them babbling about a trunk. They seemed to be struggling to get it open, banging feverishly on its surface.

He thought perhaps Twinkle would call for his assistance, but he was not summoned. He looked about the hallway and to the landing below, at the champagne glasses and half-eaten samosas and napkins smeared with lipstick abandoned in every corner, on every available surface. Then he noticed that Twinkle, in her haste, had discarded her shoes altogether, for they lay by the foot of the ladder, black patent-leather mules with heels like golf tees, open toes, and slightly soiled silk labels on the instep where her soles had rested. He placed them in the doorway of the master bedroom so that no one would trip when they descended.

He heard something creaking open slowly. The strident voices had subsided to an even murmur. It occurred to Sanjeev that he had the house all to himself. The music had ended and he could hear, if he concentrated, the hum of the refrigerator, and the rustle of the last leaves on the trees outside, and the tapping of their branches against the windowpanes. With one flick of his hand he could snap the ladder back on its spring into the ceiling, and they would have no way of getting down unless he were to pull the chain and let them. He thought of all the things he could do, undisturbed. He could sweep Twinkle's menagerie into a garbage bag and get in the car and drive it all to the dump, and tear down the poster of weeping Jesus, and take a hammer to the Virgin Mary while he was at it. Then he would return to the empty house; he could easily clear up the cups and plates in an hour's time, and pour himself a gin and tonic, and eat a plate of warmed rice and listen to his new Bach CD while reading the liner notes so as to understand it properly. He nudged the ladder slightly, but it was sturdily planted against the floor. Budging it would require some effort.

"My God, I need a cigarette," Twinkle exclaimed from above.

Sanjeev felt knots forming at the back of his neck. He felt dizzy. He needed to lie down. He walked toward the bedroom, but stopped short when he saw Twinkle's shoes facing him in the doorway. He thought of her slipping them on her feet. But instead of feeling irritated, as he had ever since they'd moved into the house together, he felt a pang of anticipation at the thought of her rushing unsteadily down the winding staircase in them, scratching the floor a bit in her path. The pang intensified as he thought of her rushing to the bathroom to brighten her lipstick, and eventually rushing to get people their coats, and finally rushing to the cherry-wood table when the last guest had left, to begin opening their housewarming presents. It was the same pang he used to feel before they were married, when he would hang up the phone after one of their conversations, or when he would drive back from the airport, wondering which ascending plane in the sky was hers.

"Sanj, you won't believe this."

She emerged with her back to him, her hands over her head, the tops of her bare shoulder blades perspiring, supporting something still hidden from view.

"You got it, Twinkle?" someone asked.

"Yes, you can let go."

Now he saw that her hands were wrapped around it: a solid silver bust of Christ, the head easily three times the size of his own. It had a patrician bump on its nose, magnificent curly hair that rested atop a pronounced collarbone, and a broad forehead that reflected in miniature the walls and doors and lampshades around them. Its expression was confident, as if assured of its devotees, the unyielding lips sensuous and full. It was also sporting Nora's feather hat. As Twinkle descended, Sanjeev put his hands around her waist to balance her, and he relieved her of the bust when she had reached the ground. It weighed a good thirty pounds. The others began lowering themselves slowly, exhausted from the hunt. Some trickled downstairs in search of a fresh drink.

She took a breath, raised her eyebrows, crossed her fingers. "Would you mind terribly if we displayed it on the mantel? Just for tonight? I know you hate it."

He did hate it. He hated its immensity, and its flawless, polished surface, and its undeniable value. He hated that it was in his house, and that he owned it. Unlike the other things they'd found, this contained dignity, solemnity, beauty even. But to his surprise these qualities made him hate it all the more. Most of all he hated it because he knew that Twinkle loved it.

"I'll keep it in my study from tomorrow," Twinkle added. "I promise."

She would never put it in her study, he knew. For the rest of their days together she would keep it on the center of the mantel, flanked on either side by the rest of the menagerie. Each time they had guests Twinkle would explain how she had found it, and they would admire her as they listened. He gazed at the crushed rose petals in her hair, at the pearl and sapphire choker at her throat, at the sparkly crimson polish on her toes. He decided these were among the things that made Prabal think she was wow. His head ached from gin and his arms ached from the weight of the statue. He said, "I put your shoes in the bedroom."

"Thanks. But my feet are killing me." Twinkle gave his elbow a little squeeze and headed for the living room.

Sanjeev pressed the massive silver face to his ribs, careful not to let the feather hat slip, and followed her.

The Treatment
of Bibi Haldar

FOR the greater number of her twenty-nine years, Bibi Haldar suffered from an ailment that baffled family, friends, priests, palmists, spinsters, gem therapists, prophets, and fools. In efforts to cure her, concerned members of our town brought her holy water from seven holy rivers. When we heard her screams and throes in the night, when her wrists were bound with ropes and stinging poultices pressed upon her, we named her in our prayers. Wise men had massaged eucalyptus balm into her temples, steamed her face with herbal infusions. At the suggestion of a blind Christian she was once taken by train to kiss the tombs of saints and martyrs. Amulets warding against the evil eye girded her arms and neck. Auspicious stones adorned her fingers.

Treatments offered by doctors only made matters worse. Allopaths, homeopaths, ayurvedics — over time, all branches of the medical arts had been consulted. Their advice was endless. After x-rays, probes, auscultations, and injections, some advised Bibi to gain weight, others to lose it. If one forbade her to sleep beyond dawn, another insisted she remain in bed till noon.

This one told her to perform headstands, that one to chant Vedic verses at specified intervals throughout the day. "Take her to Calcutta for hypnosis" was a suggestion others would offer. Shuttled from one specialist to the next, the girl had been prescribed to shun garlic, consume disproportionate quantities of bitters, meditate, drink green coconut water, and swallow raw duck's eggs beaten in milk. In short, Bibi's life was an encounter with one fruitless antidote after another.

The nature of her illness, which struck without warning, confined her world to the unpainted four-story building in which her only local family, an elder cousin and his wife, rented an apartment on the second floor. Liable to fall unconscious and enter, at any moment, into a shameless delirium, Bibi could be trusted neither to cross a street nor board a tram without supervision. Her daily occupation consisted of sitting in the storage room on the roof of our building, a space in which one could sit but not comfortably stand, featuring an adjoining latrine, a curtained entrance, one window without a grille, and shelves made from the panels of old doors. There, cross-legged on a square of jute, she recorded inventory for the cosmetics shop that her cousin Haldar owned and managed at the mouth of our courtyard. For her services, Bibi received no income but was given meals, provisions, and sufficient meters of cotton at every October holiday to replenish her wardrobe at an inexpensive tailor. At night she slept on a folding camp cot in the cousin's place downstairs.

In the mornings Bibi arrived in the storage room wearing cracked plastic slippers and a housecoat whose hem stopped some inches below the knee, a length we had not worn since we were fifteen. Her shins were hairless, and sprayed with a generous number of pallid freckles. She bemoaned her fate and challenged her stars as we hung our laundry or scrubbed scales from our fish. She was not pretty. Her upper lip was thin, her teeth too small. Her gums protruded when she spoke. "I ask you, is it fair for a girl to sit out her years, pass neglected through her prime, listing labels and prices without promise of a future?" Her voice was louder than necessary, as if she were speaking to a deaf person. "Is it wrong to envy you, all brides and mothers, busy with lives and cares? Wrong to want to shade my eyes, scent my hair? To raise a child and teach him sweet from sour, good from bad?"

Each day she unloaded her countless privations upon us, until it became unendurably apparent that Bibi wanted a man. She wanted to be spoken for, protected, placed on her path in life. Like the rest of us, she wanted to serve suppers, and scold servants, and set aside money in her *almari* to have her eyebrows threaded every three weeks at the Chinese beauty parlor. She pestered us for details of our own weddings: the jewels, the invitations, the scent of tuberoses strung over the nuptial bed. When, at her insistence, we showed her our photo albums embossed with the designs of butterflies, she pored over the snapshots that chronicled the ceremony: butter poured in fires, garlands exchanged, vermilion-painted fish, trays of shells and silver coins. "An impressive number of guests," she would observe, stroking with her finger the misplaced faces that had surrounded us. "When it happens to me, you will all be present."

Anticipation began to plague her with such ferocity that the thought of a husband, on which all her hopes were pinned, threatened at times to send her into another attack. Amid tins of talc and boxes of bobby pins she would curl up on the floor of the storage room, speaking in non sequiturs. "I will never dip my feet in milk," she whimpered. "My face will never be painted with sandalwood paste. Who will rub me with turmeric? My name will never be printed with scarlet ink on a card."

Her soliloquies mawkish, her sentiments maudlin, malaise dripped like a fever from her pores. In her most embittered moments we wrapped her in shawls, washed her face from the cistern tap, and brought her glasses of yogurt and rosewater. In moments when she was less disconsolate, we encouraged her to accompany us to the tailor and replenish her blouses and petticoats, in part to provide her with a change of scenery, and in part because we thought it might increase whatever matrimonial prospects she had. "No man wants a woman who dresses like a dishwasher," we told her. "Do you want all that fabric of yours to go to the moths?" She sulked, pouted, protested, and sighed. "Where do I go, who would I dress for?" she demanded. "Who takes me to the cinema, the zoo-garden, buys me lime soda and cashews? Admit it, are these concerns of mine? I will never be cured, never married."

But then a new treatment was prescribed for Bibi, the most outrageous of them all. One evening on her way to dinner, she collapsed on the third-floor landing, pounding her fists, kicking her feet, sweating buckets, lost to this world. Her moans echoed through the stairwell, and we rushed out of our apartments to calm her at once, bearing palm fans and sugar cubes, and tumblers of refrigerated water to pour on her head. Our children clung to the banisters and witnessed her paroxysm; our servants were sent to summon her cousin. It was ten minutes before Haldar emerged from his shop, impassive apart from the red in his face. He told us to stop fussing, and then with no efforts to repress his disdain he packed her into a rickshaw bound for the polyclinic. It was there, after performing a series of blood tests, that the doctor in charge of Bibi's case, exasperated, concluded that a marriage would cure her.

News spread between our window bars, across our clotheslines, and over the pigeon droppings that plastered the parapets of our rooftops. By the next morning, three separate palmists had examined Bibi's hand and confirmed that there was, no doubt, evidence of an imminent union etched into her skin.

Unsavory sorts murmured indelicacies at cutlet stands; grand-mothers consulted almanacs to determine a propitious hour for the betrothal. For days afterward, as we walked our children to school, picked up our cleaning, stood in lines at the ration shop, we whispered. Apparently some activity was what the poor girl needed all along. For the first time we imagined the contours below her housecoat, and attempted to appraise the pleasures she could offer a man. For the first time we noted the clarity of her complexion, the length and languor of her eyelashes, the undeniably elegant armature of her hands. "They say it's the only hope. A case of overexcitement. They say"—and here we paused, blushing—"relations will calm her blood."

Needless to say, Bibi was delighted by the diagnosis, and began at once to prepare for conjugal life. With some dam-aged merchandise from Haldar's shop she polished her toenails and softened her elbows. Neglecting the new shipments deliv-ered to the storage room, she began hounding us for recipes, for vermicelli pudding and papaya stew, and inscribed them in crooked letters in the pages of her inventory ledger. She made guest lists, dessert lists, listed lands in which she intended to honeymoon. She applied glycerine to smooth her lips, resisted sweets to reduce her measurements. One day she asked one of us to accompany her to the tailor, who stitched her a new *salwar-kameez* in an umbrella cut, the fashion that season. On the streets she dragged us to the counters of each and every jeweler, peering into glass cases, seeking our opinions of tiara designs and locket settings. In the windows of sari shops she pointed to a magenta Benarasi silk, and a turquoise one, and then one that was the color of marigolds. "The first part of the ceremony I will wear this one, then this one, then this."

But Haldar and his wife thought otherwise. Immune to her fancies, indifferent to our fears, they conducted business as usual, stuffed together in that cosmetics shop no bigger than a wardrobe, whose walls were crammed on three sides with hennas, hair oils, pumice stones, and fairness creams. "We have little time for indecent suggestions," replied Haldar to those who broached the subject of Bibi's health. "What won't be cured must be endured. Bibi has caused enough worry, added enough to expenses, sullied enough the family name." His wife, seated beside him behind the tiny glass counter, fanned the mottled skin above her breasts and agreed. She was a heavy woman whose powder, a shade too pale for her, caked in the creases of her throat. "Besides, who would marry her? The girl knows nothing about anything, speaks backward, is practically thirty, can't light a coal stove, can't boil rice, can't tell the difference between fennel and a cumin seed. Imagine her attempting to feed a man!"

They had a point. Bibi had never been taught to be a woman; the illness had left her naive in most practical matters. Haldar's wife, convinced that the devil himself possessed her, kept Bibi away from fire and flame. She had not been taught to wear a sari without pinning it in four different places, nor could she embroider slipcovers or crochet shawls with any exceptional talent. She was not allowed to watch the television (Haldar assumed its electronic properties would excite her), and was thus ignorant of the events and entertainments of our world. Her formal studies had ended after the ninth standard.

For Bibi's sake we argued in favor of finding a husband. "It's what she's wanted all along," we pointed out. But Haldar and his wife were impossible to reason with. Their rancor toward Bibi was fixed on their lips, thinner than the strings with which they tied our purchases. When we maintained that the new treatment deserved a chance, they contended, "Bibi possesses insufficient quantities of respect and self-control. She plays up her malady for the attention. The best thing is to keep her occupied, away from the trouble she invariably creates."

"Why not marry her off, then? It will get her off your hands, at least."

"And waste our profits on a wedding? Feeding guests, ordering bracelets, buying a bed, assembling a dowry?"

But Bibi's gripes persisted. Late one morning, dressed under our supervision in a sari of lavender eyelet chiffon and mirrored slippers lent to her for the occasion, she hastened in uneven steps to Haldar's shop and insisted on being taken to the photographer's studio so that her portrait, like those of other brides-in-waiting, could be circulated in the homes of eligible men. Through the shutters of our balconies we watched her; perspiration had already left black moons beneath her armpits. "Apart from my x-rays I have never been photographed," she fretted. "Potential in-laws need to know what I look like." But Haldar refused. He said that anyone who wished to see her could observe her for themselves, weeping and wailing and warding off customers. She was a bane for business, he told her, a liability and a loss. Who in this town needed a photo to know that?

The next day Bibi stopped listing inventory altogether and regaled us, instead, with imprudent details about Haldar and his wife. "On Sundays he plucks hairs from her chin. They keep their money refrigerated under lock and key." For the benefit of neighboring rooftops she strutted and shrieked; with each proclamation her audience expanded. "In the bath she applies chickpea flour to her arms because she thinks it will make her paler. The third toe on her right foot is missing. The reason they take such long siestas is that she is impossible to please."

To get her to quiet down, Haldar placed a one-line advertisement in the town newspaper, in order to solicit a groom: "GIRL, UNSTABLE, HEIGHT 152 CENTIMETRES, SEEKS HUSBAND." The identity of the prospective bride was no secret to the parents of our young men, and no family was willing to shoulder

so blatant a risk. Who could blame them? It was rumored by
many that Bibi conversed with herself in a fluent but totally incomprehensible language, and slept without dreams. Even the
lonely four-toothed widower who repaired our handbags in the
market could not be persuaded to propose. Nevertheless, to
distract her, we began to coach her in wifely ways. "Frowning like a rice pot will get you nowhere. Men require that you
caress them with your expression." As practice for the event
of encountering a possible suitor, we urged her to engage in
small conversations with nearby men. When the water bearer
arrived, at the end of his rounds, to fill Bibi's urn in the storage room, we instructed her to say "How do you do?" When
the coal supplier unloaded his baskets on the roof, we advised
her to smile and make a comment about the weather. Recalling
our own experiences, we prepared her for an interview. "Most
likely the groom will arrive with one parent, a grandparent, and
either an uncle or aunt. They will stare, ask several questions.
They will examine the bottoms of your feet, the thickness of
your braid. They will ask you to name the prime minister, recite poetry, feed a dozen hungry people on half a dozen eggs."

When two months had passed without a single reply to the
advertisement, Haldar and his wife felt vindicated. "Now do
you see that she is unfit to marry? Now do you see no man of
sane mind would touch her?"

Things had not been so bad for Bibi before her father died.
(The mother had not survived beyond the birth of the girl.) In
his final years, the old man, a teacher of mathematics in our elementary schools, had kept assiduous track of Bibi's illness in
hopes of determining some logic to her condition. "To every
problem there is a solution," he would reply whenever we inquired after his progress. He reassured Bibi. For a time he reassured us all. He wrote letters to doctors in England, spent his
evenings reading casebooks at the library, gave up eating meat

on Fridays in order to appease his household god. Eventually he gave up teaching as well, tutoring only from his room, so that he could monitor Bibi at all hours. But though in his youth he had received prizes for his ability to deduce square roots from memory, he was unable to solve the mystery of his daughter's disease. For all his work, his records led him to conclude only that Bibi's attacks occurred more frequently in summer than winter, and that she had suffered approximately twenty-five major attacks in all. He created a chart of her symptoms with directions for calming her, and distributed it throughout the neighborhood, but these were eventually lost, or turned into sailboats by our children, or used to calculate grocery budgets on the reverse side.

Apart from keeping her company, apart from soothing her woes, apart from keeping an occasional eye on her, there was little we could do to improve the situation. None of us were capable of understanding such desolation. Some days, after siesta, we combed out her hair, remembering now and then to change the part in her scalp so that it would not grow too broad. At her request we powdered the down over her lips and throat, penciled definition into her brows, and walked her to the banks of the fish pond where our children played cricket in the afternoon. She was still determined to lure a man.

"Apart from my condition I am perfectly healthy," she maintained, seating herself on a bench along the footpath where courting men and women strolled hand in hand. "I have never had a cold or flu. I have never had jaundice. I have never suffered from colic or indigestion." Sometimes we bought her smoked corn on the cob sprinkled with lemon juice, or two *paisa* caramels. We consoled her; when she was convinced a man was giving her the eye, we humored her and agreed. But she was not our responsibility, and in our private moments we were thankful for it.

• • •

In November we learned that Haldar's wife was pregnant. That morning in the storage room, Bibi wept. "She says I'm contagious, like the pox. She says I'll spoil the baby." She was breathing heavily, her pupils fixed to a peeling spot on the wall. "What will become of me?" There was still no response to the advertisement in the newspaper. "Is it not punishment enough that I bear this curse alone? Must I also be blamed for infecting another?" Dissent within the Haldar household grew. The wife, convinced that Bibi's presence would infect the unborn child, began to wrap woolen shawls around her tumid belly. In the bathroom Bibi was given separate soaps and towels. According to the scullery maid, Bibi's plates were not washed with the others.

And then one afternoon, without word or warning, it happened again. On the banks of the fish pond, Bibi fell to the footpath. She shook. She shuddered. She chewed her lips. A group encircled the convulsing girl at once, eager to assist in whatever way possible. The opener of soda bottles pinned down her thrashing limbs. The vendor of sliced cucumbers attempted to unclasp her fingers. One of us doused her with water from the pond. Another wiped her mouth with a perfumed handkerchief. The seller of jackfruits was holding Bibi's head, which struggled to toss from side to side. And the man who cranked the sugarcane press gripped the palm fan that he ordinarily used to chase away flies, agitating the air from every conceivable angle.

"Is there a doctor in the crowd?"

"Watch that she doesn't swallow her tongue."

"Has anyone informed Haldar?"

"She's hotter than coals!"

In spite of our efforts, the tumult persisted. Wrestling with her adversary, wracked with anguish, she ground her teeth and twitched at the knees. Over two minutes had passed. We watched and worried. We wondered what to do.

"Leather!" someone cried suddenly. "She needs to smell leather." Then we remembered; the last time it had happened, a cowhide sandal held under her nostrils was what had finally freed Bibi from the clutches of her torment.

"Bibi, what happened? Tell us what happened," we asked when she opened her eyes.

"I felt hot, then hotter. Smoke passed before my eyes. The world went black. Didn't you see it?"

A group of our husbands escorted her home. Dusk thickened, conch shells were blown, and the air grew dense with the incense of prayers. Bibi muttered and staggered but said nothing. Her cheeks were bruised and nicked here and there. Her hair was matted, her elbows caked with dirt, and a small piece of one front tooth was missing. We followed behind, at what we assumed to be safe distances, holding our children by the hand.

She needed a blanket, a compress, a sedative tablet. She needed supervision. But when we reached the courtyard Haldar and his wife would not have her in the flat.

"The medical risk is too great for an expectant mother to be in contact with an hysterical person," he insisted.

That night Bibi slept in the storage room.

Their baby, a girl, was delivered by forceps at the end of June. By then Bibi was sleeping downstairs again, though they kept her camp cot in the corridor, and would not let her touch the child directly. Every day they sent her to the roof to record inventory until lunch, at which point Haldar brought her receipts from the morning's sales and a bowl of yellow split peas for her lunch. At night she ate milk and bread alone in the stairwell. Another seizure, and another, went unchecked.

When we voiced our concern, Haldar said it was not our business, and flatly refused to discuss the matter. To express

our indignation we began to take our shopping elsewhere; this
provided us with our only revenge. Over the weeks the prod-
ucts on Haldar's shelves grew dusty. Labels faded and colognes
turned rank. Passing by in the evenings, we saw Haldar sitting
alone, swatting moths with the sole of his slipper. We hardly
saw the wife at all. According to the scullery maid she was still
bedridden; apparently her labor had been complicated.

Autumn came, with its promise of the October holidays, and
the town grew busy shopping and planning for the season. Film
songs blared from amplifiers strung through trees. Arcades and
markets stayed open all hours. We bought our children balloons and colored ribbons, purchased sweetmeats by the kilo,
paid calls in taxis to relatives we had not seen throughout the
year. The days grew shorter, the evenings colder. We buttoned
our sweaters and pulled up our socks. Then a chill set in that
made our throats itch. We made our children gargle with warm
saltwater and wrap mufflers around their necks. But it was the
Haldar baby who ended up getting sick.

A doctor was summoned in the middle of the night and commanded to reduce the fever. "Cure her," the wife pleaded. Her
shrill commotion had woken us all. "We can give you anything,
just cure my baby girl." The doctor prescribed a glucose for-
mula, crushed aspirins in a mortar, and told them to wrap the
child with quilts and covers.

Five days later the fever had not budged.

"It's Bibi," the wife wailed. "She's done it, she's infected our
child. We should never have let her back down here. We should
never have let her back into this house."

And so Bibi started to spend her nights in the storage room
again. At the wife's insistence Haldar even moved her camp cot
up there, along with a tin trunk that contained her belongings.
Her meals were left covered with a colander at the top of the
stairs.

"I don't mind," Bibi told us. "It's better to live apart from them, to set up house on my own." She unpacked the trunk—some housecoats, a framed portrait of her father, sewing supplies, and an assortment of fabrics—and arranged her things on a few empty shelves. By the week's end the baby had recuperated, but Bibi was not asked to return downstairs. "Don't worry, it's not as if they've locked me in here," she said in order to set us at ease. "The world begins at the bottom of the stairs. Now I am free to discover life as I please."

But in truth she stopped going out altogether. When we asked her to come with us to the fish pond or to go see temple decorations she refused, claiming that she was stitching a new curtain to hang across the entrance of the storage room. Her skin looked ashen. She needed fresh air. "What about finding your husband?" we suggested. "How do you expect to charm a man sitting up here all day?"

Nothing persuaded her.

By mid-December, Haldar cleared all the unsold merchandise off the shelves of his beauty shop and hauled them in boxes up to the storage room. We had succeeded in driving him more or less out of business. Before the year's end the family moved away, leaving an envelope containing three hundred rupees under Bibi's door. There was no more news of them.

One of us had an address for a relation of Bibi's in Hyderabad, and wrote explaining the situation. The letter was returned unopened, address unknown. Before the coldest weeks set in, we had the shutters of the storage room repaired and attached a sheet of tin to the doorframe, so that she would at least have some privacy. Someone donated a kerosene lamp; another gave her some old mosquito netting and a pair of socks without heels. At every opportunity we reminded her that we surrounded her, that she could come to us if she ever needed advice or aid of any kind. For a time we sent our children to play on the roof in the afternoons, so that they could alert us if she was having another attack. But each night we left her alone.

Some months passed. Bibi had retreated into a deep and prolonged silence. We took turns leaving her plates of rice and glasses of tea. She drank little, ate less, and began to assume an expression that no longer matched her years. At twilight she circled the parapet once or twice, but she never left the roof-top. After dark she remained behind the tin door and did not come out for any reason. We did not disturb her. Some of us began to wonder if she was dying. Others concluded that she had lost her mind.

One morning in April, when the heat had returned for drying lentil wafers on the roof, we noticed that someone had vomited by the cistern tap. When we noticed this a second morning as well, we knocked on Bibi's tin door. When there was no answer we opened it ourselves, as there was no lock to fasten it.

We found her lying on the camp cot. She was about four months pregnant.

She said she could not remember what had happened. She would not tell us who had done it. We prepared her semolina with hot milk and raisins; still she would not reveal the man's identity. In vain we searched for traces of the assault, some sign of the intrusion, but the room was swept and in order. On the floor beside the cot, her inventory ledger, open to a fresh page, contained a list of names.

She carried the baby to full term, and one evening in September, we helped her deliver a son. We showed her how to feed him, and bathe him, and lull him to sleep. We bought her an oilcloth and helped her stitch clothes and pillowcases out of the fabric she had saved over the years. Within a month Bibi had recuperated from the birth, and with the money that Haldar had left her, she had the storage room whitewashed, and placed padlocks on the window and doors. Then she dusted the shelves and arranged the leftover potions and lotions, selling Haldar's old inventory at half price. She told us to spread word of the sale, and we did. From Bibi we purchased our soaps and kohl, our combs and powders, and when she had sold the last of her merchandise, she went by taxi to the wholesale market, using her profits to restock the shelves. In this manner she raised the boy and ran a business in the storage room, and we did what we could to help. For years afterward, we wondered who in our town had disgraced her. A few of our servants were questioned, and in tea stalls and bus stands, possible suspects were debated and dismissed. But there was no point carrying out an investigation. She was, to the best of our knowledge, cured.

The Third and
Final Continent

I LEFT India in 1964 with a certificate in commerce and the equivalent, in those days, of ten dollars to my name. For three weeks I sailed on the SS *Roma*, an Italian cargo vessel, in a cabin next to the ship's engine, across the Arabian Sea, the Red Sea, the Mediterranean, and finally to England. I lived in north London, in Finsbury Park, in a house occupied entirely by penniless Bengali bachelors like myself, at least a dozen and sometimes more, all struggling to educate and establish ourselves abroad.

I attended lectures at LSE and worked at the university library to get by. We lived three or four to a room, shared a single, icy toilet, and took turns cooking pots of egg curry, which we ate with our hands on a table covered with newspapers. Apart from our jobs we had few responsibilities. On weekends we lounged barefoot in drawstring pajamas, drinking tea and smoking Rothmans, or set out to watch cricket at Lord's. Some weekends the house was crammed with still more Bengalis, to whom we had introduced ourselves at the greengrocer, or on the Tube, and we made yet more egg curry, and played Mukesh on a Grundig reel-to-reel, and soaked our dirty dishes in the bathtub. Every now and then someone in the house moved out, to live with a woman whom his family back in Calcutta had determined he was to wed. In 1969, when I was thirty-six years old, my own marriage was arranged. Around the same time I was offered a full-time job in America, in the processing department of a library at MIT. The salary was generous enough to support a wife, and I was honored to be hired by a world-famous university, and so I obtained a sixth-preference green card, and prepared to travel farther still.

By now I had enough money to go by plane. I flew first to Calcutta, to attend my wedding, and a week later I flew to Boston, to begin my new job. During the flight I read *The Student Guide to North America*, a paperback volume that I'd bought before leaving London, for seven shillings six pence on Tottenham Court Road, for although I was no longer a student I was on a budget all the same. I learned that Americans drove on the right side of the road, not the left, and that they called a lift an elevator and an engaged phone busy. "The pace of life in North America is different from Britain as you will soon discover," the guidebook informed me. "Everybody feels he must get to the top. Don't expect an English cup of tea." As the plane began its descent over Boston Harbor, the pilot announced the weather and time, and that President Nixon had declared a national holiday: two American men had landed on the moon. Several passengers cheered. "God bless America!" one of them hollered. Across the aisle, I saw a woman praying.

I spent my first night at the YMCA in Central Square, Cambridge, an inexpensive accommodation recommended by my guidebook. It was walking distance from MIT, and steps from the post office and a supermarket called Purity Supreme. The room contained a cot, a desk, and a small wooden cross on one wall. A sign on the door said cooking was strictly forbidden. A bare window overlooked Massachusetts Avenue, a major thoroughfare with traffic in both directions. Car horns, shrill and prolonged, blared one after another. Flashing sirens heralded endless emergencies, and a fleet of buses rumbled past, their doors opening and closing with a powerful hiss, throughout the night. The noise was constantly distracting, at times suffocating. I felt it deep in my ribs, just as I had felt the furious drone of the engine on the SS *Roma*. But there was no ship's deck to escape to, no glittering ocean to thrill my soul, no breeze to cool my face, no one to talk to. I was too tired to pace the gloomy corridors of the YMCA in my drawstring pajamas. Instead I sat at the desk and stared out the window, at the city hall of Cambridge and a row of small shops. In the morning I reported to my job at the Dewey Library, a beige fortlike building by Memorial Drive. I also opened a bank account, rented a post office box, and bought a plastic bowl and a spoon at Woolworth's, a store whose name I recognized from London. I went to Purity Supreme, wandering up and down the aisles, converting ounces to grams and comparing prices to things in England. In the end I bought a small carton of milk and a box of cornflakes. This was my first meal in America. I ate it at my desk. I preferred it to hamburgers or hot dogs, the only alternative I could afford in the coffee shops on Massachusetts Avenue, and, besides, at the time I had yet to consume any beef. Even the simple chore of buying milk was new to me; in London we'd had bottles delivered each morning to our door.

In a week I had adjusted, more or less. I ate cornflakes and milk, morning and night, and bought some bananas for variety, slicing them into the bowl with the edge of my spoon. In addition I bought tea bags and a flask, which the salesman in Woolworth's referred to as a thermos (a flask, he informed me, was used to store whiskey, another thing I had never consumed). For the price of one cup of tea at a coffee shop, I filled the flask with boiling water on my way to work each morning, and brewed the four cups I drank in the course of a day. I bought a larger carton of milk, and learned to leave it on the shaded part of the windowsill, as I had seen another resident at the YMCA do. To pass the time in the evenings I read the *Boston Globe* downstairs, in a spacious room with stained-glass windows. I read every article and advertisement, so that I would grow familiar with things, and when my eyes grew tired I slept. Only I did not sleep well. Each night I had to keep the window wide open; it was the only source of air in the stifling room, and the noise was intolerable. I would lie on the cot with my fingers pressed into my ears, but when I drifted off to sleep my hands fell away, and the noise of the traffic would wake me up again. Pigeon feathers drifted onto the windowsill, and one evening, when I poured milk over my cornflakes, I saw that it had soured. Nevertheless I resolved to stay at the YMCA for six weeks, until my wife's passport and green card were ready. Once she arrived I would have to rent a proper apartment, and from time to time I studied the classified section of the newspaper, or stopped in at the housing office at MIT during my lunch break, to see what was available in my price range. It was in this manner that I discovered a room for immediate occupancy, in a house on a quiet street, the listing said, for eight dollars per week. I copied the number into my guidebook and dialed from a pay telephone, sorting through the coins with which I was still unfamiliar, smaller and lighter than shillings, heavier and brighter than *paisas*.

"Who is speaking?" a woman demanded. Her voice was bold and clamorous.

"Yes, good afternoon, madame. I am calling about the room for rent."

"Harvard or Tech?"

"I beg your pardon?"

"Are you from Harvard or Tech?"

Gathering that Tech referred to the Massachusetts Institute of Technology, I replied, "I work at Dewey Library," adding tentatively, "at Tech."

"I only rent rooms to boys from Harvard or Tech!"

"Yes, madame."

I was given an address and an appointment for seven o'clock that evening. Thirty minutes before the hour I set out, my guidebook in my pocket, my breath fresh with Listerine. I turned down a street shaded with trees, perpendicular to Massachusetts Avenue. Stray blades of grass poked between the cracks of the footpath. In spite of the heat I wore a coat and a tie, regarding the event as I would any other interview; I had never lived in the home of a person who was not Indian. The house, surrounded by a chain-link fence, was off-white with dark brown trim. Unlike the stucco row house I'd lived in in London, this house, fully detached, was covered with wooden shingles, with a tangle of forsythia bushes plastered against the front and sides. When I pressed the calling bell, the woman with whom I had spoken on the phone hollered from what seemed to be just the other side of the door, "One minute, please!"

Several minutes later the door was opened by a tiny, extremely old woman. A mass of snowy hair was arranged like a small sack on top of her head. As I stepped into the house she sat down on a wooden bench positioned at the bottom of a narrow carpeted staircase. Once she was settled on the bench, in a small pool of light, she peered up at me with undivided attention. She wore a long black skirt that spread like a stiff tent to the floor, and a starched white shirt edged with ruffles at the throat and cuffs. Her hands, folded together in her lap, had long pallid fingers, with swollen knuckles and tough yellow nails. Age had battered her features so that she almost resembled a man, with sharp, shrunken eyes and prominent creases on either side of her nose. Her lips, chapped and faded, had nearly disappeared, and her eyebrows were missing altogether. Nevertheless she looked fierce.

"Lock up!" she commanded. She shouted even though I stood only a few feet away. "Fasten the chain and firmly press that button on the knob! This is the first thing you shall do when you enter, is that clear?"

I locked the door as directed and examined the house. Next to the bench on which the woman sat was a small round table, its legs fully concealed, much like the woman's, by a skirt of lace. The table held a lamp, a transistor radio, a leather change purse with a silver clasp, and a telephone. A thick wooden cane coated with a layer of dust was propped against one side. There was a parlor to my right, lined with bookcases and filled with shabby claw-footed furniture. In the corner of the parlor I saw a grand piano with its top down, piled with papers. The piano's bench was missing; it seemed to be the one on which the woman was sitting. Somewhere in the house a clock chimed seven times.

"You're punctual!" the woman proclaimed. "I expect you shall be so with the rent!"

"I have a letter, madame." In my jacket pocket was a letter confirming my employment from MIT, which I had brought along to prove that I was indeed from Tech.

She stared at the letter, then handed it back to me carefully, gripping it with her fingers as if it were a dinner plate heaped with food instead of a sheet of paper. She did not wear glasses, and I wondered if she'd read a word of it. "The last boy was always late! Still owes me eight dollars! Harvard boys aren't what they used to be! Only Harvard and Tech in this house! How's Tech, boy?"

"It is very well."

"You checked the lock?"

"Yes, madame."

She slapped the space beside her on the bench with one hand, and told me to sit down. For a moment she was silent. Then she intoned, as if she alone possessed this knowledge:

"There is an American flag on the moon!"

"Yes, madame." Until then I had not thought very much about the moon shot. It was in the newspaper, of course, article upon article. The astronauts had landed on the shores of the Sea of Tranquillity, I had read, traveling farther than anyone in the history of civilization. For a few hours they explored the moon's surface. They gathered rocks in their pockets, described their surroundings (a magnificent desolation, according to one astronaut), spoke by phone to the president, and planted a flag in lunar soil. The voyage was hailed as man's most awesome achievement. I had seen full-page photographs in the *Globe*, of the astronauts in their inflated costumes, and read about what certain people in Boston had been doing at the exact moment the astronauts landed, on a Sunday afternoon. A man said that he was operating a swan boat with a radio pressed to his ear; a woman had been baking rolls for her grandchildren.

The woman bellowed, "A flag on the moon, boy! I heard it on the radio! Isn't that splendid?"

"Yes, madame."

But she was not satisfied with my reply. Instead she commanded, "Say 'splendid'!"

I was both baffled and somewhat insulted by the request. It reminded me of the way I was taught multiplication tables as a child, repeating after the master, sitting cross-legged, without shoes or pencils, on the floor of my one-room Tollygunge school. It also reminded me of my wedding, when I had repeated endless Sanskrit verses after the priest, verses I barely understood, which joined me to my wife. I said nothing.

"Say 'splendid'!" the woman bellowed once again.

"Splendid," I murmured. I had to repeat the word a second time at the top of my lungs, so she could hear. I am soft-spoken by nature and was especially reluctant to raise my voice to an elderly woman whom I had met only moments ago, but she did not appear to be offended. If anything the reply pleased her because her next command was:

"Go see the room!"

I rose from the bench and mounted the narrow carpeted staircase. There were five doors, two on either side of an equally narrow hallway, and one at the opposite end. Only one door was partly open. The room contained a twin bed under a sloping ceiling, a brown oval rug, a basin with an exposed pipe, and a chest of drawers. One door, painted white, led to a closet, another to a toilet and a tub. The walls were covered with gray and ivory striped paper. The window was open; net curtains stirred in the breeze. I lifted them away and inspected the view: a small back yard, with a few fruit trees and an empty clothes-line. I was satisfied. From the bottom of the stairs I heard the woman demand, "What is your decision?"

When I returned to the foyer and told her, she picked up the leather change purse on the table, opened the clasp, fished about with her fingers, and produced a key on a thin wire hoop. She informed me that there was a kitchen at the back of the house, accessible through the parlor. I was welcome to use the stove as long as I left it as I found it. Sheets and towels were provided, but keeping them clean was my own responsibility. The rent was due Friday mornings on the ledge above the piano keys. "And no lady visitors!"

"I am a married man, madame." It was the first time I had announced this fact to anyone.

But she had not heard. "No lady visitors!" she insisted. She introduced herself as Mrs. Croft.

• • •

My wife's name was Mala. The marriage had been arranged by my older brother and his wife. I regarded the proposition with neither objection nor enthusiasm. It was a duty expected of me, as it was expected of every man. She was the daughter of a schoolteacher in Beleghata. I was told that she could cook, knit, embroider, sketch landscapes, and recite poems by Tagore, but these talents could not make up for the fact that she did not possess a fair complexion, and so a string of men had rejected her to her face. She was twenty-seven, an age when her parents had begun to fear that she would never marry, and so they were willing to ship their only child halfway across the world in order to save her from spinsterhood.

For five nights we shared a bed. Each of those nights, after applying cold cream and braiding her hair, which she tied up at the end with a black cotton string, she turned from me and wept; she missed her parents. Although I would be leaving the country in a few days, custom dictated that she was now a part of my household, and for the next six weeks she was to live with my brother and his wife, cooking, cleaning, serving tea and sweets to guests. I did nothing to console her. I lay on my own side of the bed, reading my guidebook by flashlight and anticipating my journey. At times I thought of the tiny room on the other side of the wall which had belonged to my mother. Now the room was practically empty; the wooden pallet on which she'd once slept was piled with trunks and old bedding. Nearly six years ago, before leaving for London, I had watched her die on that bed, had found her playing with her excrement in her final days. Before we cremated her I had cleaned each of her fingernails with a hairpin, and then, because my brother could not bear it, I had assumed the role of eldest son, and had touched the flame to her temple, to release her tormented soul to heaven.

· · ·

The next morning I moved into the room in Mrs. Croft's house. When I unlocked the door I saw that she was sitting on the piano bench, on the same side as the previous evening. She wore the same black skirt, the same starched white blouse, and had her hands folded together the same way in her lap. She looked so much the same that I wondered if she'd spent the whole night on the bench. I put my suitcase upstairs, filled my flask with boiling water in the kitchen, and headed off to work. That evening when I came home from the university, she was still there.

"Sit down, boy!" She slapped the space beside her.

I perched beside her on the bench. I had a bag of groceries with me — more milk, more cornflakes, and more bananas, for my inspection of the kitchen earlier in the day had revealed no spare pots, pans, or cooking utensils. There were only two saucepans in the refrigerator, both containing some orange broth, and a copper kettle on the stove.

"Good evening, madame."

She asked me if I had checked the lock. I told her I had.

For a moment she was silent. Then suddenly she declared, with the equal measures of disbelief and delight as the night before, "There's an American flag on the moon, boy!"

"Yes, madame."

"A flag on the moon! Isn't that splendid?"

I nodded, dreading what I knew was coming. "Yes, madame."

"Say 'splendid'!"

This time I paused, looking to either side in case anyone were there to overhear me, though I knew perfectly well that the house was empty. I felt like an idiot. But it was a small enough thing to ask. "Splendid!" I cried out.

Within days it became our routine. In the mornings when I left for the library Mrs. Croft was either hidden away in her bedroom, on the other side of the staircase, or she was sitting on the bench, oblivious to my presence, listening to the news or classical music on the radio. But each evening when I returned the same thing happened: she slapped the bench, ordered me to sit down, declared that there was a flag on the moon, and declared that it was splendid. I said it was splendid, too, and then we sat in silence. As awkward as it was, and as endless as it felt to me then, the nightly encounter lasted only about ten minutes; inevitably she would drift off to sleep, her head falling abruptly toward her chest, leaving me free to retire to my room. By then, of course, there was no flag standing on the moon. The astronauts, I had read in the paper, had seen it fall before they flew back to Earth. But I did not have the heart to tell her.

Friday morning, when my first week's rent was due, I went to the piano in the parlor to place my money on the ledge. The piano keys were dull and discolored. When I pressed one, it made no sound at all. I had put eight one-dollar bills in an envelope and written Mrs. Croft's name on the front of it. I was not in the habit of leaving money unmarked and unattended. From where I stood I could see the profile of her tent-shaped skirt. She was sitting on the bench, listening to the radio. It seemed unnecessary to make her get up and walk all the way to the piano. I never saw her walking about, and assumed, from the cane always propped against the round table at her side, that she did so with difficulty. When I approached the bench she peered up at me and demanded:

"What is your business?"

"The rent, madame."

"On the ledge above the piano keys!"

"I have it here." I extended the envelope toward her, but her fingers, folded together in her lap, did not budge. I bowed slightly and lowered the envelope, so that it hovered just above her hands. After a moment she accepted, and nodded her head.

That night when I came home, she did not slap the bench, but out of habit I sat beside her as usual. She asked me if I had checked the lock, but she mentioned nothing about the flag on the moon. Instead she said:

"It was very kind of you!"

"I beg your pardon, madame?"

"Very kind of you!"

She was still holding the envelope in her hands.

On Sunday there was a knock on my door. An elderly woman introduced herself: she was Mrs. Croft's daughter, Helen. She walked into the room and looked at each of the walls as if for signs of change, glancing at the shirts that hung in the closet, the neckties draped over the doorknob, the box of cornflakes on the chest of drawers, the dirty bowl and spoon in the basin. She was short and thick-waisted, with cropped silver hair and bright pink lipstick. She wore a sleeveless summer dress, a row of white plastic beads, and spectacles on a chain that hung like a swing against her chest. The backs of her legs were mapped with dark blue veins, and her upper arms sagged like the flesh of a roasted eggplant. She told me she lived in Arlington, a town farther up Massachusetts Avenue. "I come once a week to bring Mother groceries. Has she sent you packing yet?"

"It is very well, madame."

"Some of the boys run screaming. But I think she likes you. You're the first boarder she's ever referred to as a gentleman."

"Not at all, madame."

She looked at me, noticing my bare feet (I still felt strange wearing shoes indoors, and always removed them before entering my room). "Are you new to Boston?"

"New to America, madame."

"From?" She raised her eyebrows.

"I am from Calcutta, India."

"Is that right? We had a Brazilian fellow, about a year ago. You'll find Cambridge a very international city."

I nodded, and began to wonder how long our conversation would last. But at that moment we heard Mrs. Croft's electrifying voice rising up the stairs. When we stepped into the hallway we heard her hollering:

"You are to come downstairs immediately!"

"What is it?" Helen hollered back.

"Immediately!"

I put on my shoes at once. Helen sighed.

We walked down the staircase. It was too narrow for us to descend side by side, so I followed Helen, who seemed to be in no hurry, and complained at one point that she had a bad knee. "Have you been walking without your cane?" Helen called out. "You know you're not supposed to walk without that cane." She paused, resting her hand on the banister, and looked back at me. "She slips sometimes."

For the first time Mrs. Croft seemed vulnerable. I pictured her on the floor in front of the bench, flat on her back, staring at the ceiling, her feet pointing in opposite directions. But when we reached the bottom of the staircase she was sitting there as usual, her hands folded together in her lap. Two grocery bags were at her feet. When we stood before her she did not slap the bench, or ask us to sit down. She glared.

"What is it, Mother?"

"It's improper!"

"What's improper?"

"It is improper for a lady and gentleman who are not married to one another to hold a private conversation without a chaperone!"

Helen said she was sixty-eight years old, old enough to be my mother, but Mrs. Croft insisted that Helen and I speak to each other downstairs, in the parlor. She added that it was also improper for a lady of Helen's station to reveal her age, and to wear a dress so high above the ankle.

"For your information, Mother, it's 1969. What would you do if you actually left the house one day and saw a girl in a miniskirt?"

Mrs. Croft sniffed. "I'd have her arrested."

Helen shook her head and picked up one of the grocery bags. I picked up the other one, and followed her through the parlor and into the kitchen. The bags were filled with cans of soup, which Helen opened up one by one with a few cranks of a can opener. She tossed the old soup in the saucepans into the sink, rinsed the pans under the tap, filled them with soup from the newly opened cans, and put them back in the refrigerator. "A few years ago she could still open the cans herself," Helen said. "She hates that I do it for her now. But the piano killed her hands." She put on her spectacles, glanced at the cupboards, and spotted my tea bags. "Shall we have a cup?"

I filled the kettle on the stove. "I beg your pardon, madame. The piano?"

"She used to give lessons. For forty years. It was how she raised us after my father died." Helen put her hands on her hips, staring at the open refrigerator. She reached into the back, pulled out a wrapped stick of butter, frowned, and tossed it into the garbage. "That ought to do it," she said, and put the unopened cans of soup in the cupboard. I sat at the table and watched as Helen washed the dirty dishes, tied up the garbage bag, watered a spider plant over the sink, and poured boiling water into two cups. She handed one to me without milk, the string of the tea bag trailing over the side, and sat down at the table.

"Excuse me, madame, but is it enough?"

Helen took a sip of her tea. Her lipstick left a smiling pink stain on the inside rim of the cup. "Is what enough?"

"The soup in the pans. Is it enough food for Mrs. Croft?"

"She won't eat anything else. She stopped eating solids after she turned one hundred. That was, let's see, three years ago."

I was mortified. I had assumed Mrs. Croft was in her eighties, perhaps as old as ninety. I had never known a person who had lived for over a century. That this person was a widow who lived alone mortified me further still. It was widowhood that had driven my own mother insane. My father, who worked as a clerk at the General Post Office of Calcutta, died of encephalitis when I was sixteen. My mother refused to adjust to life without him; instead she sank deeper into a world of darkness from which neither I, nor my brother, nor concerned relatives, nor psychiatric clinics on Rash Behari Avenue could save her. What pained me most was to see her so unguarded, to hear her burp after meals or expel gas in front of company without the slightest embarrassment. After my father's death my brother abandoned his schooling and began to work in the jute mill he would eventually manage, in order to keep the household running. And so it was my job to sit by my mother's feet and study for my exams as she counted and recounted the bracelets on her arm as if they were the beads of an abacus. We tried to keep an eye on her. Once she had wandered half naked to the tram depot before we were able to bring her inside again.

"I am happy to warm Mrs. Croft's soup in the evenings," I suggested, removing the tea bag from my cup and squeezing out the liquor. "It is no trouble."

Helen looked at her watch, stood up, and poured the rest of her tea into the sink. "I wouldn't if I were you. That's the sort of thing that would kill her altogether."

That evening, when Helen had gone back to Arlington and Mrs. Croft and I were alone again, I began to worry. Now that I knew how very old she was, I worried that something would happen to her in the middle of the night, or when I was out during the day. As vigorous as her voice was, and imperious as she seemed, I knew that even a scratch or a cough could kill a person that old; each day she lived, I knew, was something of a miracle. Although Helen had seemed friendly enough, a small part of me worried that she might accuse me of negligence if anything were to happen. Helen didn't seem worried. She came and went, bringing soup for Mrs. Croft, one Sunday after the next.

In this manner the six weeks of that summer passed. I came home each evening, after my hours at the library, and spent a few minutes on the piano bench with Mrs. Croft. I gave her a bit of my company, and assured her that I had checked the lock, and told her that the flag on the moon was splendid. Some evenings I sat beside her long after she had drifted off to sleep, still in awe of how many years she had spent on this earth. At times I tried to picture the world she had been born into, in 1866 — a world, I imagined, filled with women in long black skirts, and chaste conversations in the parlor. Now, when I looked at her hands with their swollen knuckles folded together in her lap, I imagined them smooth and slim, striking the piano keys. At times I came downstairs before going to sleep, to make sure she was sitting upright on the bench, or was safe in her bedroom. On Fridays I made sure to put the rent in her hands. There was nothing I could do for her beyond these simple gestures. I was not her son, and apart from those eight dollars, I owed her nothing.

At the end of August, Mala's passport and green card were ready. I received a telegram with her flight information; my brother's house in Calcutta had no telephone. Around that time I also received a letter from her, written only a few days after we had parted. There was no salutation; addressing me by name would have assumed an intimacy we had not yet discovered. It contained only a few lines. "I write in English in preparation for the journey. Here I am very much lonely. Is it very cold there. Is there snow. Yours, Mala."

I was not touched by her words. We had spent only a handful of days in each other's company. And yet we were bound together; for six weeks she had worn an iron bangle on her wrist, and applied vermilion powder to the part in her hair, to signify to the world that she was a bride. In those six weeks I regarded her arrival as I would the arrival of a coming month, or season—something inevitable, but meaningless at the time. So little did I know her that, while details of her face sometimes rose to my memory, I could not conjure up the whole of it.

A few days after receiving the letter, as I was walking to work in the morning, I saw an Indian woman on the other side of Massachusetts Avenue, wearing a sari with its free end nearly dragging on the footpath, and pushing a child in a stroller. An American woman with a small black dog on a leash was walking to one side of her. Suddenly the dog began barking. From the other side of the street I watched as the Indian woman, startled, stopped in her path, at which point the dog leapt up and seized the end of the sari between its teeth. The American woman scolded the dog, appeared to apologize, and walked quickly away, leaving the Indian woman to fix her sari in the middle of the footpath, and quiet her crying child. She did not see me standing there, and eventually she continued on her way. Such a mishap, I realized that morning, would soon be my concern. It was my duty to take care of Mala, to welcome her and protect her. I would have to buy her her first pair of snow boots, her first winter coat. I would have to tell her which streets to avoid, which way the traffic came, tell her to wear her sari so that the free end did not drag on the footpath. A five-mile separation from her parents, I recalled with some irritation, had caused her to weep.

Unlike Mala, I was used to it all by then: used to cornflakes and milk, used to Helen's visits, used to sitting on the bench with Mrs. Croft. The only thing I was not used to was Mala. Nevertheless I did what I had to do. I went to the housing office at MIT and found a furnished apartment a few blocks away, with a double bed and a private kitchen and bath, for forty dollars a week. One last Friday I handed Mrs. Croft eight one-dollar bills in an envelope, brought my suitcase downstairs, and informed her that I was moving. She put my key into her change purse. The last thing she asked me to do was hand her the cane propped against the table, so that she could walk to the door and lock it behind me. "Good-bye, then," she said, and retreated back into the house. I did not expect any display of emotion, but I was disappointed all the same. I was only a boarder, a man who paid her a bit of money and passed in and out of her home for six weeks. Compared to a century, it was no time at all.

At the airport I recognized Mala immediately. The free end of her sari did not drag on the floor, but was draped in a sign of bridal modesty over her head, just as it had draped my mother until the day my father died. Her thin brown arms were stacked with gold bracelets, a small red circle was painted on her forehead, and the edges of her feet were tinted with a decorative red dye. I did not embrace her, or kiss her, or take her hand. Instead I asked her, speaking Bengali for the first time in America, if she was hungry.

She hesitated, then nodded yes.

I told her I had prepared some egg curry at home. "What did they give you to eat on the plane?"

"I didn't eat."

"All the way from Calcutta?"

"The menu said oxtail soup."

"But surely there were other items."

"The thought of eating an ox's tail made me lose my appetite."

When we arrived home, Mala opened up one of her suitcases, and presented me with two pullover sweaters, both made with bright blue wool, which she had knitted in the course of our separation, one with a V neck, the other covered with cables. I tried them on; both were tight under the arms. She had also brought me two new pairs of drawstring pajamas, a letter from my brother, and a packet of loose Darjeeling tea. I had no present for her apart from the egg curry. We sat at a bare table, each of us staring at our plates. We ate with our hands, another thing I had not yet done in America.

"The house is nice," she said. "Also the egg curry." With her left hand she held the end of her sari to her chest, so it would not slip off her head.

"I don't know many recipes."

She nodded, peeling the skin off each of her potatoes before eating them. At one point the sari slipped to her shoulders. She readjusted it at once.

"There is no need to cover your head," I said. "I don't mind. It doesn't matter here."

She kept it covered anyway.

I waited to get used to her, to her presence at my side, at my table and in my bed, but a week later we were still strangers. I still was not used to coming home to an apartment that smelled of steamed rice, and finding that the basin in the bathroom was always wiped clean, our two toothbrushes lying side by side, a cake of Pears soap from India resting in the soap dish. I was not used to the fragrance of the coconut oil she rubbed every other night into her scalp, or the delicate sound her bracelets made as she moved about the apartment. In the mornings she was always awake before I was. The first morning when I came into the kitchen she had heated up the leftovers and set a plate with a spoonful of salt on its edge on the table, assuming I would eat rice for breakfast, as most Bengali husbands did. I told her cereal would do, and the next morning when I came into the kitchen she had already poured the cornflakes into my bowl. One morning she walked with me down Massachusetts Avenue to MIT, where I gave her a short tour of the campus. On the way we stopped at a hardware store and I made a copy of the key, so that she could let herself into the apartment. The next morning before I left for work she asked me for a few dollars. I parted with them reluctantly, but I knew that this, too, was now normal. When I came home from work there was a potato peeler in the kitchen drawer, and a tablecloth on the table, and chicken curry made with fresh garlic and ginger on the stove. We did not have a television in those days. After dinner I read the newspaper, while Mala sat at the kitchen table, working on a cardigan for herself with more of the bright blue wool, or writing letters home.

At the end of our first week, on Friday, I suggested going out. Mala set down her knitting and disappeared into the bathroom. When she emerged I regretted the suggestion; she had put on a clean silk sari and extra bracelets, and coiled her hair with a flattering side part on top of her head. She was prepared as if for a party, or at the very least for the cinema, but I had no such destination in mind. The evening air was balmy. We walked several blocks down Massachusetts Avenue, looking into the windows of restaurants and shops. Then, without thinking, I led her down the quiet street where for so many nights I had walked alone.

"This is where I lived before you came," I said, stopping at Mrs. Croft's chain-link fence.

"In such a big house?"

"I had a small room upstairs. At the back."

"Who else lives there?"

"A very old woman."

"With her family?"

"Alone."

"But who takes care of her?"

I opened the gate. "For the most part she takes care of herself."

I wondered if Mrs. Croft would remember me; I wondered if she had a new boarder to sit with her on the bench each evening. When I pressed the bell I expected the same long wait as that day of our first meeting, when I did not have a key. But this time the door was opened almost immediately, by Helen. Mrs. Croft was not sitting on the bench. The bench was gone.

"Hello there," Helen said, smiling with her bright pink lips at Mala. "Mother's in the parlor. Will you be visiting awhile?"

"As you wish, madame."

"Then I think I'll run to the store, if you don't mind. She had a little accident. We can't leave her alone these days, not even for a minute."

I locked the door after Helen and walked into the parlor. Mrs. Croft was lying flat on her back, her head on a peach-colored cushion, a thin white quilt spread over her body. Her hands were folded together on top of her chest. When she saw me she pointed at the sofa, and told me to sit down. I took my place as directed, but Mala wandered over to the piano and sat on the bench, which was now positioned where it belonged.

"I broke my hip!" Mrs. Croft announced, as if no time had passed.

"Oh dear, madame."

"I fell off the bench!"

"I am so sorry, madame."

"It was the middle of the night! Do you know what I did, boy?"

I shook my head.

"I called the police!"

She stared up at the ceiling and grinned sedately, exposing a crowded row of long gray teeth. Not one was missing. "What do you say to that, boy?"

As stunned as I was, I knew what I had to say. With no hesitation at all, I cried out, "Splendid!"

Mala laughed then. Her voice was full of kindness, her eyes bright with amusement. I had never heard her laugh before, and it was loud enough so that Mrs. Croft had heard, too. She turned to Mala and glared.

"Who is she, boy?"

"She is my wife, madame."

Mrs. Croft pressed her head at an angle against the cushion to get a better look. "Can you play the piano?"

"No, madame," Mala replied.

"Then stand up!"

Mala rose to her feet, adjusting the end of her sari over her head and holding it to her chest, and, for the first time since her arrival, I felt sympathy. I remembered my first days in London, learning how to take the Tube to Russell Square, riding an escalator for the first time, being unable to understand that when the man cried "piper" it meant "paper," being unable to decipher, for a whole year, that the conductor said "mind the gap" as the train pulled away from each station. Like me, Mala had traveled far from home, not knowing where she was going, or what she would find, for no reason other than to be my wife. As strange as it seemed, I knew in my heart that one day her death would affect me, and stranger still, that mine would affect her. I wanted somehow to explain this to Mrs. Croft, who was still scrutinizing Mala from top to toe with what seemed to be placid disdain. I wondered if Mrs. Croft had ever seen a woman in a sari, with a dot painted on her forehead and bracelets stacked on her wrists. I wondered what she would object to. I wondered if she could see the red dye still vivid on Mala's feet, all but obscured by the bottom edge of her sari. At last Mrs. Croft declared, with the equal measures of disbelief and delight I knew well:

"She is a perfect lady!"

Now it was I who laughed. I did so quietly, and Mrs. Croft did not hear me. But Mala had heard, and, for the first time, we looked at each other and smiled.

I like to think of that moment in Mrs. Croft's parlor as the moment when the distance between Mala and me began to lessen. Although we were not yet fully in love, I like to think of the months that followed as a honeymoon of sorts. Together we explored the city and met other Bengalis, some of whom are still friends today. We discovered that a man named Bill sold fresh fish on Prospect Street, and that a shop in Harvard Square called Cardullo's sold bay leaves and cloves. In the evenings we walked to the Charles River to watch sailboats drift across the water, or had ice cream cones in Harvard Yard. We bought an Instamatic camera with which to document our life together, and I took pictures of her posing in front of the Prudential building, so that she could send them to her parents. At night we kissed, shy at first but quickly bold, and discovered pleasure and solace in each other's arms. I told her about my voyage on the SS *Roma*, and about Finsbury Park and the YMCA, and my evenings on the bench with Mrs. Croft. When I told her stories about my mother, she wept. It was Mala who consoled me when, reading the *Globe* one evening, I came across Mrs. Croft's obituary. I had not thought of her in several months—by then those six weeks of the summer were already a remote interlude in my past—but when I learned of her death I was stricken, so much so that when Mala looked up from her knitting she found me staring at the wall, the newspaper neglected in my lap, unable to speak. Mrs. Croft's was the first death I mourned in America, for hers was the first life I had admired; she had left this world at last, ancient and alone, never to return.

As for me, I have not strayed much farther. Mala and I live in a town about twenty miles from Boston, on a tree-lined street much like Mrs. Croft's, in a house we own, with a garden that saves us from buying tomatoes in summer, and room for guests. We are American citizens now, so that we can collect social security when it is time. Though we visit Calcutta every few years, and bring back more drawstring pajamas and Darjeeling tea, we have decided to grow old here. I work in a small college library. We have a son who attends Harvard University. Mala no longer drapes the end of her sari over her head, or weeps at night for her parents, but occasionally she weeps for our son. So we drive to Cambridge to visit him, or bring him home for a weekend, so that he can eat rice with us with his hands, and speak in Bengali, things we sometimes worry he will no longer do after we die.

Whenever we make that drive, I always make it a point to take Massachusetts Avenue, in spite of the traffic. I barely recognize the buildings now, but each time I am there I return instantly to those six weeks as if they were only the other day, and I slow down and point to Mrs. Croft's street, saying to my son, here was my first home in America, where I lived with a woman who was 103. "Remember?" Mala says, and smiles, amazed, as I am, that there was ever a time that we were strangers. My son always expresses his astonishment, not at Mrs. Croft's age, but at how little I paid in rent, a fact nearly as inconceivable to him as a flag on the moon was to a woman born in 1866. In my son's eyes I see the ambition that had first hurled me across the world. In a few years he will graduate and pave his way, alone and unprotected. But I remind myself that he has a father who is still living, a mother who is happy and strong. Whenever he is discouraged, I tell him that if I can survive on three continents, then there is no obstacle he cannot conquer. While the astronauts, heroes forever, spent mere hours on the moon, I have remained in this new world for nearly thirty years. I know that my achievement is quite ordinary. I am not the only man to seek his fortune far from home, and certainly I am not the first. Still, there are times I am bewildered by each mile I have traveled, each meal I have eaten, each person I have known, each room in which I have slept. As ordinary as it all appears, there are times when it is beyond my imagination.

The Namesake

For Alberto and Octavio,
whom I call by other names

ACKNOWLEDGMENTS

I wish to thank the John Simon Guggenheim Founda-
tion for its generous support. My deepest thanks also
go to Susan Choi, Carin Clevidence, Gita Daneshjoo,
Samantha Gillison, Daphne Kaloay, Cressida Leyshon,
Heidi Pitlor, Janet Silver, Eric Simonoff, and Jayne
Yaffe Kemp.

I am indebted to the following books: *Nikolai Gogol*, by
Vladimir Nabokov, and *Divided Soul: The Life of Gogol*,
by Henri Troyat. Quotations from "The Overcoat" are
from David Magarshack's translation.

The reader should realize himself that it could not have happened otherwise, and that to give him any other name was quite out of the question.

—NIKOLAI GOGOL, "The Overcoat"

I

1968

ON A sticky August evening two weeks before her due
date, Ashima Ganguli stands in the kitchen of a Central Square apartment, combining Rice Krispies and Planters
peanuts and chopped red onion in a bowl. She adds salt, lemon
juice, thin slices of green chili pepper, wishing there were mustard oil to pour into the mix. Ashima has been consuming this
concoction throughout her pregnancy, a humble approxima-
tion of the snack sold for pennies on Calcutta sidewalks and
on railway platforms throughout India, spilling from newspaper cones. Even now that there is barely space inside her, it
is the one thing she craves. Tasting from a cupped palm, she
frowns; as usual, there's something missing. She stares blankly
at the pegboard behind the countertop where her cooking
utensils hang, all slightly coated with grease. She wipes sweat
from her face with the free end of her sari. Her swollen feet
ache against speckled gray linoleum. Her pelvis aches from the
baby's weight. She opens a cupboard, the shelves lined with
a grimy yellow-and-white-checkered paper she's been meaning to replace, and reaches for another onion, frowning again
as she pulls at its crisp magenta skin. A curious warmth floods

her abdomen, followed by a tightening so severe she doubles over, gasping without sound, dropping the onion with a thud on the floor.

The sensation passes, only to be followed by a more enduring spasm of discomfort. In the bathroom she discovers, on her underpants, a solid streak of brownish blood. She calls out to her husband, Ashoke, a doctoral candidate in electrical engineering at MIT, who is studying in the bedroom. He leans over a card table; the edge of their bed, two twin mattresses pushed together under a red and purple batik spread, serves as his chair. When she calls out to Ashoke, she doesn't say his name. Ashima never thinks of her husband's name when she thinks of her husband, even though she knows perfectly well what it is. She has adopted his surname but refuses, for propriety's sake, to utter his first. It's not the type of thing Bengali wives do. Like a kiss or caress in a Hindi movie, a husband's name is something intimate and therefore unspoken, cleverly patched over. And so, instead of saying Ashoke's name, she utters the interrogative that has come to replace it, which translates roughly as "Are you listening to me?"

At dawn a taxi is called to ferry them through deserted Cambridge streets, up Massachusetts Avenue and past Harvard Yard, to Mount Auburn Hospital. Ashima registers, answering questions about the frequency and duration of the contractions, as Ashoke fills out the forms. She is seated in a wheelchair and pushed through the shining, brightly lit corridors, whisked into an elevator more spacious than her kitchen. On the maternity floor she is assigned to a bed by a window, in a room at the end of the hall. She is asked to remove her Murshidabad silk sari in favor of a flowered cotton gown that, to her mild embarrassment, only reaches her knees. A nurse offers to fold up the sari but, exasperated by the six slippery yards, ends up stuffing the material into Ashima's slate blue suitcase. Her obstetrician, Dr. Ashley, gauntly handsome in a Lord Mountbatten sort of way, with fine sand-colored hair swept back from his temples, arrives to examine her progress. The baby's head is in the proper position, has already begun its descent. She is told that she is still in early labor, three centimeters dilated, beginning to efface. "What does it mean, dilated?" she asks, and Dr. Ashley holds up two fingers side by side, then draws them apart, explaining the unimaginable thing her body must do in order for the baby to pass. The process will take some time, Dr. Ashley tells her; given that this is her first pregnancy, labor can take twenty-four hours, sometimes more. She searches for Ashoke's face, but he has stepped behind the curtain the doctor has drawn. "I'll be back," Ashoke says to her in Bengali, and then a nurse adds: "Don't you worry, Mr. Ganguli. She's got a long ways to go. We can take over from here."

Now she is alone, cut off by curtains from the three other women in the room. One woman's name, she gathers from bits of conversation, is Beverly. Another is Lois. Carol lies to her left. "Goddamnit, goddamn you, this is hell," she hears one of them say. And then a man's voice: "I love you, sweetheart." Words Ashima has neither heard nor expects to hear from her own husband; this is not how they are. It is the first time in her life she has slept alone, surrounded by strangers; all her life she has slept either in a room with her parents, or with Ashoke at her side. She wishes the curtains were open, so that she could talk to the American women. Perhaps one of them has given birth before, can tell her what to expect. But she has gathered that Americans, in spite of their public declarations of affection, in spite of their miniskirts and bikinis, in spite of their hand-holding on the street and lying on top of each other on the Cambridge Common, prefer their privacy. She spreads her fingers over the taut, enormous drum her middle has become, wondering where the baby's feet and hands are at this moment. The child is no longer restless; for the past few days, apart from the occasional flutter, she has not felt it punch or kick or press against her ribs. She wonders if she is the only Indian person in the hospital, but a gentle twitch from the baby reminds her that she is, technically speaking, not alone. Ashima thinks it's strange that her child will be born in a place most people enter either to suffer or to die. There is nothing to comfort her in the off-white tiles of the floor, the off-white panels of the ceiling, the white sheets tucked tightly into the bed. In India, she thinks to herself, women go home to their parents to give birth, away from husbands and in-laws and household cares, retreating briefly to childhood when the baby arrives.

Another contraction begins, more violent than the last. She cries out, pressing her head against the pillow. Her fingers grip the chilly rails of the bed. No one hears her, no nurse rushes to her side. She has been instructed to time the duration of the contractions and so she consults her watch, a bon voyage gift from her parents, slipped over her wrist the last time she saw them, amid airport confusion and tears. It wasn't until she was on the plane, flying for the first time in her life on a BOAC VC-10 whose deafening ascent twenty-six members of her family had watched from the balcony at Dum Dum Airport, as she was drifting over parts of India she'd never set foot in, and then even farther, outside India itself, that she'd noticed the watch among the cavalcade of matrimonial bracelets on both her arms: iron, gold, coral, conch. Now, in addition, she wears a plastic bracelet with a typed label identifying her as a patient of the hospital. She keeps the watch face turned to the inside of her wrist. On the back, surrounded by the words *waterproof, antimagnetic,* and *shock-protected,* her married initials, *A.G.,* are inscribed.

American seconds tick on top of her pulse point. For half

a minute, a band of pain wraps around her stomach, radiating toward her back and shooting down her legs. And then, again, relief. She calculates the Indian time on her hands. The tip of her thumb strikes each rung of the brown ladders etched onto the backs of her fingers, then stops at the middle of the third: it is nine and a half hours ahead in Calcutta, already evening, half past eight. In the kitchen of her parents' flat on Amherst Street, at this very moment, a servant is pouring after-dinner tea into steaming glasses, arranging Marie biscuits on a tray. Her mother, very soon to be a grandmother, is standing at the mirror of her dressing table, untangling waist-length hair, still more black than gray, with her fingers. Her father hunches over his slanted ink-stained table by the window, sketching, smoking, listening to the Voice of America. Her younger brother, Rana, studies for a physics exam on the bed. She pictures clearly the gray cement floor of her parents' sitting room, feels its solid chill underfoot even on the hottest days. An enormous black-and-white photograph of her deceased paternal grandfather looms at one end against the pink plaster wall; opposite, an alcove shielded by clouded panes of glass is stuffed with books and papers and her father's watercolor tins. For an instant the weight of the baby vanishes, replaced by the scene that passes before her eyes, only to be replaced once more by a blue strip of the Charles River, thick green treetops, cars gliding up and down Memorial Drive.

In Cambridge it is eleven in the morning, already lunch-time in the hospital's accelerated day. A tray holding warm apple juice, Jell-O, ice cream, and cold baked chicken is brought to her side. Patty, the friendly nurse with the diamond engagement ring and a fringe of reddish hair beneath her cap, tells Ashima to consume only the Jell-O and the apple juice. It's just as well. Ashima would not have touched the chicken, even if permitted; Americans eat their chicken in its skin, though

Ashima has recently found a kind butcher on Prospect Street willing to pull it off for her. Patty comes to fluff the pillows, tidy the bed. Dr. Ashley pokes in his head from time to time. "No need to worry," he chirps, putting a stethoscope to Ashima's belly, patting her hand, admiring her various bracelets. "Everything is looking perfectly normal. We are expecting a perfectly normal delivery, Mrs. Ganguli."

But nothing feels normal to Ashima. For the past eighteen months, ever since she's arrived in Cambridge, nothing has felt normal at all. It's not so much the pain, which she knows, somehow, she will survive. It's the consequence: motherhood in a foreign land. For it was one thing to be pregnant, to suffer the queasy mornings in bed, the sleepless nights, the dull throbbing in her back, the countless visits to the bathroom. Throughout the experience, in spite of her growing discomfort, she'd been astonished by her body's ability to make life, exactly as her mother and grandmother and all her great-grandmothers had done. That it was happening so far from home, unmonitored and unobserved by those she loved, had made it more miraculous still. But she is terrified to raise a child in a country where she is related to no one, where she knows so little, where life seems so tentative and spare.

"How about a little walk? It might do you good," Patty asks when she comes to clear the lunch tray.

Ashima looks up from a tattered copy of *Desh* magazine that she'd brought to read on her plane ride to Boston and still cannot bring herself to throw away. The printed pages of Bengali type, slightly rough to the touch, are a perpetual comfort to her. She's read each of the short stories and poems and articles a dozen times. There is a pen-and-ink drawing on page eleven by her father, an illustrator for the magazine: a view of the North Calcutta skyline sketched from the roof of their flat one foggy January morning. She had stood behind her father as he'd drawn it, watching as he crouched over his easel, a cigarette dangling from his lips, his shoulders wrapped in a black Kashmiri shawl.

"Yes, all right," Ashima says.

Patty helps Ashima out of bed, tucks her feet one by one into slippers, drapes a second nightgown around her shoulders. "Just think," Patty says as Ashima struggles to stand. "In a day or two you'll be half the size." She takes Ashima's arm as they step out of the room, into the hallway. After a few feet Ashima stops, her legs trembling as another wave of pain surges through her body. She shakes her head, her eyes filling with tears. "I cannot."

"You can. Squeeze my hand. Squeeze as tight as you like."

After a minute they continue on, toward the nurses' station. "Hoping for a boy or a girl?" Patty asks.

"As long as there are ten finger and ten toe," Ashima replies. For these anatomical details, these particular signs of life, are the ones she has the most difficulty picturing when she imagines the baby in her arms.

Patty smiles, a little too widely, and suddenly Ashima realizes her error, knows she should have said "fingers" and "toes." This error pains her almost as much as her last contraction. English had been her subject. In Calcutta, before she was married, she was working toward a college degree. She used to tutor neighborhood schoolchildren in their homes, on their verandas and beds, helping them to memorize Tennyson and Wordsworth, to pronounce words like *sign* and *cough*, to understand the difference between Aristotelian and Shakespearean tragedy. But in Bengali, a finger can also mean fingers, a toe toes.

It had been after tutoring one day that Ashima's mother had met her at the door, told her to go straight to the bedroom and prepare herself; a man was waiting to see her. He was the third in as many months. The first had been a widower with four children. The second, a newspaper cartoonist who knew her father, had been hit by a bus in Esplanade and lost his left arm. To her great relief they had both rejected her. She was nineteen, in the middle of her studies, in no rush to be a bride. And so, obediently but without expectation, she had untangled and rebraided her hair, wiped away the kohl that had smudged below her eyes, patted some Cuticura powder from a velvet puff onto her skin. The sheer parrot green sari she pleated and tucked into her petticoat had been laid out for her on the bed by her mother. Before entering the sitting room, Ashima had paused in the corridor. She could hear her mother saying, "She is fond of cooking, and she can knit extremely well. Within a week she finished this cardigan I am wearing."

Ashima smiled, amused by her mother's salesmanship; it had taken her the better part of a year to finish the cardigan, and still her mother had had to do the sleeves. Glancing at the floor where visitors customarily removed their slippers, she noticed, beside two sets of chappals, a pair of men's shoes that were not like any she'd ever seen on the streets and trams and buses of Calcutta, or even in the windows of Bata. They were brown shoes with black heels and off-white laces and stitching. There was a band of lentil-sized holes embossed on either side of each shoe, and at the tips was a pretty pattern pricked into the leather as if with a needle. Looking more closely, she saw the shoemaker's name written on the insides, in gold lettering that had all but faded: something and sons, it said. She saw the size, eight and a half, and the initials U.S.A. And as her mother continued to sing her praises, Ashima, unable to resist a sudden and overwhelming urge, stepped into the shoes at her feet. Lingering sweat from the owner's feet mingled with hers, causing her heart to race; it was the closest thing she had ever experienced to the touch of a man. The leather was creased, heavy, and still warm. On the left shoe she had noticed that one of the crisscrossing laces had missed a hole, and this oversight set her at ease.

She extracted her feet, entered the room. The man was sitting in a rattan chair, his parents perched on the edge of the twin bed where her brother slept at night. He was slightly plump, scholarly-looking but still youthful, with black thick-framed glasses and a sharp, prominent nose. A neatly trimmed mustache connected to a beard that covered only his chin lent him an elegant, vaguely aristocratic air. He wore brown socks and brown trousers and a green-and-white-striped shirt and was staring glumly at his knees.

He did not look up when she appeared. Though she was aware of his gaze as she crossed the room, by the time she managed to steal another look at him he was once again indifferent, focused on his knees. He cleared his throat as if to speak but then said nothing. Instead it was his father who did the talking, saying that the man had gone to St. Xavier's, and then B.E. College, graduating first-class-first from both institutions. Ashima took her seat and smoothed the pleats of her sari. She sensed the mother eyeing her with approval. Ashima was five feet four inches, tall for a Bengali woman, ninety-nine pounds. Her complexion was on the dark side of fair, but she had been compared on more than one occasion to the actress Madhabi Mukherjee. Her nails were admirably long, her fingers, like her father's, artistically slim. They inquired after her studies and she was asked to recite a few stanzas from "The Daffodils." The man's family lived in Alipore. The father was a labor officer for the customs department of a shipping company. "My son has been living abroad for two years," the man's father said, "earning a Ph.D. in Boston, researching in the field of fiber optics." Ashima had never heard of Boston, or of fiber optics. She was asked whether she was willing to fly on a plane and then if she was capable of living in a city characterized by severe, snowy winters, alone.

"Won't he be there?" she'd asked, pointing to the man whose shoes she'd briefly occupied, but who had yet to say a word to her.

It was only after the betrothal that she'd learned his name. One week later the invitations were printed, and two weeks after that she was adorned and adjusted by countless aunts, countless cousins hovering around her. These were her last moments as Ashima Bhaduri, before becoming Ashima Ganguli. Her lips were darkened, her brow and cheeks dotted with sandalwood paste, her hair wound up, bound with flowers, held in place by a hundred wire pins that would take an hour to remove once the wedding was finally over. Her head was draped with scarlet netting. The air was damp, and in spite of the pins Ashima's hair, thickest of all the cousins', would not lie flat. She wore all the necklaces and chokers and bracelets that were destined to live most of their lives in an extra-large safety deposit box in a bank vault in New England. At the designated hour she was seated on a piri that her father had decorated, hoisted five feet off the ground, carried out to meet the groom. She had hidden her face with a heart-shaped betel leaf, kept her head bent low until she had circled him seven times.

Eight thousand miles away in Cambridge, she has come to know him. In the evenings she cooks for him, hoping to please, with the unrationed, remarkably unblemished sugar, flour, rice, and salt she had written about to her mother in her very first letter home. By now she has learned that her husband likes his food on the salty side, that his favorite thing about lamb curry is the potatoes, and that he likes to finish his dinner with a small final helping of rice and dal. At night, lying beside her in bed, he listens to her describe the events of her day: her walks along Massachusetts Avenue, the shops she visits, the Hare Krishnas who pester her with their leaflets, the pistachio ice cream cones she treats herself to in Harvard Square. In spite of his meager graduate student wages he sets aside money to send every few months to his father to help put an extension on his parents' house. He is fastidious about his clothing; their first argument had been over a sweater she'd shrunk in the washing machine. As soon as he comes home from the university the first thing he does is hang up his shirt and trousers, donning a pair of drawstring pajamas and a pullover if it's cold. On Sundays he spends an hour occupied with his tins of shoe polishes and his three pairs of shoes, two black and one brown. The brown ones are the ones he'd been wearing when he'd first come to see her. The sight of him cross-legged on newspapers spread on the floor, intently whisking a brush over the leather, always reminds her of her indiscretion in her parents' corridor. It is a moment that shocks her still, and that she prefers, in spite of all she tells him at night about the life they now share, to keep to herself.

On another floor of the hospital, in a waiting room, Ashoke hunches over a *Boston Globe* from a month ago, abandoned on a neighboring chair. He reads about the riots that took place during the Democratic National Convention in Chicago and about Dr. Benjamin Spock, the baby doctor, being sentenced to two years in jail for threatening to counsel draft evaders. The Favre Leuba strapped to his wrist is running six minutes ahead of the large gray-faced clock on the wall. It is four-thirty in the morning. An hour before, Ashoke had been fast asleep, at home, Ashima's side of the bed covered with exams he'd been grading late at night, when the telephone rang. Ashima was fully dilated and being taken to the delivery room, the person on the other end had said. Upon arrival at the hospital he was told that she was pushing, that it could be any minute now. Any minute. And yet it seemed only the other day, one steel-colored winter's morning when the windows of the house were being pelted with hail, that she had spit out her tea, accusing him of mistaking the salt for sugar. To prove himself right he had taken a sip of the sweet liquid from her cup, but she had insisted on its bitterness, and poured it down the sink. That was the first thing that had caused her to suspect, and then the doctor had confirmed it, and then he would wake to the sounds, every morning when she went to brush her teeth, of her retching. Before he left for the university he would leave a cup of tea by the side of the bed, where she lay listless and silent. Often, returning in the evenings, he would find her still lying there, the tea untouched.

He now desperately needs a cup of tea for himself, not having managed to make one before leaving the house. But the machine in the corridor dispenses only coffee, tepid at best, in paper cups. He takes off his thick-rimmed glasses, fitted by a Calcutta optometrist, polishes the lenses with the cotton handkerchief he always keeps in his pocket, *A* for *Ashoke* embroidered by his mother in light blue thread. His black hair, normally combed back neatly from his forehead, is disheveled, sections of it on end. He stands and begins pacing as the other expectant fathers do. So far, the door to the waiting room has opened twice, and a nurse has announced that one of them has a boy or a girl. There are handshakes all around, pats on the back, before the father is escorted away. The men wait with cigars, flowers, address books, bottles of champagne. They smoke cigarettes, ashing onto the floor. Ashoke is indifferent to such indulgences. He neither smokes nor drinks alcohol of any kind. Ashima is the one who keeps all their addresses, in a small notebook she carries in her purse. It has never occurred to him to buy his wife flowers.

He returns to the *Globe*, still pacing as he reads. A slight limp causes Ashoke's right foot to drag almost imperceptibly with each step. Since childhood he has had the habit and the ability to read while walking, holding a book in one hand on his way to school, from room to room in his parents' three-story house in Alipore, and up and down the red clay stairs. Nothing roused him. Nothing distracted him. Nothing caused him to stumble. As a teenager he had gone through all of Dickens. He read newer authors as well, Graham Greene and Somerset Maugham, all purchased from his favorite stall on College Street with pujo money. But most of all he loved the Russians. His paternal grandfather, a former professor of European literature at Calcutta University, had read from them aloud in English translations when Ashoke was a boy. Each day at tea time, as his brothers and sisters played kabadi and cricket outside, Ashoke would go to his grandfather's room, and for an hour his grandfather would read supine on the bed, his ankles crossed and the book propped open on his chest, Ashoke curled at his side. For that hour Ashoke was deaf and blind to the world around him. He did not hear his brothers and sisters laughing on the rooftop, or see the tiny, dusty, cluttered room in which his grandfather read. "Read all the Russians, and then reread them," his grandfather had said. "They will never fail you." When Ashoke's English was good enough, he began to read the books himself. It was while walking on some of the world's noisiest, busiest streets, on Chowringhee and Gariahat Road, that he had read pages of *The Brothers Karamazov*, and *Anna Karenina*, and *Fathers and Sons*. Once, a younger cousin who had tried to imitate him had fallen down the red clay staircase in Ashoke's house and broken an arm. Ashoke's mother was always convinced that her eldest son would be hit by a bus or a tram, his nose deep into *War and Peace*. That he would be reading a book the moment he died.

One day, in the earliest hours of October 20, 1961, this nearly happened. Ashoke was twenty-two, a student at B.E. College. He was traveling on the 83 Up Howrah–Ranchi Express to visit his grandparents for the holidays; they had moved from Calcutta to Jamshedpur upon his grandfather's retirement from the university. Ashoke had never spent the holidays away from his family. But his grandfather had recently gone blind, and he had requested Ashoke's company specifically, to read him *The Statesman* in the morning, Dostoyevsky and Tolstoy in the afternoon. Ashoke accepted the invitation eagerly. He carried two suitcases, the first one containing clothes and gifts, the second empty. For it would be on this visit, his grandfather had said, that the books in his glass-fronted case, collected over a lifetime and preserved under lock and key, would be given to Ashoke. The books had been promised to Ashoke throughout his childhood, and for as long as he could remember he had coveted them more than anything else in the world. He had already received a few in recent years, given to him on birthdays and other special occasions. But now that the day had come to inherit the rest, a day his grandfather could no longer read the books himself, Ashoke was saddened, and as he placed the empty suitcase under his seat, he was disconcerted by its weightlessness, regretful of the circumstances that would cause it, upon his return, to be full.

He carried a single volume for the journey, a hardbound collection of short stories by Nikolai Gogol, which his grandfather had given him when he'd graduated from class twelve. On the title page, beneath his grandfather's signature, Ashoke had written his own. Because of Ashoke's passion for this particular book, the spine had recently split, threatening to divide the pages into two sections. His favorite story in the book was the last, "The Overcoat," and that was the one Ashoke had begun to reread as the train pulled out of Howrah Station late in the evening with a prolonged and deafening shriek, away from his parents and his six younger brothers and sisters, all of whom had come to see him off and had huddled until the last mo-

ment by the window, waving to him from the long dusky platform. He had read "The Overcoat" too many times to count,
certain sentences and phrases embedded in his memory. Each
time he was captivated by the absurd, tragic, yet oddly inspiring story of Akaky Akakyevich, the impoverished main character who spends his life meekly copying documents written by
others and suffering the ridicule of absolutely everyone. His
heart went out to poor Akaky, a humble clerk just as Ashoke's
father had been at the start of his career. Each time, reading the
account of Akaky's christening, and the series of queer names
his mother had rejected, Ashoke laughed aloud. He shuddered
at the description of the tailor Petrovich's big toe, "with its de-
formed nail as thick and hard as the shell of a tortoise." His
mouth watered at the cold veal and cream pastries and champagne Akaky consumed the night his precious coat was stolen,
in spite of the fact that Ashoke had never tasted these things
himself. Ashoke was always devastated when Akaky was robbed
in "a square that looked to him like a dreadful desert," leaving
him cold and vulnerable, and Akaky's death, some pages later,
never failed to bring tears to his eyes. In some ways the story
made less sense each time he read it, the scenes he pictured so
vividly, and absorbed so fully, growing more elusive and pro-
found. Just as Akaky's ghost haunted the final pages, so did it
haunt a place deep in Ashoke's soul, shedding light on all that
was irrational, all that was inevitable about the world.

Outside the view turned quickly black, the scattered lights
of Howrah giving way to nothing at all. He had a second-class
sleeper in the seventh bogie, behind the air-conditioned coach.
Because of the season, the train was especially crowded, especially raucous, filled with families on holiday. Small children
were wearing their best clothing, the girls with brightly colored ribbons in their hair. Though he had had his dinner before leaving for the station, a four-layer tiffin carrier packed by

his mother sat at his feet, in the event that hunger should attack him in the night. He shared his compartment with three others. There was a middle-aged Bihari couple who, he gathered from overhearing their conversation, had just married off their eldest daughter, and a friendly, potbellied, middle-aged Bengali businessman wearing a suit and tie, by the name of Ghosh. Ghosh told Ashoke that he had recently returned to India after spending two years in England on a job voucher, but that he had come back home because his wife was inconsolably miserable abroad. Ghosh spoke reverently of England. The sparkling, empty streets, the polished black cars, the rows of gleaming white houses, he said, were like a dream. Trains departed and arrived according to schedule, Ghosh said. No one spat on the sidewalks. It was in a British hospital that his son had been born.

"Seen much of this world?" Ghosh asked Ashoke, untying his shoes and settling himself cross-legged on the berth. He pulled a packet of Dunhill cigarettes from his jacket pocket, offering them around the compartment before lighting one for himself.

"Once to Delhi," Ashoke replied. "And lately once a year to Jamshedpur."

Ghosh extended his arm out the window, flicking the glowing tip of his cigarette into the night. "Not this world," he said, glancing disappointedly about the interior of the train. He tilted his head toward the window. "England. America," he said, as if the nameless villages they passed had been replaced by those countries. "Have you considered going there?"

"My professors mention it from time to time. But I have a family," Ashoke said.

Ghosh frowned. "Already married?"

"No. A mother and father and six siblings. I am the eldest."

"And in a few years you will be married and living in your parents' house," Ghosh speculated.

"I suppose."

Ghosh shook his head. "You are still young. Free," he said, spreading his hands apart for emphasis. "Do yourself a favor. Before it's too late, without thinking too much about it first, pack a pillow and a blanket and see as much of the world as you can. You will not regret it. One day it will be too late."

"My grandfather always says that's what books are for," Ashoke said, using the opportunity to open the volume in his hands. "To travel without moving an inch."

"To each his own," Ghosh said. He tipped his head politely to one side, letting the last of the cigarette drop from his fingertips. He reached into a bag by his feet and took out his diary, turning to the twentieth of October. The page was blank and on it, with a fountain pen whose cap he ceremoniously unscrewed, he wrote his name and address. He ripped out the page and handed it to Ashoke. "If you ever change your mind and need contacts, let me know. I live in Tollygunge, just behind the tram depot."

"Thank you," Ashoke said, folding up the information and putting it at the back of his book.

"How about a game of cards?" Ghosh suggested. He pulled out a well-worn deck from his suit pocket, with Big Ben's image on the back. But Ashoke politely declined, for he knew no card games, and besides which, he preferred to read. One by one the passengers brushed their teeth in the vestibule, changed into their pajamas, fastened the curtain around their compartments, and went to sleep. Ghosh offered to take the upper berth, climbing barefoot up the ladder, his suit carefully folded away, so that Ashoke had the window to himself. The Bihari couple shared some sweets from a box and drank water from the same cup without either of them putting their lips to the rim, then settled into their berths as well, switching off the lights and turning their heads to the wall.

Only Ashoke continued to read, still seated, still dressed. A single small bulb glowed dimly over his head. From time to time he looked through the open window at the inky Bengal night, at the vague shapes of palm trees and the simplest of homes. Carefully he turned the soft yellow pages of his book, a few delicately tunneled by worms. The steam engine puffed reassuringly, powerfully. Deep in his chest he felt the rough jostle of the wheels. Sparks from the smokestack passed by his window. A fine layer of sticky soot dotted one side of his face, his eyelid, his arm, his neck; his grandmother would insist that he scrub himself with a cake of Margo soap as soon as he arrived. Immersed in the sartorial plight of Akaky Akakyevich, lost in the wide, snow-white, windy avenues of St. Petersburg, unaware that one day he was to dwell in a snowy place himself, Ashoke was still reading at two-thirty in the morning, one of the few passengers on the train who was awake, when the locomotive engine and seven bogies derailed from the broad-gauge line. The sound was like a bomb exploding. The first four bogies capsized into a depression alongside the track. The fifth and sixth, containing the first-class and air-conditioned passengers, telescoped into each other, killing the passengers in their sleep. The seventh, where Ashoke was sitting, capsized as well, flung by the speed of the crash farther into the field. The accident occurred 209 kilometers from Calcutta, between the Ghatshila and Dhalbumgarh stations. The train guard's portable phone would not work; it was only after the guard ran nearly five kilometers from the site of the accident, to Ghatshila, that he was able to transmit the first message for help. Over an hour passed before the rescuers arrived, bearing lanterns and shovels and axes to pry bodies from the cars.

Ashoke can still remember their shouts, asking if anyone was alive. He remembers trying to shout back, unsuccessfully, his mouth emitting nothing but the faintest rasp. He remembers the sound of people half-dead around him, moaning and tapping on the walls of the train, whispering hoarsely for help, words that only those who were also trapped and injured could possibly hear. Blood drenched his chest and the right arm of his shirt. He had been thrust partway out the window. He remembers being unable to see anything at all; for the first hours he thought that perhaps, like his grandfather whom he was on his way to visit, he'd gone blind. He remembers the acrid odor of flames, the buzzing of flies, children crying, the taste of dust and blood on his tongue. They were nowhere, somewhere in a field. Milling about them were villagers, police inspectors, a few doctors. He remembers believing that he was dying, that perhaps he was already dead. He could not feel the lower half of his body, and so was unaware that the mangled limbs of Ghosh were draped over his legs. Eventually he saw the cold, unfriendly blue of earliest morning, the moon and a few stars still lingering in the sky. The pages of his book, which had been tossed from his hand, fluttered in two sections a few feet away from the train. The glare from a search lantern briefly caught the pages, momentarily distracting one of the rescuers. "Nothing here," Ashoke heard someone say. "Let's keep going."

But the lantern's light lingered, just long enough for Ashoke to raise his hand, a gesture that he believed would consume the small fragment of life left in him. He was still clutching a single page of "The Overcoat," crumpled tightly in his fist, and when he raised his hand the wad of paper dropped from his fingers. "Wait!" he heard a voice cry out. "The fellow by that book. I saw him move."

He was pulled from the wreckage, placed on a stretcher, transported on another train to a hospital in Tatanagar. He had broken his pelvis, his right femur, and three of his ribs on the right side. For the next year of his life he lay flat on his back, ordered to keep as still as possible as the bones of his body healed. There was a risk that his right leg might be permanently paralyzed. He was transferred to Calcutta Medical College, where two screws were put into his hips. By December he had returned to his parents' house in Alipore, carried through the courtyard and up the red clay stairs like a corpse, hoisted on the shoulders of his four brothers. Three times a day he was spoon-fed. He urinated and defecated into a tin pan. Doctors and visitors came and went. Even his blind grandfather from Jamshedpur paid a visit. His family had saved the newspaper accounts. In a photograph, he observed the train smashed to shards, piled jaggedly against the sky, security guards sitting on the unclaimed belongings. He learned that fishplates and bolts had been found several feet from the main track, giving rise to the suspicion, never subsequently confirmed, of sabotage. That bodies had been mutilated beyond recognition. "Holiday-Makers' Tryst with Death," the *Times of India* had written.

In the beginning, for most of the day, he had stared at his bedroom ceiling, at the three beige blades of the fan churning at its center, their edges grimy. He could hear the top edge of a calendar scraping against the wall behind him when the fan was on. If he moved his neck to the right he had a view of a window with a dusty bottle of Dettol on its ledge and, if the shutters were open, the concrete of the wall that surrounded the house, the pale brown geckos that scampered there. He listened to the constant parade of sounds outside, footsteps, bicycle bells, the incessant squawking of crows and of the horns of cycle rickshaws in the lane so narrow that taxis could not fit. He heard the tube well at the corner being pumped into urns. Every evening at dusk he heard a conch shell being blown in the house next door to signal the hour for prayer. He could smell but not see the shimmering green sludge that collected in the open sewer. Life within the house continued. His father came and went from work, his brothers and sisters from school. His mother worked in the kitchen, checking in on him periodically, her lap stained with turmeric. Twice daily the maid twisted rags into buckets of water and wiped the floors.

During the day he was groggy from painkillers. At night he dreamed either that he was still trapped inside the train or, worse, that the accident had never happened, that he was walking down a street, taking a bath, sitting cross-legged on the floor and eating a plate of food. And then he would wake up, coated in sweat, tears streaming down his face, convinced that he would never live to do such things again. Eventually, in an attempt to avoid his nightmares, he began to read, late at night, which was when his motionless body felt most restless, his mind agile and clear. Yet he refused to read the Russians his grandfather had brought to his bedside, or any novels, for that matter. Those books, set in countries he had never seen, reminded him only of his confinement. Instead he read his engineering books, trying his best to keep up with his courses, solving equations by flashlight. In those silent hours, he thought often of Ghosh. "Pack a pillow and a blanket," he heard Ghosh say. He remembered the address Ghosh had written on a page of his diary, somewhere behind the tram depot in Tollygunge. Now it was the home of a widow, a fatherless son. Each day, to bolster his spirits, his family reminded him of the future, the day he would stand unassisted, walk across the room. It was for this, each day, that his father and mother prayed. For this that his mother gave up meat on Wednesdays. But as the months passed, Ashoke began to envision another sort of future. He imagined not only walking, but walking away, as far as he could from the place in which he was born and in which he had nearly died. The following year, with the aid of a cane, he returned to college and graduated, and without telling his parents he applied to continue his engineering studies abroad. Only after he'd been accepted with a full fellowship, a newly issued passport in hand, did he inform them of his plans. "But we

already nearly lost you once," his bewildered father had protested. His siblings had pleaded and wept. His mother, speech-
less, had refused food for three days. In spite of all that, he'd
gone.

Seven years later, there are still certain images that wipe him
flat. They lurk around a corner as he rushes through the engineering department at MIT, checks his campus mail. They
hover by his shoulder as he leans over a plate of rice at dinnertime or nestles against Ashima's limbs at night. At every turning point in his life—at his wedding when he stood behind
Ashima, encircling her waist and peering over her shoulder as
they poured puffed rice into a fire, or during his first hours
in America, seeing a small gray city caked with snow—he has
tried but failed to push these images away: the twisted, battered,
capsized bogies of the train, his body twisted below it, the terrible crunching sound he had heard but not comprehended,
his bones crushed as fine as flour. It is not the memory of pain
that haunts him; he has no memory of that. It is the memory of
waiting before he was rescued, and the persistent fear, rising up
in his throat, that he might not have been rescued at all. To this
day he is claustrophobic, holding his breath in elevators, feels
pent-up in cars unless the windows are open on both sides. On
planes he requests the bulkhead seat. At times the wailing of
children fills him with deepest dread. At times he still presses
his ribs to make sure they are solid.

He presses them now, in the hospital, shaking his head in
relief, disbelief. Although it is Ashima who carries the child,
he, too, feels heavy, with the thought of life, of his life and the
life about to come from it. He was raised without running water, nearly killed at twenty-two. Again he tastes the dust on
his tongue, sees the twisted train, the giant overturned iron
wheels. None of this was supposed to happen. But no, he had
survived it. He was born twice in India, and then a third time,

in America. Three lives by thirty. For this he thanks his parents, and their parents, and the parents of their parents. He does not thank God; he openly reveres Marx and quietly refuses religion. But there is one more dead soul he has to thank. He cannot thank the book; the book has perished, as he nearly did, in scattered pieces, in the earliest hours of an October day, in a field 209 kilometers from Calcutta. Instead of thanking God he thanks Gogol, the Russian writer who had saved his life, when Patty enters the waiting room.

2

THE baby, a boy, is born at five past five in the morning. He measures twenty inches long, weighs seven pounds nine ounces. Ashima's initial glimpse, before the cord is clipped and they carry him away, is of a creature coated with a thick white paste, and streaks of blood, her blood, on the shoulders, feet, and head. A needle placed in the small of her back has removed all sensation from her waist to her knees, and given her a blistering headache in the final stages of the delivery. When it is all over she begins to shiver profoundly, as if beset with an acute fever. For half an hour she trembles, in a daze, covered by a blanket, her insides empty, her outside still mis-shapen. She is unable to speak, to allow the nurses to help ex-change her blood-soaked gown for a fresh one. In spite of end-less glasses of water, her throat is parched. She is told to sit on a toilet, to squirt warm water from a bottle between her legs. Eventually she is sponged clean, put into a new gown, wheeled into yet another room. The lights are soothingly dim, and there is only one other bed next to hers, empty for the time being. When Ashoke arrives, Patty is taking Ashima's blood pressure, and Ashima is reclining against a pile of pillows, the child wrapped like an oblong white parcel in her arms. Beside the bed is a bassinet, labeled with a card that says BABY BOY GANGULI.

"He's here," she says quietly, looking up at Ashoke with a weak smile. Her skin is faintly yellow, the color missing from her lips. She has circles beneath her eyes, and her hair, spilling from its braid, looks as though it has not been combed for days. Her voice is hoarse, as if she'd caught a cold. He pulls up a chair by the side of the bed and Patty helps to transfer the child from mother's to father's arms. In the process, the child pierces the silence in the room with a short-lived cry. His parents react with mutual alarm, but Patty laughs approvingly. "You see," Patty says to Ashima, "he's already getting to know you."

Ashoke does as Patty tells him, stretching out his arms, putting one hand below the neck, another below the bottom.

"Go on," Patty urges. "He wants to be held tightly. He's stronger than you think."

Ashoke lifts the minuscule parcel higher, closer to his chest. "Like this?"

"There you go," Patty says. "I'll leave you three alone for a while."

At first Ashoke is more perplexed than moved, by the pointiness of the head, the puffiness of the lids, the small white spots on the cheeks, the fleshy upper lip that droops prominently over the lower one. The skin is paler than either Ashima's or his own, translucent enough to show slim green veins at the temples. The scalp is covered by a mass of wispy black hair. He attempts to count the eyelashes. He feels gently through the flannel for the hands and feet.

"It's all there," Ashima says, watching her husband. "I already checked."

"What are the eyes like? Why won't he open them? Has he opened them?"

She nods.

"What can he see? Can he see us?"

"I think so. But not very clearly. And not in full color. Not yet."

They sit in silence, the three of them as still as stones. "How are you feeling? Was it all right?" he asks Ashima.

But there is no answer, and when Ashoke lifts his gaze from his son's face he sees that she, too, is sleeping.

When he looks back to the child, the eyes are open, staring up at him, unblinking, as dark as the hair on its head. The face is transformed; Ashoke has never seen a more perfect thing. He imagines himself as a dark, grainy, blurry presence. As a father to his son. Again he thinks of the night he was nearly killed, the memory of those hours that have forever marked him flickering and fading in his mind. Being rescued from that shattered train had been the first miracle of his life. But here, now, reposing in his arms, weighing next to nothing but changing everything, is the second.

Apart from his father, the baby has three visitors, all Bengali —Maya and Dilip Nandi, a young married couple in Cambridge whom Ashima and Ashoke met a few months ago in the Purity Supreme, and Dr. Gupta, a mathematics postdoc from Dehradun, a bachelor in his fifties, whom Ashoke has befriended in the corridors of MIT. At feeding times the gentlemen, including Ashoke, step out into the hall. Maya and Dilip give the boy a rattle and a baby book, with places for his parents to commemorate every possible aspect of his infancy. There is even a circle in which to paste a few strands from his first haircut. Dr. Gupta gives the boy a handsome illustrated copy of Mother Goose rhymes. "Lucky boy," Ashoke remarks, turning the beautifully sewn pages. "Only hours old and already the owner of books." What a difference, he thinks, from the childhood he has known.

Ashima thinks the same, though for different reasons. For as grateful as she feels for the company of the Nandis and Dr. Gupta, these acquaintances are only substitutes for the people who really ought to be surrounding them. Without a single grandparent or parent or uncle or aunt at her side, the baby's birth, like most everything else in America, feels somehow haphazard, only half true. As she strokes and suckles and studies her son, she can't help but pity him. She has never known of a person entering the world so alone, so deprived.

Because neither set of grandparents has a working telephone, their only link to home is by telegram, which Ashoke has sent to both sides in Calcutta: "With your blessings, boy and mother fine." As for a name, they have decided to let Ashima's grandmother, who is past eighty now, who has named each of her other six great-grandchildren in the world, do the honors. When her grandmother learned of Ashima's pregnancy, she was particularly thrilled at the prospect of naming the family's first sahib. And so Ashima and Ashoke have agreed to put off the decision of what to name the baby until a letter comes, ignoring the forms from the hospital about filing for a birth certificate. Ashima's grandmother has mailed the letter herself, walking with her cane to the post office, her first trip out of the house in a decade. The letter contains one name for a girl, one for a boy. Ashima's grandmother has revealed them to no one.

Though the letter was sent a month ago, in July, it has yet to arrive. Ashima and Ashoke are not terribly concerned. After all, they both know, an infant doesn't really need a name. He needs to be fed and blessed, to be given some gold and silver, to be patted on the back after feedings and held carefully behind the neck. Names can wait. In India parents take their time. It wasn't unusual for years to pass before the right name, the best possible name, was determined. Ashima and Ashoke can both cite examples of cousins who were not officially named until

they were registered, at six or seven, in school. The Nandis and
Dr. Gupta understand perfectly. Of course you must wait, they
agree, wait for the name in his great-grandmother's letter.

Besides, there are always pet names to tide one over: a practice of Bengali nomenclature granting, to every single person,
two names. In Bengali the word for pet name is *daknam*, meaning, literally, the name by which one is called, by friends, family,
and other intimates, at home and in other private, unguarded
moments. Pet names are a persistent remnant of childhood, a
reminder that life is not always so serious, so formal, so complicated. They are a reminder, too, that one is not all things to all
people. They all have pet names. Ashima's pet name is Monu,
Ashoke's is Mithu, and even as adults, these are the names by
which they are known in their respective families, the names by
which they are adored and scolded and missed and loved.

Every pet name is paired with a good name, a *bhalonam*, for
identification in the outside world. Consequently, good names
appear on envelopes, on diplomas, in telephone directories, and
in all other public places. (For this reason, letters from Ashima's
mother say "Ashima" on the outside, "Monu" on the inside.)
Good names tend to represent dignified and enlightened qualities. Ashima means "she who is limitless, without borders."
Ashoke, the name of an emperor, means "he who transcends
grief." Pet names have no such aspirations. Pet names are never
recorded officially, only uttered and remembered. Unlike good
names, pet names are frequently meaningless, deliberately silly,
ironic, even onomatopoetic. Often in one's infancy, one answers
unwittingly to dozens of pet names, until one eventually sticks.

And so at one point, when the baby screws up his rosy,
wrinkled face and regards his small circle of admirers, Mr.
Nandi leans over and calls the baby "Buro," the Bengali word
for "old man."

"What's his name? Buro?" Patty inquires brightly, bearing
another tray of baked chicken for Ashima. Ashoke lifts the lid

and polishes off the chicken; Ashima is now officially referred to by the maternity nurses as the Jell-O-and-Ice-Cream Lady.

"No, no, that is not a name," Ashima explains. "We haven't chosen. My grandmother is choosing."

Patty nods. "Will she be here soon?"

Ashima laughs, her first genuine laugh after giving birth. The thought of her grandmother, born in the previous century, a shrunken woman in widow's white and with tawny skin that refuses to wrinkle, boarding a plane and flying to Cambridge, is inconceivable to her, a thought that, no matter how welcome, how desirable, feels entirely impossible, absurd. "No. But a letter will."

That evening Ashoke goes home to the apartment, checks for the letter. Three days come and go. Ashima is shown by the nursing staff how to change diapers and how to clean the umbilical stub. She is given hot saltwater baths to soothe her bruises and stitches. She is given a list of pediatricians, and countless brochures on breast-feeding, and bonding, and immunizing, and samples of baby shampoos and Q-Tips and creams. The fourth day there is good news and bad news. The good news is that Ashima and the baby are to be discharged the following morning. The bad news is that they are told by Mr. Wilcox, compiler of hospital birth certificates, that they must choose a name for their son. For they learn that in America, a baby cannot be released from the hospital without a birth certificate. And that a birth certificate needs a name.

"But, sir," Ashima protests, "we can't possibly name him ourselves."

Mr. Wilcox, slight, bald, unamused, glances at the couple, both visibly distressed, then glances at the nameless child. "I see," he says. "The reason being?"

"We are waiting for a letter," Ashoke says, explaining the situation in detail.

"I see," Mr. Wilcox says again. "That is unfortunate. I'm

afraid your only alternative is to have the certificate read 'Baby Boy Ganguli.' You will, of course, be required to amend the permanent record when a name is decided upon."

Ashima looks at Ashoke expectantly. "Is that what we should do?"

"I don't recommend it," Mr. Wilcox says. "You will have to appear before a judge, pay a fee. The red tape is endless."

"Oh dear," Ashoke says.

Mr. Wilcox nods, and silence ensues. "Don't you have any backups?" he asks.

Ashima frowns. "What does it mean, 'backup'?"

"Well, something in reserve, in case you didn't like what your grandmother has chosen."

Ashima and Ashoke shake their heads. It has never occurred to either of them to question Ashima's grandmother's selection, to disregard an elder's wishes in such a way.

"You can always name him after yourself, or one of your ancestors," Mr. Wilcox suggests, admitting that he is actually Howard Wilcox III. "It's a fine tradition. The kings of France and England did it," he adds.

But this isn't possible, Ashima and Ashoke think to themselves. This tradition doesn't exist for Bengalis, naming a son after father or grandfather, a daughter after mother or grandmother. This sign of respect in America and Europe, this symbol of heritage and lineage, would be ridiculed in India. Within Bengali families, individual names are sacred, inviolable. They are not meant to be inherited or shared.

"Then what about naming him after another person? Someone you greatly admire?" Mr. Wilcox says, his eyebrows raised hopefully. He sighs. "Think about it. I'll be back in a few hours," he tells them, exiting the room.

The door shuts, which is when, with a slight quiver of recognition, as if he'd known it all along, the perfect pet name for his son occurs to Ashoke. He remembers the page crumpled tightly in his fingers, the sudden shock of the lantern's glare in his eyes. But for the first time he thinks of that moment not with terror, but with gratitude.

"Hello, Gogol," he whispers, leaning over his son's haughty face, his tightly bundled body. "Gogol," he repeats, satisfied. The baby turns his head with an expression of extreme consternation and yawns.

Ashima approves, aware that the name stands not only for her son's life, but her husband's. She knows the story of the accident, a story she first heard with polite newlywed sympathy, but the thought of which now, now especially, makes her blood go cold. There are nights when she has been woken by her husband's muffled screams, times they have ridden the subway together and the rhythm of the wheels on the tracks makes him suddenly pensive, aloof. She has never read any Gogol herself, but she is willing to place him on a shelf in her mind, along with Tennyson and Wordsworth. Besides, it's only a pet name, not to be taken seriously, simply something to put on the certificate for now to release them from the hospital. When Mr. Wilcox returns with his typewriter, Ashoke spells out the name. Thus Gogol Ganguli is registered in the hospital's files. "Good-bye, Gogol," Patty says, planting a quiet kiss on his shoulder, and to Ashima, dressed once again in her wrinkled silk sari, "Good luck." A first photograph, somewhat overexposed, is taken by Dr. Gupta that broiling hot, late summer's day: Gogol, an indistinct blanketed mass, reposing in his weary mother's arms. She stands on the steps of the hospital, staring at the camera, her eyes squinting into the sun. Her husband looks on from one side, his wife's suitcase in his hand, smiling with his head lowered. "Gogol enters the world," his father will eventually write on the back in Bengali letters.

Gogol's first home is a fully furnished apartment ten minutes by foot to Harvard, twenty to MIT. The apartment is on the first floor of a three-story house, covered with salmon-colored shingles, surrounded by a waist-high chain-link fence. The gray of the roof, the gray of cigarette ashes, matches the pavement of the sidewalk and the street. A row of cars parked at meters perpetually lines one side of the curb. At the corner of the block there is a small used bookstore, which one enters by going down three steps from the sidewalk, and across from it a musty shop that sells the newspaper and cigarettes and eggs, and where, to Ashima's mild disgust, a furry black cat is permitted to sit as it pleases on the shelves. Other than these small businesses, there are more shingled houses, the same shape and size and in the same state of mild decrepitude, painted mint, or lilac, or powder blue. This is the house Ashoke had brought Ashima to eighteen months ago, late one February night after her arrival at Logan Airport. In the dark, through the windows of the taxi, wide awake from jet lag, she could barely make out a thing, apart from heaps of broken snow glowing like shattered, bluish white bricks on the ground. It wasn't until morning, stepping briefly outside wearing a pair of Ashoke's socks under her thin-soled slippers, the frigid New England chill piercing her inner ears and jaw, that she'd had her first real glimpse of America: Leafless trees with ice-covered branches. Dog urine and excrement embedded in the snowbanks. Not a soul on the street.

The apartment consists of three rooms all in a row without a corridor. There is a living room at the front with a three-sided window overlooking the street, a pass-through bedroom in the middle, a kitchen at the back. It is not at all what she had expected. Not at all like the houses in *Gone With the Wind* or *The Seven-Year Itch*, movies she'd seen with her brother and cousins at the Lighthouse and the Metro. The apartment is drafty during winter, and in summer, intolerably hot. The thick glass windowpanes are covered by dreary dark brown curtains.

There are even roaches in the bathroom, emerging at night from the cracks in the tiles. But she has complained of none of this. She has kept her disappointment to herself, not wanting to offend Ashoke, or worry her parents. Instead she writes, in her letters home, of the powerful cooking gas that flares up at any time of day or night from four burners on the stove, and the hot tap water fierce enough to scald her skin, and the cold water safe enough to drink.

The top two floors of the house are occupied by their land-lords, the Montgomerys, a Harvard sociology professor and his wife. The Montgomerys have two children, both girls, Amber and Clover, aged seven and nine, whose waist-length hair is never braided, and who play on warm days for hours on a tire swing rigged to the only tree in the backyard. The professor, who has told Ashima and Ashoke to call him Alan, not Professor Montgomery as they had at first addressed him, has a wiry rust-colored beard that makes him look much older than he actually is. They see him walking to Harvard Yard in a pair of threadbare trousers, a fringed suede jacket, and rubber flip-flops. Rickshaw drivers dress better than professors here, Ashoke, who still attends meetings with his adviser in a jacket and tie, thinks frequently to himself. The Montgomerys have a dull green Volkswagen van covered with stickers: QUESTION AUTHORITY! GIVE A DAMN! BAN THE BRA! PEACE! They have a washing machine in the basement which Ashoke and Ashima are permitted to share, a television in their living room which Ashoke and Ashima can hear clearly through the ceil-ing. It had been through the ceiling one night in April, when Ashoke and Ashima were eating their dinner, that they'd heard about the assassination of Martin Luther King, Jr., and just re-cently, of Senator Robert Kennedy.

Sometimes Ashima and Alan's wife, Judy, stand side by side in the yard, clipping clothes to the line. Judy always wears blue

jeans, torn up into shorts once summer comes, and a necklace of small seashells around her throat. A red cotton scarf
over her stringy yellow hair, the same texture and shade as her
daughters', is always tied at the back of her neck. She works for
a women's health collective in Somerville a few days a week.
When she learned of Ashima's pregnancy she approved of Ashima's decision to breast-feed but had been disappointed to learn
that Ashima was going to put herself in the hands of the medical establishment for her child's delivery; Judy's daughters were
born at home, with the help of midwives at the collective. Some
nights Judy and Alan go out, leaving Amber and Clover unsu-
pervised at home. Only once, when Clover had a cold, did they
ask Ashima if she could check in on them. Ashima remembers
their apartment with abiding horror — just beyond the ceiling
yet so different from her own, piles everywhere, piles of books
and papers, piles of dirty plates on the kitchen counter, ashtrays
the size of serving platters heaped with crushed-out cigarettes.
The girls slept together on a bed piled with clothes. Sitting
momentarily on the edge of Alan and Judy's mattress, she had
cried out, falling clumsily backward, startled to discover that it
was filled with water. Instead of cereal and tea bags, there were
whiskey and wine bottles on top of the refrigerator, most of
them nearly empty. Just standing there had made Ashima feel
drunk.

They arrive home from the hospital courtesy of Dr. Gupta,
who owns a car, and sit in the sweltering living room, in front
of their only box fan, suddenly a family. Instead of a couch they
have six chairs, all of them three-legged, with oval wooden
backs and black triangular cushions. To her surprise, finding herself once again in the gloomy three-room apartment,
Ashima misses the hustle-bustle of the hospital, and Patty, and
the Jell-O and ice cream brought at regular intervals to her
side. As she walks slowly through the rooms it irks her that

there are dirty dishes stacked in the kitchen, that the bed has not been made. Until now Ashima has accepted that there is no one to sweep the floor, or do the dishes, or wash clothes, or shop for groceries, or prepare a meal on the days she is tired or homesick or cross. She has accepted that the very lack of such amenities is the American way. But now, with a baby crying in her arms, her breasts swollen with milk, her body coated with sweat, her groin still so sore she can scarcely sit, it is all suddenly unbearable.

"I can't do this," she tells Ashoke when he brings her a cup of tea, the only thing he can think to do for her, the last thing she feels like drinking.

"In a few days you'll get the hang of it," he says, hoping to encourage her, unsure of what else to do. He sets the cup beside her on the flaking windowsill. "I think he's falling asleep again," he adds, looking at Gogol, whose cheeks are working methodically at his wife's breast.

"I won't," she insists thickly, looking neither at the baby nor at him. She pulls back a bit of the curtain, then lets it fall. "Not here. Not like this."

"What are you saying, Ashima?"

"I'm saying hurry up and finish your degree." And then, impulsively, admitting it for the first time: "I'm saying I don't want to raise Gogol alone in this country. It's not right. I want to go back."

He looks at Ashima, her face leaner, the features sharper than they had been at their wedding, aware that her life in Cambridge, as his wife, has already taken a toll. On more than one occasion he has come home from the university to find her morose, in bed, rereading her parents' letters. Early mornings, when he senses that she is quietly crying, he puts an arm around her but can think of nothing to say, feeling that it is his fault, for marrying her, for bringing her here. He remembers suddenly about Ghosh, his companion on the train, who had returned from England for his wife's sake. "It is my greatest regret, coming back," Ghosh had confessed to Ashoke, mere hours before he was killed.

A soft knock on the door interrupts them: Alan and Judy and Amber and Clover, all there to see the baby. Judy holds a dish covered with a checkered cloth in her hands, says she's made a broccoli quiche. Alan sets down a garbage bag full of Amber and Clover's old baby clothes, uncorks a bottle of cold champagne. The foaming liquid splashes onto the floor, is poured into mugs. They raise their mugs to Gogol, Ashima and Ashoke only pretending to take sips. Amber and Clover flank Ashima at either side, both delighted when Gogol wraps a hand around each of their fingers. Judy scoops the baby out of Ashima's lap. "Hello, handsome," she coos. "Oh, Alan," she says, "let's have another one of these." Alan offers to bring up the girls' crib from the basement, and together he and Ashoke assemble it in the space next to Ashima and Ashoke's bed. Ashoke goes out to the corner store, and a box of disposable diapers replaces the framed black-and-white pictures of Ashima's family on the dressing table. "Twenty minutes at three-fifty for the quiche," Judy says to Ashima. "Holler if you need anything," Alan adds before they disappear.

Three days later, Ashoke is back at MIT, Alan is back at Harvard, Amber and Clover are back at school. Judy is at work at the collective as usual, and Ashima, on her own with Gogol for the first time in the silent house, suffering from a sleep deprivation far worse than the worst of her jet lag, sits by the three-sided window in the living room on one of the triangular chairs and cries the whole day. She cries as she feeds him, and as she pats him to sleep, and as he cries between sleeping and feeding. She cries after the mailman's visit because there are no letters from Calcutta. She cries when she calls Ashoke at his department and he does not answer. One day she cries when she goes to the kitchen to make dinner and discovers that they've run out of rice. She goes upstairs and knocks on Alan and Judy's door. "Help yourself," Judy says, but the rice in Judy's canister is brown. To be polite, Ashima takes a cup, but downstairs she throws it away. She calls Ashoke at his department to ask him to pick up the rice on his way home. This time, when there is no answer, she gets up, washes her face and combs her hair. She changes and dresses Gogol and puts him into the navy blue, white-wheeled pram inherited from Alan and Judy. For the first time, she pushes him through the balmy streets of Cambridge, to Purity Supreme, to buy a bag of white long-grain rice. The errand takes longer than usual; for now she is repeatedly stopped on the street, and in the aisles of the supermarket, by perfect strangers, all Americans, suddenly taking notice of her, smiling, congratulating her for what she's done. They look curiously, appreciatively, into the pram. "How old?" they ask. "Boy or girl?" "What's his name?"

She begins to pride herself on doing it alone, in devising a routine. Like Ashoke, busy with his teaching and research and dissertation seven days a week, she, too, now has something to occupy her fully, to demand her utmost devotion, her last ounce of strength. Before Gogol's birth, her days had followed no visible pattern. She would spend hours in the apartment, napping, sulking, rereading her same five Bengali novels on the bed. But now the days that had once dragged rush all too quickly toward evening—those same hours are consumed with Gogol, pacing the three rooms of the apartment with him in her arms. Now she wakes at six, pulling Gogol out of the crib for his first feeding, and then for half an hour she and Ashoke lie with the baby in bed between them, admiring the tiny person they've produced. Between eleven and one, while Gogol sleeps, she

gets dinner out of the way, a habit she will maintain for decades to come. Every afternoon she takes him out, wandering up
and down the streets, to pick up this or that, or to sit in Harvard Yard, sometimes meeting up with Ashoke on a bench on
the MIT campus, bringing him some homemade samosas and
a fresh thermos of tea. At times, staring at the baby, she sees
pieces of her family in his face—her mother's glossy eyes, her
father's slim lips, her brother's lopsided smile. She discovers a
yarn store and begins to knit for the coming winter, making
Gogol sweaters, blankets, mittens, and caps. Every few days she
gives Gogol a bath in the porcelain sink in the kitchen. Every
week she carefully clips the nails of his ten fingers and toes.
When she takes him in his pram for his immunizations at the
pediatrician's, she stands outside the room and plugs up her
ears. One day Ashoke arrives home with an Instamatic camera
to take pictures of the baby, and when Gogol is napping she
pastes the square, white-bordered prints behind plastic sheets
in an album, captions written on pieces of masking tape. To
put him to sleep, she sings him the Bengali songs her mother
had sung to her. She drinks in the sweet, milky fragrance of his
skin, the buttery scent of his breath. One day she lifts him high
over her head, smiling at him with her mouth open, and a quick
stream of undigested milk from his last feeding rises from his
throat and pours into her own. For the rest of her life she will
recall the shock of that warm, sour liquid, a taste that leaves her
unable to swallow another thing for the rest of the day.

Letters arrive from her parents, from her husband's parents,
from aunts and uncles and cousins and friends, from everyone,
it seems, but Ashima's grandmother. The letters are filled with
every possible blessing and good wish, composed in an alphabet they have seen all around them for most of their lives, on
billboards and newspapers and awnings, but which they see
now only in these precious, pale blue missives. Sometimes

two letters arrive in a single week. One week there are three. As always Ashima keeps her ear trained, between the hours of twelve and two, for the sound of the postman's footsteps on the porch, followed by the soft click of the mail slot in the door. The margins of her parents' letters, always a block of her mother's hasty penmanship followed by her father's flourishing, elegant hand, are frequently decorated with drawings of animals done by Ashima's father, and Ashima tapes these on the wall over Gogol's crib. "We are dying to see him," her mother writes. "These are the most crucial months. Every hour there is a change. Remember it." Ashima writes back with careful descriptions of her son, reporting the circumstances of his first smile, the day he first rolls over, his first squeal of delight. She writes that they are saving money for a trip home the following December, after Gogol turns one. (She does not mention the pediatrician's concern about tropical diseases. A trip to India will require a whole new set of immunizations, he has warned.)

In November, Gogol develops a mild ear infection. When Ashima and Ashoke see their son's pet name typed on the label of a prescription for antibiotics, when they see it at the top of his immunization record, it doesn't look right; pet names aren't meant to be made public in this way. But there is still no letter from Ashima's grandmother. They are forced to conclude that it is lost in the mail. Ashima decides to write to her grandmother, explaining the situation, asking her to send a second letter with the names. The very next day a letter arrives in Cambridge. Though it is from Ashima's father, no drawings for Gogol adorn the margins, no elephants or parrots or tigers. The letter is dated three weeks ago, and from it they learn that Ashima's grandmother has had a stroke, that her right side is permanently paralyzed, her mind dim. She can no longer chew, barely swallows, remembers and recognizes little of her eighty-odd years. "She is with us still, but to be honest we have already lost her," her father has written. "Prepare yourself, Ashima. Perhaps you may not see her again."

It is their first piece of bad news from home. Ashoke barely knows Ashima's grandmother, only vaguely recalls touching her feet at his wedding, but Ashima is inconsolable for days. She sits at home with Gogol as the leaves turn brown and drop from the trees, as the days begin to grow quickly, mercilessly dark, thinking of the last time she saw her grandmother, her dida, a few days before flying to Boston. Ashima had gone to visit her; for the occasion her grandmother had entered the kitchen after over a decade's retirement, to cook Ashima a light goat and potato stew. She had fed her sweets with her own hand. Unlike her parents, and her other relatives, her grandmother had not admonished Ashima not to eat beef or wear skirts or cut off her hair or forget her family the moment she landed in Boston. Her grandmother had not been fearful of such signs of betrayal; she was the only person to predict, rightly, that Ashima would never change. Before leaving, Ashima had stood, her head lowered, under her late grandfather's portrait, asking him to bless her journey. Then she bent down to touch the dust of her dida's feet to her head.

"Dida, I'm coming," Ashima had said. For this was the phrase Bengalis always used in place of good-bye.

"Enjoy it," her grandmother had bellowed in her thundering voice, helping Ashima to straighten. With trembling hands, her grandmother had pressed her thumbs to the tears streaming down Ashima's face, wiping them away. "Do what I will never do. It will all be for the best. Remember that. Now go."

As the baby grows, so, too, does their circle of Bengali acquaintances. Through the Nandis, now expecting a child of their own, Ashoke and Ashima meet the Mitras, and through the

Mitras, the Banerjees. More than once, pushing Gogol in his stroller, Ashima has been approached on the streets of Cambridge by young Bengali bachelors, shyly inquiring after her origins. Like Ashoke, the bachelors fly back to Calcutta one by one, returning with wives. Every weekend, it seems, there is a new home to go to, a new couple or young family to meet. They all come from Calcutta, and for this reason alone they are friends. Most of them live within walking distance of one another in Cambridge. The husbands are teachers, researchers, doctors, engineers. The wives, homesick and bewildered, turn to Ashima for recipes and advice, and she tells them about the carp that's sold in Chinatown, that it's possible to make halwa from Cream of Wheat. The families drop by one another's homes on Sunday afternoons. They drink tea with sugar and evaporated milk and eat shrimp cutlets fried in saucepans. They sit in circles on the floor, singing songs by Nazrul and Tagore, passing a thick yellow clothbound book of lyrics among them as Dilip Nandi plays the harmonium. They argue riotously over the films of Ritwik Ghatak versus those of Satyajit Ray. The CPIM versus the Congress party. North Calcutta versus South. For hours they argue about the politics of America, a country in which none of them is eligible to vote.

By February, when Gogol is six months old, Ashima and Ashoke know enough people to entertain on a proper scale. The occasion: Gogol's annaprasan, his rice ceremony. There is no baptism for Bengali babies, no ritualistic naming in the eyes of God. Instead, the first formal ceremony of their lives centers around the consumption of solid food. They ask Dilip Nandi to play the part of Ashima's brother, to hold the child and feed him rice, the Bengali staff of life, for the very first time. Gogol is dressed as an infant Bengali groom, in a pale yellow pajama-punjabi from his grandmother in Calcutta. The fragrance of cumin seeds, sent in the package along with the pajamas, lingers in the weave. A headpiece that Ashima cut out of paper, decorated with pieces of aluminum foil, is tied around Gogol's head with string. He wears a thin fourteen-karat gold chain around his neck. His tiny forehead has been decorated with considerable struggle with sandalwood paste to form six miniature beige moons floating above his brows. His eyes have been darkened with a touch of kohl. He fidgets in the lap of his honorary uncle, who sits on a bedcover on the floor, surrounded by guests in front and behind and beside him. The food is arranged in ten separate bowls. Ashima regrets that the plate on which the rice is heaped is melamine, not silver or brass or at the very least stainless-steel. The final bowl contains payesh, a warm rice pudding Ashima will prepare for him to eat on each of his birthdays as a child, as an adult even, alongside a slice of bakery cake.

He is photographed by his father and friends, frowning, as he searches for his mother's face in the crowd. She is busy setting up the buffet. She wears a silvery sari, a wedding gift worn for the first time, the sleeves of her blouse reaching the crook of her elbow. His father wears a transparent white Punjabi top over bell-bottom trousers. Ashima sets out paper plates that have to be tripled to hold the weight of the biryani, the carp in yogurt sauce, the dal, the six different vegetable dishes she'd spent the past week preparing. The guests will eat standing, or sitting cross-legged on the floor. They've invited Alan and Judy from upstairs, who look as they always do, in jeans and thick sweaters because it is cold, leather sandals buckled over woolly socks. Judy eyes the buffet, bites into something that turns out to be a shrimp cutlet. "I thought Indians were supposed to be vegetarian," she whispers to Alan.

Gogol's feeding begins. It's all just a touch, a gesture. No one expects the boy to eat anything more than a grain of rice here, a drop of dal there—it is all meant to introduce him to a

lifetime of consumption, a meal to inaugurate the tens of thousands of unremembered meals to come. A handful of women
ululate as the proceedings begin. A conch shell is repeatedly
tapped and passed around, but no one in the room is able to get
it to emit a sound. Blades of grass and a pradeep's slim, steady
flame are held to Gogol's head. The child is entranced, doesn't
squirm or turn away, opens his mouth obediently for each and
every course. He takes his payesh three times. Ashima's eyes
fill with tears as Gogol's mouth eagerly invites the spoon. She
can't help wishing her own brother were here to feed him, her
own parents to bless him with their hands on his head. And
then the grand finale, the moment they have all been waiting
for. To predict his future path in life, Gogol is offered a plate
holding a clump of cold Cambridge soil dug up from the backyard, a ballpoint pen, and a dollar bill, to see if he will be a landowner, scholar, or businessman. Most children will grab at one
of them, sometimes all of them, but Gogol touches nothing.
He shows no interest in the plate, instead turning away, briefly
burying his face in his honorary uncle's shoulder.

"Put the money in his hand!" someone in the group calls
out. "An American boy must be rich!"

"No!" his father protests. "The pen. Gogol, take the pen."

Gogol regards the plate doubtfully. Dozens of dark heads
hover expectantly. The material of the Punjabi pajama set begins to scratch his skin.

"Go on, Gogol, take something," Dilip Nandi says, drawing
the plate close. Gogol frowns, and his lower lip trembles. Only
then, forced at six months to confront his destiny, does he begin to cry.

Another August. Gogol is one, grabbing, walking a little, repeating words in two languages. He calls his mother "Ma," his
father "Baba." If a person in the room says "Gogol," he turns

his head and smiles. He sleeps through the night and between noon and three each day. He has seven teeth. He constantly attempts to put the tiniest scraps of paper and lint and whatever else he finds on the floor into his mouth. Ashoke and Ashima are planning their first trip to Calcutta, in December, during Ashoke's winter break. The upcoming journey inspires them to try to come up with a good name for Gogol, so they can submit his passport application. They turn to their Bengali friends for suggestions. Long evenings are devoted to considering this name or that. But nothing appeals to them. By then they've given up on the letter from Ashima's grandmother. They've given up on her grandmother remembering the name, for Ashima's grandmother, they are told, cannot even remember Ashima. Still, there is time. The trip to Calcutta is four months away. Ashima regrets that they can't go earlier, in time for Durga pujo, but it will be years before Ashoke is eligible for a sabbatical, and three weeks in December is all they can manage. "It is like going home a few months after your Christmas," Ashima explains to Judy one day over the clothesline. Judy replies that she and Alan are Buddhists.

At breakneck speed Ashima knits sweater-vests for her father, her father-in-law, her brother, her three favorite uncles. They are all the same, V-necked, pine green yarn, knit five, purl two, on number-nine needles. The exception is her father's, done in a double-seed stitch with two thick cables and buttons down the front; he prefers cardigans to pullovers, and she remembers to put in pockets for the deck of cards he always carries with him, to play patience at a moment's notice. In addition to the sweater, she buys him three sable-haired paintbrushes from the Harvard Coop, sizes he's requested by mail. Though they are wildly expensive, more so than anything else she's ever bought in America, Ashoke says nothing when he sees the bill. One day Ashima goes shopping in downtown Boston, spending hours in the basement of Jordan Marsh as she pushes Gogol in his stroller, spending every last penny. She buys mismatched teaspoons, percale pillowcases, colored candles, soaps on ropes. In a drugstore she buys a Timex watch for her father-in-law, Bic pens for her cousins, embroidery thread and thimbles for her mother and her aunts. On the train home she is exhilarated, exhausted, nervous with anticipation of the trip. The train is crowded and at first she stands, struggling to hang on to all the bags and the stroller and the overhead strap, until a young girl asks if she'd like to sit down. Ashima thanks her, sinking grate-fully into the seat, pushing the bags protectively behind her legs. She is tempted to sleep as Gogol does. She leans her head against the window and closes her eyes and thinks of home. She pictures the black iron bars in the windows of her parents' flat, and Gogol, in his American baby clothes and diapers, play-ing beneath the ceiling fan, on her parents' four-poster bed. She pictures her father missing a tooth, lost after a recent fall, her mother has written, on the stairs. She tries to imagine how it will feel when her grandmother doesn't recognize her.

When she opens her eyes she sees that the train is stand-ing still, the doors open at her stop. She leaps up, her heart racing. "Excuse me, please," she says, pushing the stroller and herself through the tightly packed bodies. "Ma'am," some-one says as she struggles past, about to step onto the platform, "your things." The doors of the subway clamp shut as she re-alizes her mistake, and the train rolls slowly away. She stands there watching until the rear car disappears into the tunnel, until she and Gogol are the only people remaining on the plat-form. She pushes the stroller back down Massachusetts Ave-nue, weeping freely, knowing that she can't possibly afford to go back and buy it all again. For the rest of the afternoon she is furious with herself, humiliated at the prospect of arriving in Calcutta empty-handed apart from the sweaters and the paintbrushes. But when Ashoke comes home he calls the MBTA lost and found; the following day the bags are returned, not a teaspoon missing. Somehow, this small miracle causes Ashima to feel connected to Cambridge in a way she has not previously thought possible, affiliated with its exceptions as well as its rules. She has a story to tell at dinner parties. Friends listen, amazed at her luck. "Only in this country," Maya Nandi says.

One night not long after, they are fast asleep when the telephone rings. The sound rouses them instantly, their hearts hammering as if from the same frightening dream. Ashima knows even before Ashoke answers that it's a call from India. A few months ago, her family had asked in a letter for the phone number in Cambridge, and she had sent it reluctantly in her reply, aware that it would only be a way for bad news to reach her. As Ashoke sits up and takes the receiver, answering in a weary, weakened voice, Ashima prepares herself. She pushes down the crib railing to comfort Gogol, who has begun stirring as a result of the telephone's rings, and reviews the facts in her head. Her grandmother is in her eighties, bedridden, all but senile, unable to eat or talk. The last few months of her life, according to her parents' most recent letter, have been painful, for her grandmother, for those who know her. It was no way to live. She pictures her mother saying all this gently into the next-door neighbors' phone, standing in the neighbors' sitting room. Ashima prepares herself for the news, to accept the fact that Gogol will never meet his great-grandmother, the giver of his lost name.

The room is unpleasantly cold. She picks up Gogol and gets back into bed, under the blanket. She presses the baby to her body for strength, puts him to her breast. She thinks of the cream-colored cardigan bought with her grandmother in mind, sitting in a shopping bag in the closet. She hears Ashoke speaking, saying soberly but loudly enough so that she fears he will wake Alan and Judy upstairs, "Yes, all right, I see. Don't worry, yes, I will." For a while he is silent, listening. "They want to talk to you," he says to Ashima, briefly putting a hand to her shoulder. In the dark, he hands her the phone, and after a moment's hesitation, he gets out of bed.

She takes the phone in order to hear the news for herself, to console her mother. She can't help but wonder who will console her the day her own mother dies, if that news will also come to her in this way, in the middle of the night, wresting her from dreams. In spite of her dread she feels a thrill; this will be the first time she's heard her mother's voice in nearly three years. The first time, since her departure from Dum Dum Airport, that she will be called Monu. Only it isn't her mother but her brother, Rana, on the other end. His voice sounds small, threaded into a wire, barely recognizable through the holes of the receiver. Ashima's first question is what time it is there. She has to repeat the question three times, shouting in order to be heard. Rana tells her it is lunchtime. "Are you still planning to visit in December?" he asks.

She feels her chest ache, moved after all this time to hear her brother call her Didi, his older sister, a term he alone in the world is entitled to use. At the same time she hears water running in the Cambridge kitchen, her husband opening a cupboard for a glass. "Of course we're coming," she says, unsettled when she hears her echo saying it faintly, less convincingly, once again. "How is Dida? Has anything else happened to her?"

"Still alive," Rana says. "But still the same."

Ashima rests back on her pillow, limp with relief. She would see her grandmother, after all, even if for one last time. She kisses Gogol on the top of his head, presses her cheek to his. "Thank goodness. Put Ma on," she says, crossing her ankles. "Let me talk to her."

"She's not at home now," Rana says after a static-filled pause.

"And Baba?"

A patch of silence follows before his voice returns. "Not here."

"Oh." She remembers the time difference—her father must be at work already at the *Desh* offices, her mother at the market, a burlap bag in hand, buying vegetables and fish.

"How is little Gogol?" Rana asks her. "Does he only speak English?"

She laughs. "He doesn't speak much of anything, at the moment." She begins to tell Rana that she is teaching Gogol to say "Dida" and "Dadu" and "Mamu," to recognize his grandparents and his uncle from photographs. But another burst of static, longer this time, quiets her in midsentence.

"Rana? Can you hear me?"

"I can't hear you, Didi," Rana says, his voice growing fainter. "Can't hear. Let's speak later."

"Yes," she says, "later. See you soon. Very soon. Write to me." She puts down the phone, invigorated by the sound of her brother's voice. An instant later she is confused and somewhat irritated. Why had he gone to the trouble of calling, only to ask an obvious question? Why call while both her parents were out?

Ashoke returns from the kitchen, a glass of water in his hand. He sets down the water and switches on the small lamp by the side of the bed.

"I'm awake," Ashoke says, though his voice is still small from fatigue.

"Me too."

"What about Gogol?"

"Asleep again." She gets up and puts him back in the crib, drawing the blanket to his shoulders, then returns to bed, shivering. "I don't understand it," she says, shaking her head at the rumpled sheet. "Why did Rana go to the trouble of calling just now? It's so expensive. It doesn't make sense." She turns to look at Ashoke. "What did he say to you, exactly?"

Ashoke shakes his head from side to side, his profile lowered.

"He told you something you're not telling me. Tell me, what did he say?"

He continues to shake his head, and then he reaches across to her side of the bed and presses her hand so tightly that it is slightly painful. He presses her to the bed, lying on top of her, his face to one side, his body suddenly trembling. He holds her this way for so long that she begins to wonder if he is going to turn off the light and caress her. Instead he tells her what Rana told him a few minutes ago, what Rana couldn't bear to tell his sister, over the telephone, himself: that her father died yesterday evening, of a heart attack, playing patience on his bed.

They leave for India six days later, six weeks before they'd planned. Alan and Judy, waking the next morning to Ashima's sobs, then hearing the news from Ashoke, leave a vase filled with flowers by the door. In those six days, there is no time to think of a good name for Gogol. They get an express passport with "Gogol Ganguli" typed across the United States of America seal, Ashoke signing on his son's behalf. The day before leaving, Ashima puts Gogol in his stroller, puts the sweater she'd knit for her father and the paintbrushes in a shopping bag, and walks to Harvard Square, to the subway station. "Excuse me," she asks a gentleman on the street, "I must get on the train." The man helps her carry down the stroller, and Ashima waits on the platform. When the train comes she heads immediately back to Central Square. This time she is wide awake. There are only a half-dozen people in the car, their faces hidden behind the *Globe*, or looking down at paperback books, or staring straight through her, at nothing. As the train slows to a halt she stands, ready to disembark. She does not turn back to look at the shopping bag, left purposely beneath her seat. "Hey, the Indian lady forgot her stuff," she hears as the doors shut, and as the train pulls away she hears a fist pounding on glass, but she keeps walking, pushing Gogol along the platform.

The following evening they board a Pan Am flight to London, where after a five-hour layover they will board a second flight to Calcutta, via Tehran and Bombay. On the runway in Boston, her seat belt buckled, Ashima looks at her watch and calculates the Indian time on her fingers. But this time no image of her family comes to mind. She refuses to picture what she shall see soon enough: her mother's vermilion erased from her part, her brother's thick hair shaved from his head in mourning. The wheels begin to move, causing the enormous metal wings to flap gently up and down. Ashima looks at Ashoke, who is double-checking to make sure their passports and green cards are in order. She watches him adjust his watch in anticipation of their arrival, the pale silver hands scissoring into place.

"I don't want to go," she says, turning toward the dark oval window. "I don't want to see them. I can't."

Ashoke puts his hand over hers as the plane begins to gather speed. And then Boston tilts away and they ascend effortlessly over a blackened Atlantic. The wheels retract and the cabin shakes as they struggle upward, through the first layer of clouds. Though Gogol's ears have been stuffed with cotton, he screams nevertheless in the arms of his grieving mother as they climb farther still, as he flies for the first time in his life across the world.

3

1971

THE Gangulis have moved to a university town outside Boston. As far as they know, they are the only Bengali residents. The town has a historic district, a brief strip of colonial architecture visited by tourists on summer weekends. There is a white steepled Congregational church, a stone courthouse with an adjoining jail, a cupolaed public library, a wooden well from which Paul Revere is rumored to have drunk. In winter, tapers burn in the windows of homes after dark. Ashoke has been hired as an assistant professor of electrical engineering at the university. In exchange for teaching five classes, he earns sixteen thousand dollars a year. He is given his own office, with his name etched onto a strip of black plastic by the door. He shares, along with the other members of his department, the services of an elderly secretary named Mrs. Jones, who often puts a plate of homemade banana bread by the coffee percolator in the staff room. Ashoke suspects that Mrs. Jones, whose husband used to teach in the English department until his death, is about his own mother's age. Mrs. Jones leads a life that Ashoke's mother would consider humiliating: eating alone, driving herself to work in snow and sleet, seeing her children and grandchildren, at most, three or four times a year.

The job is everything Ashoke has ever dreamed of. He has always hoped to teach in a university rather than work for a corporation. What a thrill, he thinks, to stand lecturing before a roomful of American students. What a sense of accomplishment it gives him to see his name printed under "Faculty" in the university directory. What joy each time Mrs. Jones says to him, "Professor Ganguli, your wife is on the phone." From his fourth-floor office he has a sweeping view of the quadrangle, surrounded by vine-covered brick buildings, and on pleasant days he takes his lunch on a bench, listening to the melody of bells chiming from the campus clock tower. On Fridays, after he has taught his last class, he visits the library, to read international newspapers on long wooden poles. He reads about U.S. planes bombing Vietcong supply routes in Cambodia, Naxalites being murdered on the streets of Calcutta, India and Pakistan going to war. At times he wanders up to the library's sun-filled, unpopulated top floor, where all the literature is shelved. He browses in the aisles, gravitating most often toward his beloved Russians, where he is particularly comforted, each time, by his son's name stamped in golden letters on the spines of a row of red and green and blue hardbound books.

For Ashima, migrating to the suburbs feels more drastic, more distressing than the move from Calcutta to Cambridge had been. She wishes Ashoke had accepted the position at Northeastern so that they could have stayed in the city. She is stunned that in this town there are no sidewalks to speak of, no streetlights, no public transportation, no stores for miles at a time. She has no interest in learning how to drive the new Toyota Corolla it is now necessary for them to own. Though no longer pregnant, she continues, at times, to mix Rice Krispies and peanuts and onions in a bowl. For being a foreigner, Ashima is beginning to realize, is a sort of lifelong pregnancy—a perpetual wait, a constant burden, a continuous feeling out of sorts. It is an ongoing responsibility, a parenthesis in what had once been ordinary life, only to discover that that previous life has vanished, replaced by something more complicated and demanding. Like pregnancy, being a foreigner, Ashima believes, is something that elicits the same curiosity from strangers, the same combination of pity and respect.

Her forays out of the apartment, while her husband is at work, are limited to the university within which they live, and to the historic district that flanks the campus on one edge. She wanders around with Gogol, letting him run across the quadrangle, or sitting with him on rainy days to watch television in the student lounge. Once a week she makes thirty samosas to sell at the international coffeehouse, for twenty-five cents each, next to the linzer squares baked by Mrs. Etzold, and baklava by Mrs. Cassolis. On Fridays she takes Gogol to the public library for children's story hour. After he turns four, she drops him off and fetches him from the university-run nursery school three mornings a week. For the hours that Gogol is at nursery school, finger-painting and learning the English alphabet, Ashima is despondent, unaccustomed, all over again, to being on her own. She misses her son's habit of always holding on to the free end of her sari as they walk together. She misses the sound of his sulky, high-pitched little-boy voice, telling her that he is hungry, or tired, or needs to go to the bathroom. To avoid being alone at home she sits in the reading room of the public library, in a cracked leather armchair, writing letters to her mother, or reading magazines or one of her Bengali books from home. The room is cheerful, filled with light, with a tomato-colored carpet on the floor and people reading the paper around a big, round wooden table with forsythias or cattails arranged at its center. When she misses Gogol especially, she wanders into the children's room; there, pinned to a bulletin board, is a picture of him in profile, sitting cross-legged on a cushion during story hour, listening to the children's librarian, Mrs. Aiken, reading *The Cat in the Hat.*

After two years in an overheated university-subsidized apartment, Ashima and Ashoke are ready to purchase a home. In the evenings, after dinner, they set out in their car, Gogol in the back seat, to look at houses for sale. They do not look in the historic district, where the chairman of Ashoke's department lives, in an eighteenth-century mansion to which he and Ashima and Gogol are invited once a year for Boxing Day tea. Instead they look on ordinary roads where plastic wading pools and baseball bats are left out on the lawns. All the houses belong to Americans. Shoes are worn inside, trays of cat litter are placed in the kitchens, dogs bark and jump when Ashima and Ashoke ring the bell. They learn the names of the different architectural styles: cape, saltbox, raised ranch, garrison. In the end they decide on a shingled two-story colonial in a recently built development, a house previously occupied by no one, erected on a quarter acre of land. This is the small patch of America to which they lay claim. Gogol accompanies his parents to banks, sits waiting as they sign the endless papers. The mortgage is approved and the move is scheduled for spring. Ashoke and Ashima are amazed, when moving by U-Haul to the new house, to discover how much they possess; each of them had come to America with a single suitcase, a few weeks' worth of clothes. Now there are enough old issues of the *Globe* stacked in the corners of the apartment to wrap all their plates and glasses. There are whole years of *Time* magazine to toss out.

The walls of the new house are painted, the driveway sealed with pitch, the shingles and sun deck weatherproofed and stained. Ashoke takes photographs of every room, Gogol standing somewhere in the frame, to send to relatives in India.

There are pictures of Gogol opening up the refrigerator, pretending to talk on the phone. He is a sturdily built child, with full cheeks but already pensive features. When he poses for the camera he has to be coaxed into a smile. The house is fifteen minutes from the nearest supermarket, forty minutes from a mall. The address is 67 Pemberton Road. Their neighbors are the Johnsons, the Mertons, the Aspris, the Hills. There are four modest bedrooms, one and a half bathrooms, eight-foot ceilings, a one-car garage. In the living room is a brick fireplace and a bay window overlooking the yard. In the kitchen there are matching yellow appliances, a lazy Susan, linoleum made to look like tiles. A watercolor by Ashima's father, of a caravan of camels in a desert in Rajasthan, is framed at the local print shop and hung on the living room wall. Gogol has a room of his own, a bed with a built-in drawer in its base, metal shelves that hold Tinkertoys, Lincoln Logs, a View-Master, an Etch-A-Sketch. Most of Gogol's toys come from yard sales, as does most of the furniture, and the curtains, and the toaster, and a set of pots and pans. At first Ashima is reluctant to introduce such items into her home, ashamed at the thought of buying what had originally belonged to strangers, American strangers at that. But Ashoke points out that even his chairman shops at yard sales, that in spite of living in a mansion an American is not above wearing a pair of secondhand pants, bought for fifty cents.

When they first move into the house, the grounds have yet to be landscaped. No trees grow on the property, no shrubs flank the front door, so that the cement of the foundation is clearly visible to the eye. And so for the first few months, four-year-old Gogol plays on an uneven, dirt-covered yard littered with stones and sticks, soiling his sneakers, leaving footprints in his path. It is among his earliest memories. For the rest of his life he will remember that cold, overcast spring, digging in the dirt, collecting rocks, discovering black and yellow salamanders beneath an overturned slab of slate. He will remember the sounds of the other children in the neighborhood, laughing and pedaling their Big Wheels down the road. He will remember the warm, bright summer's day when the topsoil was poured from the back of a truck, and stepping onto the sun deck a few weeks later with both of his parents to see thin blades of grass emerge from the bald black lawn.

In the beginning, in the evenings, his family goes for drives, exploring their new environs bit by bit: the neglected dirt lanes, the shaded back roads, the farms where one could pick pumpkins in autumn and buy berries sold in green cardboard boxes in July. The back seat of the car is sheathed with plastic, the ashtrays on the doors still sealed. They drive until it grows dark, without destination in mind, past hidden ponds and graveyards, culs-de-sac and dead ends. Sometimes they drive out of the town altogether, to one of the beaches along the North Shore. Even in summer, they never go to swim or to turn brown beneath the sun. Instead they go dressed in their ordinary clothes. By the time they arrive, the ticket collector's booth is empty, the crowds gone; there is only a handful of cars in the parking lot, and the only other visitors are people walking their dogs or watching the sun set or dragging metal detectors through the sand. Together, as the Gangulis drive, they anticipate the moment the thin blue line of ocean will come into view. On the beach Gogol collects rocks, digs tunnels in the sand. He and his father wander barefoot, their pant legs rolled halfway up their calves. He watches his father raise a kite within minutes into the wind, so high that Gogol must tip his head back in order to see a rippling speck against the sky. The wind whips around their ears, turning their faces cold. Snowy gulls hover with wings spread, low enough to touch. Gogol darts in and out of the ocean, making faint, temporary footprints, soaking his rolled-up cuffs. His mother cries out, laughing, as she lifts her sari a few inches above her ankles, her slippers in one hand, and places her feet in foaming, ice-cold water. She reaches out to Gogol, takes his hand. "Not so far," she tells him. The waves retract, gathering force, the soft, dark sand seeming to shift away instantly beneath their feet, causing them to lose their balance. "I'm falling. It's pulling me in," she always says.

The August that Gogol turns five, Ashima discovers she is pregnant again. In the mornings she forces herself to eat a slice of toast, only because Ashoke makes it for her and watches her while she chews it in bed. Her head constantly spins. She spends her days lying down, a pink plastic wastepaper basket by her side, the shades drawn, her mouth and teeth coated with the taste of metal. She watches *The Price Is Right* and *Guiding Light* and *The $10,000 Pyramid* on the television Ashoke moves in from the living room to her side of the bed. Staggering out to the kitchen at lunchtime, to prepare a peanut butter and jelly sandwich for Gogol, she is revolted by the odor of the fridge, convinced that the contents of her vegetable drawers have been replaced with garbage, that meat is rotting on the shelves. Sometimes Gogol lies beside her in his parents' bedroom, reading a picture book, or coloring with crayons. "You're going to be an older brother," she tells him one day. "There'll be someone to call you Dada. Won't that be exciting?" Sometimes, if she is feeling energetic, she asks Gogol to go and get a photo album, and together they look at pictures of Gogol's grandparents, and his uncles and aunts and cousins, of whom, in spite of his one visit to Calcutta, he has no memory. She teaches him to memorize a four-line children's poem by Tagore, and the names of the deities adorning the ten-handed goddess Durga during pujo: Saraswati with her swan and Kartik with his peacock to her left, Lakshmi with her owl and Ganesh with his mouse to her right. Every afternoon Ashima sleeps, but before nodding off she switches the television to Channel 2, and tells Gogol to watch *Sesame Street* and *The Electric Company*, in order to keep up with the English he uses at nursery school.

In the evenings Gogol and his father eat together, alone, a week's worth of chicken curry and rice, which his father cooks in two battered Dutch ovens every Sunday. As the food reheats, his father tells Gogol to shut the bedroom door because his mother cannot tolerate the smell. It is odd to see his father presiding in the kitchen, standing in his mother's place at the stove. When they sit down at the table, the sound of his parents' conversation is missing, as is the sound of the television in the living room, playing the news. His father eats with his head bent over his plate, flipping through the latest issue of *Time*, occasionally glancing at Gogol to make sure he is eating as well. Though his father remembers to mix up the rice and curry for Gogol beforehand, he doesn't bother to shape it into individual balls the way his mother does, lining them around his plate like the numbers on a clockface. Gogol has already been taught to eat on his own with his fingers, not to let the food stain the skin of his palm. He has learned to suck the marrow from lamb, to extract the bones from fish. But without his mother at the table he does not feel like eating. He keeps wishing, every evening, that she would emerge from the bedroom and sit between him and his father, filling the air with her sari and cardigan smell. He grows bored of eating the same thing day after day, and one evening he discreetly pushes the remaining food to the side. With his index finger, in the traces of leftover sauce, he begins to draw on his plate. He plays tic-tac-toe.

"Finish," his father says, glancing up from his magazine. "Don't play with food that way."

"I'm full, Baba."

"There's still some food on your plate."

"Baba, I can't."

His father's plate is polished clean, the chicken bones denuded of cartilage and chewed to a pinkish pulp, the bay leaf and cinnamon stick as good as new. Ashoke shakes his head at Gogol, disapproving, unyielding. Each day Ashoke is pained by the half-eaten sandwiches people toss into garbage cans on campus, apples abandoned after one or two bites. "Finish it, Gogol. At your age I ate tin."

Because his mother tends to vomit the moment she finds herself in a moving car, she is unable to accompany her husband to take Gogol, in September of 1973, to his first day of kindergarten at the town's public elementary school. By the time Gogol starts, it is already the second week of the school year. But for the past week, Gogol has been in bed, just like his mother, listless, without appetite, claiming to have a stomachache, even vomiting one day into his mother's pink wastepaper basket. He doesn't want to go to kindergarten. He doesn't want to wear the new clothes his mother has bought him from Sears, hanging on a knob of his dresser, or carry his Charlie Brown lunch box, or board the yellow school bus that stops at the end of Pemberton Road. The school, unlike the nursery school, is several miles from the house, several miles from the university. On numerous occasions he's been driven to see the building, a low, long, brick structure with a perfectly flat roof and a flag that flaps at the top of a tall white pole planted on the lawn.

There is a reason Gogol doesn't want to go to kindergarten. His parents have told him that at school, instead of being called Gogol, he will be called by a new name, a good name, which his parents have finally decided on, just in time for him to begin his formal education. The name, Nikhil, is artfully connected to the old. Not only is it a perfectly respectable Bengali good name, meaning "he who is entire, encompassing all," but it also bears a satisfying resemblance to Nikolai, the first name of the Russian Gogol. Ashoke had thought of it recently, staring mindlessly at the Gogol spines in the library, and he had rushed back to the house to ask Ashima her opinion. He pointed out that it was relatively easy to pronounce, though there was the danger that Americans, obsessed with abbreviation, would truncate it to Nick. She told him she liked it well enough, though later, alone, she'd wept, thinking of her grandmother, who had died earlier in the year, and of the letter, forever hovering somewhere between India and America, containing the good name she'd chosen for Gogol. Ashima still dreams of the letter at times, discovering it after all these years in the mailbox on Pemberton Road, opening it up only to find it blank.

But Gogol doesn't want a new name. He can't understand why he has to answer to anything else. "Why do I have to have a new name?" he asks his parents, tears springing to his eyes. It would be one thing if his parents were to call him Nikhil, too. But they tell him that the new name will be used only by the teachers and children at school. He is afraid to be Nikhil, someone he doesn't know. Who doesn't know him. His parents tell him that they each have two names, too, as do all their Bengali friends in America, and all their relatives in Calcutta. It's a part of growing up, they tell him, part of being a Bengali. They write it for him on a sheet of paper, ask him to copy it over ten times. "Don't worry," his father says. "To me and your mother, you will never be anyone but Gogol."

At school, Ashoke and Gogol are greeted by the secretary, Mrs. McNab, who asks Ashoke to fill out a registration form. He provides a copy of Gogol's birth certificate and immunization record, which Mrs. McNab puts in a folder along with the registration. "This way," Mrs. McNab says, leading them to the principal's office. CANDACE LAPIDUS, the name on the door says. Mrs. Lapidus assures Ashoke that missing the first week of kindergarten is not a problem, that things have yet to settle down. Mrs. Lapidus is a tall, slender woman with short white-blond hair. She wears frosted blue eye shadow and a lemon yellow suit. She shakes Ashoke's hand and tells him that there are two other Indian children at the school, Jayadev Modi in the third grade and Rekha Saxena in fifth. Perhaps the Gangulis know them? Ashoke tells Mrs. Lapidus that they do not. She looks at the registration form and smiles kindly at the boy, who is clutching his father's hand. Gogol is dressed in powder blue pants, red and white canvas sneakers, a striped turtleneck top.

"Welcome to elementary school, Nikhil. I am your principal, Mrs. Lapidus."

Gogol looks down at his sneakers. The way the principal pronounces his new name is different from the way his parents say it, the second part of it longer, sounding like "heel."

She bends down so that her face is level with his, and extends a hand to his shoulder. "Can you tell me how old you are, Nikhil?"

When the question is repeated and there is still no response, Mrs. Lapidus asks, "Mr. Ganguli, does Nikhil follow English?"

"Of course he follows," Ashoke says. "My son is perfectly bilingual."

In order to prove that Gogol knows English, Ashoke does something he has never done before, and addresses his son in careful, accented English. "Go on, Gogol," he says, patting him on the head. "Tell Mrs. Lapidus how old you are."

"What was that?" Mrs. Lapidus says.

"I beg your pardon, madam?"

"That name you called him. Something with a *G*."

"Oh that, that is what we call him at home only. But his good name should be — is" — he nods his head firmly — "Nikhil."

Mrs. Lapidus frowns. "I'm afraid I don't understand. Good name?"

"Yes."

Mrs. Lapidus studies the registration form. She has not had to go through this confusion with the other two Indian children. She opens up the folder and examines the immunization record, the birth certificate. "There seems to be some confusion, Mr. Ganguli," she says. "According to these documents, your son's legal name is Gogol."

"That is correct. But please allow me to explain—"

"That you want us to call him Nikhil."

"That is correct."

Mrs. Lapidus nods. "The reason being?"

"That is our wish."

"I'm not sure I follow you, Mr. Ganguli. Do you mean that Nikhil is a middle name? Or a nickname? Many of the children go by nicknames here. On this form there is a space—"

"No, no, it's not a middle name," Ashoke says. He is beginning to lose patience. "He has no middle name. No nickname. The boy's good name, his school name, is Nikhil."

Mrs. Lapidus presses her lips together and smiles. "But clearly he doesn't respond."

"Please, Mrs. Lapidus," Ashoke says. "It is very common for a child to be confused at first. Please give it some time. I assure you he will grow accustomed."

He bends down and this time in Bengali, calmly and quietly, asks Gogol to please answer when Mrs. Lapidus asks a question. "Don't be scared, Gogol," he says, raising his son's chin with his finger. "You're a big boy now. No tears."

Though Mrs. Lapidus does not understand a word, she listens carefully, hears that name again. Gogol. Lightly, in pencil, she writes it down on the registration form.

Ashoke hands over the lunch box, a windbreaker in case it

gets cold. He thanks Mrs. Lapidus. "Be good, Nikhil," he says in English. And then, after a moment's hesitation, he is gone.

When they are alone, Mrs. Lapidus asks, "Are you happy to be entering elementary school, Gogol?"

"My parents want me to have another name in school."

"And what about you, Gogol? Do you want to be called by another name?"

After a pause, he shakes his head.

"Is that a no?"

He nods. "Yes."

"Then it's settled. Can you write your name on this piece of paper?"

Gogol picks up a pencil, grips it tightly, and forms the letters of the only word he has learned thus far to write from memory, getting the "L" backward due to nerves. "What beautiful penmanship you have," Mrs. Lapidus says. She tears up the old registration form and asks Mrs. McNab to type up a new one. Then she takes Gogol by the hand, down a carpeted hallway with painted cement walls. She opens a door, and Gogol is introduced to his teacher, Miss Watkins, a woman with hair in two braids, wearing overalls and clogs. Inside the classroom it's a small universe of nicknames—Andrew is Andy, Alexandra Sandy, William Billy, Elizabeth Lizzy. It is nothing like the schooling Gogol's parents have known, fountain pens and polished black shoes and notebooks and good names and sir or madam at a tender age. Here the only official ritual is pledging allegiance first thing in the morning to the American flag. For the rest of the day, they sit at a communal round table, drinking punch and eating cookies, taking naps on little orange cushions on the floor. At the end of his first day he is sent home with a letter to his parents from Mrs. Lapidus, folded and stapled to a string around his neck, explaining that due to their son's preference he will be known as Gogol at school. What about the parents' preference? Ashima and Ashoke wonder, shaking their heads. But since neither of them feels comfortable pressing the issue, they have no choice but to give in.

And so Gogol's formal education begins. At the top of sheets of scratchy pale yellow paper he writes out his pet name again and again, and the alphabet in capitals and lowercase. He learns to add and subtract, and to spell his first words. In the front covers of the textbooks from which he is taught to read he leaves his legacy, writing his name in number-two pencil below a series of others. In art class, his favorite hour of the week, he carves his name with paper clips into the bottoms of clay cups and bowls. He pastes uncooked pasta to cardboard, and leaves his signature in fat brush strokes below paintings. Day after day he brings his creations home to Ashima, who hangs them proudly on the refrigerator door. "Gogol G," he signs his work in the lower right-hand corner, as if there were a need to distinguish him from any other Gogol in the school.

In May his sister is born. This time the labor happens quickly. They are thinking about going to a yard sale in the neighborhood one Saturday morning, playing Bengali songs on the stereo. Gogol is eating frozen waffles for breakfast, wishing his parents would turn off the music so that he could hear the cartoons he is watching, when his mother's water breaks. His father switches off the music and calls Dilip and Maya Nandi, who now live in a suburb twenty minutes away and have a little boy of their own. Then he calls the next-door neighbor, Mrs. Merton, who has offered to look after Gogol until the Nandis arrive. Though his parents have prepared him for the event, when Mrs. Merton shows up with her needlepoint he feels stranded, no longer in the mood for cartoons. He stands on the front step, watching his father help his mother into the car, waving as they pull away. To pass the time he draws a picture of himself and his parents and his new sibling, standing in a row in front of their house. He remembers to put a dot on his mother's forehead, glasses on his father's face, a lamppost by the flagstone path in front of the house. "Well, if that's not the spitting image," Mrs. Merton says, looking over his shoulder.

That evening Maya Nandi, whom he calls Maya Mashi, as if she were his own mother's sister, his own aunt, is heating up the dinner she's brought over, when his father calls to say the baby has arrived. The next day Gogol sees his mother sitting in an angled bed, a plastic bracelet around her wrist, her stomach no longer as hard and round. Through a big glass window, he sees his sister asleep, lying in a small glass bed, the only one of the babies in the nursery to have a thick head of black hair. He is introduced to his mother's nurses. He drinks the juice and eats the pudding off his mother's tray. Shyly he gives his mother the picture he's drawn. Underneath the figures he's written his own name, and Ma, and Baba. Only the space under the baby is blank. "I didn't know the baby's name," Gogol says, which is when his parents tell him. This time, Ashoke and Ashima are ready. They have the names lined up, for a boy or a girl. They've learned their lesson after Gogol. They've learned that schools in America will ignore parents' instructions and register a child under his pet name. The only way to avoid such confusion, they have concluded, is to do away with the pet name altogether, as many of their Bengali friends have already done. For their daughter, good name and pet name are one and the same: Sonali, meaning "she who is golden."

Two days later, coming back from school, Gogol finds his mother at home again, wearing a bathrobe instead of a sari, and sees his sister awake for the first time. She is dressed in pink pajamas that conceal her hands and feet, with a pink bonnet tied around her moon-shaped face. His father is home, too. His parents sit Gogol on the living room sofa and place Sonali in his lap, telling him to hold her against his chest, a hand cupped under her head, and his father takes pictures with a new Nikon 35-millimeter camera. The shutter advances softly, repeatedly; the room is bathed in rich afternoon light. "Hi, Sonali," Gogol says, sitting stiffly, looking down at her face, and then up at the lens. Though Sonali is the name on her birth certificate, the name she will carry officially through life, at home they begin to call her Sonu, then Sona, and finally Sonia. Sonia makes her a citizen of the world. It's a Russian link to her brother, it's European, South American. Eventually it will be the name of the Indian prime minister's Italian wife. At first Gogol is disappointed by the fact that he can't play with her, that all she does is sleep and soil her diapers and cry. But eventually she begins to respond to him, cackling when he tickles her stomach, or pushes her in a swing operated by a noisy crank, or when he cries out "Peekaboo." He helps his mother to bathe her, fetching the towel and the shampoo. He entertains her in the back seat of the car when they drive on the highway on Saturday evenings, on the way to dinner parties thrown by their parents' friends. For by now all the Cambridge Bengalis have moved to places like Dedham and Framingham and Lexington and Winchester, to houses with backyards and driveways. They have met so many Bengalis that there is rarely a Saturday free, so that for the rest of his life Gogol's childhood memories of Saturday evenings will consist of a single, repeated scene: thirty-odd people in a three-bedroom suburban house, the children watching television or playing board games in a basement, the parents eating and conversing in the Bengali their children don't speak among themselves. He will remember eating watered-down curry off paper plates, sometimes pizza or Chinese ordered specially for the kids. There are so many guests invited to Sonia's rice ceremony that Ashoke arranges to rent a building on campus, with twenty folding tables and an industrial stove. Unlike her compliant older brother, Sonia, seven months old, refuses all the food. She plays with the dirt they've dug up from the yard and threatens to put the dollar bill into her mouth. "This one," one of the guests remarks, "this one is the true American."

As their lives in New England swell with fellow Bengali friends, the members of that other, former life, those who know Ashima and Ashoke not by their good names but as Monu and Mithu, slowly dwindle. More deaths come, more telephone calls startle them in the middle of the night, more letters arrive in the mailbox informing them of aunts and uncles no longer with them. The news of these deaths never gets lost in the mail as other letters do. Somehow, bad news, however ridden with static, however filled with echoes, always manages to be conveyed. Within a decade abroad, they are both orphaned; Ashoke's parents both dead from cancer, Ashima's mother from kidney disease. Gogol and Sonia are woken by these deaths in the early mornings, their parents screaming on the other side of thin bedroom walls. They stumble into their parents' room, uncomprehending, embarrassed at the sight of their parents' tears, feeling only slightly sad. In some senses Ashoke and Ashima live the lives of the extremely aged, those for whom everyone they once knew and loved is lost, those who survive and are consoled by memory alone. Even those family members who continue to live seem dead somehow, always invisible, impossible to touch. Voices on the phone, occasionally bearing news of births and weddings, send chills down their spines. How could it be, still alive, still talking? The sight of them when they visit Calcutta every few years feels stranger still, six or eight weeks passing like a dream. Once back on Pemberton Road, in the modest house that is suddenly mammoth, there is nothing to remind them; in spite of the hundred or so relatives they've just seen, they feel as if they are the only Gangulis in the world. The people they have grown up with will never see this life, of this they are certain. They will never breathe the air of a damp New England morning, see smoke rising from a neighbor's chimney, shiver in a car waiting for the glass to defrost and the engine to warm.

And yet to a casual observer, the Gangulis, apart from the name on their mailbox, apart from the issues of *India Abroad* and *Sangbad Bichitra* that are delivered there, appear no different from their neighbors. Their garage, like every other, contains shovels and pruning shears and a sled. They purchase a barbecue for tandoori on the porch in summer. Each step, each acquisition, no matter how small, involves deliberation, consultation with Bengali friends. Was there a difference between a plastic rake and a metal one? Which was preferable, a live Christmas tree or an artificial one? They learn to roast turkeys, albeit rubbed with garlic and cumin and cayenne, at Thanksgiving, to nail a wreath to their door in December, to wrap woolen scarves around snowmen, to color boiled eggs violet and pink at Easter and hide them around the house. For the sake of Gogol and Sonia they celebrate, with progressively increasing fanfare, the birth of Christ, an event the children look forward to far more than the worship of Durga and Saraswati. During pujos, scheduled for convenience on two Saturdays a year, Gogol and Sonia are dragged off to a high school or a Knights of Columbus hall overtaken by Bengalis, where they are required to throw marigold petals at a cardboard effigy of a goddess and eat bland vegetarian food. It can't compare to Christmas, when they hang stockings on the fireplace mantel, and set out cookies and milk for Santa Claus, and receive heaps of presents, and stay home from school.

There are other ways in which Ashoke and Ashima give in. Though Ashima continues to wear nothing but saris and sandals from Bata, Ashoke, accustomed to wearing tailor-made pants and shirts all his life, learns to buy ready-made. He trades in fountain pens for ballpoints, Wilkinson blades and his boar-bristled shaving brush for Bic razors bought six to a pack. Though he is now a tenured full professor, he stops wearing jackets and ties to the university. Given that there is a clock everywhere he turns, at the side of his bed, over the stove where he prepares tea, in the car he drives to work, on the wall opposite his desk, he stops wearing a wristwatch, resigning his Favre Leuba to the depths of his sock drawer. In the supermarket they let Gogol fill the cart with items that he and Sonia, but not they, consume: individually wrapped slices of cheese, mayonnaise, tuna fish, hot dogs. For Gogol's lunches they stand at the deli to buy cold cuts, and in the mornings Ashima makes sandwiches with bologna or roast beef. At his insistence, she concedes and makes him an American dinner once a week as a treat, Shake 'n Bake chicken or Hamburger Helper prepared with ground lamb.

Still, they do what they can. They make a point of driving into Cambridge with the children when the Apu Trilogy plays at the Orson Welles, or when there is a Kathakali dance performance or a sitar recital at Memorial Hall. When Gogol is in the third grade, they send him to Bengali language and culture lessons every other Saturday, held in the home of one of their friends. For when Ashima and Ashoke close their eyes it never fails to unsettle them, that their children sound just like Americans, expertly conversing in a language that still at times confounds them, in accents they are accustomed not to trust. In Bengali class, Gogol is taught to read and write his ancestral alphabet, which begins at the back of his throat with an unaspirated K and marches steadily across the roof of his mouth, ending with elusive vowels that hover outside his lips. He is taught to write letters that hang from a bar, and eventually to cobble these intricate shapes into his name. They read hand-outs written in English about the Bengali Renaissance, and the revolutionary exploits of Subhas Chandra Bose. The children in the class study without interest, wishing they could be at ballet or softball practice instead. Gogol hates it because it keeps him from attending every other session of a Saturday-morning drawing class he's enrolled in, at the suggestion of his art teacher. The drawing class is held on the top floor of the public library; on nice days they are taken for walks through the historic district, carrying large sketchpads and pencils, and told to draw the facade of this building or that. In Bengali class they read from hand-sewn primers brought back by their teacher from Calcutta, intended for five-year-olds, printed, Gogol can't help noticing, on paper that resembles the folded toilet paper he uses at school.

As a young boy Gogol doesn't mind his name. He recognizes pieces of himself in road signs: GO LEFT, GO RIGHT, GO SLOW. For birthdays his mother orders a cake on which his name is piped across the white frosted surface in a bright blue sugary script. It all seems perfectly normal. It doesn't bother him that his name is never an option on key chains or metal pins or refrigerator magnets. He has been told that he was named after a famous Russian author, born in a previous century. That the author's name, and therefore his, is known throughout the world and will live on forever. One day his father takes him to the university library, and shows him, on a shelf well beyond his reach, a row of Gogol spines. When his father opens up one of the books to a random page, the print is far smaller than in the Hardy Boys series Gogol has begun recently to enjoy. "In a few years," his father tells him, "you'll be ready to read them." Though substitute teachers at school always pause, looking apologetic when they arrive at his name on the roster, forcing Gogol to call out, before even being summoned, "That's me," teachers in the school system know not to give it a second thought. After a year or two, the students no longer tease and say "Giggle" or "Gargle." In the programs of the school Christmas plays, the parents are accustomed to seeing his name among the cast. "Gogol is an outstanding student, curious and cooperative," his teachers write year after year on report cards. "Go, Gogol!" his classmates shout on golden autumn days as he runs the bases or sprints in a dash.

As for his last name, Ganguli, by the time he is ten he has been to Calcutta three more times, twice in summer and once during Durga pujo, and from the most recent trip he still remembers the sight of it etched respectably into the white-washed exterior of his paternal grandparents' house. He remembers the astonishment of seeing pages full of Gangulis, three columns to a page, in the Calcutta telephone directory. He'd wanted to rip out the page as a souvenir, but when he'd told this to one of his cousins, the cousin had laughed. On taxi rides through the city, going to visit the various homes of his relatives, his father had pointed out the name elsewhere, on the awnings of confectioners, and stationers, and opticians. He had told Gogol that Ganguli is a legacy of the British, an anglicized way of pronouncing his real surname, Gangopadhyay.

Back home on Pemberton Road, he helps his father paste individual golden letters bought from a rack in the hardware store, spelling out GANGULI on one side of their mailbox. One morning, the day after Halloween, Gogol discovers, on his way to the bus stop, that it has been shortened to GANG, with the word GRENE scrawled in pencil following it. His ears burn at the sight, and he runs back into the house, sickened, certain of the insult his father will feel. Though it is his last name, too, something tells Gogol that the desecration is intended for his parents more than Sonia and him. For by now he is aware, in stores, of cashiers smirking at his parents' accents, and of salesmen who prefer to direct their conversation to Gogol, as though his parents were either incompetent or deaf. But his father is unaffected at such moments, just as he is unaffected by the mailbox. "It's only boys having fun," he tells Gogol, flicking the matter away with the back of a hand, and that evening they drive back to the hardware store, to buy the missing letters again.

Then one day the peculiarity of his name becomes apparent. He is eleven years old, in the sixth grade, on a school field trip of some historical intent. They set off in their school bus, two classes, two teachers, two chaperones along for the ride, driving straight through the town and onto the highway. It is a chilly, spectacular November day, the blue sky cloudless, the trees shedding bright yellow leaves that blanket the ground. The children scream and sing and drink cans of soda wrapped in aluminum foil. First they visit a textile mill somewhere in Rhode Island. The next stop is a small unpainted wooden house with tiny windows, sitting on a large plot of land. Inside, after adjusting to the diminished light, they stare at a desk with an inkwell at its top, a soot-stained fireplace, a washtub, a short, narrow bed. It was once the home of a poet, they are told. All the furniture is roped off from the center of the room, with little signs telling them not to touch. The ceiling is so low that the teachers duck their heads as they walk from darkened room to room. They look at the kitchen, with its iron stove and stone sink, and file along a dirt path to look at the outhouse. The students shriek with disgust at the sight of a tin pan hanging from the bottom of a wooden chair. In the gift shop, Gogol buys a postcard of the house and a ballpoint pen disguised as a quill.

The final stop on the field trip, a short distance by bus from the poet's house, is a graveyard where the writer lies buried. They take a few minutes wandering from stone to stone, among thick and thin tablets, some leaning back as if pressed by a wind. The stones are square and arched, black and gray, more often plain than shiny, caked with lichen and moss. On many of the stones the inscriptions have faded. They find the stone that bears the poet's name. "Line up," the teachers say, "it's time for a project." The students are each given several sheets of newsprint and thick colored crayons whose labels have been peeled. Gogol can't help but feel a chill. He's never set foot in a graveyard before, only glimpsed them in passing, riding in cars. There is a large one on the outskirts of their town; once, stuck in traffic, he and his family had witnessed a burial from a distance, and ever since then, whenever they drive by, his mother always tells them to avert their eyes.

To Gogol's surprise they are told not to draw the gravestones, but to rub their surfaces. A teacher crouches down, one hand holding the newsprint in place, and shows them how. The children begin to scamper between rows of the dead, over leathery leaves, looking for their own names, a handful triumphant when they are able to claim a grave they are related to. "Smith!" they holler. "Collins!" "Wood!" Gogol is old enough to know that there is no Ganguli here. He is old enough to know that he himself will be burned, not buried, that his body will occupy no plot of earth, that no stone in this country will bear his name beyond life. In Calcutta, from taxis and once from the roof of his grandparents' house, he has seen the dead bodies of strangers carried on people's shoulders through streets, decked with flowers, wrapped in sheets.

He walks over to a slim, blackened stone with a pleasing shape, rounded at the top before rising into a cross. He kneels on the grass and holds up the newsprint, then begins to rub gently with the side of his crayon. The sun is already sinking and his fingers are stiff with cold. The teachers and chaperones sit on the ground, legs extended, leaning back against the headstones, the aroma of their menthol cigarettes drifting through the air. At first nothing appears apart from a grainy, featureless wash of midnight blue. But then, suddenly, the crayon meets with slight resistance, and letters, one after another, emerge magically on the page: ABIJAH CRAVEN, 1701–45. Gogol has never met a person named Abijah, just as, he now realizes, he has never met another Gogol. He wonders how to pronounce Abijah, whether it's a man's or a woman's name. He walks to another tombstone, less than a foot tall, and presses another sheet of paper to its surface. This one says ANGUISH MATHER, A CHILD. He shudders, imagining bones no larger than his below the ground. Some of the other children in the class, already bored with the project, begin chasing one another around the stones, pushing and teasing and snapping gum. But Gogol goes from grave to grave with paper and crayon in hand, bringing to life one name after another. PEREGRINE WOTTON, D. 1699. EZEKIEL AND URIAH LOCKWOOD, BROTHERS, R.I.P. He likes these names, likes their oddness, their flamboyance. "Now those are some names you don't see very often these days," one of the chaperones, passing by and looking down at his rubbings, remarks. "Sort of like yours." Until now it has not occurred to Gogol that names die over time, that they perish just as people do. On the ride back to school the rubbings made by the other children are torn up, crumpled, tossed at one another's heads, abandoned below the dark green seats. But Gogol is silent, his rubbings rolled up carefully like parchment in his lap.

At home, his mother is horrified. What type of field trip was this? It was enough that they applied lipstick to their corpses and buried them in silk-lined boxes. Only in America (a phrase she has begun to resort to often these days), only in America are children taken to cemeteries in the name of art. What's next, she demands to know, a trip to the morgue? In Calcutta the burning ghats are the most forbidden of places, she tells Gogol, and though she tries her best not to, though she was here, not there, both times it happened, she sees her parents' bodies, swallowed by flames. "Death is not a pastime," she says, her voice rising unsteadily, "not a place to make paintings." She refuses to display the rubbings in the kitchen alongside his other creations, his charcoal drawings and his magazine collages, his pencil sketch of a Greek temple copied from an encyclopedia, his pastel image of the public library's facade, awarded first place in a contest sponsored by the library trustees. Never before has she rejected a piece of her son's art. The guilt she feels at Gogol's deflated expression is leavened by common sense. How can she be expected to cook dinner for her family with the names of dead people on the walls?

But Gogol is attached to them. For reasons he cannot explain or necessarily understand, these ancient Puritan spirits, these very first immigrants to America, these bearers of unthinkable, obsolete names, have spoken to him, so much so that in spite of his mother's disgust he refuses to throw the rubbings away. He rolls them up, takes them upstairs, and puts them in his room, behind his chest of drawers, where he knows his mother will never bother to look, and where they will remain, ignored but protected, gathering dust for years to come.

4

1982

GOGOL'S fourteenth birthday. Like most events in his life, it is another excuse for his parents to throw a party for their Bengali friends. His own friends from school were invited the previous day, a tame affair, with pizzas that his father picked up on his way home from work, a baseball game watched together on television, some Ping-Pong in the den. For the first time in his life he has said no to the frosted cake, the box of harlequin ice cream, the hot dogs in buns, the balloons and streamers taped to the walls. The other celebration, the Bengali one, is held on the closest Saturday to the actual date of his birth. As usual his mother cooks for days beforehand, cramming the refrigerator with stacks of foil-covered trays. She makes sure to prepare his favorite things: lamb curry with lots of potatoes, luchis, thick channa dal with swollen brown raisins, pineapple chutney, sandeshes molded out of saffron-tinted ricotta cheese. All this is less stressful to her than the task of feeding a handful of American children, half of whom always claim they are allergic to milk, all of whom refuse to eat the crusts of their bread.

Close to forty guests come from three different states.

Women are dressed in saris far more dazzling than the pants and polo shirts their husbands wear. A group of men sit in a circle on the floor and immediately start a game of poker. These are his mashis and meshos, his honorary aunts and uncles. They all bring their children; his parents' crowd does not believe in baby-sitters. As usual, Gogol is the oldest child in the group. He is too old to be playing hide-and-seek with eight-year-old Sonia and her ponytailed, gap-toothed friends, but not old enough to sit in the living room and discuss Reaganomics with his father and the rest of the husbands, or to sit around the dining room table, gossiping, with his mother and the wives. The closest person to him in age is a girl named Moushumi, whose family recently moved to Massachusetts from England, and whose thirteenth birthday was celebrated in a similar fashion a few months ago. But Gogol and Moushumi have nothing to say to each other. Moushumi sits cross-legged on the floor, in glasses with maroon plastic frames and a puffy polka-dotted headband holding back her thick, chin-length hair. In her lap is a kelly green Bermuda bag with pink piping and wooden handles; inside the bag is a tube of 7UP-flavored lip balm that she draws from time to time across her mouth. She is reading a well-thumbed paperback copy of *Pride and Prejudice* while the other children, Gogol included, watch *The Love Boat* and *Fantasy Island*, piled together on top and around the sides of his parents' bed. Occasionally one of the children asks Moushumi to say something, anything, in her English accent. Sonia asks if she's ever seen Princess Diana on the street. "I detest American television," Moushumi eventually declares to everyone's delight, then wanders into the hallway to continue her reading.

Presents are opened when the guests are gone. Gogol receives several dictionaries, several calculators, several Cross pen-and-pencil sets, several ugly sweaters. His parents give him an Instamatic camera, a new sketchbook, colored pencils and the mechanical pen he'd asked for, and twenty dollars to spend as he wishes. Sonia has made him a card with Magic Markers, on paper she's ripped out of one of his own sketchbooks, which says "Happy Birthday Goggles," the name she insists on calling him instead of Dada. His mother sets aside the things he doesn't like, which is most everything, to give to his cousins the next time they go to India. Later that night he is alone in his room, listening to side 3 of the White Album on his parents' cast-off RCA turntable. The album is a present from his American birthday party, given to him by one of his friends at school. Born when the band was near death, Gogol is a passionate devotee of John, Paul, George, and Ringo. In recent years he has collected nearly all their albums, and the only thing tacked to the bulletin board on the back of his door is Lennon's obituary, already yellow and brittle, clipped from the *Boston Globe*. He sits cross-legged on the bed, hunched over the lyrics, when he hears a knock on the door.

"Come in," he hollers, expecting it to be Sonia in her pajamas, asking if she can borrow his Magic 8 Ball or his Rubik's Cube. He is surprised to see his father, standing in stocking feet, a small potbelly visible beneath his oat-colored sweater vest, his mustache turning gray. Gogol is especially surprised to see a gift in his father's hands. His father has never given him birthday presents apart from whatever his mother buys, but this year, his father says, walking across the room to where Gogol is sitting, he has something special. The gift is covered in red-and-green-and-gold-striped paper left over from Christmas the year before, taped awkwardly at the seams. It is obviously a book, thick, hardcover, wrapped by his father's own hands. Gogol lifts the paper slowly, but in spite of this the tape leaves a scab. *The Short Stories of Nikolai Gogol*, the jacket says. Inside, the price has been snipped away on the diagonal.

"I ordered it from the bookstore, just for you," his father says, his voice raised in order to be heard over the music. "It's difficult to find in hardcover these days. It's a British publication, a very small press. It took four months to arrive. I hope you like it."

Gogol leans over toward the stereo to turn the volume down a bit. He would have preferred *The Hitchhiker's Guide to the Galaxy*, or even another copy of *The Hobbit* to replace the one he lost last summer in Calcutta, left on the rooftop of his father's house in Alipore and snatched away by crows. In spite of his father's occasional suggestions, he has never been inspired to read a word of Gogol, or any Russian writer, for that matter. He has never been told why he was really named Gogol, doesn't know about the accident that had nearly killed his father. He thinks his father's limp is the consequence of an injury playing soccer in his teens. He's been told only half the truth about Gogol: that his father is a fan.

"Thanks, Baba," Gogol says, eager to return to his lyrics. Lately he's been lazy, addressing his parents in English though they continue to speak to him in Bengali. Occasionally he wanders through the house with his running sneakers on. At dinner he sometimes uses a fork.

His father is still standing there in his room, watching expectantly, his hands clasped together behind his back, so Gogol flips through the book. A single picture at the front, on smoother paper than the rest of the pages, shows a pencil drawing of the author, sporting a velvet jacket, a billowy white shirt and cravat. The face is foxlike, with small, dark eyes, a thin, neat mustache, an extremely large pointy nose. Dark hair slants steeply across his forehead and is plastered to either side of his head, and there is a disturbing, vaguely supercilious smile set into long, narrow lips. Gogol Ganguli is relieved to see no resemblance. True, his nose is long but not so long, his hair dark

but surely not so dark, his skin pale but certainly not so pale.
The style of his own hair is altogether different—thick Beatle-
like bangs that conceal his brows. Gogol Ganguli wears a Harvard sweatshirt and gray Levi's corduroys. He has worn a tie
once in his life, to attend a friend's bar mitzvah. No, he concludes confidently, there is no resemblance at all.

For by now, he's come to hate questions pertaining to his
name, hates having constantly to explain. He hates having to
tell people that it doesn't mean anything "in Indian." He hates
having to wear a nametag on his sweater at Model United Nations Day at school. He even hates signing his name at the bottom of his drawings in art class. He hates that his name is both
absurd and obscure, that it has nothing to do with who he is,
that it is neither Indian nor American but of all things Russian.
He hates having to live with it, with a pet name turned good
name, day after day, second after second. He hates seeing it on
the brown paper sleeve of the *National Geographic* subscription
his parents got him for his birthday the year before and perpetually listed in the honor roll printed in the town's newspaper.
At times his name, an entity shapeless and weightless, manages
nevertheless to distress him physically, like the scratchy tag of
a shirt he has been forced permanently to wear. At times he
wishes he could disguise it, shorten it somehow, the way the
other Indian boy in his school, Jayadev, had gotten people to
call him Jay. But Gogol, already short and catchy, resists muta-
tion. Other boys his age have begun to court girls already, asking them to go to the movies or the pizza parlor, but he cannot imagine saying, "Hi, it's Gogol" under potentially romantic
circumstances. He cannot imagine this at all.

From the little he knows about Russian writers, it dismays
him that his parents chose the weirdest namesake. Leo or An-
ton, he could have lived with. Alexander, shortened to Alex, he
would have greatly preferred. But Gogol sounds ludicrous to

his ears, lacking dignity or gravity. What dismays him most is the irrelevance of it all. Gogol, he's been tempted to tell his father on more than one occasion, was his father's favorite author, not his. Then again, it's his own fault. He could have been known, at school at least, as Nikhil. That one day, that first day of kindergarten, which he no longer remembers, could have changed everything. He could have been Gogol only fifty percent of the time. Like his parents when they went to Calcutta, he could have had an alternative identity, a B-side to the self. "We tried," his parents explain to friends and relatives who ask why their son lacks a good name, "but he would only respond to Gogol. The school insisted." His parents would add, "We live in a country where a president is called Jimmy. Really, there was nothing we could do."

"Thanks again," Gogol tells his father now. He shuts the cover and swings his legs over the edge of the bed, to put the book away on his shelves. But his father takes the opportunity to sit beside him on the bed. For a moment he rests a hand on Gogol's shoulder. The boy's body, in recent months, has grown tall, nearly as tall as Ashoke's. The childhood pudginess has vanished from his face. The voice has begun to deepen, is slightly husky now. It occurs to Ashoke that he and his son probably wear the same size shoe. In the glow of the bedside lamp, Ashoke notices a scattered down emerging on his son's upper lip. An Adam's apple is prominent on his neck. The pale hands, like Ashima's, are long and thin. Ashoke wonders how closely Gogol resembles himself at this age. But there are no photographs to document Ashoke's childhood; not until his passport, not until his life in America, does visual documentation exist. On the night table Ashoke sees a can of deodorant, a tube of Clearasil. He lifts the book from where it lies on the bed between them, running a hand protectively over the cover. "I took the liberty of reading it first. It has been many years since I have read these stories. I hope you don't mind."

"No problem," Gogol says.

"I feel a special kinship with Gogol," Ashoke says, "more than with any other writer. Do you know why?"

"You like his stories."

"Apart from that. He spent most of his adult life outside his homeland. Like me."

Gogol nods. "Right."

"And there is another reason." The music ends and there is silence. But then Gogol flips the record, turning the volume up on "Revolution 1."

"What's that?" Gogol says, a bit impatiently.

Ashoke looks around the room. He notices the Lennon obituary pinned to the bulletin board, and then a cassette of classical Indian music he'd bought for Gogol months ago, after a concert at Kresge, still sealed in its wrapper. He sees the pile of birthday cards scattered on the carpet, and remembers a hot August day fourteen years ago in Cambridge when he held his son for the first time. Ever since that day, the day he became a father, the memory of his accident has receded, diminishing over the years. Though he will never forget that night, it no longer lurks persistently in his mind, stalking him in the same way. It no longer looms over his life, darkening it without warning as it used to do. Instead, it is affixed firmly to a distant time, to a place far from Pemberton Road. Today, his son's birthday, is a day to honor life, not brushes with death. And so, for now, Ashoke decides to keep the explanation of his son's name to himself.

"No other reason. Good night," he says to Gogol, getting up from the bed. At the door he pauses, turns around. "Do you know what Dostoyevsky once said?"

Gogol shakes his head.

"'We all came out of Gogol's overcoat.'"

"What's that supposed to mean?"

"It will make sense to you one day. Many happy returns of the day."

Gogol gets up and shuts the door behind his father, who has the annoying habit of always leaving it partly open. He fastens the lock on the knob for good measure, then wedges the book on a high shelf between two volumes of the Hardy Boys. He settles down again with his lyrics on the bed when something occurs to him. This writer he is named after—Gogol isn't his first name. His first name is Nikolai. Not only does Gogol Ganguli have a pet name turned good name, but a last name turned first name. And so it occurs to him that no one he knows in the world, in Russia or India or America or anywhere, shares his name. Not even the source of his namesake.

The following year Ashoke is up for a sabbatical, and Gogol and Sonia are informed that they will all be going to Calcutta for eight months. When his parents tell him, one evening after dinner, Gogol thinks they're joking. But then they tell them that the tickets have already been booked, the plans already made. "Think of it as a long vacation," Ashoke and Ashima say to their crestfallen children. But Gogol knows that eight months is no vacation. He dreads the thought of eight months without a room of his own, without his records and his stereo, without friends. In Gogol's opinion, eight months in Calcutta is practically like moving there, a possibility that, until now, has never even remotely crossed his mind. Besides, he's a sophomore now. "What about school?" he points out. His parents remind him that in the past his teachers have never minded Gogol missing school now and again. They've given him math and language workbooks that he's ignored, and when he returns, a month or two later, they praise him for keeping up with things. But Gogol's guidance counselor expresses concern when Gogol informs him that he will be missing the entire second half of the tenth grade. A meeting is called with Ashima and Ashoke to discuss the options. The guidance counselor asks if it's possible to enroll Gogol in one of the American Schools in India. But the nearest one is in Delhi, over eight hundred miles from Calcutta. The guidance counselor suggests that perhaps Gogol could join his parents later, after the school year ends, stay with a relative until June. "We have no relatives in this country," Ashima informs the guidance counselor. "That is why we are going to India in the first place."

And so after barely four months of tenth grade, after an early supper of rice and boiled potatoes and eggs that his mother insists they eat even though they will be served another supper on the plane, he is off, geometry and U.S. history books packed into his suitcase, which is locked, along with the others, with padlocks and bound with ropes, labeled with the address of his father's house in Alipore. Gogol always finds the labels unsettling, the sight of them making him feel that his family doesn't really live on Pemberton Road. They depart Christmas Day, driving with their massive collection of luggage to Logan when they should be home opening gifts. Sonia is morose, running a slight fever from her typhoid shot, still expecting, when she enters the living room in the morning, to see a tree trimmed with lights. But the only thing in the living room is debris: price tags from all the gifts they've packed for their relatives, plastic hangers, cardboard from shirts. They shiver as they leave the house, without coats or gloves; they won't need them where they're going, and it will be August by the time they return. The house has been rented to some American students his father has found through the university, an unmarried couple named Barbara and Steve. In the airport Gogol stands in the check-in line with his father, who is dressed in a jacket and tie, clothes he still thinks to wear when riding on planes. "Four in the family," his father says when it is their turn, producing two U.S. passports and two Indian ones. "Two Hindu meals, please."

On the plane Gogol is seated several rows behind his parents and Sonia, in another section altogether. His parents are distressed by this, but Gogol is secretly pleased to be on his own. When the stewardess approaches with her cart of beverages he tries his luck and asks for a Bloody Mary, tasting the metallic bite of alcohol for the first time in his life. They fly first to London, and then to Calcutta via Dubai. When they fly over the Alps, his father gets out of his seat to take pictures of the snowcapped peaks through the window. On past trips, it used to thrill Gogol that they were flying over so many countries; again and again he would trace their itinerary on the map in the seat pocket below his tray and feel somehow adventurous. But this time it frustrates him that it is to Calcutta that they always go. Apart from visiting relatives there was nothing to do in Calcutta. He's already been to the planetarium and the Zoo Garden and the Victoria Memorial a dozen times. They have never been to Disneyland or the Grand Canyon. Only once, when their connecting flight in London was delayed, did they leave Heathrow and take a double-decker bus tour of the city.

On the final leg of the trip there are only a few non-Indians left on the plane. Bengali conversation fills the cabin; his mother has already exchanged addresses with the family across the aisle. Before landing she slips into the bathroom and changes, miraculously in that minuscule space, into a fresh sari. A final meal is served, an herbed omelette topped with a slice of grilled tomato. Gogol savors each mouthful, aware that for the next eight months nothing will taste quite the same. Through the window he sees palm trees and banana trees, a damp, drab sky. The wheels touch the ground, the aircraft is sprayed with disinfectant, and then they descend onto the tarmac of Dum Dum Airport, breathing in the sour, stomach-turning, early morning air. They stop to wave back at the row of relatives waving madly from the observation deck, little cousins propped up on uncles' shoulders. As usual the Gangulis are relieved to learn that all their luggage has arrived, together and unmolested, and relieved further still when customs doesn't make a fuss. And then the frosted doors slide open and once again they are officially there, no longer in transit, swallowed by hugs and kisses and pinched cheeks and smiles. There are endless names Gogol and Sonia must remember to say, not aunt this and uncle that but terms far more specific: *mashi* and *pishi*, *mama* and *maima*, *kaku* and *jethu*, to signify whether they are related on their mother's or their father's side, by marriage or by blood. Ashima, now Monu, weeps with relief, and Ashoke, now Mithu, kisses his brothers on both cheeks, holds their heads in his hands. Gogol and Sonia know these people, but they do not feel close to them as their parents do. Within minutes, before their eyes Ashoke and Ashima slip into bolder, less complicated versions of themselves, their voices louder, their smiles wider, revealing a confidence Gogol and Sonia never see on Pemberton Road. "I'm scared, Goggles," Sonia whispers to her brother in English, seeking his hand and refusing to let go.

They are ushered into waiting taxis and down VIP Road, past a colossal landfill and into the heart of North Calcutta. Gogol is accustomed to the scenery, yet he still stares, at the short, dark men pulling rickshaws and the crumbling buildings side by side with fretwork balconies, hammers and sickles painted on their facades. He stares at the commuters who cling precariously to trams and buses, threatening at any moment to spill onto the street, and at the families who boil rice and shampoo their hair on the sidewalk. At his mother's flat

on Amherst Street, where his uncle's family lives now, neighbors look from their windows and roofs as Gogol and his family emerge from the taxi. They stand out in their bright, expensive sneakers, American haircuts, backpacks slung over one
shoulder. Once inside, he and Sonia are given cups of Horlick's,
plates of syrupy, spongy rossogollas for which they have no appetite but which they dutifully eat. They have their feet traced
onto pieces of paper, and a servant is sent to Bata to bring back
rubber slippers for them to wear indoors. The suitcases are unlocked and unbound and all the gifts are unearthed, admired,
tried on for size.

In the days that follow they adjust once again to sleeping
under a mosquito net, bathing by pouring tin cups of water
over their heads. In the mornings Gogol watches his cousins
put on their white and blue school uniforms and strap water
bottles across their chests. His aunt, Uma Maima, presides in
the kitchen all morning, harassing the servants as they squat by
the drain scouring the dirty dishes with ash, or pound heaps
of spices on slabs that resemble tombstones. At the Ganguli
house in Alipore, he sees the room in which they would have
lived had his parents remained in India, the ebony four-poster
bed on which they would have slept all together, the armoire in
which they would have stored their clothes.

Instead of renting an apartment of their own, they spend
eight months with their various relatives, shuttling from home
to home. They stay in Ballygunge, Tollygunge, Salt Lake,
Budge Budge, ferried by endless bumpy taxi rides back and
forth through the city. Every few weeks there is a different bed
to sleep in, another family to live with, a new schedule to learn.
Depending on where they are, they eat sitting on red clay or
cement or terrazzo floors, or at marble-topped tables too cold
to rest their elbows on. Their cousins and aunts and uncles ask
them about life in America, about what they eat for breakfast,

about their friends at school. They look at the pictures of their house on Pemberton Road. "Carpets in the bathroom," they say, "imagine that." His father keeps busy with his research, delivering lectures at Jadavpur University. His mother shops in New Market and goes to movies and sees her old school friends. For eight months she does not set foot in a kitchen. She wanders freely around a city in which Gogol, in spite of his many visits, has no sense of direction. Within three months Sonia has read each of her Laura Ingalls Wilder books a dozen times. Gogol occasionally opens up one of his textbooks, bloated from the heat. Though he's brought his sneakers with him, hoping to keep up with cross-country training, it is impossible, on these cracked, congested, chock-a-block streets, to run. The one day he tries, Uma Maima, watching from the rooftop, sends a servant to follow him so that Gogol doesn't get lost.

It's easier to surrender to confinement. On Amherst Street, Gogol sits at his grandfather's drawing table, poking through a tin full of dried-out nibs. He sketches what he sees through the iron window bars: the crooked skyline, the courtyards, the cobblestone square where he watches maids filling brass urns at the tube well, people passing under the soiled canopies of rickshaws, hurrying home with parcels in the rain. On the roof one day, with its view of Howrah Bridge in the distance, he smokes a bidi tightly rolled in olive green leaves with one of the servants. Of all the people who surround them at practically all times, Sonia is his only ally, the only person to speak and sit and see as he does. While the rest of the household sleeps, he and Sonia fight over the Walkman, over the melting collection of tapes Gogol recorded back in his room at home. From time to time, they privately admit to excruciating cravings, for hamburgers or a slice of pepperoni pizza or a cold glass of milk.

They are surprised, in the summer, to learn that their father has planned a trip for them, first to Delhi to visit an un-

cle, and then to Agra to see the Taj Mahal. It will be Gogol and
Sonia's first journey outside of Calcutta, their first time on an
Indian train. They depart from Howrah, that immense, soar-
ing, echoing station, where barefoot coolies in red cotton shirts
pile the Gangulis' Samsonite luggage on their heads, where entire families sleep, covered, in rows on the floor. Gogol is aware
of the dangers involved: his cousins have told him about the
bandits that lurk in Bihar, so that his father wears a special garment under his shirt, with hidden pockets to carry cash, and
his mother and Sonia remove their gold jewels. On the platform they walk from compartment to compartment, looking
for their four names on the passenger list pasted to the outside
wall of the train. They settle onto their blue berths, the top two
swinging down from the walls when it is time to sleep and held
in place by sliding latches during the day. A conductor gives
them their bedding, heavy white cotton sheets and thin woolen
blankets. In the morning they look at the scenery through the
tinted window of their air-conditioned car. As a result, the view,
no matter how bright the day, is gloomy and gray.

They are unaccustomed, after all these months, to being just
the four of them. For a few days, in Agra, which is as foreign to
Ashima and Ashoke as it is to Gogol and Sonia, they are tourists, staying at a hotel with a swimming pool, sipping bottled
water, eating in restaurants with forks and spoons, paying by
credit card. Ashima and Ashoke speak in broken Hindi, and
when young boys approach to sell postcards or marble trinkets
Gogol and Sonia are forced to say, "English, please." Gogol notices in certain restaurants that they are the only Indians apart
from the serving staff. For two days they wander around the
marble mausoleum that glows gray and yellow and pink and
orange depending on the light. They admire its perfect sym-
metry and pose for photographs beneath the minarets from
which tourists used to leap to their deaths. "I want a picture

here, just the two of us," Ashima says to Ashoke as they wander around the massive plinth, and so under the blinding Agra sun, overlooking the dried-up Yamuna, Ashoke teaches Gogol how to use the Nikon, how to focus and advance the film. A tour guide tells them that after the Taj was completed, each of the builders, twenty-two thousand men, had his thumbs cut off so that the structure could never be built again. That night in the hotel Sonia wakes up screaming that her own thumbs are missing. "It's just legend," her parents tell her. But the idea of it haunts Gogol as well. No other building he's seen has affected him so powerfully. Their second day at the Taj he attempts to sketch the dome and a portion of the facade, but the building's grace eludes him and he throws the sketch away. Instead, he immerses himself in the guidebook, studying the history of Mughal architecture, learning the succession of emperors' names: Babur, Humayun, Akbar, Jahangir, Shah Jahan, Aurangzeb. At Agra Fort he and his family look through the window of the room where Shah Jahan was imprisoned by his own son. At Sikandra, Akbar's tomb, they gaze at gilded frescoes in the entryway, chipped, ransacked, burned, the gems gouged out with penknives, graffiti etched into the stone. At Fatehpur Sikri, Akbar's abandoned sandstone city, they wander among courtyards and cloisters as parrots and hawks fly overhead, and in Salim Chishti's tomb Ashima ties red threads for good luck to a marble lattice screen.

But bad luck trails them on the trip back to Calcutta. At Benares station, Sonia asks her father to buy her a slice of jackfruit, which makes her lips itch unbearably, then swell to three times their size. Somewhere in Bihar, in the middle of the night, a businessman in another compartment is stabbed in his sleep and robbed of three hundred thousand rupees, and the train stops for five hours while the local police investigate. The Gangulis learn the cause of the delay the following morning, as breakfast is being served, the passengers agitated and horrified, all speaking of the same thing. "Wake up. Some guy on the train got murdered," Gogol says to Sonia from his top berth to hers. No one is more horrified than Ashoke, who privately recalls that other train, on that other night, and that other field where he'd been stopped. This time he'd heard nothing. He'd slept through the whole thing.

Upon returning to Calcutta, Gogol and Sonia both get terribly ill. It is the air, the rice, the wind, their relatives casually remark; they were not made to survive in a poor country, they say. They have constipation followed by the opposite. Doctors come to the house in the evening with stethoscopes in black leather bags. They are given courses of Entroquinol, ajowan water that burns their throats. And once they've recovered it's time to go back: the day they were convinced would never come is just two weeks away. Kashmiri pencil cups are bought for Ashoke to give to his colleagues at the university. Gogol buys Indian comic books to give to his American friends. On the evening of their departure he watches his parents standing in front of framed pictures of his dead grandparents on the walls, heads bowed, weeping like children. And then the caravan of taxis and Ambassadors comes to whisk them one last time across the city. Their flight is at dawn and so they must leave in darkness, driving through streets so empty they are unrecognizable, a tram with its small single headlight the only other thing that moves. At the airport the row of people who had greeted them, have hosted and fed and fawned over them for all these months, those with whom he shares a name if not his life, assemble once more on the balcony, to wave good-bye. Gogol knows that his relatives will stand there until the plane has drifted away, until the flashing lights are no longer visible in the sky. He knows that his mother will sit silently, staring at the clouds, as they journey back to Boston. But for Gogol, relief quickly replaces any lingering sadness. With relief he peels back the foil covering his breakfast, extracts the silverware from its sealed plastic packaging, asks the British Airways stewardess for a glass of orange juice. With relief he puts on his headset to watch *The Big Chill* and listen to top-forty songs all the way home.

Within twenty-four hours he and his family are back on Pemberton Road, the late August grass in need of trimming, a quart of milk and some bread left by their tenants in the re-frigerator, four grocery bags on the staircase filled with mail. At first the Gangulis sleep most of the day and are wide awake at night, gorging themselves on toast at three in the morning, unpacking the suitcases one by one. Though they are home they are disconcerted by the space, by the uncompromising si-lence that surrounds them. They still feel somehow in tran-sit, still disconnected from their lives, bound up in an alter-nate schedule, an intimacy only the four of them share. But by the end of the week, after his mother's friends come to ad-mire her new gold and saris, after the eight suitcases have been aired out on the sun deck and put away, after the chanachur is poured into Tupperware and the smuggled mangoes eaten for breakfast with cereal and tea, it's as if they've never been gone. "How dark you've become," his parents' friends say re-gretfully to Gogol and Sonia. On this end, there is no effort in-volved. They retreat to their three rooms, to their three sepa-rate beds, to their thick mattresses and pillows and fitted sheets. After a single trip to the supermarket, the refrigerator and the cupboards fill with familiar labels: Skippy, Hood, Bumble Bee, Land O' Lakes. His mother enters the kitchen and prepares their meals once again; his father mows the lawn and drives the car and returns to the university. Gogol and Sonia sleep for as long as they want, watch television, make themselves peanut butter and jelly sandwiches at any time of day. Once again they are free to quarrel, to tease each other, to shout and holler and say shut up. They take hot showers, speak to each other in English, ride their bicycles around the neighborhood. They call up their American friends, who are happy enough to see them but ask them nothing about where they've been. And so the eight months are put behind them, quickly shed, quickly forgotten, like clothes worn for a special occasion, or for a season that has passed, suddenly cumbersome, irrelevant to their lives.

In September, Gogol returns to high school to begin his junior year: honors biology, honors U.S. history, advanced trigonometry, Spanish, honors English. In his English class he reads *Ethan Frome*, *The Great Gatsby*, *The Good Earth*, *The Red Badge of Courage*. He takes his turn at the podium and recites the "Tomorrow, and tomorrow, and tomorrow" speech from *Macbeth*, the only lines of poetry he will know by heart for the rest of his life. His teacher, Mr. Lawson, is a slight, wiry, shamelessly preppy man with a surprisingly deep voice, reddish blond hair, smallish but penetrating green eyes, horn-rimmed glasses. He is the subject of schoolwide speculation, and slight scandal, having once been married to Ms. Sagan, who teaches French. He wears khakis and Shetland sweaters in bright solid colors, kelly green and yellow and red, sips black coffee continually from the same chipped blue mug, cannot survive the fifty-minute class without excusing himself to go to the teachers' lounge for a cigarette. In spite of his diminutive stature he has a commanding, captivating presence in the room. His handwriting is famously illegible; student compositions are regularly returned stamped with tan rings of coffee, sometimes golden rings of Scotch. Every year he gives everyone either a D or an F on the first assignment, an analysis of Blake's "The Tiger." A number of girls in the class insist that Mr. Lawson is indescribably sexy and have raging crushes on him.

Mr. Lawson is the first of Gogol's teachers to know and to care about Gogol the author. The first day of class he had looked up from the podium when he came to Gogol's name on the roster, an expression of benign amazement on his face. Unlike other teachers he did not ask, Was that really his name, was that the last name, was it short for something else? He did not ask, as many foolishly did, "Wasn't he a writer?" Instead he called out the name in a perfectly reasonable way, without pause, without doubt, without a suppressed smile, just as he had called out Brian and Erica and Tom. And then: "Well, we're going to have to read 'The Overcoat.' Either that or 'The Nose.'"

One January morning, the week after Christmas vacation, Gogol sits at his desk by the window and watches a thin, sugary snow fall inconsistently from the sky. "We're going to devote this quarter to the short story," Mr. Lawson announces, and instantly Gogol knows. With growing dread and a feeling of slight nausea, he watches as Mr. Lawson distributes the books piled on his desk, giving half a dozen well-worn copies of an anthology, *Short Story Classics*, to each of the students at the front of the rows. Gogol's copy is particularly battered, the corner blunted, the cover spotted as if by a whitish mold. He looks at the table of contents, sees Gogol listed after Faulkner, before Hemingway. The sight of it printed in capital letters on the crinkly page upsets him viscerally. It's as though the name were a particularly unflattering snapshot of himself that makes him want to say in his defense, "That's not really me." Gogol wants to excuse himself, to raise his hand and take a trip to the lavatory, but at the same time he wants to draw as little attention to himself as possible. And so he sits, avoiding eye contact with any of his classmates, and pages through the book. A number of the authors' names have been starred with penciled asterisks by previous readers, but there is no sign or mark by Nikolai Gogol's name. A single story corresponds with each author's name. The one by Gogol is called "The Overcoat." But for the rest of the class, Mr. Lawson does not mention Gogol. Instead, to Gogol Ganguli's relief, they take turns reading aloud from "The Necklace," by Guy de Maupassant. Perhaps, Gogol begins to wonder hopefully, Mr. Lawson has no intention of assigning the Gogol story. Perhaps he's forgotten about it. But as the bell rings, and the students rise collectively from their desks, Mr. Lawson holds up a hand. "Read the Gogol for tomorrow," he hollers as they shuffle through the door.

The following day, Mr. Lawson writes "Nikolai Vasilievich Gogol" in capital letters on the board, draws a box around it, then writes the dates of the author's birth and death in parentheses. Gogol opens the binder on his desk, reluctantly copies the information down. He tells himself it isn't so strange; there is, after all, a William in the class, if not an Ernest. Mr. Lawson's left hand guides the chalk rapidly across the board, but Gogol's pen begins to lag. The loose-leaf pages remain blank as those of his classmates fill up with facts on which he will most likely soon be quizzed: Born 1809 in the province of Poltava to a family of Ukrainian Cossack gentry. Father a small landowner who also wrote plays, died when Gogol was sixteen. Studied at the Lyceum of Nezhin, went to St. Petersburg in 1828 where he entered, in 1829, the civil service, in the Department of Public Works for the Ministry of the Interior. From 1830 to 1831, transferred to the Court Ministry in the Department of Royal Estates, after which time he became a teacher, lecturing on history at the Young Ladies' Institute, and later at the University of St. Petersburg. At the age of twenty-two, established a close friendship with Alexander Pushkin. In 1830, published his first short story. In 1836, a comic play, *The Government Inspector*, was produced in St. Petersburg. Dismayed by the play's mixed reception, left Russia. For the next twelve years lived abroad, in Paris, Rome, and elsewhere, composing the first volume of *Dead Souls*, the novel considered to be his finest work.

Mr. Lawson sits on the edge of his desk, crosses his legs, turns a few pages in a yellow legal pad covered with notes. Beside the legal pad is a biography of the author, a thick book called *Divided Soul*, the pages marked by numerous scraps of torn-up paper.

"Not your ordinary guy, Nikolai Gogol," Mr. Lawson says. "He is celebrated today as one of Russia's most brilliant writers. But during his life he was understood by no one, least of all himself. One might say he typified the phrase 'eccentric genius.' Gogol's life, in a nutshell, was a steady decline into madness. The writer Ivan Turgenev described him as an intelligent, queer, and sickly creature. He was reputed to be a hypochondriac and a deeply paranoid, frustrated man. He was, in addition, by all accounts, morbidly melancholic, given to fits of severe depression. He had trouble making friends. He never married, fathered no children. It's commonly believed he died a virgin."

Warmth spreads from the back of Gogol's neck to his cheeks and his ears. Each time the name is uttered, he quietly winces. His parents have never told him any of this. He looks at his classmates, but they seem indifferent, obediently copying down the information as Mr. Lawson continues to speak, looking over one shoulder, his sloppy handwriting filling up the board. He feels angry at Mr. Lawson suddenly. Somehow he feels betrayed.

"Gogol's literary career spanned a period of about eleven years, after which he was more or less paralyzed by writer's block. The last years of his life were marked by physical deterioration and emotional torment," Mr. Lawson says. "Desperate to restore his health and creative inspiration, Gogol sought refuge in a series of spas and sanatoriums. In 1848 he made a pilgrimage to Palestine. Eventually he returned to Russia. In 1852, in Moscow, disillusioned and convinced of his failure as a writer, he renounced all literary activity and burned the manuscript to the second volume of *Dead Souls*. He then pronounced a death sentence on himself, and proceeded to commit slow suicide by starvation."

"Gross," someone says from the back of the classroom. "Why would someone want to do that to himself?"

A few people glance at Emily Gardener, rumored to have anorexia.

Mr. Lawson, holding up a finger, goes on. "In attempts to revive him on the day before his death, doctors immersed him in a bath of broth while ice water was poured over his head, and then affixed seven leeches to his nose. His hands were pinned down so that he could not tear the worms away."

The class, all but one, begins to moan in unison, so that Mr. Lawson has to raise his voice considerably in order to be heard. Gogol stares at his desk, seeing nothing. He is convinced that the entire school is listening to Mr. Lawson's lecture. That it's on the PA. He lowers his head over his desk, discreetly presses his hands against his ears. It's not enough to block out Mr. Lawson: "By the following evening he was no longer fully conscious, and so wasted that his spine could be felt through his stomach." Gogol shuts his eyes. Please, stop, he wishes he could say to Mr. Lawson. Please stop, he says, mouthing the words. And then, suddenly, there is silence. Gogol looks up, sees Mr. Lawson drop his chalk on the blackboard ledge.

"I'll be right back," he says, and disappears to have a cigarette. The students, accustomed to this routine, begin talking among themselves. They complain about the story, saying that it's too long. They complain that it was hard to get through. There is talk of the difficulty of Russian names, students confessing merely to skimming them. Gogol says nothing. He has not read the story himself. He has never touched the Gogol book his father gave him on his fourteenth birthday. And yesterday, after class, he'd shoved the short story anthology deep into his locker, refusing to bring it home. To read the story, he believes, would mean paying tribute to his namesake, accepting it somehow. Still, listening to his classmates complain, he feels perversely responsible, as if his own work were being attacked.

Mr. Lawson returns, sitting once more on his desk. Gogol hopes that perhaps the biographical portion of the lecture is over. What else could he possibly have left to say? But Mr. Lawson picks up *Divided Soul.* "Here is an account of his final moments," he says, and, turning toward the end of the book, he reads:

"'His feet were icy. Tarasenkov slid a hot-water bottle into the bed, but it had no effect: he was shivering. Cold sweat covered his emaciated face. Blue circles appeared under his eyes. At midnight Dr. Klimentov relieved Dr. Tarasenkov. To ease the dying man, he administered a dose of calomel and placed loaves of hot bread around his body. Gogol began to moan again. His mind wandered, quietly, all night long. "Go on!" he whispered. "Rise up, charge, charge the mill!" Then he became still weaker, his face hollowed and darkened, his breathing became imperceptible. He seemed to grow calm; at least he was no longer suffering. At eight in the morning of February 21, 1852, he breathed his last. He was not yet forty-three years old.'"

Gogol does not date anyone in high school. He suffers quiet crushes, which he admits to no one, on this girl or that girl with whom he is already friends. He does not attend dances or parties. He and his group of friends, Colin and Jason and Marc, prefer to listen to records together, to Dylan and Clapton and The Who, and read Nietzsche in their spare time. His parents do not find it strange that their son doesn't date, does not rent a tuxedo for his junior prom. They have never been on a date in their lives and therefore they see no reason to encourage Gogol, certainly not at his age. Instead they urge him to join the math team and maintain his A average. His father presses him to pursue engineering, perhaps at MIT. Assured by his grades and his apparent indifference to girls, his parents don't suspect Gogol of being, in his own fumbling way, an American teenager. They don't suspect him, for instance, of smoking pot, which he does from time to time when he and his friends get together to listen to records at one another's homes. They don't suspect him, when he goes to spend the night at a friend's house, of driving to a neighboring town to see *The Rocky Horror Picture Show*, or into Boston to see bands in Kenmore Square.

One Saturday, soon before he is scheduled to take the SAT, his family drives to Connecticut for the weekend, leaving Gogol at home alone overnight for the first time in his life. It never crosses his parents' minds that instead of taking timed practice tests in his room, Gogol will drive with Colin and Jason and Marc to a party. They are invited by Colin's older brother, who is a freshman at the university where Gogol's father teaches. He dresses for the party as he normally does, in Levi's and boat shoes and a checkered flannel shirt. For all the times he's been to the campus, to visit his father at the engineering department or for swimming lessons or to run laps around the track, he has never been in a dorm before. They approach nervously, a bit giddy, afraid to be caught. "If anyone asks, my brother said to say we're freshmen at Amherst," Colin advises them in the car.

The party occupies an entire hallway, the doors of the individual rooms all open. They enter the first room they can manage to, crowded, dark, hot. No one notices as Gogol and his three friends make their way across the room to the keg. For a while, they stand in a circle, holding their plastic cups of beer, shouting over the music in order to be heard. But then Colin sees his brother in the hallway, and Jason needs to find a bathroom, and Marc needs another beer already. Gogol drifts into the hallway as well. Everyone seems to know everyone else, embroiled in conversations that are impossible to join. Music playing from the different rooms mingles unpleasantly in Gogol's ears. He feels too wholesome in this ripped jeans and T-shirt crowd, fears his hair was too recently washed and is too neatly combed. And yet it doesn't seem to matter, no one seems to care. At the end of the hallway, he climbs a set of stairs, and at the top there is another hallway, equally crowded and loud. In the corner he sees a couple kissing, pressed up against the wall. Instead of pushing his way through to the other end of the hallway, he decides to climb another set of stairs. This time the hallway is deserted, an expanse of dark blue carpeting and white wooden doors. The only presence in the space is the sound of muffled music and voices coming from below. He is about to turn back down the staircase when one of the doors opens and a girl emerges, a pretty, slender girl wearing a buttoned-up polka-dotted thrift store dress and scuffed Doc Martens. She has short, dark brown hair, curving in toward her cheeks and cut in a high fringe over her brows. Her face is heart-shaped, her lips painted a glamorous red.

"Sorry," Gogol says. "Am I not supposed to be up here?"

"Well, it's technically a girls' floor," the girl says. "But that's never stopped a guy before." She studies him thoughtfully, as no other girl has looked at him. "You don't go here, do you?"

"No," he says, his heart pounding. And then he remembers his surreptitious identity for the evening: "I'm a freshman at Amherst."

"That's cool," the girl says, walking toward him. "I'm Kim."

"Nice to meet you." He extends his hand, and Kim shakes it, a bit longer than necessary. For a moment she looks at him expectantly, then smiles, revealing two front teeth that are slightly overlapping.

"Come on," she says. "I can show you around." They walk together down the staircase. She leads him to a room where she gets herself a beer and he pours himself another. He stands awkwardly at her side as she pauses to say hello to friends. They work their way to a common area where there is a television, a Coke machine, a shabby sofa, and an assortment of chairs. They sit on the sofa, slouching, a considerable space between them. Kim notices a stray pack of cigarettes on the coffee table and lights one.

"Well?" she says, turning to look at him, somewhat suspiciously this time.

"What?"

"Aren't you going to introduce yourself to me?"

"Oh," he says. "Yeah." But he doesn't want to tell Kim his name. He doesn't want to endure her reaction, to watch her lovely blue eyes grow wide. He wishes there were another name he could use, just this once, to get him through the evening. It wouldn't be so terrible. He's lied to her already, about being at Amherst. He could introduce himself as Colin or Jason or Marc, as anybody at all, and their conversation could continue, and she would never know or care. There were a million names to choose from. But then he realizes there's no need to lie. Not technically. He remembers the other name that had once been chosen for him, the one that should have been.

"I'm Nikhil," he says for the first time in his life. He says it tentatively, his voice sounding strained to his ears, the statement turning without his meaning to into a question. He looks at Kim, his eyebrows furrowed, prepared for her to challenge him, to correct him, to laugh in his face. He holds his breath. His face tingles, whether from triumph or terror he isn't sure.

But Kim accepts it gladly. "Nikhil," she says, blowing a thin plume of smoke toward the ceiling. Again she turns to him and smiles. "Nikhil," she repeats. "I've never heard that before. That's a lovely name."

They sit awhile longer, the conversation continuing, Gogol stunned at how easy it is. His mind floats; he only half listens as Kim talks about her classes, about the town in Connecticut where she's from. He feels at once guilty and exhilarated, protected as if by an invisible shield. Because he knows he will never see her again, he is brave that evening, kissing her lightly on the mouth as she is talking to him, his leg pressing gently against her leg on the sofa, briefly running a hand through her hair. It is the first time he's kissed anyone, the first time he's felt a girl's face and body and breath so close to his own. "I can't believe you kissed her, Gogol," his friends exclaim as they drive home from the party. He shakes his head in a daze, as astonished as they are, elation still welling inside him. "It wasn't me," he nearly says. But he doesn't tell them that it hadn't been Gogol who'd kissed Kim. That Gogol had had nothing to do with it.

5

PLENTY of people changed their names: actors, writers, revolutionaries, transvestites. In history class, Gogol has learned that European immigrants had their names changed at Ellis Island, that slaves renamed themselves once they were emancipated. Though Gogol doesn't know it, even Nikolai Gogol renamed himself, simplifying his surname at the age of twenty-two from Gogol-Yanovsky to Gogol upon publication in the *Literary Gazette*. (He had also published under the name Yanov, and once signed his work "OOOO" in honor of the four *o*'s in his full name.)

One day in the summer of 1986, in the frantic weeks before moving away from his family, before his freshman year at Yale is about to begin, Gogol Ganguli does the same. He rides the commuter rail into Boston, switching to the Green Line at North Station, getting out at Lechmere. The area is somewhat familiar: he has been to Lechmere countless times with his family, to buy new televisions and vacuum cleaners, and he has been to the Museum of Science on field trips from school. But he has never been to this neighborhood on his own, and in spite of the directions he's written on a sheet of paper he gets briefly lost on his way to the Middlesex Probate and Family

Court. He wears a blue oxford shirt, khakis, a camel-colored corduroy blazer bought for his college interviews that is too warm for the sultry day. Knotted around his neck is his only tie, maroon with yellow stripes on the diagonal. By now Gogol is just shy of six feet tall, his body slender, his thick brown-black hair slightly in need of a cut. His face is lean, intelligent, suddenly handsome, the bones more prominent, the pale gold skin clean-shaven and clear. He has inherited Ashima's eyes, large, penetrating, with bold, elegant brows, and shares with Ashoke the slight bump at the very top of his nose.

The courthouse is an imposing, old, pillared brick building occupying a full city block, but the entrance is off to the side, down a set of steps. Inside, Gogol empties his pockets and steps through a metal detector, as if he were at an airport, about to embark on a journey. He is soothed by the chill of the air-conditioning, by the beautifully carved plaster ceiling, by the voices that echo pleasantly in the marbled interior. He had pictured a setting far less grand. And yet this is a place, he gathers, that people come to seek divorces, dispute wills. A man at the information booth tells him to wait upstairs, in an area filled with round tables, where people sit eating their lunch. Gogol sits impatiently, one long leg jiggling up and down. He has forgotten to bring a book to read and so he picks up a discarded section of the *Globe*, skimming an article in the "Arts" section about Andrew Wyeth's Helga paintings. Eventually he begins to practice his new signature in the margins of the paper. He tries it in various styles, his hand unaccustomed to the angles of the *N*, the dotting of the two *i*'s. He wonders how many times he has written his old name, at the tops of how many tests and quizzes, how many homework assignments, how many year-book inscriptions to friends. How many times does a person write his name in a lifetime — a million? Two million?

The idea to change his name had first occurred to him a few

months ago. He was sitting in the waiting room of his dentist, flipping through an issue of *Reader's Digest*. He'd been turning the pages at random until he came to an article that caused him to stop. The article was called "Second Baptisms." "Can you identify the following famous people?" was written beneath the headline. A list of names followed and, at the bottom of the page, printed in tiny letters upside down, the famous personalities they corresponded to. The only one he guessed correctly was Robert Zimmerman, Bob Dylan's real name. He had no idea that Molière had been born Jean-Baptiste Poquelin and that Leon Trotsky was born Lev Davidovich Bronstein. That Gerald Ford's name was Leslie Lynch King, Jr., and that Engelbert Humperdinck's was Arnold George Dorsey. They had all renamed themselves, the article said, adding that it was a right belonging to every American citizen. He read that tens of thousands of Americans had their names changed each year. All it took was a legal petition, the article had said. And suddenly he envisioned "Gogol" added to the list of names, "Nikhil" printed in tiny letters upside down.

That night at the dinner table, he brought it up with his parents. It was one thing for Gogol to be the name penned in calligraphy on his high school diploma, and printed below his picture in the yearbook, he'd begun. It was one thing, even, for it to be typed on his applications to five Ivy League colleges, as well as to Stanford and Berkeley. But engraved, four years from now, on a bachelor of arts degree? Written at the top of a résumé? Centered on a business card? It would be the name his parents picked out for him, he assured them, the good name they'd chosen for him when he was five.

"What's done is done," his father had said. "It will be a hassle. Gogol has, in effect, become your good name."

"It's too complicated now," his mother said, agreeing. "You're too old."

"I'm not," he persisted. "I don't get it. Why did you have to give me a pet name in the first place? What's the point?"

"It's our way, Gogol," his mother maintained. "It's what Bengalis do."

"But it's not even a Bengali name."

He told his parents what he'd learned in Mr. Lawson's class, about Gogol's lifelong unhappiness, his mental instability, about how he'd starved himself to death. "Did you know all this stuff about him?" he asked.

"You forgot to mention that he was also a genius," his father said.

"I don't get it. How could you guys name me after someone so strange? No one takes me seriously," Gogol said.

"Who? Who does not take you seriously?" his father wanted to know, lifting his fingers from his plate, looking up at him.

"People," he said, lying to his parents. For his father had a point; the only person who didn't take Gogol seriously, the only person who tormented him, the only person chronically aware of and afflicted by the embarrassment of his name, the only person who constantly questioned it and wished it were otherwise, was Gogol. And yet he'd continued, saying that they should be glad, that his official name would be Bengali, not Russian.

"I don't know, Gogol," his mother had said, shaking her head. "I really don't know." She got up to clear the dishes. Sonia slinked away, up to her room. Gogol remained at the table with his father. They sat there together, listening to his mother scraping the plates, the water running in the sink.

"Then change it," his father said simply, quietly, after a while.

"Really?"

"In America anything is possible. Do as you wish."

And so he had obtained a Commonwealth of Massachusetts

change-of-name form, to submit along with a certified copy of
his birth certificate and a check to the Middlesex Probate and
Family Court. He'd brought the form to his father, who had
glanced at it only briefly before signing his consent, with the
same resignation with which he signed a check or a credit card
receipt, his eyebrows slightly raised over his glasses, inwardly
calculating the loss. He'd filled out the rest of the form in his
room, late at night when his family was asleep. The application consisted of a single side of a cream-colored sheet, and
yet it had taken him longer to fill out than his applications for
college. On the first line he filled out the name he wished to
change, and his place and date of birth. He wrote in the new
name he wished to adopt, then signed the form with his old
signature. Only one part of the form had given him pause: in
approximately three lines, he was asked to provide a reason for
seeking the change. For nearly an hour he'd sat there, wondering what to write. He'd left it blank in the end.

At the appointed time, his case is called. He enters a room
and sits on an empty wooden bench at the back. The judge,
a middle-aged, heavyset black woman wearing half-moon
glasses, sits opposite, on a dais. The clerk, a thin young woman
with bobbed hair, asks for his application, reviewing it before
handing it to the judge. There is nothing decorating the room
apart from the Massachusetts state and American flags and an
oil portrait of a judge. "Gogol Ganguli," the clerk says, motioning for Gogol to approach the dais, and as eager as he is to go
through with it, he is aware, with a twinge of sadness, that this
is the last time in his life he will hear that name uttered in an
official context. In spite of his parents' sanction he feels that he
is overstepping them, correcting a mistake they've made.

"What is the reason you wish to change your name, Mr.
Ganguli?" the judge asks.

The question catches him off-guard, and for several seconds

he has no idea what to say. "Personal reasons," he says eventually.

The judge looks at him, leaning forward, her chin cupped in her hand. "Would you care to be more specific?"

At first he says nothing, unprepared to give any further explanation. He wonders whether to tell the judge the whole convoluted story, about his great-grandmother's letter that never made it to Cambridge, and about pet names and good names, about what had happened on the first day of kindergarten. But instead he takes a deep breath and tells the people in the courtroom what he has never dared admit to his parents. "I hate the name Gogol," he says. "I've always hated it."

"Very well," the judge says, stamping and signing the form, then returning it to the clerk. He is told that notice of the new name must be given to all other agencies, that it's his responsibility to notify the Registry of Motor Vehicles, banks, schools. He orders three certified copies of the name change decree, two for himself, and one for his parents to keep in their safe-deposit box. No one accompanies him on this legal rite of passage, and when he steps out of the room no one is waiting to commemorate the moment with flowers and Polaroid snapshots and balloons. In fact the procedure is entirely unmomentous, and when he looks at his watch he sees that from the time he'd entered the courtroom it had taken all of ten minutes. He emerges into the muggy afternoon, perspiring, still partly convinced it is a dream. He takes the T across the river to Boston. He walks with his blazer clasped by a finger over his shoulder, across the Common, through the Public Garden, over the bridges and along the curving paths that rim the lagoon. Thick clouds conceal the sky, which appears only here and there like the small lakes on a map, and the air threatens rain.

He wonders if this is how it feels for an obese person to become thin, for a prisoner to walk free. "I'm Nikhil," he wants to tell the people who are walking their dogs, pushing children in their strollers, throwing bread to the ducks. He wanders up Newbury Street as drops begin to fall. He dashes into Newbury Comics, buys himself *London Calling* and *Talking Heads: 77* with his birthday money, a Che poster for his dorm room. He pockets an application for a student American Express card, grateful that his first credit card will not say Gogol in raised letters at the bottom. "I'm Nikhil," he is tempted to tell the attractive, nose-ringed cashier with dyed black hair and skin as pale as paper. The cashier hands him his change and looks past him to the next customer, but it doesn't matter; instead he thinks of how many more women he can now approach, for the rest of his life, with this same unobjectionable, uninteresting fact. Still, for the next three weeks, even though his new driver's license says "Nikhil," even though he's sliced up the old one with his mother's sewing scissors, even though he's ripped out the pages in front of his favorite books in which he'd written his name until now, there's a snag: everyone he knows in the world still calls him Gogol. He is aware that his parents, and their friends, and the children of their friends, and all his own friends from high school, will never call him anything but Gogol. He will remain Gogol during holidays and in summer; Gogol will revisit him on each of his birthdays. Everyone who comes to his going-away-to-college party writes "Good Luck, Gogol" on the cards.

It isn't until his first day in New Haven, after his father and teary mother and Sonia are heading back up 95 toward Boston, that he begins to introduce himself as Nikhil. The first people to call him by his new name are his suitemates, Brandon and Jonathan, both of whom had been notified by mail over the summer that his name is Gogol. Brandon, lanky and blond, grew up in Massachusetts not far from Gogol, and went to Andover. Jonathan, who is Korean and plays the cello, comes from L.A.

"Is Gogol your first name or your last?" Brandon wants to know.

Normally that question agitates him. But today he has a new answer. "Actually, that's my middle name," Gogol says by way of explanation, sitting with them in the common room to their suite. "Nikhil is my first name. It got left out for some reason."

Jonathan nods in acceptance, distracted by the task of setting up his stereo components. Brandon nods, too. "Hey, Nikhil," Brandon says awhile later, after they have arranged the furniture in the common room to their liking. "Want to smoke a bowl?" Since everything else is suddenly so new, going by a new name doesn't feel so terribly strange to Gogol. He lives in a new state, has a new telephone number. He eats his meals off a tray in Commons, shares a bathroom with a floor full of people, showers each morning in a stall. He sleeps in a new bed, which his mother had insisted on making before she left.

He spends the days of orientation rushing around campus, back and forth along the intersecting flagstone path, past the clock tower, and the turreted, crenelated buildings. He is too harried, at first, to sit on the grass in Old Campus as the other students do, perusing their course catalogues, playing Frisbee, getting to know one another among the verdigris-covered statues of robed, seated men. He makes a list of all the places he has to go, circling the buildings on his campus map. When he is alone in his room he types out a written request on his Smith Corona, notifying the registrar's office of his name change, providing examples of his former and current signatures side by side. He gives these documents to a secretary, along with a copy of the change-of-name form. He tells his freshman counselor about his name change; he tells the person in charge of processing his student ID and his library card. He corrects the error in stealth, not bothering to explain to Jonathan and Brandon what he's so busy doing all day, and then suddenly it is over. After so much work it is no work at all. By the time the upperclassmen arrive and classes begin, he's paved the way for a whole university to call him Nikhil: students and professors and TAs and girls at parties. Nikhil registers for his first four classes: Intro to the History of Art, Medieval History, a semester of Spanish, Astronomy to fulfill his hard science requirement. At the last minute he registers for a drawing class in the evenings. He doesn't tell his parents about the drawing class, something they would consider frivolous at this stage of his life, in spite of the fact that his own grandfather was an artist. They are already distressed that he hasn't settled on a major and a profession. Like the rest of their Bengali friends, his parents expect him to be, if not an engineer, then a doctor, a lawyer, an economist at the very least. These were the fields that brought them to America, his father repeatedly reminds him, the professions that have earned them security and respect.

But now that he's Nikhil it's easier to ignore his parents, to tune out their concerns and pleas. With relief, he types his name at the tops of his freshman papers. He reads the telephone messages his suitemates leave for Nikhil on assorted scraps in their rooms. He opens up a checking account, writes his new name into course books. *"Me llamo Nikhil,"* he says in his Spanish class. It is as Nikhil, that first semester, that he grows a goatee, starts smoking Camel Lights at parties and while writing papers and before exams, discovers Brian Eno and Elvis Costello and Charlie Parker. It is as Nikhil that he takes Metro-North into Manhattan one weekend with Jonathan and gets himself a fake ID that allows him to be served liquor in New Haven bars. It is as Nikhil that he loses his virginity at a party at Ezra Stiles, with a girl wearing a plaid woolen skirt and combat boots and mustard tights. By the time he wakes up, hung-over, at three in the morning, she has vanished from the room, and he is unable to recall her name.

There is only one complication: he doesn't feel like Nikhil. Not yet. Part of the problem is that the people who now know him as Nikhil have no idea that he used to be Gogol. They know him only in the present, not at all in the past. But after eighteen years of Gogol, two months of Nikhil feel scant, inconsequential. At times he feels as if he's cast himself in a play, acting the part of twins, indistinguishable to the naked eye yet fundamentally different. At times he still feels his old name, painfully and without warning, the way his front tooth had unbearably throbbed in recent weeks after a filling, threatening for an instant to sever from his gums when he drank coffee, or iced water, and once when he was riding in an elevator. He fears being discovered, having the whole charade somehow unravel, and in nightmares his files are exposed, his original name printed on the front page of the *Yale Daily News*. Once, he signs his old name by mistake on a credit card slip at the college bookstore. Occasionally he has to hear Nikhil three times before he answers.

Even more startling is when those who normally call him Gogol refer to him as Nikhil. For example, when his parents call on Saturday mornings, if Brandon or Jonathan happens to pick up the phone, they ask if Nikhil is there. Though he has asked his parents to do precisely this, the fact of it troubles him, making him feel in that instant that he is not related to them, not their child. "Please come to our home with Nikhil one weekend," Ashima says to his roommates when she and Ashoke visit campus during parents weekend in October, the suite hastily cleared of liquor bottles and ashtrays and Brandon's bong for the occasion. The substitution sounds wrong to Gogol, correct but off-key, the way it sounds when his parents speak English to him instead of Bengali. Stranger still is when one of his parents addresses him, in front of his new friends, as Nikhil directly: "Nikhil, show us the buildings where you have your classes," his father suggests. Later that evening, out to dinner with Jonathan at a restaurant on Chapel Street, Ashima slips, asking, "Gogol, have you decided yet what your major will be?" Though Jonathan, listening to something his father is saying, doesn't hear, Gogol feels helpless, annoyed yet unable to blame his mother, caught in the mess he's made.

During his first semester, obediently but unwillingly, he goes home every other weekend, after his last Friday class. He rides Amtrak to Boston and then switches to a commuter rail, his duffel bag stuffed with course books and dirty laundry. Somewhere along the two-and-a-half-hour journey, Nikhil evaporates and Gogol claims him again. His father comes to the station to fetch him, always calling ahead to check whether the train is on time. Together they drive through the town, along the familiar tree-lined roads, his father asking after his studies. Between Friday night and Sunday afternoon the laundry, thanks to his mother, gets done, but the course books are neglected; in spite of his intentions, Gogol finds himself capable of doing little at his parents' but eat and sleep. The desk in his room feels too small. He is distracted by the telephone ringing, by his parents and Sonia talking and moving through the house. He misses Sterling Library, where he studies every night after dinner, and the nocturnal schedule of which he is now a part. He misses being in his suite in Farnam, smoking one of Brandon's cigarettes, listening to music with Jonathan, learning how to tell the classical composers apart.

At home he watches MTV with Sonia as she doctors her jeans, cutting inches off the bottoms and inserting zippers at the newly narrowed ankles. One weekend, the washing machine is occupied because Sonia is in the process of dyeing the vast majority of her clothing black. She is in high school now, taking Mr. Lawson's English class, going to the dances Gogol never went to himself, already going to parties at which both boys and girls are present. Her braces have come off her teeth, revealing a confident, frequent, American smile. Her formerly shoulder-length hair has been chopped asymmetrically by one of her friends. Ashima lives in fear that Sonia will color a streak of it blond, as Sonia has threatened on more than one occasion to do, and that she will have additional holes pierced in her earlobes at the mall. They argue violently about such things, Ashima crying, Sonia slamming doors. Some weekends his parents are invited to parties, and they insist that both Gogol and Sonia go with them. The host or hostess shows him to a room where he can study alone while the party thunders below, but he always ends up watching television with Sonia and the other children, just as he has done all his life. "I'm eighteen," he says once to his parents as they drive back from a party, a fact that makes no difference to them. One weekend Gogol makes the mistake of referring to New Haven as home. "Sorry, I left it at home," he says when his father asks if he remembered to buy the Yale decal his parents want to paste to the rear window of their car. Ashima is outraged by the remark, dwelling on it all day. "Only three months, and listen to you," she says, telling him that after twenty years in America, she still cannot bring herself to refer to Pemberton Road as home.

But now it is his room at Yale where Gogol feels most comfortable. He likes its oldness, its persistent grace. He likes that so many students have occupied it before him. He likes the solidity of its plaster walls, its dark wooden floorboards, however battered and stained. He likes the dormer window he sees first thing in the mornings when he opens his eyes and looking at Battell Chapel. He has fallen in love with the Gothic architecture of the campus, always astonished by the physical beauty that surrounds him, that roots him to his environs in a way he had never felt growing up on Pemberton Road. For his drawing class, in which he is required to make half a dozen sketches every week, he is inspired to draw the details of buildings: flying buttresses, pointed archways filled with flowing tracery, thick rounded doorways, squat columns of pale pink stone. In the spring semester he takes an introductory class in architecture. He reads about how the pyramids and Greek temples and Medieval cathedrals were built, studying the plans of churches and palaces in his textbook. He learns the endless terms, the vocabulary that classifies the details of ancient buildings, writing them on separate index cards and making illustrations on the back: architrave, entablature, tympanum, voussoir. Together the words form another language he longs to know. He files these index cards in a shoebox, reviews them before the exam, memorizing far more terms than he needs to, keeping the box of cards even after the exam is done, adding to them in his spare time.

In the autumn of his sophomore year, he boards a particularly crowded train at Union Station. It is the Wednesday before Thanksgiving. He edges through the compartments, his duffel bag heavy with books for his Renaissance architecture class, for which he has to write a paper over the next five days. Passengers have already staked out parts of the vestibule, sitting glumly on their luggage. "Standing room only," the conductor hollers. "I want my money back," a passenger complains. Gogol keeps walking, from one compartment to the next, looking for an uncrowded vestibule in which he might sit. In the very last car of the train he sees an empty seat. A girl is seated next to the window, reading a folded-back issue of *The New Yorker*. Arranged on the seat beside her is a chocolate brown, shearling-lined suede coat, which is what had caused the person in front of Gogol to move on. But something tells Gogol the coat belongs to the girl, and so he stops and says, "Is that yours?"

She lifts up her narrow body and in a single, swift motion arranges the coat beneath her buttocks and legs. It's a face he recognizes from campus, someone he's crossed paths with in the corridors of buildings as he walks to and from class. He remembers that freshman year she'd had hair dyed an emphatic shade of cranberry red, cut to her jaw. She's grown it to her shoulders now, and allowed it to resume what appears to be its natural shade, light brown with bits of blond here and there. It is parted just off-center, a bit crooked at the base. The hair of her eyebrows is darker, lending her otherwise friendly features a serious expression. She wears a pair of nicely faded jeans, brown leather boots with yellow laces and thick rubber soles. A cabled sweater the same flecked gray of her eyes is too large for her, the sleeves coming partway up her hands. A man's billfold bulges prominently from the front pocket of her jeans.

"Hi, I'm Ruth," she says, recognizing him in that same vague way.

"I'm Nikhil." He sits, too exhausted to put his duffel bag away in the luggage rack overhead. He shoves it as best he can under his seat, his long legs bent awkwardly, aware that he is perspiring. He unzips his blue down parka. He massages his fingers, crisscrossed with welts from the leather straps of the bag.

"Sorry," Ruth says, watching him. "I guess I was just trying to put off the inevitable."

Still seated, he pries his arms free of the parka. "What do you mean?"

"Making it look like someone was sitting here. With the coat."

"It's pretty brilliant, actually. Sometimes I pretend to fall asleep for the same reason," he admits. "No one wants to sit next to me if I'm sleeping."

She laughs softly, putting a strand of her hair behind her ear. Her beauty is direct, unassuming. She wears no make-up apart from something glossy on her lips; two small brown moles by her right cheekbone are the only things that distract from the pale peach of her complexion. She has slim, small hands with unpolished nails and ragged cuticles. She leans over to put the magazine away and get a book from the bag at her feet, and he briefly glimpses the skin above her waistband.

"Are you going to Boston?" he asks.

"Maine. That's where my dad lives. I have to switch to a bus at South Station. It's another four hours from there. What college are you in?"

"J. E."

He learns that she is in Silliman, that she is planning to be an English major. Comparing notes of their experiences at college so far, they discover that they had both taken Psychology 110 the previous spring. The book in her hands is a paperback copy of *Timon of Athens*, and though she keeps a finger marking her page she never reads a word of it. Nor does he bother to open up the volume on perspective he's pulled out of his duffel. She tells him she was raised on a commune in Vermont, the child of hippies, educated at home until the seventh grade. Her parents are divorced now. Her father lives with her stepmother, raising llamas on a farm. Her mother, an anthropologist, is doing field-work on midwives in Thailand.

He cannot imagine coming from such parents, such a background, and when he describes his own upbringing it feels bland by comparison. But Ruth expresses interest, asking about his visits to Calcutta. She tells him her parents went to India once, to an ashram somewhere, before she was born. She asks what the streets are like, and the houses, and so on the blank back page of his book on perspective Gogol draws a floor plan of his maternal grandparents' flat, navigating Ruth along the verandas and the terrazzo floors, telling her about the chalky blue walls, the narrow stone kitchen, the sitting room with cane furniture that looked as if it belonged on a porch. He draws with confidence, thanks to the drafting course he is taking this term. He shows her the room where he and Sonia sleep when they visit, and describes the view of the tiny lane lined with corrugated tin–roofed businesses. When he is finished, Ruth takes the book from him and looks at the drawing he's made, trailing her finger through the rooms. "I'd love to go," she says, and suddenly he imagines her face and arms tan, a back-pack strapped to her shoulders, walking along Chowringhee as other Western tourists do, shopping in New Market, staying at the Grand.

As they are talking a woman across the aisle reprimands them; she's been trying to take a nap, she says. This only goads them into talking further, in lowered voices, their heads leaning in toward each other. Gogol is unaware of which state they are in, which stations they've passed. The train rumbles over a bridge; the setting sun is feverishly beautiful, casting a striking pink glow on the facades of the clapboard houses that dot the water's edge. In minutes these shades fade, replaced by the pallor that precedes dusk. When it is dark he sees that their images are reflected at an angle in the glass, hovering as if outside the train. Their throats are parched from talking and at one point he offers to go to the café car. She asks him to get her a bag of potato chips and a cup of tea with milk. He likes that she doesn't bother to pull the billfold out of her jeans, that she allows him to buy them for her. He returns with a coffee for himself, and the chips and the tea, along with a paper cup of milk the bartender has given him instead of the regulation container of cream. They continue talking, Ruth eating the chips, brushing the salt from around her lips with the back of her hand. She offers some to Gogol, pulling them out for him one by one. He tells her about the meals he'd eaten on Indian trains the time he traveled with his family to Delhi and Agra, the rotis and slightly sour dal ordered at one station and delivered hot at the next, the thick vegetable cutlets served with bread and butter for breakfast. He tells her about the tea, how it was bought through the window from men on the platform who poured it from giant aluminum kettles, the milk and sugar already mixed in, and how it was drunk in crude clay cups that were smashed afterward on the tracks. Her appreciation for these details flatters him; it occurs to him that he has never spoken of his experiences in India to any American friend.

They part suddenly, Gogol working up the nerve to ask for her number at the last minute, writing it into the same book where he'd drawn her the floor plan. He wishes he could wait with her at South Station for her bus to Maine, but he has a commuter train to catch in ten minutes to take him to the suburbs. The days of the holiday feel endless; all he can think of is getting back to New Haven and calling Ruth. He wonders how many times they've crossed paths, how many meals they've unwittingly shared in Commons. He thinks back to Psychology 110, wishing his memory would yield some image of her, taking notes on the other side of the law school auditorium, her head bent over her desk. Most often he thinks of the train, longs to sit beside her again, imagines their faces flushed from the heat of the compartment, their bodies cramped in the same way, her hair shining from the yellow lights overhead. On the ride back he looks for her, combing each and every compartment, but she is nowhere and he ends up sitting next to an elderly nun with a brown habit and prominent white down on her upper lip, who snores all the way.

The following week, back at Yale, Ruth agrees to meet him

for coffee at the Atticus bookshop. She is a few minutes late and dressed in the same jeans and boots and chocolate suede coat she'd worn when they met. Again she asks for tea. At first he senses an awkwardness he hadn't felt on the train. The café feels loud and hectic, the table between them too wide. Ruth is quieter than before, looking down at her cup and playing with the sugar packets, her eyes occasionally wandering to the books that line the walls. But soon enough they are conversing easily, as they had before, exchanging tales of their respective holidays. He tells her about how he and Sonia occupied the kitchen on Pemberton Road for a day, stuffing a turkey and rolling out dough for pies, things his mother did not particularly like to do. "I looked for you on my way back," he admits to her, telling her about the snoring nun. Afterward they walk together through the Center for British Art; there is an exhibit of Renaissance works on paper, which they've both been meaning to see. He walks her back to Silliman, and they arrange to have coffee a few days later. After saying good night, Ruth lingers by the gate, looking down at the books pressed up to her chest, and he wonders if he should kiss her, which is what he's been wanting to do for hours, or whether, in her mind, they are only friends. She starts walking backward toward her entryway, smiling at him, taking an impressive number of steps before giving a final wave and turning away.

He begins to meet her after her classes, remembering her schedule, looking up at the buildings and hovering casually under the archways. She always seems pleased to see him, stepping away from her girlfriends to say hello. "Of course she likes you," Jonathan tells Gogol, patiently listening to a minute account of their acquaintance one night in the dining hall. A few days later, following Ruth back to her room because she's forgotten a book she needs for a class, he places his hand over hers as she reaches for the doorknob. Her roommates are out. He

waits for her on the sofa in the common room as she searches
for the book. It is the middle of the day, overcast, lightly raining. "Found it," she says, and though they both have classes,
they remain in the room, sitting on the sofa and kissing until it
is too late to bother going.

Every evening they study together at the library, sitting at
either end of a table to keep from whispering. She takes him
to her dining hall, and he to hers. He takes her to the sculpture garden. He thinks of her constantly, while leaning over
the slanted board in his drafting class, under the strong white
lights of the studio, and in the darkened lecture hall of his Renaissance architecture class, as images of Palladian villas flash
onto the screen from a slide projector. Within weeks the end of
the semester is upon them, and they are besieged by exams and
papers and hundreds of pages of reading. Far more than the
amount of work he faces, he dreads the month of separation
they will have to endure at winter break. One Saturday afternoon, just before exams, she mentions to him in the library that
both her roommates will be out all day. They walk together
through Cross Campus, back to Silliman, and he sits with her
on her unmade bed. The room smells as she does, a powdery
floral smell that lacks the acridness of perfume. Postcards of
authors are taped to the wall over her desk, Oscar Wilde and
Virginia Woolf. Their lips and faces are still numb from the
cold, and at first they still keep their coats on. They lie together
against the shearling lining of hers, and she guides his hand beneath her bulky sweater. It had not been like this the first time,
the only other time, that he'd been with a girl. He recalled
nothing from that episode, only being thankful, afterward, that
he was no longer a virgin.

But this time he is aware of everything, the warm hollow of
Ruth's abdomen, the way her lank hair rests in thick strands on
the pillow, the way her features change slightly when she is ly-

ing down. "You're great, Nikhil," she whispers as he touches small breasts set wide apart, one pale nipple slightly larger than the other. He kisses them, kisses the moles scattered on her stomach as she arcs gently toward him, feels her hands on his head and then on his shoulders, guiding him between her parted legs. He feels inept, clumsy, as he tastes and smells her there, and yet he hears her whispering his name, telling him it feels wonderful. She knows what to do, unzipping his jeans, standing up at one point and getting a diaphragm case from her bureau drawer.

A week later he is home again, helping Sonia and his mother decorate the tree, shoveling the driveway with his father, going to the mall to buy last-minute gifts. He mopes around the house, restless, pretending to be coming down with a cold. He wishes he could simply borrow his parents' car and drive up to Maine to see Ruth after Christmas, or that she could visit him. He was perfectly welcome, she'd assured him, her father and stepmother wouldn't mind. They'd put him in the guest room, she'd said; at night he'd creep into her bed. He imagines himself in the farmhouse she's described to him, waking up to eggs frying in a skillet, walking with her through snowy, abandoned fields. But such a trip would require telling his parents about Ruth, something he has no desire to do. He has no patience for their surprise, their nervousness, their quiet disappointment, their questions about what Ruth's parents did and whether or not the relationship was serious. As much as he longs to see her, he cannot picture her at the kitchen table on Pemberton Road, in her jeans and her bulky sweater, politely eating his mother's food. He cannot imagine being with her in the house where he is still Gogol.

He speaks to her when his family is asleep, quietly in the empty kitchen, charging the calls to his telephone at school. They arrange to meet one day in Boston and spend the day

together in Harvard Square. There is a foot of snow on the
ground, and the sky is a piercing blue. They go first to a movie
at the Brattle, buying tickets for whatever is about to begin, sitting at the back of the balcony and kissing, causing people to
turn back and stare. They have lunch at Cafe Pamplona, eating
pressed ham sandwiches and bowls of garlic soup off in a corner. They exchange presents: she gives him a small used book
of drawings by Goya, and he gives her a pair of blue woolen
mittens and a mixed tape of his favorite Beatles songs. They
discover a store just above the café that sells nothing but architecture books, and he browses the aisles, treating himself to a
paperback edition of Le Corbusier's *Journey to the East*, for he
is thinking of declaring himself an architecture major in the
spring. Afterward they wander hand in hand, kissing now and
then against a building, along the very streets he was pushed up
and down in his stroller as a child. He shows her the American
professor's house where he and his parents once lived, a time
before Sonia was born, years that he has no memory of. He's
seen the house in pictures, knows from his parents the name
of the street. Whoever lives there now appears to be away; the
snow hasn't been cleared from the porch steps, and a number of rolled-up newspapers have collected on the doormat. "I
wish we could go inside," he says. "I wish we could be alone together." Looking at the house now, with Ruth at his side, her
mittened hand in his, he feels strangely helpless. Though he
was only an infant at the time, he feels nevertheless betrayed by
his inability to know then that one day, years later, he would return to the house under such different circumstances, and that
he would be so happy.

By the following year his parents know vaguely about Ruth.
Though he has been to the farmhouse in Maine twice, meeting
her father and her stepmother, Sonia, who secretly has a boy-

friend these days, is the only person in his family to have met Ruth, during a weekend when Sonia came to New Haven. His parents have expressed no curiosity about his girlfriend. His relationship with her is one accomplishment in his life about which they are not in the least bit proud or pleased. Ruth tells him she doesn't mind his parents' disapproval, that she finds it romantic. But Gogol knows it isn't right. He wishes his parents could simply accept her, as her family accepts him, without pressure of any kind. "You're too young to get involved this way," Ashoke and Ashima tell him. They've even gone so far as to point out examples of Bengali men they know who've married Americans, marriages that have ended in divorce. It only makes things worse when he says that marriage is the last thing on his mind. At times he hangs up on them. He pities his parents when they speak to him this way, for having no experience of being young and in love. He suspects that they are secretly glad when Ruth goes away to Oxford for a semester. She'd mentioned her interest in going there long ago, in the first weeks of their courtship, when the spring of junior year had felt like a remote speck on the horizon. She'd asked him if he minded if she applied, and though the idea of her being so far had made him queasy he'd said no, of course not, that twelve weeks would go like that.

He is lost that spring without her. He spends all his time in the studio, especially the Friday nights and weekends he would normally have been with her, the two of them eating at Naples and going to see movies in the law school auditorium. He listens to the music she loves: Simon and Garfunkel, Neil Young, Cat Stevens, buying himself brand-new copies of the albums she'd inherited from her parents. It sickens him to think of the physical distance between them, to think that when he is asleep at night she is leaning over a sink somewhere, brushing her teeth and washing her face to start the next day. He longs for her as his parents have longed, all these years, for the people they love in India—for the first time in his life, he knows this feeling. But his parents refuse to give him the money to fly to England on his spring break. He spends what little money he has from working in the dining hall on transatlantic phone calls to Ruth twice a week. Twice a day he checks his campus mailbox for letters and postcards stamped with the multicolored profiles of the queen. He carries these letters and postcards wherever he goes, stuck into his books. "My Shakespeare class is the best I've ever taken," she's written in violet-colored ink. "The coffee is undrinkable. Everyone constantly says 'cheers.' I think of you all the time."

One day he attends a panel discussion about Indian novels written in English. He feels obligated to attend; one of the presenters on the panel, Amit, is a distant cousin who lives in Bombay, whom Gogol has never met. His mother has asked him to greet Amit on her behalf. Gogol is bored by the panelists, who keep referring to something called "marginality," as if it were some sort of medical condition. For most of the hour, he sketches portraits of the panelists, who sit hunched over their papers along a rectangular table. "Teleologically speaking, ABCDs are unable to answer the question 'Where are you from?'" the sociologist on the panel declares. Gogol has never heard the term *ABCD*. He eventually gathers that it stands for "American-born confused deshi." In other words, him. He learns that the *C* could also stand for "conflicted." He knows that *deshi*, a generic word for "countryman," means "Indian," knows that his parents and all their friends always refer to India simply as *desh*. But Gogol never thinks of India as desh. He thinks of it as Americans do, as India.

Gogol slouches in his seat and ponders certain awkward truths. For instance, although he can understand his mother tongue, and speak it fluently, he cannot read or write it with even modest proficiency. On trips to India his American-accented English is a source of endless amusement to his relatives, and when he and Sonia speak to each other, aunts and uncles and cousins always shake their heads in disbelief and say, "I didn't understand a word!" Living with a pet name and a good name, in a place where such distinctions do not exist—surely that was emblematic of the greatest confusion of all. He searches the audience for someone he knows, but it isn't his crowd—lots of lit majors with leather satchels and gold-rimmed glasses and fountain pens, lots of people Ruth would have waved to. There are also lots of ABCDs. He has no idea there are this many on campus. He has no ABCD friends at college. He avoids them, for they remind him too much of the way his parents choose to live, befriending people not so much because they like them, but because of a past they happen to share. "Gogol, why aren't you a member of the Indian association here?" Amit asks later when they go for a drink at the Anchor. "I just don't have the time," Gogol says, not telling his well-meaning cousin that he can think of no greater hypocrisy than joining an organization that willingly celebrates occasions his parents forced him, throughout his childhood and adolescence, to attend. "I'm Nikhil now," Gogol says, suddenly depressed by how many more times he will have to say this, asking people to remember, reminding them to forget, feeling as if an errata slip were perpetually pinned to his chest.

Thanksgiving of his senior year he takes the train, alone, up to Boston. He and Ruth are no longer together. Instead of coming back from Oxford after those twelve weeks, she'd stayed on to do a summer course, explaining that a professor she admired would be retiring after that. Gogol had spent the summer on Pemberton Road. He had had an unpaid internship at a small architecture firm in Cambridge, where he'd run errands at Charrette for the designers, been sent to photograph nearby sites, lettered a few drawings. To make money he worked nights washing dishes at an Italian restaurant in his parents' town. Late in August he'd gone to Logan to welcome Ruth home. He had waited for her at the arrival gate, taken her to a hotel for one night, paying for it with the money he'd made at the restaurant. The room overlooked the Public Garden, its walls covered with thickly striped pink-and-cream paper. They'd made love for the first time in a double bed. They'd gone out for their meals, neither of them able to afford the items on the room service menu. They walked up Newbury Street and went to a Greek restaurant with tables on the sidewalk. The day was blazing hot. Ruth looked the same, but her speech was peppered with words and phrases she'd picked up in England, like "I imagine" and "I suppose" and "presumably." She spoke of her semester and how much she'd liked England, the traveling she'd done in Barcelona and Rome. She wanted to go back to England for graduate school, she said. "I imagine they've got good architecture schools," she'd added. "You could come as well." The next morning he'd put her on the bus to Maine. But within days of being together again in New Haven, in an apartment he'd rented on Howe Street with friends, they'd begun fighting, both admitting in the end that something had changed.

They avoid each other now, when they happen to cross paths in the library and on the streets. He's scratched out her phone number and the addresses he'd written down for her at Oxford and in Maine. But boarding the train it is impossible not to think of the afternoon, two years ago, they'd met. As usual the train is incredibly crowded, and this time he sits for half the journey in the vestibule. After Westerly he finds a seat, and settles down with the course selection guide for next semester. But he feels distracted for some reason, gloomy, impatient to be off the train; he does not bother to remove his coat, does not bother to go to the café car for something to drink even though he is thirsty. He puts away the course guide and opens up a library book that might be helpful for his senior thesis project, a comparison between Renaissance Italian and Mughal palace design. But after a few paragraphs he closes this book as well. His stomach growls and he wonders what there will be for dinner at home, what his father has prepared. His mother and Sonia have gone to India for three weeks, to attend a cousin's wedding, and this year Gogol and his father will spend Thanksgiving at the home of friends.

He angles his head against the window and watches the autumnal landscape pass: the spewing pink and purple waters of a dye mill, electrical power stations, a big ball-shaped water tank covered with rust. Abandoned factories, with rows of small square windows partly bashed in, ravaged as if by moths. On the trees the topmost branches are bare, the remaining leaves yellow, paper-thin. The train moves more slowly than usual, and when he looks at his watch he sees that they are running well behind schedule. And then, somewhere outside Providence, in an abandoned, grassy field, the train stops. For over an hour they stand there as a solid, scarlet disk of sun sinks into the tree-lined horizon. The lights turn off, and the air inside the train turns uncomfortably warm. The conductors rush anxiously through the compartments. "Probably a broken wire," the gentleman sitting beside Gogol remarks. Across the aisle a gray-haired woman reads, a coat clutched like a blanket to her chest. Behind him two students discuss the poems of Ben Jonson. Without the sound of the engine Gogol can hear an opera playing faintly on someone's Walkman. Through the window he admires the darkening sapphire sky. He sees spare lengths of rusted rails heaped in piles. It isn't until they start moving again that an announcement is made on the loudspeaker about a medical emergency. But the truth, overheard by one of the passengers from a conductor, quickly circulates: a suicide had been committed, a person had jumped in front of the train.

He is shocked and discomfited by the news, feeling bad about his irritation and impatience, wondering if the victim had been a man or a woman, young or old. He imagines the person consulting the same schedule that's in his backpack, determining exactly when the train would be passing through. The approach of the train's headlights. As a result of the delay he misses his commuter rail connection in Boston, waits another forty minutes for the next one. He puts a call through to his parents' house, but no one answers. He tries his father's department at the university, but there too the phone rings and rings. At the station he sees his father waiting on the darkened platform, wearing sneakers and corduroys, anxiousness in his face. A trench coat is belted around his waist, a scarf knitted by Ashima wrapped at his throat, a tweed cap on his head.

"Sorry I'm late," Gogol says. "How long have you been waiting?"

"Since quarter to six," his father says. Gogol looks at his watch. It is nearly eight.

"There was an accident."

"I know. I called. What happened? Were you hurt?"

Gogol shakes his head. "Someone jumped onto the tracks. Somewhere in Rhode Island. I tried to call you. They had to wait for the police, I think."

"I was worried."

"I hope you haven't been standing out in the cold all this time," Gogol says, and from his father's lack of response he knows that this is exactly what he has done. Gogol wonders what it is like for his father to be without his mother and Sonia. He wonders if he is lonely. But his father is not the type to admit such things, to speak openly of his desires, his moods, his needs. They walk to the parking lot, get into the car, and begin the short drive home.

The night is windy, so much so that the car jostles slightly from time to time, and brown leaves as large as human feet fly across the road in the headlights' glare. Normally on these rides back from the station his father asks questions, about his classes, about his finances, about his plans after graduation. But tonight they are silent, Ashoke concentrating on driving. Gogol fidgets with the radio, switching from the AM news station to NPR.

"I want to tell you something," his father says when the piece ends, once they have already turned onto Pemberton Road.

"What?" Gogol asks.

"It's about your name."

Gogol looks at his father, puzzled. "My name?"

His father shuts off the radio. "Gogol."

These days he is called Gogol so seldom that the sound of it no longer upsets him as it used to. After three years of being Nikhil the vast majority of the time, he no longer minds.

"There is a reason for it, you know," his father continues.

"Right, Baba. Gogol's your favorite author. I know."

"No," his father says. He pulls into the driveway and switches off the engine, then the headlights. He undoes his seat belt, guiding it with his hand as it retracts, back behind his left shoulder. "Another reason."

And as they sit together in the car, his father revisits a field 209 kilometers from Howrah. With his fingers lightly grasping the bottom of the steering wheel, his gaze directed through the windshield at the garage door, he tells Gogol the story of the train he'd ridden twenty-eight years ago, in October 1961, on his way to visit his grandfather in Jamshedpur. He tells him about the night that had nearly taken his life, and the book that had saved him, and about the year afterward, when he'd been unable to move.

Gogol listens, stunned, his eyes fixed on his father's profile. Though there are only inches between them, for an instant his father is a stranger, a man who has kept a secret, has survived a tragedy, a man whose past he does not fully know. A man who is vulnerable, who has suffered in an inconceivable way. He imagines his father, in his twenties as Gogol is now, sitting on a train as Gogol had just been, reading a story, and then suddenly nearly killed. He struggles to picture the West Bengal countryside he has seen on only a few occasions, his father's mangled body, among hundreds of dead ones, being carried on a stretcher, past a twisted length of maroon compartments. Against instinct he tries to imagine life without his father, a world in which his father does not exist.

"Why don't I know this about you?" Gogol says. His voice sounds harsh, accusing, but his eyes well with tears. "Why haven't you told me this until now?"

"It never felt like the right time," his father says.

"But it's like you've lied to me all these years." When his father doesn't respond, he adds, "That's why you have that limp, isn't it?"

"It happened so long ago. I didn't want to upset you."

"It doesn't matter. You should have told me."

"Perhaps," his father concedes, glancing briefly in Gogol's direction. He removes the keys from the ignition. "Come, you must be hungry. The car is getting cold."

But Gogol doesn't move. He sits there, still struggling to absorb the information, feeling awkward, oddly ashamed, at fault. "I'm sorry, Baba."

His father laughs softly. "You had nothing to do with it."

"Does Sonia know?"

His father shakes his head. "Not yet. I'll explain it to her one day. In this country, only your mother knows. And now you. I've always meant for you to know, Gogol."

And suddenly the sound of his pet name, uttered by his father as he has been accustomed to hearing it all his life, means something completely new, bound up with a catastrophe he has unwittingly embodied for years. "Is that what you think of when you think of me?" Gogol asks him. "Do I remind you of that night?"

"Not at all," his father says eventually, one hand going to his ribs, a habitual gesture that has baffled Gogol until now. "You remind me of everything that followed."

6

1994

HE lives in New York now. In May he graduated from the
architecture program at Columbia. He's been working
since then for a firm in midtown, with celebrated large-scale
commissions to its name. It's not the sort of job he'd envisioned
for himself as a student; designing and renovating private resi-
dences was what he'd wanted to do. That might come later, his
advisers have told him; for now, it was important to apprentice
with the big names. And so, facing the tawny brick wall of a
neighboring building across the air shaft, he works with a team
on designs for hotels and museums and corporate headquarters
in cities he's never seen: Brussels, Buenos Aires, Abu Dhabi,
Hong Kong. His contributions are incidental, and never fully
his own: a stairwell, a skylight, a corridor, an air-conditioning
duct. Still, he knows that each component of a building, however small, is nevertheless essential, and he finds it gratifying
that after all his years of schooling, all his crits and unbuilt
projects, his efforts are to have some practical end. He typically works late into his evenings, and on most of his weekends,
drawing designs on the computer, drafting plans, writing spec-
ifications, building Styrofoam and cardboard models to scale.

He goes home to a studio in Morningside Heights, with two windows facing west, on Amsterdam Avenue. The entrance is easy to miss, a scratched-up glass door between a newsstand and a nail salon. It's the first apartment he has to himself, after an evolving chain of roommates all through college and graduate school. There is so much street noise that when he is on the phone and the windows are open, people often ask if he is calling from a pay phone. The kitchen is built into what should have been an entryway, a space so small that the refrigerator stands several feet away, over by the bathroom door. On the stove sits a teakettle he has never filled with water, and on the countertop a toaster he's never plugged in.

His parents are distressed by how little money he makes, and occasionally his father sends him checks in the mail to help him with his rent, his credit card bills. They had been disappointed that he'd gone to Columbia. They'd hoped he would choose MIT, the other architecture program to which he'd been accepted. But after four years in New Haven he didn't want to move back to Massachusetts, to the one city in America his parents know. He didn't want to attend his father's alma mater, and live in an apartment in Central Square as his parents once had, and revisit the streets about which his parents speak nostalgically. He didn't want to go home on the weekends, to go with them to pujos and Bengali parties, to remain unquestionably in their world.

He prefers New York, a place which his parents do not know well, whose beauty they are blind to, which they fear. He'd come to know the city slightly during his years at Yale, on visits with architecture classes. He'd been to a few parties at Columbia. Sometimes he and Ruth would ride in on Metro-North, and they would go to museums, or to the Village, or to browse for books at the Strand. But as a child he'd been to New York only once with his family, a trip that had given him no sense of what the city was like. They had gone one weekend to visit Bengali friends who lived in Queens. The friends had given his family a tour of Manhattan. Gogol had been ten years old, Sonia four. "I want to see Sesame Street," Sonia had said, believing that it was an actual landmark in the city, and she had cried when Gogol had laughed at her, saying it didn't exist. On the tour they were driven past sites like Rockefeller Center and Central Park and the Empire State Building, and Gogol had ducked his head below the car's window to try to see how tall the buildings were. His parents had remarked endlessly at the amount of traffic, the pedestrians, the noise. Calcutta was no worse, they had said. He remembered wanting to get out and go to the top of one of the skyscrapers, the way his father had once taken him to the top of the Prudential Center in Boston when he was little. But they were allowed out of the car only once they got to Lexington Avenue, to eat lunch at an Indian restaurant and then to buy Indian groceries, and polyester saris and 220-volt appliances to give to relatives in Calcutta. This, to his parents, was what one came to Manhattan to do. He remembered wishing that his parents would walk through the park, take him to the Museum of Natural History to see the dinosaurs, ride the subway even. But they had had no interest in such things.

One night, Evan, one of the draftsmen at work with whom he is friendly, talks him into going to a party. Evan tells Gogol that it's an apartment worth seeing, a Tribeca loft that happens to be designed by one of the partners at the firm. The host of the party, Russell, an old friend of Evan's, works for the UN and has spent several years in Kenya, and as a result the loft is filled with an impressive collection of African furniture and sculpture and masks. Gogol imagines that it will be a party of hundreds filling up a vast space, the sort of party where he might arrive and leave undetected. But by the time Gogol and Evan get there, the party is nearly over, and there are only a dozen or so people sitting around a low coffee table surrounded by cushions, eating picked-over grapes and cheese. At one point Russell, who is diabetic, raises his shirt and injects himself in the stomach with insulin. Beside Russell is a woman Gogol can't stop looking at. She is kneeling on the floor at Russell's side, spreading a generous amount of brie on a cracker, paying no attention to what Russell is doing. Instead she is arguing with a man on the other side of the coffee table about a movie by Buñuel. "Oh, come on," she keeps saying, "it was brilliant." At once strident and flirtatious, she is a little bit drunk. She has dirty blond hair gathered sloppily into a bun, strands falling randomly, attractively, around her face. Her forehead is high and smooth, her jawbones sloping and unusually long. Her eyes are greenish, the irises encased by thin rings of black. She is dressed in silk capri pants and a sleeveless white shirt that shows off her tan. "What did you think of it?" she asks Gogol, drawing him without warning into the discussion. When he tells her he hasn't seen the film she looks away.

She approaches him again as he is standing idle, looking up at an imposing wooden mask that hangs above a suspended metal staircase, the hollow diamond-shaped eyes and mouth of the mask revealing the white brick wall behind it. "There's an even scarier one in the bedroom," she says, making a face, shuddering. "Imagine opening your eyes and seeing something like that first thing in the morning." The way she says this makes him wonder if she speaks from experience, if she's Russell's lover, or ex-lover, if that is what she is implying.

Her name is Maxine. She asks him about the program at Columbia, mentioning that she'd gone to Barnard for college, majoring in art history. She leans back against a column as she speaks, smiling at him easily, drinking a glass of champagne.

At first he assumes she is older than he is, closer to thirty than twenty. He is surprised to learn that she'd graduated from college the year after he started graduate school, that for a year they overlapped at Columbia, living just three blocks away from each other, and that they have in all likelihood crossed paths on Broadway or walking up the steps of Low Library or in Avery. It reminds him of Ruth, of the way they, too, had once lived in such close proximity as strangers. Maxine tells him she works as an assistant editor for a publisher of art books. Her current project is a book on Andrea Mantegna, and he impresses her, remembering correctly that his frescoes are in Mantua, in the Palazzo Ducale. They speak in that slightly strained, silly way that he associates now with flirtation — the exchange feels desperately arbitrary, fleeting. It is the sort of conversation he might have had with anybody, but Maxine has a way of focusing her attention on him completely, her pale, watchful eyes holding his gaze, making him feel, for those brief minutes, the absolute center of her world.

The next morning she calls, waking him; at ten on a Sunday he is still in bed, his head aching from the Scotch and sodas he'd consumed throughout the evening. He answers gruffly, a bit impatiently, expecting it to be his mother calling to ask how his week has been. He has the feeling, from the tone of Maxine's voice, that she's been up for hours, that her breakfast has already been eaten, her *Times* thoroughly read. "It's Maxine. From last night," she says, not bothering to apologize for waking him. She tells him she'd found his number in the phone book, though he doesn't remember telling her his last name. "God, your apartment's noisy," she remarks. Then, without awkwardness or pause, she invites him to dinner at her place. She specifies the evening, a Friday, tells him the address, somewhere in Chelsea. He assumes it will be a dinner party, asks if there's anything he can bring, but she says no, it will be just him.

"I should probably warn you that I live with my parents," she adds.

"Oh." This unexpected piece of information deflates him, confuses him. He asks if her parents will mind his coming over, if perhaps they should meet at a restaurant instead.

But she laughs at this suggestion in a way that makes him feel vaguely foolish. "Why on earth would they mind?"

He takes a cab from his office to her neighborhood, getting out at a liquor store to buy a bottle of wine. It is a cool evening in September, raining steadily, the summer's leaves still plentiful on the trees. He turns onto a remote, tranquil block between Ninth and Tenth Avenues. It is his first date in a long time; with the exception of a few forgettable affairs at Columbia he's been with no one seriously since Ruth. He doesn't know what to make of the whole arrangement with Maxine, but as odd as the terms of the invitation seem he'd been unable to refuse. He is curious about her, attracted, flattered by the boldness of her pursuit.

He is stunned by the house, a Greek Revival, admiring it for several minutes like a tourist before opening the gate. He notes the pedimented window lintels, the Doric pilasters, the bracketed entablature, the black cruciform paneled door. He climbs a low stoop with cast-iron railings. The name below the bell is Ratliff. Several minutes after he presses it, enough to make him double-check the address on the scrap of paper in his jacket pocket, Maxine arrives. She kisses him on the cheek, leaning toward him on one foot, the other leg extended, slightly raised behind her. She is barefoot, wearing flowing black wool pants and a thin beige cardigan. As far as he can tell she wears nothing under the cardigan apart from her bra. Her hair is done up in the same careless way. His raincoat is draped on a coat rack, his folding umbrella dropped into a stand. He glimpses himself quickly in a mirror in the foyer, smoothing his hair and his tie.

She leads him down a flight of stairs to a kitchen that appears to occupy an entire floor of the house, with a large farmhouse table at one end, and beyond that French doors leading to a garden. The walls are adorned with prints of roosters and herbs and an arrangement of copper skillets. Ceramic plates and platters are displayed on open shelves, along with what seem to be hundreds of cookbooks, food encyclopedias, and volumes of essays about eating. A woman stands at a butcher-block island by the appliances, snipping the ends of a pile of green beans with a pair of scissors.

"This is my mother, Lydia," Maxine says. "And this is Silas," she tells him, pointing to a reddish brown cocker spaniel dozing under the table.

Lydia is tall and slender like her daughter, with straight iron-colored hair cut youthfully to frame her face. She is carefully dressed, with gold jewelry at her ears and throat, a navy apron wrapped around her waist, gleaming black leather shoes. Though her face is lined and her complexion a bit splotchy, she is more beautiful even than Maxine, her features more regular, the cheekbones higher, the eyes more elegantly defined.

"Lovely to meet you, Nikhil," she says, smiling brightly, and though she looks at him with interest, she does not pause in her work or offer to shake his hand.

Maxine pours him a glass of wine, not asking if perhaps he might prefer something else. "Come on," she says, "I'll show you the house." She leads him up five flights of uncarpeted stairs that creak noisily beneath their combined weight. The plan of the house is simple, two immense rooms per floor, each of which, he is certain, is larger than his own apartment. Politely he admires the plaster cove moldings, the ceiling medallions, the marble mantelpieces, things he knows how to speak intelligently and at length about. The walls are painted in flamboyant colors: hibiscus pink, lilac, pistachio, and are crowded with clusters of paintings and drawings and photographs. In one room he sees an oil portrait of a small girl he assumes is Maxine, sitting in the lap of a stunning, youthful Lydia, wearing a yellow sleeveless dress. Along the hallways on every floor shelves ascend to the ceiling, crammed with all the novels one should read in a lifetime, biographies, massive monographs of every artist, all the architecture books Gogol has ever coveted. Alongside the clutter there is a starkness about the place that appeals to him: the floors are bare, the woodwork stripped, many of the windows without curtains to highlight their generous proportions.

Maxine has the top floor to herself: a peach-colored bedroom with a sleigh bed at the back, a long black and red bathroom. The shelf above the sink is full of different creams for her neck, her throat, her eyes, her feet, daytime, nighttime, sun and shade. Through the bedroom is a gray sitting room she treats as a closet, her shoes and handbags and clothes scattered across the floor, piled on a fainting couch, spilling over the backs of chairs. These patches of disorder make no difference—it is a house too spectacular to suffer distraction, forgiving of oversight and mess.

"Lovely frieze-band windows," he comments, looking toward the ceiling.

She turns to him, puzzled. "What?"

"That's what those are called," he explains, pointing. "They're fairly common in houses from this period."

She looks up, and then at him, seeming impressed. "I never knew that."

He sits with Maxine on the fainting couch, leafing through a coffee table book she'd helped to edit on eighteenth-century French wallpapers, one side of the book resting on each of their knees. She tells him this is the house she's grown up in, mentioning casually that she'd moved back six months ago after living with a man in Boston, an arrangement that had not worked out. When he asks if she plans to look for a place of her own she says it hasn't occurred to her. "It's such a bother renting a place in the city," she says. "Besides, I love this house. There's really nowhere else I'd rather live." For all her sophistication he finds the fact that she's moved back with her parents after a love affair has soured endearingly old-fashioned; it is something he cannot picture himself doing at this stage in his life.

At dinner he meets her father, a tall, good-looking man with luxuriant white hair, Maxine's pale green-gray eyes, thin rectangular glasses perched halfway down his nose. "How do you do. I'm Gerald," he says, nodding, shaking Gogol's hand. Gerald gives him a bunch of cutlery and cloth napkins and asks him to set the table. Gogol does as he is told, aware that he is touching the everyday possessions of a family he barely knows. "You'll sit here, Nikhil," Gerald says, pointing to a chair once the silverware is laid. Gogol takes his place on one side of the table, across from Maxine. Gerald and Lydia are at either end. Gogol had skipped lunch that day in order to leave the office in time for the date with Maxine, and already the wine, at once heavier and smoother than what he is used to drinking, has gone to his head. He feels a pleasant ache at his temples, and a sudden gratitude for the day and where it has brought him. Maxine lights a pair of candles. Gerald tops off the wine. Lydia serves the food on broad white plates: a thin piece of steak rolled into a bundle and tied with string, sitting in a pool of dark sauce, the green beans boiled so that they are still crisp. A bowl of small, round, roasted red potatoes is passed around, and afterward a salad. They eat appreciatively, commenting on the tenderness of the meat, the freshness of the beans. His own mother would never have served so few dishes to a guest. She would have kept her eyes trained on Maxine's plate, insisting she have seconds and then thirds. The table would have been lined with a row of serving bowls so that people could help themselves. But Lydia

pays no attention to Gogol's plate. She makes no announcement indicating that there is more. Silas sits at Lydia's feet as
they eat, and at one point Lydia slices off a generous portion of
her meat and feeds it to him off of her palm.

The four of them go quickly through two bottles of wine,
then move on to a third. The Ratliffs are vociferous at the table, opinionated about things his own parents are indifferent
to: movies, exhibits at museums, good restaurants, the design
of everyday things. They speak of New York, of stores and
neighborhoods and buildings they either despise or love, with
an intimacy and ease that make Gogol feel as if he barely knows
the city. They speak about the house, which Gerald and Lydia
bought back in the seventies, when no one wanted to live in the
area, about the history of the neighborhood, and about Clement Clarke Moore, who Gerald explains was a professor of classics at the seminary across the street. "He was the person responsible for local residential zoning," Gerald says. "That and
writing ''Twas the Night Before Christmas,' of course." Gogol
is unaccustomed to this sort of talk at mealtimes, to the indulgent ritual of the lingering meal, and the pleasant aftermath
of bottles and crumbs and empty glasses that clutter the table.
Something tells him that none of this is for his benefit, that this
is the way the Ratliffs eat every night. Gerald is a lawyer. Lydia
is a curator of textiles at the Met. They are at once satisfied and
intrigued by his background, by his years at Yale and Columbia, his career as an architect, his Mediterranean looks. "You
could be Italian," Lydia remarks at one point during the meal,
regarding him in the candle's glow.

Gerald remembers a bar of French chocolate he bought on
his way home, and this is unwrapped, broken apart, and passed
around the table. Eventually the talk turns to India. Gerald
asks questions about the recent rise of Hindu fundamentalism,
a topic Gogol knows little about. Lydia talks at length about

Indian carpets and miniatures, Maxine about a college class she'd once taken on Buddhist stupas. They have never known a person who has been to Calcutta. Gerald has an Indian colleague at work who just went to India for his honeymoon. He'd brought back spectacular photographs, of a palace built on a lake. Was that in Calcutta?

"That's Udaipur," Gogol tells them. "I've never been there. Calcutta's in the east, closer to Thailand."

Lydia peers into the salad bowl, fishing out a stray piece of lettuce and eating it with her fingers. She seems more relaxed now, quicker to smile, her cheeks rosy from the wine. "What's Calcutta like? Is it beautiful?"

The question surprises him. He is accustomed to people asking about the poverty, about the beggars and the heat. "Parts of it are beautiful," he tells her. "There's a lot of lovely Victorian architecture left over from the British. But most of it's decaying."

"That sounds like Venice," Gerald says. "Are there canals?"

"Only during monsoons. That's when the streets flood. I guess that's the closest it comes to resembling Venice."

"I want to go to Calcutta," Maxine says, as if this has been a thing denied to her all her life. She gets up and walks over to the stove. "I feel like tea. Who wants tea?"

But Gerald and Lydia decide against tea tonight; there is an *I, Claudius* video they want to watch before bed. Without tending to the dishes they stand up, Gerald taking their two glasses and the rest of the wine. "Good night, dear," Lydia says, kissing Gogol lightly on the cheek. And then their footsteps creak noisily up the stairs.

"I suppose you've never been subjected to someone's parents on the first date before," Maxine says once they are alone, sipping milky cups of Lapsang Souchong from heavy white mugs.

"I enjoyed meeting them. They're charming."

"That's one way of putting it."

They remain awhile at the table, talking, the sound of the rain echoing quietly in the enclosed space behind the house. The candles shrink to stubs, and specks of wax drip onto the table. Silas, who has been softly pacing on the floor, comes and presses his head against Gogol's leg, looking up at him, wagging his tail. Gogol bends over, pats him tentatively.

"You've never had a dog, have you?" Maxine says, observing him.

"No."

"Didn't you ever want one?"

"When I was a kid. But my parents never wanted the responsibility. Plus we had to go to India every couple of years."

He realizes it's the first time he's mentioned his parents to her, his past. He wonders if perhaps she'll ask him more about these things. Instead she says, "Silas likes you. He's very picky."

He looks at her, watching as she undoes her hair, letting it hang loose for a moment over her shoulders before wrapping it thoughtlessly around her hand. She looks back at him, smiling. Once again he is aware of her nakedness beneath the cardigan.

"I should go," he says. But he is glad that she accepts his offer to help her clean up before leaving. They loiter over the task, loading the dishwasher, wiping down the table and the butcher-block island, washing and drying the pots and pans. They agree to go to the Film Forum on Sunday afternoon, to see the Antonioni double feature that Lydia and Gerald have recently been to and recommended over dinner.

"I'll walk you to the subway," Maxine says when they are finished, putting a leash around Silas. "He needs to go out." They go up to the parlor level, put on their coats. He hears the sound

of a television faintly through the ceiling. He pauses at the foot
of the stairs. "I forgot to thank your parents," he says.

"For what?"

"For having me over. For dinner."

She links elbows with him. "You can thank them next time."

From the very beginning he feels effortlessly incorporated into
their lives. It is a different brand of hospitality from what he is
used to; for though the Ratliffs are generous, they are people
who do not go out of their way to accommodate others, assured, in his case correctly, that their life will appeal to him.
Gerald and Lydia, busy with their own engagements, keep out
of the way. Gogol and Maxine come and go as they please, from
movies and dinners out. He goes shopping with her on Madison Avenue at stores they must be buzzed into, for cashmere
cardigans and outrageously expensive English colognes that
Maxine buys without deliberation or guilt. They go to darkened, humble-looking restaurants downtown where the tables
are tiny, the bills huge. Almost without fail they wind up back
at her parents' place. There is always some delicious cheese or
pâté to snack on, always some good wine to drink. It is in her
claw-footed tub that they soak together, glasses of wine or sin-
gle-malt Scotch on the floor. At night he sleeps with her in the
room she grew up in, on a soft, sagging mattress, holding her
body, as warm as a furnace, through the night, making love to
her in a room just above the one in which Gerald and Lydia
lie. On nights he has to stay late at work he simply comes over;
Maxine keeps dinner waiting for him, and then they go upstairs
to bed. Gerald and Lydia think nothing, in the mornings, when
he and Maxine join them downstairs in the kitchen, their hair
uncombed, seeking bowls of café au lait and toasted slices of
French bread and jam. The first morning he'd slept over he'd
been mortified to face them, showering beforehand, putting on

his wrinkled shirt and trousers from the day before, but they'd merely smiled, still in their bathrobes, and offered him warm sticky buns from their favorite neighborhood bakery and sections of the paper.

Quickly, simultaneously, he falls in love with Maxine, the house, and Gerald and Lydia's manner of living, for to know her and love her is to know and love all of these things. He loves the mess that surrounds Maxine, her hundreds of things always covering her floor and her bedside table, her habit, when they are alone on the fifth floor, of not shutting the door when she goes to the bathroom. Her unkempt ways, a challenge to his increasingly minimalist taste, charm him. He learns to love the food she and her parents eat, the polenta and risotto, the bouillabaisse and osso buco, the meat baked in parchment paper. He comes to expect the weight of their flatware in his hands, and to keep the cloth napkin, still partially folded, on his lap. He learns that one does not grate Parmesan cheese over pasta dishes containing seafood. He learns not to put wooden spoons in the dishwasher, as he had mistakenly done one evening when he was helping to clean up. The nights he spends there, he learns to wake up earlier than he is used to, to the sound of Silas barking downstairs, wanting to be taken for his morning walk. He learns to anticipate, every evening, the sound of a cork emerging from a fresh bottle of wine.

Maxine is open about her past, showing him photographs of her ex-boyfriends in the pages of a marble-papered album, speaking of those relationships without embarrassment or regret. She has the gift of accepting her life; as he comes to know her, he realizes that she has never wished she were anyone other than herself, raised in any other place, in any other way. This, in his opinion, is the biggest difference between them, a thing far more foreign to him than the beautiful house she'd grown up in, her education at private schools. In addition, he is continually amazed by how much Maxine emulates her parents, how much she respects their tastes and their ways. At the dinner table she argues with them about books and paintings and people they know in common the way one might argue with a friend. There is none of the exasperation he feels with his own parents. No sense of obligation. Unlike his parents, they pressure her to do nothing, and yet she lives faithfully, happily, at their side.

She is surprised to hear certain things about his life: that all his parents' friends are Bengali, that they had had an arranged marriage, that his mother cooks Indian food every day, that she wears saris and a bindi. "Really?" she says, not fully believing him. "But you're so different. I would never have thought that." He doesn't feel insulted, but he is aware that a line has been drawn all the same. To him the terms of his parents' marriage are something at once unthinkable and unremarkable; nearly all their friends and relatives had been married in the same way. But their lives bear no resemblance to that of Gerald and Lydia: expensive pieces of jewelry presented on Lydia's birthday, flowers brought home for no reason at all, the two of them kissing openly, going for walks through the city, or to dinner, just as Gogol and Maxine do. Seeing the two of them curled up on the sofa in the evenings, Gerald's head resting on Lydia's shoulder, Gogol is reminded that in all his life he has never witnessed a single moment of physical affection between his parents. Whatever love exists between them is an utterly private, uncelebrated thing. "That's so depressing," Maxine says when he confesses this fact to her, and though it upsets him to hear her reaction, he can't help but agree. One day Maxine asks him if his parents want him to marry an Indian girl. She poses the question out of curiosity, without hoping for a particular response. He feels angry at his parents then, wishing they could be otherwise, knowing in his heart what the answer is.

"I don't know," he tells her. "I guess so. It doesn't matter what they want."

She visits him infrequently; she and Gogol are never close to his neighborhood for any reason, and even the absolute privacy they would have had there is of no appeal. Still, some nights when her parents have a dinner party she has no interest in, or simply to be fair, she appears, quickly filling up the small space with her gardenia perfume, her coat, her big brown leather bag, her discarded clothes, and they make love on his futon as the traffic rumbles below. He is nervous to have her in his place, aware that he has put nothing up on his walls, that he has not bothered to buy lamps to replace the dismal glow of the ceiling light. "Oh, Nikhil, it's too awful," she eventually says on one of these occasions, barely three months after they've met. "I won't let you live here." When his mother had said more or less the same thing, the first time his parents had visited the apartment, he'd argued with her, hotly defending the merits of his spartan, solitary existence. But when Maxine says it, adding "you should just stay with me," he is quietly thrilled. By then he knows enough about her to know that she is not one to offer things if she doesn't mean them. Still, he demurs; what would her parents think? She shrugs. "My parents love you," she says matter-of-factly, definitively, just as she says everything else. And so he moves in with her in a way, bringing a few bags of his clothes, nothing else. His futon and his table, his kettle and toaster and television and the rest of his things, remain on Amsterdam Avenue. His answering machine continues to record his messages. He continues to receive his mail there, in a nameless metal box.

Within six months he has the keys to the Ratliffs' house, a set of which Maxine presents to him on a silver Tiffany chain. Like her parents, he has come to call her Max. He drops off his shirts at the dry cleaner around the corner from her place. He keeps a toothbrush and razor on her cluttered pedestal sink. In the mornings a few times a week he gets up early and goes running before work with Gerald along the Hudson, down to Battery Park City and back. He volunteers to take Silas out for walks, holding the leash as the dog sniffs and pokes at trees, and he picks up Silas's warm shit with a plastic bag. He spends entire weekends holed up in the house, reading books from Gerald and Lydia's shelves, admiring the sunlight that filters through the enormous unadorned windows during the course of the day. He comes to prefer certain sofas and chairs to others; when he is not there, he can conjure the paintings and photographs arrayed on the walls. He has to make a point of going to his studio, of resetting the tape on his answering machine, paying his rent check and his bills.

Often, on weekends, he helps to shop and prepare for Gerald and Lydia's dinner parties, peeling apples and deveining shrimp with Lydia, helping to shuck oysters, going down to the cellar with Gerald to bring up the extra chairs, the wine. He has fallen the tiniest bit in love with Lydia and with the understated, unflustered way she entertains. He is always struck by these dinners: only a dozen or so guests sitting around the candlelit table, a carefully selected mix of painters, editors, academics, gallery owners, eating the meal course by course, talking intelligently until the evening's end. How different they are from his own parents' parties, cheerfully unruly evenings to which there were never fewer than thirty people invited, small children in tow. Fish and meat served side by side, so many courses that people had to eat in shifts, the food still in the pans they were cooked in crowding the table. They sat where they could, in the different rooms of the house, half the people having finished before the other half began. Unlike Gerald and Lydia, who preside at the center of their dinners, his parents behaved more like caterers in their own home, solicitous and watchful, waiting until most of their guests' plates were stacked by the sink in order finally to help themselves. At times, as the laughter at Gerald and Lydia's table swells, and another bottle of wine is opened, and Gogol raises his glass to be filled yet again, he is conscious of the fact that his immersion in Maxine's family is a betrayal of his own. It isn't simply the fact that his parents don't know about Maxine, that they have no idea how much time he spends with her and Gerald and Lydia. Instead it is his knowledge that apart from their affluence, Gerald and Lydia are secure in a way his parents will never be. He cannot imagine his parents sitting at Lydia and Gerald's table, enjoying Lydia's cooking, appreciating Gerald's selection of wine. He cannot imagine them contributing to one of their dinner party conversations. And yet here he is, night after night, a welcome addition to the Ratliffs' universe, doing just that.

In June, Gerald and Lydia disappear to their lake house in New Hampshire. It is an unquestioned ritual, a yearly migration to the town where Gerald's parents live year-round. For a few days a series of canvas tote bags accumulate in the hallway, cardboard boxes full of liquor, shopping bags full of food, cases of wine. Their departure reminds Gogol of his family's preparations for Calcutta every few years, when the living room would be crowded with suitcases that his parents packed and repacked, fitting in as many gifts as possible for their relatives. In spite of his parents' excitement, there was always a solemnity accompanying these preparations, Ashima and Ashoke at once apprehensive and eager, steeling themselves to find fewer faces at the airport in Calcutta, to confront the deaths of relatives since the last time they were there. No matter how many times they'd been to Calcutta, his father was always anxious about the job of transporting the four of them such a great distance. Gogol was aware of an obligation being fulfilled; that it was, above all else, a sense of duty that drew his parents back. But it is the call of pleasure that summons Gerald and Lydia to New Hampshire. They leave without fanfare, in the middle of the day, when Gogol and Maxine are both at work. In Gerald and Lydia's wake, certain things are missing: Silas, some of the cookbooks, the food processor, novels and CDs, the fax machine so that Gerald can keep in touch with his clients, the red Volvo station wagon they keep parked on the street. A note is left on the island in the kitchen: "We're off!" Lydia has written, followed by X's and O's.

Suddenly Gogol and Maxine have the house in Chelsea to themselves. They stray to the lower stories, making love on countless pieces of furniture, on the floor, on the island in the kitchen, once even on the pearl gray sheets of Gerald and Lydia's bed. On weekends they wander naked from room to room, up and down the five flights of stairs. They eat in different places according to their moods, spreading an old cotton quilt on the floor, sometimes eating take-out on Gerald and Lydia's finest china, falling asleep at odd hours as the strong summer light of the lengthened days pours through the enormous windows onto their bodies. As the days grow warmer, they stop cooking complicated things. They live off sushi and salads and cold poached salmon. They switch from red wine to white. Now that it is just the two of them it seems to him, more than ever, that they are living together. And yet for some reason it is dependence, not adulthood, he feels. He feels free of expectation, of responsibility, in willing exile from his own life. He is responsible for nothing in the house; in spite of their absence, Gerald and Lydia continue to lord, however blindly, over their days. It is their books he reads, their music he listens to. Their front door he unlocks when he gets back from work. Their telephone messages he takes down.

He learns that the house, for all its beauty, has certain faults in the summer months, so that it makes all the more sense that it is a place Gerald and Lydia annually avoid. It lacks air-conditioning, something Gerald and Lydia have never bothered to install because they are never there when it's hot, and the enormous windows lack screens. As a result, the rooms are sweltering during the day, and at night, because it is necessary to leave the windows wide open, he is ambushed by mosquitoes that shriek in his ears and leave angry, lumpen welts between his toes, on his arms and thighs. He longs for a mosquito net to drape over Maxine's bed, remembers the filmy blue nylon boxes that he and Sonia would sleep inside of on their visits to Calcutta, the corners hooked onto the four posts of the bed, the edges tucked tightly beneath the mattress, creating a temporary, tiny, impenetrable room for the night. There are times when he cannot bear it, turning on the light and standing on the bed, looking for them, a rolled-up magazine or a slipper in his hand, as Maxine, unbothered and unbitten, begs him to get back to sleep. He sees them sometimes against the peach-colored paint on the wall, faint specks engorged with his blood, just inches below the ceiling, always too high up to kill.

With work as an excuse he does not go home to Massachusetts all summer. The firm is entering a competition, submitting designs for a new five-star hotel to be built in Miami. At eleven at night, he is still there, along with most of the other designers on his team, all rushing to finish drawings and models by the month's end. When his phone rings, he hopes it's Maxine, calling to coax him into leaving the office. Instead it's his mother.

"Why are you calling me here so late?" he asks her, distracted, his eyes still focused on the computer screen.

"Because you are not at your apartment," his mother says. "You are never at your apartment, Gogol. In the middle of the night I have called and you are not there."

"I am, Ma," he lies. "I need my sleep. I shut off the phone."

"I cannot imagine why anyone would want to have a phone only to shut it off," his mother says.

"So, is there a reason you're calling me?"

She asks him to visit the following weekend, the Saturday before his birthday.

"I can't," he says. He tells her he has a deadline at work, but it's not true—that's the day that he and Maxine are leaving for New Hampshire, for two weeks. But his mother insists; his father is leaving for Ohio the following day—doesn't Gogol want to go with them to the airport, to see him off?

He knows vaguely of his father's plans to spend nine months at a small university somewhere outside Cleveland, that he and a colleague have received a grant funded by the colleague's university, to direct research for a corporation there. His father had sent him a clipping about the grant printed in the campus newspaper, with a photograph of his father standing outside the engineering building: "Prestigious grant for Professor Ganguli," the caption read. At first it was assumed that his parents would shut up the house, or rent it out to students, and that his mother would go too. But then his mother had surprised them, pointing out that there would be nothing for her to do in Ohio for nine months, that his father would be busy all day at the lab, and that she preferred to stay in Massachusetts, even if it meant staying in the house alone.

"Why do I have to see him off?" Gogol asks his mother now. He knows that for his parents, the act of travel is never regarded casually, that even the most ordinary of journeys is seen off and greeted at either end. And yet he continues, "Baba and I already live in different states. I'm practically as far from Ohio as I am from Boston."

"That's no way to think," his mother says. "Please, Gogol. You haven't been home since May."

"I have a job, Ma. I'm busy. Besides, Sonia's not coming."

"Sonia lives in California. You are so close."

"Listen, I can't come home that weekend," he says. The truth seeps out of him slowly. He knows it's his only defense at this point. "I'm going on a vacation. I've already made plans."

"Why do you wait to tell us these things at the last minute?" his mother asks. "What sort of vacation? What plans?"

"I'm going to spend a couple of weeks in New Hampshire."

"Oh," his mother says. She sounds at once unimpressed and relieved. "Why do you want to go there, of all places? What's the difference between New Hampshire and here?"

"I'm going with a girl I'm seeing," he tells her. "Her parents have a place there."

Though she says nothing for a while, he knows what his mother is thinking, that he is willing to go on vacation with someone else's parents but not see his own.

"Where is this place, exactly?"

"I don't know. Somewhere in the mountains."

"What's her name?"

"Max."

"That's a boy's name."

He shakes his head. "No, Ma. It's Maxine."

And so, on the way to New Hampshire, they stop off at Pemberton Road for lunch, which is what, in the end, he has agreed to. Maxine doesn't mind, it's on their way, after all, and she is curious by now to meet his parents. They drive up from New York in a rented car, the trunk packed with more supplies that Gerald and Lydia have asked them for on the back of a postcard: wine, bags of a particular imported pasta, a large tin of olive oil, thick wedges of Parmesan and Asiago cheese. When he asks Maxine why these things are necessary, she explains that they are going to the middle of nowhere, that if they were to depend on the general store they would have nothing to live on but potato chips and Wonder bread and Pepsi. On the way to Massachusetts, he tells her things he figures she should know in advance—that they will not be able to touch or kiss each other in front of his parents, that there will be no wine with lunch.

"There's plenty of wine in the trunk of the car," Maxine points out.

"It doesn't matter," he tells her. "My parents don't own a corkscrew."

The restrictions amuse her; she sees them as a single afternoon's challenge, an anomaly never to be repeated. She does not associate him with his parents' habits; she still cannot believe that she is to be the first girlfriend he's ever brought home. He feels no excitement over this prospect, wants simply to be done with it. Once they get off at his parents' exit he senses that the landscape is foreign to her: the shopping plazas, the sprawling brick-faced public high school from which he and Sonia graduated, the shingled houses, uncomfortably close to one another, on their grassy quarter-acre plots. The sign that says CHILDREN AT PLAY. He knows that this sort of life, one which is such a proud accomplishment for his own parents, is of no relevance, no interest, to her, that she loves him in spite of it.

A van from a company that installs security systems blocks his parents' driveway, and so he parks on the street, by the mailbox on the edge of the lawn. He leads Maxine up the flagstone path, ringing the bell because his parents always keep the front door locked. His mother opens the door. He can tell she is nervous, dressed in one of her better saris, wearing lipstick and perfume, in contrast to the khakis and T-shirts and soft leather moccasins Gogol and Maxine both wear.

"Hi, Ma," he says, leaning over, giving his mother a quick kiss. "This is Maxine. Max, this is my mother. Ashima."

"It's so nice to finally meet you, Ashima," Maxine says, leaning over and giving his mother a kiss as well. "These are for

you," she says, handing Ashima a cellophane-wrapped basket
full of tinned pâtés and jars of cornichons and chutneys that
Gogol knows his parents will never open or enjoy. And yet
when Maxine had shopped for the things to put in the basket, at Dean and DeLuca, he'd said nothing to dissuade her.
He walks in with his shoes on instead of changing into a pair
of flip-flops that his parents keep in the hall closet. They follow his mother across the living room and around the corner
into the kitchen. His mother returns to the stove, where she
is deep-frying a batch of samosas, filling the air with a haze of
smoke.

"Nikhil's father is upstairs," his mother says to Maxine,
lifting out a samosa with a slotted spatula and putting it on a
paper-towel-lined plate. "With the man from the alarm company. Sorry, lunch will be ready in a minute," she adds. "I was
not expecting you to arrive for another half an hour."

"Why on earth are we getting a security system?" Gogol
wants to know.

"It was your father's idea," his mother says, "now that I will
be on my own." She says that there have been two burglaries
recently in the neighborhood, both of them in the middle of
the afternoon. "Even in good areas like this, these days there
are crimes," she says to Maxine, shaking her head.

His mother offers them glasses of frothy pink lassi, thick and
sweet-tasting, flavored with rose water. They sit in the formal
living room, where they normally never sit. Maxine sees the
school pictures of Sonia and him in front of blue-gray backgrounds arranged on the mantel of the brick fireplace, the family portraits from Olan Mills. She looks at his childhood photo
albums with his mother. She admires the material of his mother's sari, mentioning that her mother curates textiles at the
Met.

"The Met?"

"The Metropolitan Museum of Art," Maxine explains.

"You've been there, Ma," Gogol says. "It's the big museum on Fifth Avenue. With all the steps. I took you there to see the Egyptian temple, remember?"

"Yes, I remember. My father was an artist," she tells Maxine, pointing to one of his grandfather's watercolors on the wall.

They hear footsteps coming down the stairs, and then his father enters the living room, along with a uniformed man holding a clipboard. Unlike his mother, his father is not dressed up at all. He wears a pair of thin brown cotton pants, an untucked, slightly wrinkled short-sleeved shirt, and flip-flops. His gray hair looks more sparse than the last time Gogol remembers, his potbelly more pronounced. "Here's your copy of the receipt. Any problems, you just call the eight hundred number," the uniformed man says. He and his father shake hands. "Have a nice day," the man calls out before leaving.

"Hi, Baba," Gogol says. "I'd like you to meet Maxine."

"Hello," his father says, putting up a hand, looking as if he is about to take an oath. He does not sit down with them. Instead he asks Maxine, "That is your car outside?"

"It's a rental," she says.

"Better to put it in the driveway," his father tells her.

"It doesn't matter," Gogol says. "It's fine where it is."

"But better to be careful," his father persists. "The neighborhood children, they are not very careful. One time my car was on the road and a baseball went through the window. I can park it for you if you like."

"I'll do it," Gogol says, getting up, irritated by his parents' perpetual fear of disaster. When he returns to the house, the lunch is set out, too rich for the weather. Along with the samosas, there are breaded chicken cutlets, chickpeas with tamarind sauce, lamb biryani, chutney made with tomatoes from the garden. It is a meal he knows it has taken his mother over a day to prepare, and yet the amount of effort embarrasses him. The water glasses are already filled, plates and forks and paper napkins set on the dining room table they use only for special occasions, with uncomfortable high-backed chairs and seats upholstered in gold velvet.

"Go ahead and start," his mother says, still hovering between the dining room and the kitchen, finishing up the last of the samosas.

His parents are diffident around Maxine, at first keeping their distance, not boisterous as they typically are around their Bengali friends. They ask where she went to college, what it is her parents do. But Maxine is immune to their awkwardness, drawing them out, devoting her attention to them fully, and Gogol is reminded of the first time he'd met her, when she'd seduced him in the same way. She asks his father about his research project in Cleveland, his mother about her part-time job at the local public library, which she's recently begun. Gogol is only partly attentive to the conversation. He is overly aware that they are not used to passing things around the table, or to chewing food with their mouths fully closed. They avert their eyes when Maxine accidentally leans over to run her hand through his hair. To his relief she eats generously, asking his mother how she made this and that, telling her it's the best Indian food she's ever tasted, accepting his mother's offer to pack them some extra cutlets and samosas for the road.

When his mother confesses that she is nervous to be in the house alone, Maxine tells her she'd be nervous, too. She mentions a break-in at her parents' once when she was by herself. When she tells them that she lives with her parents, Ashima says, "Really? I thought no one did that in America." When she tells them she was born and raised in Manhattan, his father shakes his head. "New York is too much," he says, "too many cars, too many tall buildings." He tells the story of the time they'd driven in for Gogol's graduation from Columbia, the trunk of the car broken into in just five minutes, their suitcase stolen, having to attend the commencement without a jacket and tie.

"It's a pity you can't stay for dinner," his mother says as the meal comes to an end.

But his father urges them to get going. "Better not to drive in the dark," he says.

Afterward there is tea, and bowls of payesh made in honor of his birthday. He receives a Hallmark card signed by both of his parents, a check for one hundred dollars, a navy blue cotton sweater from Filene's.

"He'll need that where we're going," Maxine says approvingly. "The temperature can really drop at night."

In the driveway there are hugs and kisses good-bye, initiated by Maxine, his parents reciprocating clumsily. His mother invites Maxine to please come again. He is given a piece of paper with his father's new phone number in Ohio, and the date on which it will be activated.

"Have a good trip to Cleveland," he tells his father. "Good luck with the project."

"Okay," his father says. He pats Gogol on the shoulder. "I'll miss you," he says. In Bengali he adds, "Remember to check in on your mother now and again."

"Don't worry, Baba. See you at Thanksgiving."

"Yes, see you," his father says. And then: "Drive safely, Gogol."

At first he's unaware of the slip. But as soon as they're in the car, buckling their seat belts, Maxine says, "What did your dad just call you?"

He shakes his head. "It's nothing. I'll explain it later." He turns on the ignition and begins to back out of the driveway, away from his parents, who stand there, waving, until the last possible moment. "Call to let us know you've arrived there safely," his mother says to Gogol in Bengali. But he waves and drives off, pretending not to hear.

It's a relief to be back in her world, heading north across the state border. For a while it's nothing different, the same expanse of sky, the same strip of highway, large liquor stores and fast-food chains on either side. Maxine knows the way, so there is no need to consult a map. He has been to New Hampshire once or twice with his family, to see the leaves, driving for the day to places one could pull off the road and take pictures of and admire the view. But he's never been so far north. They pass farms, spotted cows grazing in fields, red silos, white wooden churches, barns with rusted tin roofs. Small, scattered towns. The names of the towns mean nothing to him. They leave the highway behind and drive on steep, slender, two-lane ribbons of road, the mountains appearing like enormous milky waves suspended against the sky. Wisps of cloud hang low over the summits, like smoke rising from the trees. Other clouds cast broad shadows across the valley. Eventually there are only a few cars on the road, no signs for tourist facilities or campgrounds, just more farms and woods, the fields full of blue and purple flowers. He has no idea where he is, or how far they've traveled. Maxine tells him they aren't far from Canada, that if they're motivated they could drive into Montreal for the day.

They turn down a long dirt road in the middle of a forest, dense with hemlock and birch. There is nothing to mark where they turned, no mailbox or sign. At first there is no house visible, nothing but large lime-colored ferns covering the ground. Small stones spray wildly under the tires and the trees throw patterns of shade onto the hood of the car. They come to a partial clearing, to a humble house covered with bleached brown shingles and surrounded by a low wall of flat stones. Gerald and Lydia's Volvo is parked on the grass because there is no driveway. Gogol and Maxine step out, and he is led by the hand to the back of the house, his limbs stiff from the hours in the car. Though the sun is beginning to set, its warmth is still palpable, the air lazy and mild. As they approach he sees that after a certain expanse the yard falls away, and then he sees the lake, a blue a thousand times deeper, more brilliant, than the sky and girded by pines. The mountains rise up behind them. The lake is bigger than he'd expected, a distance he cannot imagine swimming across.

"We're here," Maxine calls out, waving, her arms in a V. They walk toward her parents, who are sitting on Adirondack chairs on the grass, their legs and feet bare, drinking cocktails and admiring the view. Silas comes bounding toward them, barking across the lawn. Gerald and Lydia are tanner, leaner, a bit scantily dressed, Lydia in a white tank top and a denim wrap skirt, Gerald in wrinkled blue shorts, a green polo shirt faded with use. Lydia's arms are nearly as dark as his own. Gerald has burned. Discarded books lie at their feet, facedown on the grass. A turquoise dragonfly hovers above them, then darts crookedly away. They turn their heads in greeting, shielding their eyes from the sun's glare. "Welcome to paradise," Gerald says.

It is the opposite of how they live in New York. The house is dark, a bit musty, full of primitive, mismatched furniture. There are exposed pipes in the bathrooms, wires stapled over doorsills, nails protruding from beams. On the walls are clusters of local butterflies, mounted and framed, a map of the region on thin white paper, photographs of the family at the lake over the years. Checkered cotton curtains hang in the windows on thin white rods. Instead of staying with Gerald and Lydia, he and Maxine sleep in an unheated cabin down a path from the main house. No bigger than a cell, the space was originally built for Maxine to play in when she was a girl. There is a small chest of drawers, a crude night table between two twin beds, a lamp with a plaid paper shade, two wooden chests in which extra quilts are stored. The beds are covered with ancient electric blankets. In the corner is a device whose hum is supposed to keep the bats away. Hairy, unfinished logs hold up the roof, and there is a gap between where the floor ends and the wall begins, so that one can see a thin line of grass. There are insect carcasses everywhere, squashed against the windowpanes and walls, languishing in pools of water behind the taps of the sink. "It's sort of like being at camp," Maxine says as they unpack their things, but Gogol has never been to camp, and though he is only three hours away from his parents' house, this is an unknown world to him, a kind of holiday he's never been on.

During the days he sits with Maxine's family on a thin strip of beach, looking out onto the glittering jade lake, surrounded by other homes, overturned canoes. Long docks jut into the water. Tadpoles dart close to shore. He does as they do, sitting on a folding chair, a cotton cap on his head, applying sunblock at intervals to his arms, reading, falling asleep after barely a page. He wades into the water and swims to the dock when his shoulders grow too warm, the sand free of stones or growth, smooth and yielding under his feet. Occasionally they are joined by Maxine's grandparents, Hank and Edith, who live on the lake several houses away. Hank, a retired professor of classical archaeology, always brings a small volume of Greek poetry to read, his long sun-spotted fingers curling over the tops of the pages. At some point he gets up, laboriously removing his shoes and socks, and walks calf-deep into the water, regarding the surroundings with his hands on his hips, his chin thrust pridefully into the air. Edith is small and thin, proportioned like a girl, her white hair cut in a bob and her face deeply wrinkled. They have traveled a bit of the world together, Italy, Greece, Egypt, Iran. "We never got as far as India," Edith tells him. "We would certainly have loved to have seen that."

All day he and Maxine walk about the property barefoot in their bathing suits. Gogol goes for runs around the lake with Gerald, arduous laps along steep hilly dirt roads, so infrequently traveled that they can occupy the dead center. Halfway around is a small private graveyard where members of the Ratliff family lie buried, where Gerald and Gogol always stop to catch their breath. Where Maxine will be buried one day. Gerald spends most of his time in his vegetable garden, his nails permanently blackened from his careful cultivation of lettuce and herbs. One day, Gogol and Maxine swim over to Hank and Edith's for lunch, for egg salad sandwiches and canned tomato soup. Some nights, when it's too warm in the cabin, he and Maxine take a flashlight and walk to the lake in their pajamas to go skinny-dipping. They swim in the dark water, under the moonlight, weeds catching their limbs, out to the neighboring dock. The unfamiliar sensation of the water surrounding his unclothed body arouses Gogol, and when they come back to shore they make love on the grass that is wet from their bodies. He looks up at her, and behind her, at the sky, which holds more stars than he ever has seen at one time, crowded together, a mess of dust and gems.

In spite of the fact that there is nothing in particular to do, the days assume a pattern. There is a certain stringency to life, a willful doing without. In the mornings they wake early to the frenzied chirping of birds, when the eastern sky is streaked with the thinnest of pink clouds. Breakfast is eaten by seven, on the screened-in porch overlooking the lake where they have all their meals, homemade preserves slathered on thick slices of bread. Their news of the world comes from the thin local paper Gerald brings back each day from the general store. In the late afternoons, they shower and dress for dinner. They sit with their drinks on the lawn, eating pieces of the cheese Gogol and Maxine brought from New York, and watch the sun set behind the mountains, bats darting between the pines that soar as tall as ten-story buildings, all the bathing suits hung to dry on a line. Dinners are simple: boiled corn from a farm stand, cold chicken, pasta with pesto, tomatoes from the garden sliced and salted on a plate. Lydia bakes pies and cobblers with berries picked by hand. Occasionally she disappears for the day, to go antiquing in the surrounding towns. There is no television to watch in the evenings, just an old stereo on which they sometimes play a symphony or jazz. On the first rainy day Gerald and Lydia teach him to play cribbage. They are often in bed by nine. The phone, in the main house, seldom rings.

He grows to appreciate being utterly disconnected from the world. He grows used to the quiet, the scent of sun-warmed wood. The only sounds are the occasional motorboat cutting across the water, screen doors snapping shut. He presents Gerald and Lydia with a sketch of the main house done one afternoon down at the beach, the first thing he's drawn in years that hasn't been for work. They set it atop the crowded mantel of the stone fireplace, next to piles of books and photographs, promise to have it framed. The family seems to possess every piece of the landscape, not only the house itself but every tree and blade of grass. Nothing is locked, not the main house, or the cabin that he and Maxine sleep in. Anyone could walk in. He thinks of the alarm system now installed in his parents' house, wonders why they cannot relax about their physical surroundings in the same way. The Ratliffs own the moon that floats over the lake, and the sun and the clouds. It is a place that has been good to them, as much a part of them as a member of the family. The idea of returning year after year to a single place appeals to Gogol deeply. Yet he cannot picture his family occupying a house like this, playing board games on rainy afternoons, watching shooting stars at night, all their relatives gathered neatly on a small strip of sand. It is an impulse his parents have never felt, this need to be so far from things. They would have felt lonely in this setting, remarking that they were the only Indians. They would not want to go hiking, as he and Maxine and Gerald and Lydia do almost every day, up the rocky mountain trails, to watch the sun set over the valley. They would not care to cook with the fresh basil that grows rampant in Gerald's garden or to spend a whole day boiling blueberries for jam. His mother would not put on a bathing suit or swim. He feels no nostalgia for the vacations he's spent with his family, and he realizes now that they were never really true vacations at all. Instead they were overwhelming, disorienting expeditions, either going to Calcutta, or sightseeing in places they did not belong to and intended never to see again. Some summers there had been road trips with one or two Bengali families, in rented vans, going to Toronto or Atlanta or Chicago, places where they had other Bengali friends. The fathers would be huddled at the front, taking turns at the wheel, consulting maps highlighted by AAA. All the children would sit in the back with plastic tubs of aloo dum and cold flattened luchis wrapped in foil, fried the day before, which they would stop in state parks to eat on picnic tables. They had stayed in motels, slept whole families to a single room, swum in pools that could be seen from the road.

One day they canoe across the lake. Maxine teaches him how to paddle properly, angling the oar and drawing it back through the still, gray water. She speaks reverently of her summers here. This is her favorite place in the world, she tells him, and he understands that this landscape, the water of this particular lake in which she first learned to swim, is an essential part of her, even more so than the house in Chelsea. This was where she lost her virginity, she confesses, when she was fourteen years old, in a boathouse, with a boy whose family once summered here. He thinks of himself at fourteen, his life nothing like it is now, still called Gogol and nothing else. He remembers Maxine's reaction to his telling her about his other name, as they'd driven up from his parents' house. "That's the cutest thing I've ever heard," she'd said. And then she'd never mentioned it again, this essential fact about his life slipping from her mind as so many others did. He realizes that this is a place that will always be here for her. It makes it easy to imagine her past, and her future, to picture her growing old. He sees her with streaks of gray in her hair, her face still beautiful, her long body slightly widened and slack, sitting on a beach chair with a floppy hat on her head. He sees her returning here, grieving, to bury her parents, teaching her children to swim in the lake, leading them with two hands into the water, showing them how to dive cleanly off the edge of the dock.

It is here that his twenty-seventh birthday is celebrated, the first birthday in his life that he hasn't spent with his own parents, either in Calcutta or on Pemberton Road. Lydia and Maxine plan a special dinner, curling up with cookbooks for days beforehand on the beach. They decide to make a paella, drive to Maine for the mussels and clams. An angel food cake is baked from scratch. They bring the dining table out onto the lawn, a few card tables added on to make room for everyone. In addition to Hank and Edith, a number of friends from around the lake are invited. The women arrive in straw hats and linen dresses. The front lawn fills up with cars, and small children scamper among them. There is talk of the lake, the temperature dropping, the water turning cooler, summer coming to an end. There are complaints about motorboats, gossip about the owner of the general store, whose wife has run off with another man and is seeking a divorce. "Here's the architect Max brought up with her," Gerald says at one point, leading him over to a couple interested in building an addition to their cottage. Gogol speaks to the couple about their plans, promises to come down and have a look at their place before he leaves. At dinner he is asked by his neighbor, a middle-aged woman named Pamela, at what age he moved to America from India.

"I'm from Boston," he says.

It turns out Pamela is from Boston as well, but when he tells her the name of the suburb where his parents live Pamela shakes her head. "I've never heard of that." She goes on, "I once had a girlfriend who went to India."

"Oh? Where did she go?"

"I don't know. All I remember is that she came back thin as a rail, and that I was horribly envious of her." Pamela laughs. "But you must be lucky that way."

"What do you mean?"

"I mean, you must never get sick."

"Actually, that's not true," he says, slightly annoyed. He looks over at Maxine, trying to catch her eye, but she's speaking intently with her neighbor. "We get sick all the time. We have to get shots before we go. My parents devote the better part of a suitcase to medicine."

"But you're Indian," Pamela says, frowning. "I'd think the climate wouldn't affect you, given your heritage."

"Pamela, Nick's American," Lydia says, leaning across the table, rescuing Gogol from the conversation. "He was born here." She turns to him, and he sees from Lydia's expression that after all these months, she herself isn't sure. "Weren't you?"

Champagne is poured with the cake. "To Nikhil," Gerald announces, raising his glass. Everybody sings "Happy Birthday," this group who has known him for only one evening. Who will forget him the next day. It is in the midst of the laughter of these drunken adults, and the cries of their children running barefoot, chasing fireflies on the lawn, that he remembers that his father left for Cleveland a week ago, that by now he is there, in a new apartment, alone. That his mother is alone on Pemberton Road. He knows he should call to make sure his father has arrived safely, and to find out how his mother is faring on her own. But such concerns make no sense here among Maxine and her family. That night, lying in the cabin beside Maxine, he is woken by the sound of the phone ringing persistently in the main house. He gets out of bed, convinced that it's his parents calling to wish him a happy birthday, mortified that it will wake Gerald and Lydia from sleep. He stumbles onto the lawn, but when his bare feet strike the cold grass there is silence, and he realizes the ringing he'd heard had been a dream. He returns to bed, squeezing in beside Maxine's warm, sleeping body, and drapes his arm around her narrow waist, fits his knees behind hers. Through the window he sees that dawn is creeping into the sky, only a handful of stars still visible, the shapes of the surrounding pines and cabins growing distinct. A bird begins to call. And then he remembers that his parents can't possibly reach him: he has not given them the number, and the Ratliffs are unlisted. That here at Maxine's side, in this cloistered wilderness, he is free.

7

ASHIMA sits at the kitchen table on Pemberton Road, addressing Christmas cards. A cup of Lipton tea grows slowly cold by her hand. Three different address books are open before her, along with some calligraphy pens she's found in the desk drawer in Gogol's room, and the stack of cards, and a bit of dampened sponge to seal the envelopes with. The oldest of the address books, bought twenty-eight years ago at a stationery store in Harvard Square, has a pebbly black cover and blue pages, bound together by a rubber band. The other two are larger, prettier, the alphabetical tabs still intact. One has a padded dark green cover and pages edged in gilt. Her favorite, a birthday gift from Gogol, features paintings that hang in the Museum of Modern Art. On the endpapers of all these books are phone numbers corresponding to no one, and the 800 numbers of all the airlines they've flown back and forth to Calcutta, and reservation numbers, and her ballpoint doodles as she was kept on hold.

Having three separate address books makes her current task a bit complicated. But Ashima does not believe in crossing out names, or consolidating them into a single book. She prides herself on each entry in each volume, for together they form a record of all the Bengalis she and Ashoke have known over the years, all the people she has had the fortune to share rice with in a foreign land. She remembers the day she bought the oldest book, soon after arriving in America, one of her first trips out of the apartment without Ashoke at her side, the five-dollar bill in her purse feeling like a fortune. She remembers selecting the smallest and cheapest style, saying "I would like to buy this one, please" as she placed the item on the counter, her heart pounding for fear that she would not be understood. The salesperson had not even glanced at her, had said nothing other than the price. She had come back to the apartment and written into the book's blank blue pages her parents' address in Calcutta, on Amherst Street, and then her in-laws' in Alipore, and finally her own, the apartment in Central Square, so that she would remember it. She had written in Ashoke's extension at MIT, conscious of writing his name for the first time in her life, writing his last name as well. That had been her world.

She has made her own Christmas cards this year, an idea she picked up from a book in the crafts section of the library. Normally she buys boxes of cards, marked fifty percent off at department stores in January, always forgetting, by the following winter, exactly where in the house she's put them. She is careful to choose ones that say "Happy Holidays" or "Season's Greetings" as opposed to "Merry Christmas," to avoid angels or nativity scenes in favor of what she considers firmly secular images—a sleigh being pulled through a snow-covered field, or skaters on a pond. This year's card is a drawing she has done herself, of an elephant decked with red and green jewels, glued onto silver paper. The elephant is a replica of a drawing her father had done for Gogol over twenty-seven years ago, in the margins of an aerogramme. She has saved her dead parents' letters on the top shelf of her closet, in a large white purse she used to carry in the seventies until the strap broke. Once a year she dumps the letters onto her bed and goes through them, devoting an entire day to her parents' words, allowing herself a good cry. She revisits their affection and concern, conveyed weekly, faithfully, across continents — all the bits of news that had had nothing to do with her life in Cambridge but which had sustained her in those days nevertheless. Her ability to reproduce the elephant has surprised her. She has not drawn a thing since she was a child, has assumed she'd long forgotten what her father had once taught her, and what her son has inherited, about holding the pen with confidence and making bold, swift strokes. She spent a whole day redoing the drawing on different sheets of paper, coloring it in, trimming it to size, taking it to the university copy center. For an entire evening she had driven herself to different stationery stores in the town, looking for red envelopes that the cards would fit into.

She has time to do things like this now that she is alone. Now that there is no one to feed or entertain or talk to for weeks at a time. At forty-eight she has come to experience the solitude that her husband and son and daughter already know, and which they claim not to mind. "It's not such a big deal," her children tell her. "Everyone should live on their own at some point." But Ashima feels too old to learn such a skill. She hates returning in the evenings to a dark, empty house, going to sleep on one side of the bed and waking up on another. At first she was wildly industrious, cleaning out closets and scrubbing the insides of kitchen cupboards and scraping the shelves of the refrigerator, rinsing out the vegetable bins. In spite of the security system she would sit up startled in the middle of the night by a sound somewhere in the house, or the rapid taps that traveled through the baseboards when heat flowed through the pipes. For nights on end, she would double-check all the window locks, making sure that they were fastened tightly. There was the night she'd been roused by a repetitive banging outside

the front door and called Ashoke in Ohio. With the cordless
phone pressed to her ear, she'd gone downstairs and looked
through the peephole, and when she'd finally opened the door
she saw that it was only the screen door, which she'd forgotten
to latch, swinging wildly in the wind.

Now she does the laundry once a month. She no longer
dusts, or notices dust, for that matter. She eats on the sofa, in
front of the television, simple meals of buttered toast and dal,
a single pot lasting her a week and an omelette to go with it if
she has energy to bother. Sometimes she eats the way Gogol
and Sonia do when they visit, standing in front of the refrigerator, not bothering to heat up the food in the oven or to put
it on a plate. Her hair is thinning, graying, still parted in the
middle, worn in a bun instead of a braid. She's been fitted for
bifocals recently, and they hang against the folds of her sari on
a chain around her neck. Three afternoons a week and two Saturdays a month, she works at the public library, just as Sonia
had done when she was in high school. It is Ashima's first job
in America, the first since before she was married. She signs
her small paychecks over to Ashoke, and he deposits them for
her at the bank into their account. She works at the library to
pass the time — she has been going regularly for years, taking
her children to story hour when they were young and checking out magazines and books of knitting patterns for herself,
and one day Mrs. Buxton, the head librarian, asked if she would
be interested in a part-time position. At first her responsibilities were the same as those of the high school girls, shelving
the books that people returned, making sure that sections of
shelves were in precise alphabetical order, sometimes running
a feather duster along the spines. She mended old books, put
protective covers on new arrivals, organized monthly displays
on subjects such as gardening, presidential biographies, poetry,
African-American history. Lately she's begun to work at the

main desk, greeting the regular patrons by name as they walk through the doors, filling out forms for interlibrary loans. She is friendly with the other women who work at the library, most of them also with grown children. A number of them live alone, as Ashima does now, because they are divorced. They are the first American friends she has made in her life. Over tea in the staff room, they gossip about the patrons, about the perils of dating in middle age. On occasion she has her library friends over to the house for lunch, goes shopping with them on weekends to outlet stores in Maine.

Every three weekends her husband comes home. He arrives by taxi — though she is willing to drive herself around their town, she is not willing to get on the highway and drive to Logan. When her husband is in the house, she shops and cooks as she used to. If there is a dinner invitation at friends', they go together, driving along the highway without the children, sadly aware that Gogol and Sonia, now both grown, will never sit with them in the back seat again. During his visits, Ashoke keeps his clothes in his suitcase, his shaving things in a bag by the sink. He does the things she still doesn't know how to do. He pays all the bills, and rakes the leaves on the lawn, and puts gas from the self-service station into her car. His visits are too short to make a difference, and, within hours it seems, Sunday comes, and she is on her own again. When they are apart, they speak by phone every night, at eight o'clock. Sometimes, not knowing what to do with herself after dinner, she is already in bed by then, in her nightgown, watching the small black-and-white television they've owned for decades that lives on her side of the bed, the picture gradually disappearing, a rim of black perpetually framing the screen. If there is nothing decent on television she leafs through books she takes out of the library, books that occupy the space Ashoke normally does on the bed.

Now it is three in the afternoon, the sun's strength already draining from the sky. It is the sort of day that seems to end minutes after it begins, defeating Ashima's intentions to spend it fruitfully, the inevitability of nightfall distracting her. The sort of day when Ashima craves her dinner by five. It's one of the things she's always hated about life here: these chilly, abbreviated days of early winter, darkness descending mere hours after noon. She expects nothing of days such as this, simply waits for them to end. She is resigned to warming dinner for herself in a little while, changing into her nightgown, switching on the electric blanket on her bed. She takes a sip of her tea, now stone cold. She gets up to refill the kettle, make another cup. The petunias in her window box, planted Memorial Day weekend, the last time Gogol and Sonia were home together, have withered to shuddering brown stalks that she's been meaning, for weeks, to root from the soil. Ashoke will do it, she thinks to herself, and when the phone rings, and her husband says hello, this is the first thing she tells him. She hears noises in the background, people speaking. "Are you watching television?" she asks him.

"I'm in the hospital," he tells her.

"What's happened?" She turns off the whistling kettle, startled, her chest tightening, terrified that he's been in some sort of accident.

"My stomach's been bothering me since morning." He tells Ashima it's probably something he's eaten, that he'd been invited the previous evening to the home of some Bengali students he'd met in Cleveland who are still teaching themselves to cook, where he was subjected to a suspicious-looking chicken biryani.

She exhales audibly, relieved that it's nothing serious. "So take an Alka-Seltzer."

"I did. It didn't help. I just came to the emergency room because all the doctors' offices are closed today."

"You're working too hard. You're no longer a student, you know. I hope you're not getting an ulcer," she says.

"No. I hope not."

"Who drove you there?"

"No one. I'm here on my own. Really, it's not that bad."

Nevertheless she feels a wave of sympathy for him, at the thought of him driving to the hospital alone. She misses him suddenly, remembering afternoons years ago when they'd first moved to this town, when he would surprise her and come home from the university in the middle of the day. They would indulge in a proper Bengali lunch instead of the sandwiches they'd gotten used to by then, boiling rice and warming the previous night's leftovers, filling their stomachs, sitting and talking at the table, sleepy and sated, as their palms turned yellow and dry.

"What does the doctor say?" she asks Ashoke now.

"I'm waiting to see him. It's a rather long wait. Do me one thing."

"What?"

"Call Dr. Sandler tomorrow. I'm due for a physical anyway. Make an appointment for me next Saturday, if he has an opening."

"All right."

"Don't worry. I'm feeling better already. I'll call you when I get home."

"All right." She hangs up the phone, prepares her tea, returns to the table. She writes "Call Dr. Sandler" on one of the red envelopes, propping it up against the salt and pepper shakers. She takes a sip of tea and winces, detecting a faint film of dishwashing liquid on this section of the rim, chiding herself for being careless about rinsing. She wonders if she ought to call Gogol and Sonia, to tell them that their father is in the hospital. But quickly she reminds herself that he is not technically in the hospital, that if this were any other day but Sunday he'd be at a doctor's office having an ordinary checkup. He had spoken to her normally, sounding a bit tired, perhaps, but not in great pain.

And so she returns to her project. At the bottom of the cards, over and over, she signs their names: her husband's name, which she has never once uttered in his presence, followed by her own, and then the names of her children, Gogol and Sonia. She refuses to write Nikhil, even though she knows that's what he would prefer. No parent ever called a child by his good name. Good names had no place within a family. She writes the names one below the other, in order of age, Ashoke Ashima Gogol Sonia. She decides to send a card to each of them, shifting the respective name to the top of the card: to her husband's apartment in Cleveland, to Gogol in New York, adding Maxine's name, too. Though she'd been polite enough the one time Gogol had brought Maxine to the house, Ashima doesn't want her for a daughter-in-law. She'd been startled that Maxine had addressed her as Ashima, and her husband as Ashoke. And yet Gogol has been dating her for over a year now. By now Ashima knows that Gogol spends his nights with Maxine, sleeping under the same roof as her parents, a thing Ashima refuses to admit to her Bengali friends. She even has his number there; she'd called it once, listening to the voice of the woman who must be Maxine's mother, not leaving any message. She knows the relationship is something she must be willing to accept. Sonia has told her this, and so have her American friends at the library. She addresses a card to Sonia and the two girlfriends she lives with in San Francisco. Ashima looks forward to Christmas, the four of them being together. It still bothers her that neither Gogol nor Sonia had come home for Thanksgiving this year. Sonia, who is working for an environmental agency and studying for her LSAT, had said it was too far to travel. Gogol, who had to work the following day because of a project at his firm, had spent the holiday with Maxine's family in New York. Having been deprived of the company of her own parents upon moving to America, her children's independence, their need to keep their distance from her, is something she will never understand. Still, she had not argued with them. This, too, she is beginning to learn. She had complained to her friends at the library, and they had told her it was inevitable, that eventually parents had to stop assuming that their children would return faithfully for the holidays. And so she and Ashoke had spent Thanksgiving together, not bothering, for the first time in years, to buy a turkey. "Love, Ma," she writes now at the bottom of the cards to her children. And at the bottom of the one for Ashoke, simply, "Ashima."

She passes over two pages filled only with the addresses of her daughter, and then her son. She has given birth to vagabonds. She is the keeper of all these names and numbers now, numbers she once knew by heart, numbers and addresses her children no longer remember. She thinks of all the dark, hot apartments Gogol has inhabited over the years, beginning with his first dorm room in New Haven, and now the apartment in Manhattan with the peeling radiator and cracks in the walls. Sonia has done the same as her brother, a new room every year ever since she was eighteen, new roommates Ashima must keep track of when she calls. She thinks of her husband's apartment in Cleveland, which she had helped him settle into one weekend when she visited. She'd bought him inexpensive pots and plates, the kind she used back in Cambridge, as opposed to the gleaming ones from Williams-Sonoma her children buy for her these days as gifts. Sheets and towels, some sheer curtains for the windows, a big sack of rice. In her own life Ashima has lived in only five houses: her parents' flat in Calcutta, her in-laws' house for one month, the house they rented in Cambridge, living below the Montgomerys, the faculty apartment on campus, and, lastly, the one they own now. One hand, five homes. A lifetime in a fist.

From time to time, she looks out the window, at the lilac sky of early evening, vividly tinged with two parallel stripes of pink. She looks up at the phone on the wall, wishing it would ring. She will buy her husband a cell phone for Christmas, she decides. She continues to work in the silent house, in the waning light, not bothering to rest, though her wrist has begun to ache, not bothering to get up and turn on the lamp over the table, or the lights on the lawn or in any of the other rooms, until the telephone rings. She answers after half a ring, but it's only a telemarketer, some poor soul on weekend duty, asking reluctantly if a Mrs., um—

"Ganguli," Ashima replies tartly before hanging up.

At twilight the sky turns a pale but intense blue, and the trees on the lawn and the shapes of the neighboring houses become silhouettes, solidly black. At five o'clock her husband still hasn't called. She calls his apartment and gets no answer. She calls ten minutes later, then ten minutes after that. It is her own voice on the answering machine, reciting the number and asking the caller to leave a message. Each time she calls she listens to the tone, but she doesn't leave a message. She considers the places he may have stopped on his way home—the pharmacy to pick up a prescription, the supermarket for food. By six o'clock she can no longer distract herself by sealing and stamping the envelopes she's spent all day addressing. She calls directory assistance, asking for an operator in Cleveland, then calls the number of the hospital he told her he'd gone to. She asks for the emergency room, is connected to one part of the hospital after another. "He's just there for an examination," she tells the people who answer and tell her to hold. She spells the last name as she has hundreds of thousands of times by now, "G like green," "N like napkin." She holds the line until she is tempted to hang up, wondering all the while if her husband is trying to reach her from home, regretting not having call waiting. She is disconnected, calls again. "Ganguli," she says. Again she is told to hold. Then a person comes on the line, a young woman's voice, no older than Sonia probably. "Yes. I do apologize for the wait. To whom am I speaking?"

"Ashima Ganguli," Ashima says. "Ashoke Ganguli's wife. To whom am I speaking, please?"

"I see. I'm sorry, ma'am. I'm the intern who first examined your husband."

"I've been holding on for nearly half an hour. Is my husband still there or has he gone?"

"I'm very sorry, ma'am," the young woman repeats. "We've been trying to reach you."

And then the young woman tells her that the patient, Ashoke Ganguli, her husband, has expired.

Expired. A word used for library cards, for magazine subscriptions. A word which, for several seconds, has no effect whatsoever on Ashima.

"No, no, it must be a mistake," Ashima says calmly, shaking her head, a small laugh escaping from her throat. "My husband is not there for an emergency. Only for a stomachache."

"I'm sorry, Mrs. . . . . Ganguli, is it?"

She listens to something about a heart attack, that it had been massive, that all attempts to revive him had failed. Did she wish to have any of her husband's organs donated? she is asked. And then, is there anyone in the Cleveland area to identify and claim the body? Instead of answering, Ashima hangs up the phone as the woman is still speaking, pressing down the receiver as hard as she can into the cradle, keeping her hand there for a full minute, as if to smother the words she's just heard. She stares at her empty teacup, and then at the kettle on the stove, which she'd had to turn off in order to hear her husband's voice just a few hours ago. She begins to shiver violently, the house instantly feeling twenty degrees colder. She pulls her sari tightly around her shoulders, like a shawl. She gets up and walks systematically through the rooms of the house, turning on all the light switches, turning on the lamppost on the lawn and the floodlight over the garage, as if she and Ashoke are expecting company. She returns to the kitchen and stares at the pile of cards on the table, in the red envelopes it had pleased her so much to buy, most of them ready to be dropped in the mailbox. Her husband's name is on all of them. She opens her address book, suddenly unable to remember her son's phone number, a thing she can normally dial in her sleep. There is no answer at his office or at his apartment and so she tries the number she has written down for Maxine. It's listed, along with the other numbers, under *G*, both for *Ganguli* and for *Gogol*.

Sonia flies back from San Francisco to be with Ashima. Gogol flies from LaGuardia to Cleveland alone. He leaves early the next morning, boarding the first flight he can get. On the plane he stares through the window at the land below, at the snow-covered patches of the Midwest and at curving rivers that seem covered with tinfoil glinting under the sun. The plane's shape darkens a shifting length of ground. The flight is more than half empty, men and a few women in business suits, people used to such flights and to traveling at such hours, typing on laptops or reading the news of the day. He is unaccustomed to the banality of domestic flights, the narrow cabin, the single bag he's packed, small enough to stow overhead. Maxine has offered to go with him, but he has told her no. He doesn't want to be with someone who barely knew his father, who's met him only once. She walked him to Ninth Avenue, stood with him at dawn, her hair uncombed, her face still thick with sleep, her coat and a pair of boots slipped on over her pajamas. He withdrew cash from an ATM, hailed a cab. Most of the city, including Gerald and Lydia, were still asleep in their beds.

He and Maxine had been at a book party for one of Maxine's writer friends the night before. Afterward they'd gone out to dinner with a small group. At about ten o'clock they returned to her parents' house as usual, tired as if it were much later, pausing on their way upstairs to say good night to Gerald and Lydia, who were sitting under a blanket on the sofa, watching a French film on video, sipping glasses of after-dinner wine. The lights had been turned off, but from the glow of the television screen Gogol could see that Lydia was resting her head on Gerald's shoulder, that they both had their feet propped against the edge of the coffee table. "Oh, Nick. Your mother called," Gerald had said, glancing up from the screen. "Twice," Lydia added. He felt a sting of embarrassment. No, she hadn't left any message, they said. His mother called him more often these days, now that she was living on her own. Every day, it seemed, she needed to hear the voices of her children. But she had never called him at Maxine's parents'. She called him at work, or left messages at his apartment that he would receive days later. He decided that whatever it was could wait until morning. "Thanks, Gerald," he'd said, his arm around Maxine's waist, turning to leave the room. But then the phone had rung again. "Hello," Gerald had said, and then to Gogol, "It's your sister this time."

He takes a cab from the airport to the hospital, shocked by how much colder it is in Ohio than in New York, by the thick layer of snow that cakes the ground. The hospital is a compound of beige stone buildings situated on the crest of a softly sloping hill. He enters the same emergency room his father had entered the day before. After giving his name, he is told to take the elevator to the sixth floor, and then to wait in an empty room, the walls painted a rich dark blue. He watches the clock on the wall, donated, along with the rest of the furnishings in the room, by the loving family of someone named Eugene Arthur. There are no magazines in the waiting room, no television, only a collection of matching wing chairs lined up against the walls and a water fountain at one end. Through the glass door he sees a white hallway, a few empty hospital beds. There is little commotion, no doctors or nurses scurrying down the halls. He keeps his eyes on the elevator, half expecting his father to walk out and fetch him, to indicate, with a slight tilt of the head, that it is time to go. When the elevator doors eventually open, he sees a cart stacked with breakfast trays, most of their contents hidden under domes, and tiny cartons of milk. He feels hungry all of a sudden, wishes he'd thought to save the bagel the stewardess had handed him on the plane. His last meal had been at the restaurant the night before, a bright, bustling place in Chinatown. They had waited nearly an hour on the sidewalk for their table and then feasted on flowering chives and salted squid and the clams in black bean sauce that Maxine loved best. They were already drunk from the book party, lazily sipping their beers, their cold cups of jasmine tea. All that time, his father was in the hospital, already dead.

The door opens and a short, pleasant-looking man with a salt-and-pepper beard steps into the room. He wears a white knee-length coat over his clothing and carries a clipboard. "Hello," he says, smiling kindly at Gogol.

"Are you—were you my father's doctor?"

"No. I'm Mr. Davenport. I'll be taking you downstairs."

Mr. Davenport escorts Gogol in an elevator reserved for patients and doctors, to the subbasement of the hospital. He stands with Gogol in the morgue as a sheet is pulled back to show his father's face. The face is yellow and waxy, a thickened, oddly bloated image. The lips, nearly colorless, are set in an expression of uncharacteristic haughtiness. Below the sheet,

Gogol realizes, his father is unclothed. The fact shames him, causes him to turn briefly away. When he looks again he studies the face more closely, still thinking that perhaps it's a mistake, that a tap on his father's shoulder will wake him. The only thing that feels familiar is the mustache, the excess hair on his cheeks and chin shaved less than twenty-four hours ago.

"His glasses are missing," Gogol says, looking up at Mr. Davenport.

Mr. Davenport does not reply. After a few minutes he says, "Mr. Ganguli, are you able to positively identify the body? Is this your father?"

"Yes, that's him," Gogol hears himself saying. After a few moments he realizes that a chair has been brought for him to sit in, that Mr. Davenport has stepped aside. Gogol sits down. He wonders if he should touch his father's face, lay a hand on his forehead as his father used to do to Gogol when he was unwell, to see if he had a fever. And yet he feels terrified to do so, unable to move. Eventually, with his index finger, he grazes his father's mustache, an eyebrow, a bit of the hair on his head, those parts of him, he knows, that are still quietly living.

Mr. Davenport asks Gogol if he's ready, and then the sheet is replaced, and he is led from the room. A resident arrives, explaining exactly how and when the heart attack happened, why there was nothing the doctors could do. Gogol is given the clothes his father had been wearing, navy slacks, a white shirt with brown stripes, a gray L. L. Bean sweater vest that Gogol and Sonia had gotten him for Christmas one year. Dark brown socks, light brown shoes. His glasses. A trench coat and a scarf. The items brim to the top of a large paper shopping bag. There is a book in the pocket of the trench coat, a copy of *The Comedians* by Graham Greene, with yellow pages and tiny print. Opening the cover, he sees that the book had been bought used; a stranger's name, Roy Goodwin, is written inside. In a separate envelope he is given his father's wallet, his car keys. He tells the hospital that no religious services are necessary, is told that the ashes would be ready in a few days. He could pick them up personally, at the funeral home the hospital suggests, or have them sent, along with the death certificate, directly to Pemberton Road. Before leaving he asks to see the exact place in the emergency room his father was last alive. The bed number is looked up on a chart; a young man with his arm in a sling lies in it now, otherwise in good spirits, talking on the telephone. Gogol glimpses the curtains that had partly girded his father when life left him, green and gray flowers with a section of white mesh at the top; metal hooks hang from the ceiling, traveling on a white U-shaped rail.

His father's leased car, described to him by his mother on the telephone last night, is still parked in the visitors' parking lot. AM news fills his ears as soon as he turns on the ignition, startling him; his father had always been particular about turning off the radio at the end of a drive. In fact, there is no sign of his father in the car. No maps or scraps of paper, no empty cups or loose change or receipts. All he finds in the glove compartment is the registration and the owner's manual. He spends a few minutes reading through the manual, comparing the features of the dashboard to the illustration in the book. He turns the wipers on and off and tests the headlights even though it's still daylight. He shuts off the radio, drives in silence through the cold, bleak afternoon, through the flat, charmless town he will never visit again. He follows directions a nurse at the hospital gave him to the apartment where his father had lived, wondering if this route is the same one his father had taken when he drove himself to the hospital. Each time he passes a restaurant he considers turning off the road, but then he finds himself in a residential section, blocks of Victorian mansions on snow-covered lawns, sidewalks covered with lacy patches of ice.

His father's apartment is part of a complex called Baron's Court. Beyond the gate, oversized silver mailboxes, spacious enough to hold a month's worth of mail, stand in a row. A man outside the first of the buildings, marked RENTAL OF- FICE, nods to him as he drives past, seeming to recognize the car. Has he mistaken him for his father? Gogol wonders, the thought comforting. The only thing to distinguish each build- ing is a number and a name; to either side of it are more units, absolutely identical, each three stories tall, arranged around a vast looping road. Tudor facades, tiny metal balconies, wood chips under the stairs. The relentless uniformity of it upsets him profoundly, more so than even the hospital, and the sight of his father's face. Thinking of his father living here alone these past three months, he feels the first threat of tears, but he knows that his father did not mind, that he was not offended by such things. He parks in front of his father's building, remain- ing long enough in the car to see an elderly, sprightly couple emerge with tennis rackets. He remembers his father telling him that the residents are mostly retired, or divorced. There are paths for walking, a small exercise complex, a man-made pond surrounded by benches and willow trees.

His father's apartment is on the second floor. He unlocks the door, takes off his shoes, puts them on the plastic runner that his father must have placed there to protect the plush off-white wall-to-wall carpeting. He sees a pair of his father's sneakers, and a pair of flip-flops for wearing around the house. The door opens onto a spacious living room, with a sliding glass door to the right, a kitchen to the left. Nothing hangs on the freshly painted ivory walls. The kitchen is separated on one side by a half wall, one of the things his mother always wanted in their own house, so that it would be possible to cook and still see and speak to people in another room. Against the refrigera- tor is a picture of himself and his mother and Sonia, behind a magnet from a local bank. They are standing at Fatehpur

Sikri with cloths tied over their feet to protect them from the hot stone surface. He was a freshman in high school, thin and glum, Sonia just a girl, his mother in a salwar kameeze, something she was too shy to wear in front of their relatives in Calcutta, who always expected her to be in a sari. He opens the cupboards, first the ones above the countertop, then the ones below. Most of them are empty. He finds four plates, two mugs, four glasses. In a drawer he finds one knife and two forks, a pattern recognizable from home. In another cupboard are a box of tea bags, Peek Freans shortbread biscuits, a five-pound bag of sugar that has not been poured into a bowl, a tin of evaporated milk. There are several small bags of yellow split peas and a large plastic bag of rice. A rice cooker sits mindfully unplugged on the counter. The ledge of the stove is lined with a few spice jars, labeled in his mother's hand. Below the sink he finds a bottle of Windex, a box of trash bags, a single sponge.

He walks through the rest of the apartment. Behind the living room is a small bedroom with nothing in it but a bed, and across from it a windowless bathroom. A jar of Pond's cold cream, his father's lifelong answer to after-shave, sits at the side of the sink. He goes to work immediately, going through the room and putting things into garbage bags: the spices, the cold cream, the issue of *Time* magazine by his father's bed. "Don't bring anything back," his mother had told him on the phone. "It's not our way." He lingers over nothing at first, but in the kitchen he pauses. He feels guilty throwing out the food; were it his father in his place, he would have packed the spare rice and tea bags into his suitcase. His father had abhorred waste of any kind, to the point where he complained to Ashima if a kettle had been filled with too much water.

On his first trip to the basement, Gogol sees a table on which other tenants have left things up for grabs: books, videotapes, a white casserole with a clear glass lid. Soon the table is filled with his father's hand-held vacuum, the rice cooker, the tape player, the television, the curtains still attached to their collapsible plastic rods. From the bag he'd brought back from the hospital, he saves his father's wallet, containing forty dollars, three credit cards, a wad of receipts, photographs of Gogol and Sonia when they were babies. He saves the photograph on the fridge.

Everything takes much longer than he expects. The task of emptying three rooms, practically empty to begin with, leaves him exhausted. He is surprised to see how many garbage bags he's managed to fill up, how many trips up and down the stairs he's had to make. By the time he is finished, it is already beginning to get dark. He has a list with him of the people he has to call before the business day is over: Call rental office. Call university. Cancel utilities. "We're so very sorry," he is told by a series of people he's never met. "We just saw him Friday," one of his father's colleagues says. "What a shock it must be." The rental office tells him not to worry, that they will send someone by to remove the couch and the bed. When he finishes, he drives through town to the dealer who leased his father the car, and then he takes a cab back to Baron's Court. In the lobby he notices a menu for pizza delivery. He orders a pizza, calls home as he waits for it to arrive. For an hour the line is busy; by the time he gets through, his mother and Sonia are both asleep, a friend of the family informs him. The house is filled with noise, and it is only then that he realizes how quiet it is on his end. He considers going back down to the basement to get the tape player or the television. Instead he calls Maxine, describing the details of his day, amazed to think she'd been with him at the beginning of it, that it was in her arms, in her bed, that he'd woken.

"I should have come with you," she says. "I could still make it out there by morning."

"I'm finished. There's nothing else to do. I'm taking the first flight back tomorrow."

"You're not going to spend the night there, are you, Nick?" she asks him.

"I have to. There aren't any other flights tonight."

"In that apartment, I mean."

He feels defensive; after all his efforts, he feels protective of the three empty rooms. "I don't know anyone here."

"For God's sake, get out of there. Check yourself into a hotel."

"Okay," he says. He thinks of the last time he'd seen his father, three months ago: the image of him waving good-bye as he and Maxine pulled out of the driveway on their way to New Hampshire. He cannot remember the last time he and his father had spoken. Two weeks ago? Four? His father was not one to make frequent phone calls the way his mother does.

"You were with me," he tells her.

"What?"

"The last time I saw my father. You were there."

"I know. I'm so sorry, Nick. Just promise me you'll go to a hotel."

"Yeah. I promise." He hangs up and opens the phone book, looking at his choices of places to stay. He is accustomed to obeying her, to taking her advice. He dials one of the numbers. "Good evening, may I help you?" a voice inquires. He asks if there are any rooms available for the night, but while he is on hold he hangs up. He doesn't want to inhabit an anonymous room. As long as he is here, he doesn't want to leave his father's apartment empty. He lies on the couch in the dark, in his clothes, his body covered by his jacket, preferring that to the stripped mattress in the bedroom. For hours he lies in the dark, falling in and out of sleep. He thinks of his father, in the apartment just yesterday morning. What had he been doing when he'd begun to feel badly? Was he at the stove making tea? Sitting on the sofa, where Gogol sits now? Gogol imagines his father by the door, bending over to tie his shoelaces for the last time. Putting on his coat and scarf and driving to the hospital. Stopping at a traffic light, listening to the weather report on the radio, the thought of death absent from his mind. Eventually Gogol is aware of bluish light creeping into the room. He feels strangely vigilant, as if, were he to pay close enough attention, some sign of his father might manifest itself, putting a stop to the events of the day. He watches the sky whiten, listens as the perfect silence is replaced by the faintest hum of distant traffic, until suddenly he succumbs, for a few hours, to the deepest sleep possible, his mind blank and undisturbed, his limbs motionless, weighted down.

It is nearly ten in the morning when he wakes up again, unobstructed sunlight brightening the room. A dull, steady ache persists on the right side of his head, emanating from deep inside his skull. He opens the sliding glass door to the balcony and stands outside. His eyes burn from fatigue. He gazes at the man-made pond, which, his father had told Gogol during a phone conversation, he walked around twenty times each evening before eating his dinner, that it equaled a distance of two miles. A few people are out there now, walking their dogs, couples exercising side by side, swinging their arms, thick fleece bands covering their ears. Gogol puts on his coat, goes outside and attempts to walk around the pond once. At first he welcomes the cold air on his face, but the chill turns brutal, unforgiving, slicing through his body and pressing the backs of his pants against his legs, and so he returns to the apartment. He takes a shower, changing into the same clothes he'd worn the day before. He calls himself a cab and goes to the basement one last time to throw away the towel he'd used to dry off, the gray push-button phone. He is taken to the airport, boards a flight to Boston. Sonia and his mother will be there, along with a few friends of the family, waiting for him at the arrival gate. He wishes it could be otherwise. Wishes he could simply get into another cab, and ride along another highway, deferring the moment he must face them. He is terrified to see his mother, more than he had been to see his father's body in the morgue. He knows now the guilt that his parents carried inside, at being able to do nothing when their parents had died in India, of arriving weeks, sometimes months later, when there was nothing left to do.

On the way to Cleveland, the journey had felt endless, but this time, staring out the plane window, seeing nothing, all too quickly he feels the plane's descent in his chest. Just before landing he goes into the bathroom, retches into the tiny metal basin. He rinses his face and looks at himself in the mirror. Apart from a day's growth on his face, he looks exactly the same. He remembers when his paternal grandfather died, sometime in the seventies, remembers his mother screaming when she walked in on his father, who was shaving off all his hair with a disposable razor. In the process his scalp had bled in numerous places, and for weeks he had worn a cap to work to hide the scabs. "Stop it, you're hurting yourself," his mother had said. His father had shut the door, and locked it, and emerged shrunken and bald. Years later Gogol had learned the significance, that it was a Bengali son's duty to shave his head in the wake of a parent's death. But at the time Gogol was too young to understand; when the bathroom door opened he had laughed at the sight of his hairless, grief-stricken father, and Sonia, just a baby, had cried.

For the first week they are never alone. No longer a family of four, they become a household of ten, sometimes twenty, friends coming by to sit with them quietly in the living room, their heads bent, drinking cups of tea, a cluster of people attempting to make up for his father's loss. His mother has shampooed the vermilion from her part. She has taken off her iron wedding bracelet, forcing it from her hand with cold cream, along with all the other bracelets she's always worn. Cards and flowers come continually to the house, from his father's colleagues at the university, from the women who work with his mother at the library, from neighbors who normally do little but wave from their lawns. People call from the West Coast, from Texas, from Michigan and D.C. All the people in his mother's address books, always added to, never crossed out, all of them are stricken by the news. Who had forsaken everything to come to this country, to make a better life, only to die here? The phone rings constantly, and their ears ache from speaking to all these people, their throats turning weak from explaining again and again. No he wasn't ill, they say; yes, it was completely unexpected. A short obituary runs in the town paper, citing the names of Ashima and Gogol and Sonia, mentioning that the children had been educated at the local schools. In the middle of the night, they call their relatives in India. For the first time in their lives, it's they who have bad news to bear.

For ten days following his father's death, he and his mother and Sonia eat a mourner's diet, forgoing meat and fish. They eat only rice and dal and vegetables, plainly prepared. Gogol remembers having to do the same thing when he was younger, when his grandparents died, his mother yelling at him when he forgot one day and had a hamburger at school. He remembers, back then, being bored by it, annoyed at having to observe a ritual no one else he knew followed, in honor of people he had seen only a few times in his life. He remembers his father sitting unshaven on a chair, staring through them, speaking to no one. He remembers those meals eaten in complete silence, the television turned off. Now, sitting together at the kitchen table at six-thirty every evening, the hour feeling more like midnight through the window, his father's chair empty, this meatless meal

is the only thing that seems to make sense. There is no question of skipping this meal; on the contrary, for ten evenings the
three of them are strangely hungry, eager to taste the blandness
on their plates. It is the one thing that structures their days:
the sound of the food being warmed in the microwave, three
plates lowered from the cupboard, three glasses filled. The rest
of it—the calls, the flowers that are everywhere, the visitors,
the hours they spend sitting together in the living room unable
to say a word, mean nothing. Without articulating it to one another, they draw comfort from the fact that it is the only time
in the day that they are alone, isolated, as a family; even if there
are visitors lingering in the house, only the three of them par-
take of this meal. And only for its duration is their grief slightly
abated, the enforced absence of certain foods on their plates
conjuring his father's presence somehow.

On the eleventh day they invite their friends to mark the end
of the mourning period. There is a religious ceremony conducted on the floor in one corner of the living room; Gogol is
asked to sit in front of a picture of his father, as a priest chants
verses in Sanskrit. Before the ceremony they had spent a whole
day looking for a picture to frame, going through albums. But
there are almost no pictures of his father alone, his father who
was forever behind the lens. They decide to crop one, of him
and Ashima standing together years ago in front of the sea. He
is dressed like a New Englander, in a parka and a scarf. Sonia
takes it to CVS to have it enlarged. They prepare an elaborate
meal, fish and meat bought one bitterly cold morning at Chinatown and Haymarket, cooked as his father liked them best,
with extra potatoes and fresh coriander leaves. When they shut
their eyes, it's as if it is just another party, the house smelling of
food. All those years of entertaining have prepared them somehow. Ashima frets that there will not be enough rice; Gogol
and Sonia take people's coats and put them upstairs, on the
guest room bed. The friends his parents have collected for al-

most thirty years are in attendance, to pay their respects, cars from six different states lining the whole of Pemberton Road.

Maxine drives up from New York, bringing Gogol the clothes he normally keeps at her house, his laptop, his mail. His bosses have given him a month off from work. It's a bit of a shock to see Maxine, to introduce her to Sonia. This time he doesn't care how the house, how the pile of guests' shoes heaped by the doorway, might appear to her eyes. He can tell that she feels useless, a bit excluded in this house full of Bengalis. And yet he doesn't bother to translate what people are saying, to introduce her to everyone, to stay close by her side. "I'm so sorry," he hears her say to his mother, aware that his father's death does not affect Maxine in the least. "You guys can't stay with your mother forever," Maxine says when they are alone for a moment after the ceremony, upstairs in his room, sitting side by side on the edge of the bed. "You know that." She says it gently, puts her hand to his cheek. He stares at her, takes her hand and puts it back in her lap.

"I miss you, Nikhil."

He nods.

"What about New Year's Eve?" she says.

"What about it?"

"Do you still want to try to go up to New Hampshire?" For they had talked of this, going away together, just the two of them, Maxine picking him up after Christmas, staying at the lake house. Maxine was going to teach him how to ski.

"I don't think so."

"It might do you good," she says, tilting her head to one side. She glances around the room. "To get away from all this."

"I don't want to get away."

In the weeks that follow, as their neighbors' hedges and windows are decorated with strings of colored lights, as piles of Christmas cards arrive at the house, each of them assumes a task his father normally had done. In the mornings his mother goes to the mailbox and brings in the paper. Sonia drives into town and does the weekly grocery shopping. Gogol pays the bills, shovels the driveway when it snows. Instead of arranging the Christmas cards on the fireplace mantel, Ashima glances at the return addresses and then, without opening the envelopes, she throws them away.

Each small event seems like an enormous accomplishment. His mother spends hours on the phone and has all the names changed on the bank account, the mortgage, the bills. She is unable to stem the tide of junk mail that will continue to arrive for years, addressed to her dead husband. In the wan, dreary afternoons Gogol goes running. Sometimes he drives to the university, parking behind his father's department, running along the campus roads, through the confined, picturesque universe that had been his father's world for most of the past twenty-five years. Eventually, on weekends, they begin to visit the homes of their parents' friends who live in surrounding suburbs. Gogol drives one way, Sonia the other. Ashima sits in the back seat. At the homes of their friends, his mother tells the story of calling the hospital. "He went in for a stomachache," she says each time, reciting the details of the afternoon, the pink streaks that had been in the sky, the pile of cards, the cup of tea at her side, reciting it in a way that Gogol cannot bear to have repeated, a way he quickly comes to dread. Friends suggest she go to India, see her brother and her cousins for a while. But for the first time in her life, Ashima has no desire to escape to Calcutta, not now. She refuses to be so far from the place where her husband made his life, the country in which he died. "Now I know why he went to Cleveland," she tells people, refusing, even in death, to utter her husband's name. "He was teaching me how to live alone."

• • •

Early in January, after holidays they don't celebrate, in the first days of a year that his father does not live to see, Gogol boards a train and goes back to New York. Sonia is staying on with Ashima, thinking of getting an apartment in Boston or Cambridge so that she will be nearby. They come to the station to see him off, standing on the platform in the cold, his diminished family, straining but failing to see Gogol, who waves at them through the tinted glass. He remembers them all coming to see him off each time, in his first year of college, he would head back to Yale. And though, over the years, his departures had become mundane, his father would always stand on the platform until the moment the train was out of sight. Now Gogol raps his knuckles on the window, but the train begins to move as his mother and Sonia are still struggling to spot him.

The train rattles forward, jostles from side to side, its engine making a sound like the propeller of a plane. The whistle blares intermittently in a minor key. He sits on the left side of the train, the winter sunlight strong on his face. Instructions for removing the window in the event of an emergency, in three steps, are pasted to the glass. Snow covers the straw-colored ground. Trees stand like spears, dried copper leaves from the previous season still clinging to a few of the branches. He sees the backs of houses made of brick and wood. Small snowy lawns. A solid shelf of winter clouds stops just short of the horizon. More snow, possibly heavy, is expected by evening. He hears a young woman somewhere in the compartment, talking to her boyfriend on a cell phone, softly laughing. She talks about where they should meet for dinner once she gets into the city. "I'm so bored," she complains. Gogol will arrive in New York in time for dinner as well. Maxine will be there to greet him at Penn Station, something she has never bothered to do in the past, waiting for him under the arrivals-and-departures board.

The landscape jerks forward, falls away, the train casting a passing shadow on an expanse of nondescript buildings. The tracks resemble endless ladders that stretch ahead rather than upward, rooted to the ground. Between Westerly and Mystic, the tracks are at an angle, embedded into the sloping land, so that the whole train threatens, ever so slightly, to topple over. Though the other passengers seldom comment on this, the way they do, for example, when the engine changes at New Haven from diesel to electric with a sudden jolt, this momentary shift never fails to rouse Gogol from his nap, or the book he is reading, or the conversation he is engaged in, or the thought that has gathered in his head. The train tilts to the left heading south to New York, to the right on the way to Boston. In that brief period of suggested peril, he thinks, always, of that other train he has never seen, the one that had nearly killed his father. Of the disaster that has given him his name.

The train rights itself, the angle falls behind. Again he feels its motion at the small of his back. For several miles the tracks hug the ocean, which is close enough to touch. The shallowest waves lap against mere inches of shore. He sees a stone bridge, scattered islands the size of rooms, gracious gray and white homes with pleasant views. Boxy houses built on stilts. Lone herons and cormorants perched on bleached wooden posts. Boats with naked masts crowd the marina. It is a view his father would have appreciated, and Gogol is reminded of the many times he had driven with his family, on cold Sunday afternoons, to the sea. There were times when it had been so cold that they had simply sat in the car, in the parking lot, looking at the water, his parents sharing tea from a thermos in the front seat, the engine running to keep them warm. Once they had gone to Cape Cod, driving along that curving piece of land until they could drive no farther. He and his father had walked to the very tip, across the breakwater, a string of giant gray slanted stones, and then on the narrow, final inward crescent of sand. His mother had stopped after a few stones and waited with Sonia, too young to go with them, at her side. "Don't go too far," his mother had warned, "don't go so that I can't see you." His legs began to ache halfway there, but his father marched ahead, stopping at times to lend Gogol an arm, his body slightly tilted when he rested on a rock. While on these rocks, some far apart enough to make them pause and consider the best way to reach the next one, water had surrounded them on both sides. It was early winter. Ducks swam in the tide pools. The waves flowed in two directions. "He's too little," his mother had called out. "Are you listening? He's too little to go so far." Gogol had stopped then, thinking that perhaps his father would agree. "What do you say?" his father had said instead. "Are you too little? No, I didn't think so."

At the end of the breakwater, there was a field of yellow reeds to the right, and dunes beyond, and the ocean behind it all. He had expected his father to turn back, but still they had continued, stepping onto the sand. They walked along the water to the left, heading toward the lighthouse, past rusted boat frames, fish spines as thick as pipes attached to yellow skulls, a dead gull whose feathery white breast was freshly stained with blood. They began to pick up small, faded black stones with white stripes running around them, stuffing them into their pockets so that they drooped on either side. He remembers his father's footprints in the sand; because of his limp, the right toe of his shoe was always turned outward, the left straight ahead. Their shadows that day were unnaturally slender and long, leaning in toward each other, the late afternoon sun at their backs. They paused to regard a cracked wooden buoy painted blue and white, shaped like an old parasol. The surface was wrapped with thin brown strands of seaweed and encrusted with barnacles. His father lifted and inspected it, pointing to a live mussel underneath. Finally they stood by the lighthouse, exhausted, surrounded by water on three sides, pale green in the harbor, azure behind. Overheated from the exertion, they unzipped their coats. His father stepped away to urinate. He heard his father cry out—they had left the camera with his mother. "All this way, and no picture," he'd said, shaking his head. He reached into his pocket and began to throw the striped stones into the water. "We will have to remember it, then." They looked around, at the gray and white town that glowed across the harbor. Then they started back again, for a while trying not to make an extra set of footsteps, inserting their shoes into the ones they had just made. A wind had picked up, so strong that it forced them to stop now and then.

"Will you remember this day, Gogol?" his father had asked, turning back to look at him, his hands pressed like earmuffs to either side of his head.

"How long do I have to remember it?"

Over the rise and fall of the wind, he could hear his father's laughter. He was standing there, waiting for Gogol to catch up, putting out a hand as Gogol drew near.

"Try to remember it always," he said once Gogol had reached him, leading him slowly back across the breakwater, to where his mother and Sonia stood waiting. "Remember that you and I made this journey, that we went together to a place where there was nowhere left to go."

8

A YEAR has passed since his father's death. He still lives in New York, rents the apartment on Amsterdam Avenue. He works for the same firm. The only significant difference in his life, apart from the permanent absence of his father, is the additional absence of Maxine. At first she'd been patient with him, and for a while he'd allowed himself to fall back into her life, going home after work to her parents' house, to their world in which nothing had changed. Initially she'd tolerated his silences at the dinner table, his indifference in bed, his need to speak to his mother and Sonia every evening, and to visit them, on weekends, without her. But she had not understood being excluded from the family's plans to travel to Calcutta that summer to see their relatives and scatter Ashoke's ashes in the Ganges. Quickly they began to argue about this, and about other things, Maxine going so far one day as to admit that she felt jealous of his mother and sister, an accusation that struck Gogol as so absurd that he had no energy to argue anymore. And so, a few months after his father's death, he stepped out of Maxine's life for good. Recently, bumping into Gerald and Lydia in a gallery, he learned of their daughter's engagement to another man.

On weekends he takes the train to Massachusetts, to the house in which his father's photograph, the one used during the funeral, hangs in a frame on a wall in the upstairs hallway. On the anniversary of his father's death, and on his father's birthday, a day they never celebrated when his father was alive, they stand together in front of the photograph and drape a garland of rose petals around the frame and anoint his father's forehead with sandalwood paste through the glass. It is the photograph more than anything that draws Gogol back to the house again and again, and one day, stepping out of the bathroom on his way to bed and glancing at his father's smiling face, he realizes that this is the closest thing his father has to a grave.

His visits home are different now; often it's Sonia who does the cooking. Sonia is still living there with their mother, settled back into the room she had occupied as a girl. Four days a week she leaves the house at five-thirty in the morning, takes a bus to a train that takes her to downtown Boston. She works as a paralegal, is applying to law schools nearby. It is she who drives their mother to weekend parties, and to Haymarket on Saturday mornings. Their mother has become thinner, her hair gray. The white column of her part, the sight of her bare wrists, pains Gogol when he first catches sight of her. From Sonia he learns of how their mother spends her evenings, alone in her bed, unable to sleep, watching television without sound. One weekend he suggests going to one of the beaches where his father had liked to walk. At first his mother agrees, cheered by the prospect, but as soon as they step out into the windy parking lot she gets back into the car, saying she will wait.

He is preparing to take his registration exam, the two-day ordeal that will enable him to become a licensed architect, to stamp drawings and design things under his own name. He studies in his apartment, and occasionally up at one of the libraries at Columbia, learning about the matter-of-fact aspects of his profession: electricity, materials, lateral forces. He enrolls in a review class to help him prepare for the exam. The class meets twice a week in the evenings, after work. He enjoys the passivity of sitting in a classroom again, listening to an instructor, being told what to do. He is reminded of being a student, of a time when his father was still alive. It's a small class, and afterward several of them soon begin going out for drinks. Though he is invited to join them, he always says no. Then one day, as they are all filing out of the classroom, one of the women approaches him, and says, "So what's your excuse?" and because he has none, that night he tags along. The woman's name is Bridget, and at the bar she sits beside him. She is starkly attractive, with brown hair cut extremely short, the sort of style that would have looked disastrous on most women. She speaks slowly, deliberately, her speech unhurried. She was raised in the south, in New Orleans. She tells him that she works for a small firm, a husband-and-wife team who operate out of a brownstone in Brooklyn Heights. For a while they talk about the projects they are working on, the architects they both admire: Gropius, van der Rohe, Saarinen. She is his age, married. She sees her husband on weekends; he is a professor at a college in Boston. He thinks of his parents then, living apart for the final months of his father's life. "That must be difficult," he tells her. "It can be," she says. "But it was either that or adjuncting in New York." She tells him about the house her husband rents in Brookline, a sprawling Victorian that costs less than half of their one-bedroom apartment in Murray Hill. She says that her husband had insisted on putting her name on the mailbox, her voice on the answering machine. He had even insisted on hanging a few items of her clothing in the closet, putting a tube of her lipstick in the medicine cabinet. She tells Gogol that her husband delights in illusions like these, is consoled by them, whereas she finds them simply to be reminders of what is missing.

That night they share a cab back to his apartment. Bridget

excuses herself to use the bathroom and when she emerges her wedding ring is absent from her finger. When they are together, he is ravenous; it has been a long time since he's made love. And yet he never thinks about seeing her at any other time. The day he sets out with his *AIA Guide to New York City* to explore Roosevelt Island, it doesn't occur to him to ask her to come along. Only twice a week, the nights the review class meets, does he look forward to her company. They do not have each other's phone numbers. He does not know exactly where she lives. She always goes with him to his apartment. She never spends the night. He likes the limitations. He has never been in a situation with a woman in which so little of him is involved, so little expected. He does not know, nor does he want to know, her husband's name. Then one weekend, when he is on the train to Massachusetts to see his mother and Sonia, a southbound train slices by, and he wonders if perhaps the husband is on the other train, on his way to see Bridget. Suddenly he imagines the house where Bridget's husband lives alone, longing for her, with his unfaithful wife's name on the mailbox, her lipstick beside his shaving things. Only then does he feel guilty.

From time to time his mother asks him if he has a new girlfriend. In the past she broached the topic defensively, but now she is hopeful, quietly concerned. She even asks once whether it is possible to patch things up with Maxine. When he points out to her that she had disliked Maxine, his mother says that that isn't the point, the point is for him to move on with his life. He works to remain calm during these conversations, not to accuse her of meddling, as he once would have done. When he tells her that he isn't even thirty, she tells him that by that age she had already celebrated her tenth wedding anniversary. He is aware, without having to be told, that his father's death has accelerated certain expectations, that by now his mother wants him settled. The fact that he is single doesn't worry him, and yet he is conscious of the degree to which it troubles his mother. She makes a point of mentioning the engagements and weddings of the Bengali children he's grown up with in Massachusetts, and his cousins in India. She mentions grandchildren being born.

One day when he is speaking to her on the phone, she asks him if he might be willing to call someone. He had known her as a girl, his mother explains. Her name is Moushumi Mazoomdar. He remembers her vaguely. She was the daughter of friends of his parents who had lived for a while in Massachusetts, then moved to New Jersey when he was in high school. She had a British accent. Always with a book in her hand at parties. This is all he remembers about her—details neither appealing nor unappealing. His mother tells him that she is a year younger than he is, that she has a much younger brother, that her father is a renowned chemist with a patent to his name. That he called her mother Rina Mashi, her father Shubir Mesho. Her parents had driven up for his father's funeral, his mother says, from New Jersey, but Gogol has no memory of them there. Moushumi lives in New York City these days, is a graduate student at NYU. She was supposed to have been married a year ago, a wedding that he and his mother and Sonia had been invited to, but her fiancé, an American, had backed out of the engagement, well after the hotel had been booked, the invitations sent, the gift registry selected. Her parents are a bit worried about her. She could use a friend, his mother says. Why doesn't he give her a call?

When his mother asks if he has a pen to take down the number he lies, telling her yes, not listening as she recites it to him. He has no intention of calling Moushumi; his exam is coming up, besides which, as much as he wants to make his mother happy, he refuses to let her set him up with someone. He refuses to go that far. The next time he is home for the weekend, his mother brings it up again. This time, because he is in the same room with her, he writes down the number, still with no intention of calling. But his mother persists, reminding him, the next time they speak, that her parents had come to his father's funeral, that it was the least he could do. A cup of tea, a conversation—did he have no time for that?

They meet at a bar in the East Village, a place Moushumi had suggested when they'd spoken on the phone. It's a small, dark, silent space, a single square room with just three booths against one wall. She's there, sitting at the bar reading a paperback book, when he arrives, and when she looks up from its pages, though it is she who is waiting for him, he has the feeling that he is interrupting her. She has a slender face, pleasingly feline features, spare, straight brows. Her eyes are heavy-lidded and boldly lined on the top lids, in the manner of 1960s movie stars. Her hair is middle-parted, gathered into a chignon, and she wears stylishly narrow tortoiseshell glasses. A gray wool skirt and a thin blue sweater cling suggestively to her sides. Opaque black tights cover her calves. A collection of white shopping bags lie at the base of her stool. On the phone, he hadn't bothered to ask what she looked like, assuming he'd recognize her, but now he is no longer sure.

"Moushumi?" he says, approaching her.

"Hey there," she says, closing the cover of the book and kissing him casually on both sides of his face. The book has a plain ivory cover, a title written in French. Her British accent, one of the few things he clearly remembers about her, is gone; she sounds as American as he does, with the low, gravelly voice that had surprised him on the phone. She has ordered herself a martini with olives. Beside it is a blue packet of Dunhills.

"Nikhil," she says as he sits down on the stool beside her, and orders a single malt.

"Yes."

"As opposed to Gogol."

"Yes." It had annoyed him, when he'd called her, that she hadn't recognized him as Nikhil. This is the first time he's been out with a woman who'd once known him by that other name. On the phone, she'd sounded guarded, faintly suspicious, as he had. The conversation had been brief and thoroughly awkward. "I hope you don't mind my calling," he'd begun, after explaining to her that he'd changed his name. "Let me check my book," she'd told him when he'd asked if she was free Sunday evening for a drink, and then he'd listened to her footsteps clicking across a bare wooden floor.

She studies him for a moment, playfully twisting her lips. "As I recall, given that you're a year older than me, I was taught by my parents to call you Gogol Dada."

He is aware of the bartender glancing at them briefly, assessing their potential. He can smell Moushumi's perfume, something slightly overpowering that makes him think of wet moss and prunes. The silence and the intimacy of the room disconcerts him. "Let's not dwell on that."

She laughs. "I'll drink to that," she says, lifting her glass.

"I never did, of course," she adds.

"Did what?"

"Call you Gogol Dada. I don't remember our ever talking, really."

He sips his drink. "Neither do I."

"So, I've never done this before," she says after a pause. She speaks matter-of-factly, but nevertheless she averts her gaze.

He knows what she is referring to. In spite of this he asks, "Done what?"

"Gone out on a blind date that's been engineered by my mom."

"Well, it's not a blind date, exactly," he says.

"No?"

"We already know each other, in a way."

She shrugs and gives a quick smile, as if she has yet to be convinced. Her teeth are crowded together, not entirely straight. "I guess. I guess we do."

Together they watch as the bartender puts a CD into the player mounted to the wall. Some jazz. He is thankful for the distraction.

"I was sorry to hear about your father," she says.

Though she sounds genuinely sympathetic, he wonders whether she even remembers his father. He is tempted to ask her, but instead he nods. "Thanks," he says, all he can ever think to say.

"How is your mother getting along?"

"All right, I guess."

"Is she okay on her own?"

"Sonia's living with her now."

"Oh. That's good. That must be a relief to you." She reaches for the Dunhills, opening the box and peeling back the gold foil. After offering one to him, she reaches for the book of matches that lies in an ashtray on the bar and lights a cigarette for herself. "Do you guys still live in that same house I used to visit?" she asks.

"Yeah."

"I remember it."

"Do you?"

"I remember that the driveway was to the right of the house as you faced it. There was a flagstone path cut into the lawn."

The fact that she can recall these details so precisely is at once startling and endearing to him. "Wow. I'm impressed."

"I also remember watching lots of television in a room covered with really thick brownish gold carpeting."

He groans. "It still is."

She apologizes for not being at the funeral, she'd been in

Paris at the time. It was where she'd lived after graduating from Brown, she explains. Now she is a candidate for a Ph.D. in French literature at NYU. She's been living in the city for almost two years. She's spent the past summer temping, working for two months in the business office of an expensive midtown hotel. Her job was to review and file all the exit surveys left by the guests, make copies, distribute them to the appropriate people. This simple task had taken up her day. She'd been amazed by the energy people put into the surveys. They complained about the pillows being too hard or too soft, or that there wasn't enough space around the sinks for their toiletries, or that the bedskirt had a loose thread. Most of the people didn't even pay for the rooms themselves. They were at conventions, everything expensed. One person had complained that an architectural print above the desk had a visible speck of dust under the glass.

The anecdote amuses him. "That might have been me," he speculates.

She laughs.

"Why did you leave Paris for New York?" he asks. "I'd think you'd rather study French literature in France."

"I moved here for love," she says. Her frankness surprises him. "Surely you know about my prenuptial disaster."

"Not really," he lies.

"Well, you ought to." She shakes her head. "Every other Bengali living on the East Coast does." She speaks of it lightly, but he detects a bitterness in her voice. "In fact, I'm pretty sure you and your family were invited to the wedding."

"When was the last time we saw each other?" he says, in an effort to change the subject.

"Correct me if I'm wrong, but I think it was your high school graduation party."

His mind goes back to a brightly lit space in the basement of a church his parents and their friends sometimes rented for especially large parties. It was where Sunday school classes were normally held. In the hallways were felt hangings, mottoes about Jesus. He remembers the big, long folding tables that he'd helped his father to set up, chalkboards on the walls, Sonia standing up on a chair, writing "Congratulations."

"You were there?"

She nods. "It was right before we moved to New Jersey. You sat with your American friends from high school. A few of your teachers were there. You seemed a little embarrassed by it all."

He shakes his head. "I don't remember you there. Did I speak to you?"

"You ignored me thoroughly. But it doesn't matter." She smiles. "I'm sure I brought a book with me."

They have a second round of drinks. The bar is beginning to fill up, small groups occupying each of the booths, people sitting on either side of them. A large party enters, and now there are patrons standing behind them to order drinks. When he'd arrived, he'd been bothered by the lack of people, of sounds, feeling on display, but now the crowd bothers him even more.

"It's getting pretty crazy in here," he says.

"It's not usually like this on a Sunday. Should we leave?"

He considers. "Maybe."

They ask for the bill, step out together into the cool October evening. Glancing at his watch, he sees that not even an hour has passed.

"Where are you headed?" she asks in a way that makes him realize that she assumes the date is over.

He hadn't planned to take her to dinner. He had intended to go back to his apartment after the drink, and study, and order in some Chinese food. But now he finds himself saying that he is thinking of getting something to eat, did she want to join him?

"I'd like that," she says.

Neither can think of a place to go and so they decide to walk a bit. He offers to carry her shopping bags, and though they weigh nothing at all she allows him to, telling him she'd been to a sample sale in SoHo just before they'd met. They stop in front of a small place that looks as if it has just opened. They study the handwritten menu taped to the window, the review that was printed a few days ago in the *Times*. He is distracted by her reflection in the glass, a more severe version of herself, for some reason more stunning.

"Shall we try it?" he asks, stepping away and reaching for the door. Inside, the walls are painted red. They are surrounded by old posters advertising wine, and street signs and photographs of Paris arranged above the picture rails.

"This place must seem silly to you," he acknowledges, watching her gaze up at the walls.

She shakes her head. "It's pretty authentic, actually."

She asks for a glass of champagne and looks carefully at the wine list. He asks for another single malt, but is told that there is only beer and wine.

"Shall we have a bottle?" she says, handing him the list.

"You choose."

She orders a salad and the bouillabaisse and a bottle of Sancerre. He orders the cassoulet. She doesn't speak French to the waiter, who is French himself, but the way she pronounces the items on the menu makes it clear that she is fluent. It impresses him. Apart from Bengali, he has never bothered to master another language. The meal passes quickly. He speaks of his work, the projects he is involved in, his upcoming exam. They comment on each other's dishes, trading tastes on their bread plates. They order espresso and share a crème brûlée, their two teaspoons cracking the hard amber surface from either side.

She offers to pay her share when the bill comes, as she'd done in the bar, but this time he insists on treating. He walks her to her apartment, which is on a run-down but pretty residential block, close to the bar where they'd met. Her building has a crumbling stoop, a terra cotta–colored facade with a gaudy green cornice. She thanks him for the dinner, says she's had a great time. Again she kisses him on both cheeks, then begins to search for the keys in her purse.

"Don't forget these." He gives her the shopping bags, watches as she loops them over her wrist. Now that he is no longer carrying them he feels awkward, unsure of what to do with his hands. He is parched from the alcohol he has consumed. "So, should we make our parents happy and see each other again?"

She looks at him, studying his face intently. "Maybe." Her eyes stray to a passing car on the street, the headlights briefly shining on their bodies, but then her gaze returns to his face. She smiles at him, nodding. "Give me a call."

He watches as she ascends quickly up the stoop with her shopping bags, her heels suspended over the treads in a way that looks precarious. She turns briefly to wave at him and then she goes through a second glass door, not waiting to see him waving back. For a minute longer he stands there, watching as the door opens again and a tenant emerges to deposit something into one of the trash cans below the stoop. Gogol looks up at the building, wondering which of the apartments is hers, waiting to see if a light will turn on in one of the windows.

He had not expected to enjoy himself, to be attracted to her in the least. It strikes him that there is no term for what they once were to each other. Their parents were friends, not they. She is a family acquaintance but she is not family. Their contact until tonight has been artificial, imposed, something like his re-

lationship to his cousins in India but lacking even the justifica-
tion of blood ties. Until they'd met tonight, he had never seen
her outside the context of her family, or she his. He decides
that it is her very familiarity that makes him curious about her,
and as he begins to walk west, to the subway, he wonders when
he might see her again. When he reaches Broadway he changes
his mind and hails a cab. The decision feels indulgent, as it is
not particularly late, or cold, or raining, and he is in no great
rush to be home. But he has the urge to be alone all of a sudden,
to be thoroughly passive, to revisit the evening in solitude. The
driver of the cab is a Bangladeshi; the name on the registration
card pasted to the plexiglass behind the front seat says Mustafa
Sayeed. He is talking in Bengali on his cell phone, complaining
of traffic on the FDR, of difficult passengers, as they sail uptown, past the shuttered shops and restaurants on Eighth Avenue. If his parents were in the cab they would have struck up
a conversation with the driver, asking what part of Bangladesh
he was from, how long he'd been in this country, whether his
wife and children lived here or there. Gogol sits silently, as if
he were any other passenger, lost in his own thoughts, thinking
of Moushumi. But as they near his apartment, he leans toward
the plexiglass and says to the driver, in Bengali, "It's that one,
up on the right."

The driver turns around, surprised, smiling. "I didn't realize," he says.

"That's okay," Gogol says, reaching for his wallet. He tips
the driver excessively and steps out of the car.

In the days that follow, he begins to remember things about
Moushumi, images that come to him without warning while
he is sitting at his desk at work, or during a meeting, or drifting off to sleep, or standing in the mornings under the shower.
They are scenes he has carried within him, buried but intact,

scenes he has never thought about or had reason to conjure up until now. He is grateful that his mind has retained these images of her, pleased with himself, as if he has just discovered an innate talent for a sport or a game he's never played. He remembers her mainly at the pujos he had attended every year, twice a year, with his family, where she would be dressed in a sari carefully pinned to the top of her shoulder. Sonia would have to do the same, but she would always take off her sari after an hour or two and put on her jeans, stuffing the sari into a plastic bag and telling Gogol or their father to put it away for her in the car. He does not remember Moushumi ever accompanying the other teenagers to the McDonald's that was across the street from the building in Watertown where the pujos often were, or eventually sitting in someone's car in the parking lot, listening to the radio and drinking beer from a can. He struggles but fails to recall her presence at Pemberton Road; still, he is secretly pleased that she has seen those rooms, tasted his mother's cooking, washed her hands in the bathroom, however long ago.

He remembers once going to a Christmas party at her parents' home. He and Sonia had not wanted to go; Christmas was supposed to be spent with just family. But their parents had replied that in America, Bengali friends were the closest thing they had to family, and so they had gone to Bedford, where the Mazoomdars lived. Her mother, Rina Mashi, had served cold pound cake and warmed-up frozen doughnuts that deflated at the touch. Her brother, Samrat, now a senior in high school, had been a boy of four, obsessed with Spider-Man. Rina Mashi had gone to a great deal of trouble to organize an anonymous gift exchange. Each family was asked to bring as many gifts as there were members, so that there would be something for everyone to open. Gogol had been asked to write numbers on squares of paper, one set to tape onto the gifts and another to pass around, folded up in a drawstring pouch, to the guests. Everyone gathered in a single room, cramming through the two doorways. He remembers sitting in their living room, listening with all the other guests to Moushumi play something on the piano. On the wall above her was a framed reproduction of Renoir's girl with a green watering can. After great deliberation, just as people were beginning to fidget, she had played a short piece by Mozart, adapted for children, but the guests wanted her to play "Jingle Bells." She shook her head no, but her mother said, "Oh, Moushumi's just being shy, she knows very well how to play 'Jingle Bells.'" For an instant she had glared at her mother, but then she'd played the song, again and again, as the numbers were called out and people claimed their gifts, sitting with her back to the room.

A week later they meet for lunch. It is the middle of the week and she has offered to meet him someplace near his office, so he's told her to come to the building where he works. When the receptionist tells him she is waiting in the lobby he feels the anticipation rise in his chest; all morning he'd been unable to concentrate on the elevation he was working on. He spends a few minutes showing her around, pointing out photographs of projects he's worked on, introducing her to one of the principal designers, showing her the room where the partners meet. His coworkers in the drafting room look up from their desks as she passes by. It is early November, a day on which the temperature has suddenly dropped, bringing the first true cold of the year. Outside, unprepared pedestrians scurry past unhappily, arms folded across their chests. Fallen leaves, battered and bleached, scuttle in swirls on the pavement. Gogol has no hat or gloves, and as they walk he puts his hands into the pockets of his jacket. Moushumi, in contrast, seems enviably protected, at ease in the cold. She wears a navy wool coat, a black wool scarf at her throat, long black leather boots that zip up the sides.

He takes her to an Italian restaurant where he goes from time to time with people at work, to celebrate birthdays and promotions and projects well done. The entrance is a few steps below street level, the windows shielded with panels of lace. The waiter recognizes him, smiles. They are led to a small table at the back as opposed to the long one in the center that he normally sits at. Underneath the coat he sees that she is wearing a nubbly gray suit, with large buttons on the jacket and a bell-shaped skirt that stops short of her knees.

"I taught today," she explains, aware that he is looking at her—she preferred to wear a suit when she taught, she says, given that her students were only a decade younger than she was. Otherwise she feels no sense of authority. He envies her students suddenly, seeing her without fail, three times a week, pictures them gathered together around a table, staring at her continuously as she writes on the board.

"The pastas are usually pretty good here," he says as the waiter hands them menus.

"Join me for a glass of wine," she says. "I'm done for the day."

"Lucky you. I have a stressful meeting to go to after this."

She looks at him, closing the menu. "All the more reason for a drink," she points out cheerfully.

"True," he concedes.

"Two glasses of the merlot," he says when the waiter returns. She orders what he does, porcini ravioli and a salad of arugula and pears. He's nervous that she'll be disappointed by the choice, but when the food arrives she eyes it approvingly, and she eats heartily, quickly, sopping up the leftover sauce on her plate with bread. As they drink their wine and eat their meal, he admires the light on her face, the faint pale hairs that shine against the contours of her cheek. She speaks of her students, the topic for the dissertation she plans to write, about twentieth-century francophone poets from Algeria. He tells her about his memory of the Christmas party, of her being forced to play "Jingle Bells."

"Do you remember that night?" he asks, hopeful that she will.

"No. My mother was always forcing me to do things like that."

"Do you still play?"

She shakes her head. "I never wanted to learn in the first place. My mother had this fantasy. One of many. I think my mother's taking lessons now."

The room is quiet again, the lunch crowd has come and gone. He looks around for the waiter, signals for the check, dismayed that their plates are empty, that the hour has passed.

"She is your sister, *signore*?" the waiter asks as he sets the check between them, glancing at Moushumi and then back at Gogol.

"Oh, no," Gogol says, shaking his head, laughing, at once insulted and oddly aroused. In a way, he realizes, it's true — they share the same coloring, the straight eyebrows, the long, slender bodies, the high cheekbones and dark hair.

"You are sure?" the waiter persists.

"Quite sure," Gogol says.

"But you could be," the waiter says. "*Sì, sì*, there is quite a resemblance."

"You think so?" Moushumi says. She appears to be at ease with the comparison, looking comically askance at Gogol. And yet he notices that some color has risen to her cheeks, whether from the wine or from self-consciousness he doesn't know.

"It's funny he should say that," she says, once they have stepped out into the cold.

"What do you mean?"

"Well, it's just funny to think that all our lives our parents raised us according to the illusion that we were cousins, that we were all part of some makeshift extended Bengali family, and now here we are, years later, and someone actually thinks we're related."

He does not know what to say. The waiter's comment has discomfited him, making his attraction to Moushumi feel mildly illicit.

"You're not dressed warmly enough," she observes, twisting the woolen scarf securely around her neck.

"It's so damn hot in my apartment all the time," he says. "The heat just got turned on. For some reason I can never get my mind around the fact that it won't be the same temperature outside."

"Don't you check the paper?"

"I get it on my way to work."

"I always check the weather by phone when I leave the house," Moushumi says.

"You're joking." He stares at her, surprised that she should actually be the type to go to such lengths. "Please tell me you're joking."

She laughs. "I don't admit that to just anyone, you know." She finishes arranging her scarf, and then, without removing her hands from it, she says, "Why don't you borrow this?" and begins to untie it again.

"Please, I'm fine." He puts a hand to his throat, against the knot of his tie.

"Sure?"

He nods, half tempted to say yes, to feel her scarf against his skin.

"Well, at the very least you need a hat," she tells him. "I know a place nearby. Do you need to be back at work right away?"

She leads him to a little boutique on Madison. The window is crowded with women's hats perched on gray, featureless heads, with sloping necks nearly a foot long.

"They have men's stuff in the back," she says. The shop is crowded with women. The back is relatively tranquil, stacks of fedoras and berets arrayed on curved wooden shelves. He picks up a fur hat, a top hat, trying them on as a joke. The glass of wine has made him tipsy. Moushumi begins rummaging through a basket.

"This will be warm," she says, placing her fingers inside a thick navy cap with yellow stripes on the brim. She stretches the hat with her fingers. "What do you think?" She puts it on his head, touching his hair, his scalp. She smiles, pointing to the mirror. She watches as he studies himself.

He is aware that she is looking at him rather than at his reflection. He wonders what her face looks like without her glasses, when her hair is loose. He wonders what it might be like to kiss her on the mouth. "I like it," he says. "I'll take it."

She pulls it off his head quickly, spoiling his hair.

"What are you doing?"

"I want to buy it for you."

"You don't have to do that."

"I want to," she says, already heading toward the register. "It was my idea, anyway. You were perfectly happy freezing to death."

At the register the cashier notices Moushumi eyeing a brown wool and velvet hat decorated with feathers. "It's an exquisite piece," the cashier says, carefully lifting it off the bust. "Handmade by a woman in Spain. No two are alike. Would you like to try it?"

Moushumi places it on her head. A customer compliments her. So does the cashier. "Not many women can pull off a hat like that," the cashier says.

Moushumi blushes, glances at the price tag dangling from a thread on one side of her face. "I'm afraid it's out of my budget for today," she says.

The cashier replaces the hat on the shelf. "Well, now you know what to get her for her birthday," she says, looking at Gogol.

He puts on the new cap and they step out of the store. He is late for his meeting. If it weren't for that, he would be tempted to stay with her, to walk through the streets beside her, or disappear with her into the dark of a movie theater. The day has turned even colder, the wind more forceful, the sun a faint white patch. She walks him back to his office. For the rest of the day, throughout his meeting and as he struggles, afterward, to get back to work, he thinks of her. When he leaves the office, instead of walking to the subway, he retraces the steps they'd taken together earlier, past the restaurant where people are now having their dinners, and finds his way to the hat store, the sight of it lifting his spirits. It is nearly eight o'clock, dark outside. He assumes the store will be closed, is surprised to see the lights still on inside, the grate only partly lowered. He studies the items in the window, and his reflection in the glass, wearing the cap she'd bought for him. Eventually he walks in. He is the only customer; he can hear the sound of a vacuum cleaner running at the rear of the store.

"I knew you'd be back," the saleswoman says as he walks through the door. She takes the brown velvet hat off the Styrofoam head without his having to ask. "He was here earlier today with his girlfriend," she explains to her assistant. "Shall I wrap it for you?"

"That would be great." It excites him to hear himself referred to that way. He watches as the hat is placed in a round chocolate-colored box, tied with a thick, creamy ribbon. He realizes that he has not asked the price, but without a thought he signs the receipt for two hundred dollars. He takes the hat back to his apartment, hiding it at the back of his closet even though Moushumi has never been there. He would give it to her on her birthday, in spite of the fact that he has no idea when her birthday is.

And yet he has the feeling that he has been to a few of her birthdays, and she to his. That weekend, at his parents' house, he confirms this; at night, after his mother and Sonia have gone up to bed, he hunts for her in the photo albums that his mother has assembled over the years. Moushumi is there, lined up behind a blazing cake in his parents' dining room. She is looking away, a pointed paper hat on her head. He stares straight at the lens, the knife in his hand, poised, for the camera's benefit, over the cake, his face shining with impending adolescence. He tries to peel the image from the sticky yellow backing, to show her the next time he sees her, but it clings stubbornly, refusing to detach cleanly from the past.

The following weekend she invites him over for dinner at her place. She has to come downstairs in order to let him into the building; the buzzer is broken, she'd warned him when they'd made their plans.

"Nice cap," she says. She wears a sleeveless black dress tied loosely at the back. Her legs are bare, her feet slim, her toenails, exposed at the tops of her sandals, painted maroon. Strands of hair have come loose from her chignon. She holds half a cigarette between her fingers, but just before she leans forward to kiss him on the cheeks she lets it drop and crushes it with the toe of her sandal. She leads him up the steps to an apartment on the third floor. She's left the door open. The apartment smells strongly of cooking; on the stove, a few large pieces of chicken are browning in a pan full of oil. Music is playing, a man singing songs in French. Gogol gives her a bunch of sunflowers whose massive stems are heavier in his arms than the bottle of wine he's also brought. She does not know where to put the flowers; the countertops, limited to begin with, are crammed with evidence of the meal she is preparing, onions and mushrooms, flour, a stick of butter rapidly softening in the heat, a glass of wine she is in the process of drinking, plastic grocery bags she has not had time to put away.

"I should have brought something more manageable," he says as she looks around the kitchen, the flowers resting against her shoulder, as if expecting a surface miraculously to clear.

"I've been meaning for weeks to buy myself some sunflowers," she says. She glances quickly at the pan on the stove and takes him through the kitchen and into the living room. She unwraps the flowers. "There's a vase up there," she says, pointing to the top of a bookcase. "Would you mind getting it down?"

She carries the vase into the bathroom, and he can hear water running in the tub. He takes the opportunity to remove his coat and cap, drape them over the back of the sofa. He has dressed with care, a blue-and-white-striped Italian shirt that Sonia had bought for him at Filene's Basement, a pair of black jeans. She returns and fills the vase with the flowers, putting it on the coffee table. The place is nicer than he expected from the grimy look of the lobby. The floors have been redone, the walls freshly painted, the ceiling dotted with track lights. The living room has a square dining table in one corner, and a desk and file cabinets set up in another. Three particleboard bookcases line one wall. On the dining table, there is a pepper mill, a saltcellar, bright, clear-skinned clementines arranged in a bowl. He recognizes versions of things he knows from home: a Kashmiri crewelwork carpet on the floor, Rajasthani silk pillows on the sofa, a cast-iron Natraj on one of the bookcases.

Back in the kitchen she sets out some olives and some goat

cheese coated with ash. She hands him a corkscrew and asks him to open the bottle he's brought, to pour himself a glass. She dredges more of the chicken on a plate of flour. The pan is sputtering loudly and has showered the wall behind the stove with oil. He stands there as she refers to a cookbook by Julia Child. He is overwhelmed by the production taking place for his benefit. In spite of the meals they've already shared, he is nervous about eating with her.

"When would you like to eat?" she says. "Are you hungry?"

"Whenever. What are you making?"

She looks at him doubtfully. "Coq au vin. I haven't made it before. I just found out that you're supposed to cook it twenty-four hours in advance. I'm afraid I'm running a bit behind."

He shrugs. "It already smells great. I'll help you." He rolls up his sleeves. "What can I do?"

"Let's see," she says, reading. "Oh. Okay. You can take those onions, and make X's in the bottom with a knife, and drop them into that pan."

"In with the chicken?"

"No. Shoot." She kneels down and retrieves a pot from one of the lower cupboards. "In here. They need to boil for a minute and then you take them out."

He does as he is told, filling the pan with water and turning on the flame. He finds a knife and scores the onions, as he had once been taught to do with Brussels sprouts in the Ratliffs' kitchen. He watches her measure wine and tomato paste into the pan containing the chicken. She searches in a cupboard for a stainless-steel spice caddy and throws in a bay leaf.

"Of course, my mother is appalled that I'm not making you Indian food," she says, studying the contents of the pan.

"You told her I was coming over?"

"She happened to call today." Then she asks him, "What about you? Have you been giving your mother updates?"

"I haven't gone out of my way. But she probably suspects something given that it's a Saturday and I'm not at home with her and Sonia."

Moushumi leans over the pan, watching the contents come to a simmer, prodding the pieces of chicken with a wooden spoon. She glances back at the recipe. "I think I need to add more liquid," she says, pouring water from a teakettle into the pan, causing her glasses to steam. "I can't see." She laughs, stepping away so that she stands a bit closer to him. The CD has ended and the apartment is silent apart from the sounds on the stove. She turns to him, still laughing, her eyes still obscured. She holds up her hands, messy from cooking, coated with flour and chicken fat. "Would you mind taking these off for me?"

With both hands he pries the glasses from her face, clasping the frames where they meet her temples. He puts them on the counter. And then he leans over and kisses her. He touches his fingers to her bare arms, cool in spite of the warmth of the kitchen. He presses her close, a hand at the small of her back, against the knot of her dress, tasting the warm, slightly sour tang of her mouth. They make their way through the living room, to the bedroom. He sees a box spring and mattress without a frame. He unties the knot at the back of her dress with difficulty, then swiftly undoes the long zipper, leaving a small black pool at her feet. In the light cast from the living room, he glimpses black mesh underwear and a matching bra. She is curvier than she appears clothed, her breasts fuller, her hips generously flared. They make love on top of the covers, quickly, efficiently, as if they've known each other's bodies for years. But when they are finished she switches on the lamp by her bed and they examine each other, quietly discovering moles and marks and ribs.

"Who would have thought," she says, her voice tired, satisfied. She is smiling, her eyes partly closed.

He looks down at her face. "You're beautiful."

"And you."

"Can you even see me without those glasses?"

"Only if you stay close," she says.

"Then I'd better not move."

"Don't."

They peel back the covers and lie together, sticky and spent, in each other's arms. He begins to kiss her again, and she wraps her legs around him. But the smell of something burning causes them to bolt naked from the bed, rushing comically to the kitchen, laughing. The sauce has evaporated and the chicken is irreparably scorched, so much so that the pan itself has to be thrown away. By then they are starving and because they lack the energy either to go out or to prepare another meal they end up ordering in, feeding each other tart, tiny wedges of clementines as they wait for Chinese food to arrive.

Within three months they have clothes and toothbrushes at each other's apartments. He sees her for entire weekends without make-up, sees her with gray shadows under her eyes as she types papers at her desk, and when he kisses her head he tastes the oil that accumulates on her scalp between shampoos. He sees the hair that grows on her legs between waxings, the black roots that emerge between appointments at the salon, and in these moments, these glimpses, he believes he has known no greater intimacy. He learns that she sleeps, always, with her left leg straight and her right leg bent, ankle over knee, in the shape of a 4. He learns that she is prone to snoring, ever so faintly, sounding like a lawn mower that will not start, and to gnashing her jaws, which he massages for her as she sleeps. At restaurants and bars, they sometimes slip Bengali phrases into their conversation in order to comment with impunity on another diner's unfortunate hair or shoes.

They talk endlessly about how they know and do not know each other. In a way there is little to explain. There had been the same parties to attend when they were growing up, the same episodes of *The Love Boat* and *Fantasy Island* the children watched as the parents feasted in another part of the house, the same meals served to them on paper plates, the carpets lined with newspapers when the hosts happened to be particularly fastidious. He can imagine her life, even after she and her family moved away to New Jersey, easily. He can imagine the large suburban house her family owned; the china cabinet in the dining room, her mother's prized possession; the large public high school in which she had excelled but that she had miserably attended. There had been the same frequent trips to Calcutta, being plucked out of their American lives for months at a time. They calculate the many months that they were in that distant city together, on trips that had overlapped by weeks and once by months, unaware of each other's presence. They talk about how they are both routinely assumed to be Greek, Egyptian, Mexican—even in this misrendering they are joined.

She speaks with nostalgia of the years her family had spent in England, living at first in London, which she barely remembers, and then in a brick semidetached house in Croydon, with rosebushes in front. She describes the narrow house, the gas fireplaces, the dank odor of the bathrooms, eating Weetabix and hot milk for breakfast, wearing a uniform to school. She tells him that she had hated moving to America, that she had held on to her British accent for as long as she could. For some reason, her parents feared America much more than England, perhaps because of its vastness, or perhaps because in their minds it had less of a link to India. A few months before their arrival in Massachusetts, a child had disappeared while playing in his yard and was never found; for a long time afterward there were posters in the supermarket. She remembers always having to call her mother every time she and her friends moved to another house in the neighborhood, a house visible from her own, to play with another girl's toys, to have another family's cookies and punch. She would have to excuse herself upon entering and ask for the telephone. The American mothers were at once charmed and perplexed by her sense of duty. "I'm at Anna's house," she would report to her mother in English. "I'm at Sue's."

He does not feel insulted when she tells him that for most of her life he was exactly the sort of person she had sought to avoid. If anything it flatters him. From earliest girlhood, she says, she had been determined not to allow her parents to have a hand in her marriage. She had always been admonished not to marry an American, as had he, but he gathers that in her case these warnings had been relentless, and had therefore plagued her far more than they had him. When she was only five years old, she was asked by her relatives if she planned to get married in a red sari or a white gown. Though she had refused to indulge them, she knew, even then, what the correct response was. By the time she was twelve she had made a pact, with two other Bengali girls she knew, never to marry a Bengali man. They had written a statement vowing never to do so, and spit on it at the same time, and buried it somewhere in her parents' backyard.

From the onset of adolescence she'd been subjected to a series of unsuccessful schemes; every so often a small group of unmarried Bengali men materialized in the house, young colleagues of her father's. She never spoke to them; she strutted upstairs with the excuse of homework and did not come downstairs to say good-bye. During summer visits to Calcutta, strange men mysteriously appeared in the sitting room of her grandparents' flat. Once on a train to Durgapur to visit an uncle, a couple had been bold enough to ask her parents if she was engaged; they had a son doing his surgical residency in Michi-

gan. "Aren't you going to arrange a wedding for her?" relatives
would ask her parents. Their inquiries had filled her with a cold
dread. She hated the way they would talk of the details of her
wedding, the menu and the different colors of saris she would
wear for the different ceremonies, as if it were a fixed certainty
in her life. She hated when her grandmother would unlock her
almari, showing her which jewels would be hers when the day
came.

The shameful truth was that she was not involved, was in
fact desperately lonely. She had rebuffed the Indian men she
wasn't interested in, and she had been forbidden as a teenager to date. In college she had harbored lengthy infatuations,
with students with whom she never spoke, with professors and
TAs. In her mind she would have relationships with these men,
structuring her days around chance meetings in the library, or
a conversation during office hours, or the one class she and a
fellow student shared, so that even now she associated a particular year of college with the man or boy she had silently,
faithfully, absurdly, desired. Occasionally one of her infatuations would culminate in a lunch or coffee date, an encounter
on which she would pin all her hopes but which would lead to
nothing. In reality there had been no one, so that toward the
end of college, as graduation loomed, she was convinced in her
bones that there would be no one at all. Sometimes she wondered if it was her horror of being married to someone she
didn't love that had caused her, subconsciously, to shut herself
off. She shakes her head as she speaks, irritated with having re-
visited this aspect of her past. Even now she regrets herself as
a teenager. She regrets her obedience, her long, unstyled hair,
her piano lessons and lace-collared shirts. She regrets her mor-
tifying lack of confidence, the extra ten pounds she carried on
her frame during puberty. "No wonder you never talked to me
back then," she says. He feels tenderness toward her when she

disparages herself this way. And though he had witnessed that stage of her himself, he can no longer picture it; those vague recollections of her he's carried with him all his life have been wiped clean, replaced by the woman he knows now.

At Brown her rebellion had been academic. At her parents' insistence, she'd majored in chemistry, for they were hopeful she would follow in her father's footsteps. Without telling them, she'd pursued a double major in French. Immersing herself in a third language, a third culture, had been her refuge—she approached French, unlike things American or Indian, without guilt, or misgiving, or expectation of any kind. It was easier to turn her back on the two countries that could claim her in favor of one that had no claim whatsoever. Her four years of secret study had prepared her, at the end of college, to escape as far as possible. She told her parents she had no intention of being a chemist and, deaf to their protests, she'd scraped together all the money she had and moved to Paris, with no specific plans.

Suddenly it was easy, and after years of being convinced she would never have a lover she began to fall effortlessly into affairs. With no hesitation, she had allowed men to seduce her in cafés, in parks, while she gazed at paintings in museums. She gave herself openly, completely, not caring about the consequences. She was exactly the same person, looked and behaved the same way, and yet suddenly, in that new city, she was transformed into the kind of girl she had once envied, had believed she would never become. She allowed the men to buy her drinks, dinners, later to take her in taxis to their apartments, in neighborhoods she had not yet discovered on her own. In retrospect she saw that her sudden lack of inhibition had intoxicated her more than any of the men had. Some of them had been married, far older, fathers to children in secondary school. The men had been French for the most part, but also German, Persian, Italian, Lebanese. There were days she slept with one man after lunch, another after dinner. They were a bit excessive, she tells Gogol with a roll of her eyes, the type to lavish her with perfume and jewels.

She found a job working for an agency, helping American businesspeople learn conversational French, and French businesspeople learn conversational English. She would meet with them in cafés, or speak with them by phone, asking questions about their families, their backgrounds, their favorite books and foods. She began to socialize with other American expatriates. Her fiancé was part of that crowd. He was an investment banker from New York, living in Paris for a year. His name was Graham. She had fallen in love and very quickly moved in with him. It was for Graham that she'd applied to NYU. They took a place together on York Avenue. They lived there in secret, with two telephone lines so that her parents would never know. When her parents came to the city, he'd disappear to a hotel, removing all traces of himself from the apartment. It had been exciting at first, maintaining such an elaborate lie. But then it had gotten tiresome, impossible. She brought him home to New Jersey, prepared herself for battle, but in fact, to her enormous surprise, her parents were relieved. By then she was old enough so that it didn't matter to them that he was an American. Enough of their friends' children had married Americans, had produced pale, dark-haired, half-American grandchildren, and none of it was as terrible as they had feared. And so her parents did their best to accept him. They told their Bengali friends that Graham was well behaved, Ivy educated, earned an impressive salary. They learned to overlook the fact that his parents were divorced, that his father had remarried not once but twice, that his second wife was only ten years older than Moushumi.

One night, in a taxi stuck in midtown traffic, she had impulsively asked him to marry her. Looking back on it, she supposed it was all those years of people attempting to claim her, choose her, of feeling an invisible net cast around her, that had led her to this proposal. Graham had accepted, gave her his grandmother's diamond. He had agreed to fly with her and her parents to Calcutta, to meet her extended family and ask for her grandparents' blessing. He had charmed them all, learned to sit on the floor and eat with his fingers, take the dust from her grandparents' feet. He had visited the homes of dozens of her relatives, eaten the plates full of syrupy mishti, patiently posed for countless photographs on rooftops, surrounded by her cousins. He had agreed to a Hindu wedding, and so she and her mother had gone shopping in Gariahat and New Market, selected a dozen saris, gold jewelry in red cases with purple velvet linings, a dhoti and a topor for Graham that her mother carried by hand on the plane ride back. The wedding was planned for summer in New Jersey, an engagement party thrown, a few gifts already received. Her mother had typed up an explanation of Bengali wedding rituals on the computer and mailed it to all the Americans on the guest list. A photograph of the two of them was taken for the local paper in her parents' town.

A few weeks before the wedding, they were out to dinner with friends, getting happily drunk, and she heard Graham talking about their time in Calcutta. To her surprise, he was complaining about it, commenting that he found it taxing, found the culture repressed. All they did was visit her relatives, he said. Though he thought the city was fascinating, the society, in his opinion, was somewhat provincial. People tended to stay at home most of the time. There was nothing to drink. "Imagine dealing with fifty in-laws without alcohol. I couldn't even hold her hand on the street without attracting stares," he had said. She had listened to him, partly sympathetic, partly horrified. For it was one thing for her to reject her background, to be critical of her family's heritage, another to hear it from him.

She realized that he had fooled everyone, including her. On their walk home from the restaurant, she brought it up, saying that his comments had upset her, why hadn't he told her these things? Was he only pretending to enjoy himself all that time? They'd begun to argue, a chasm opening up between them, swallowing them, and suddenly, in a rage, she had removed his grandmother's ring from her finger and tossed it into the street, into oncoming traffic, and then Graham had struck her on the face as pedestrians watched. By the end of the week, he had moved out of the apartment they shared. She stopped going to school, filed for incompletes in all her classes. She swallowed half a bottle of pills, was forced to drink charcoal in an emergency room. She was given a referral to a therapist. She called her adviser at NYU, told him she'd had a nervous breakdown, took off the rest of the semester. The wedding was canceled, hundreds of phone calls made. They lost the deposit they'd paid to Shah Jahan caterers, as well as to their honeymoon destination, Palace on Wheels. The gold was taken to a bank vault, the saris and blouses and petticoats put away in a mothproof box.

Her first impulse was to move back to Paris. But she was in school, too invested to drop out, and besides, she had no money for that. She fled the apartment on York Avenue, unable to afford it on her own. She refused to go home to her parents. Some friends in Brooklyn took her in. It was painful, she told him, living with a couple at that particular time, listening to them shower together in the mornings, watching them kiss and shut the door to their bedroom at the end of each night, but in the beginning she could not face being alone. She started temping. By the time she'd saved enough to move to her own place in the East Village, she was thankful to be alone. All summer she went to movies by herself, sometimes as many as three a day. She bought *TV Guide* every week and read it from cover to cover, planning her nights around her favorite shows. She began to subsist on a diet of raita and Triscuits. She grew thinner than she'd ever been in her life, so that in the few pictures taken of her in that period her face is faintly unrecognizable. She went to end-of-summer sales and bought everything in a size four; six months later she would be forced to donate it all to a thrift shop. When autumn came, she threw herself into her studies, catching up on all the work she had abandoned that spring, began every now and then to date. And then one day her mother called, asking if she remembered a boy named Gogol.

9

THEY marry within a year, at a DoubleTree hotel in New Jersey, close to the suburb where her parents live. It's not the type of wedding either of them really wants. They would have preferred the sorts of venues their American friends choose, the Brooklyn Botanic Garden or the Metropolitan Club or the Boat House in Central Park. They would have preferred a sit-down dinner, jazz played during the reception, black-and-white photographs, keeping things small. But their parents insist on inviting close to three hundred people, and serving Indian food, and providing easy parking for all the guests. Gogol and Moushumi agree that it's better to give in to these expectations than to put up a fight. It's what they deserve, they joke, for having listened to their mothers, and for getting together in the first place, and the fact that they are united in their resignation makes the consequences somewhat bearable. Within weeks of announcing their engagement, the date is settled, the hotel booked, the menu decided, and though for a while there are nightly phone calls, her mother asking if they prefer a sheet cake or layers, sage- or rose-colored napkins, Chardonnay or Chablis, there is little for either Gogol or Moushumi to do other than listen and say yes, whichever seems

best, it all sounds fine. "Consider yourselves lucky," Gogol's coworkers tell him. Planning a wedding is incredibly stressful, the
first real trial of a marriage, they say. Still, it feels a little strange
to be so uninvolved in his own wedding, and he is reminded of
the many other celebrations in his life, all the birthdays and
graduation parties his parents had thrown when he was growing up, in his honor, attended by his parents' friends, occasions
from which he had always felt at a remove.

The Saturday of the wedding they pack suitcases, rent a car,
and drive down to New Jersey, separating only when they get
to the hotel, where they are claimed one last time by their respective families. Starting tomorrow, he realizes with a shock,
he and Moushumi will be regarded as a family of their own.
They have not seen the hotel beforehand. Its most memora-
ble feature is a glass elevator that rises and falls ceaselessly at
its center, much to the amusement of children and adults alike.
The rooms are gathered around successive elliptical balconies
that can be seen from the lobby, reminding Gogol of a parking
garage. He has a room to himself, on a floor with his mother
and Sonia and a few of the Gangulis' closest family friends.
Moushumi stays chastely on the floor above, next door to her
parents, though by now she and Gogol are practically living
together at her place. His mother has brought him the things
he is to wear, a parchment-colored Punjabi top that had once
belonged to his father, a prepleated dhoti with a drawstring
waist, a pair of nagrai slippers with curling toes. His father had
never worn the punjabi, and Gogol has to hang it in the bathroom, hot water running in the shower, to get the creases out.
"His blessings are always with you," his mother says, reaching
up and placing both her hands for a moment on his head. For
the first time since his father's death, she is dressed with care,
wearing a pretty pale green sari, a pearl necklace at her throat,
has agreed to let Sonia put some lipstick on her lips. "Is it too

much?" his mother worries, regarding herself in the mirror. Still, he has not seen her looking this lovely, this happy, this excited, in years. Sonia wears a sari, too, fuchsia with silver embroidery, a red rose stuck into her hair. She gives him a box wrapped in tissue.

"What's this?" he asks.

"You didn't think I forgot your thirtieth birthday, did you?"

It had been a few days ago, a weeknight he and Moushumi had both been too busy to celebrate properly. Even his mother, preoccupied with last-minute wedding details, had forgotten to call him first thing in the morning, as she normally did.

"I think I'm officially at the age when I want people to forget my birthday," he says, accepting the gift.

"Poor Goggles."

Inside he finds a small bottle of bourbon and a red leather flask. "I had it engraved," she says, and when he turns the flask over he sees the letters NG. He remembers poking his head into Sonia's room years ago, telling her about his decision to change his name to Nikhil. She'd been thirteen or so, doing her homework on her bed. "You can't do that," she'd told him then, shaking her head, and when he'd asked her why not she'd simply said, "Because you can't. Because you're Gogol." He watches her now, applying her make-up in his room, pulling at the skin next to her eye and painting a thin black line on the lid, and he recalls photographs of his mother at her own wedding.

"You're next, you know," he says.

"Don't remind me." She grimaces, then laughs. Their shared giddiness, the excitement of the preparations, saddens him, all of it reminding him that his father is dead. He imagines his father wearing an outfit similar to his own, a shawl draped over one shoulder, as he used to during pujo. The ensemble he fears looks silly on himself would have looked dignified, elegant, befitting his father in a way he knows it does not him. The nagrais are a size too large and need to be stuffed with tissues. Unlike Moushumi, who is having her hair and make-up professionally styled and applied, Gogol is ready in a matter of minutes. He regrets not having brought his running shoes along; he could have done a few miles on the treadmill before preparing himself for the event.

There is an hour-long watered-down Hindu ceremony on a platform covered with sheets. Gogol and Moushumi sit cross-legged, first opposite each other, then side by side. The guests sit facing them in folding metal chairs; the accordion wall between two windowless banquet rooms, with dropped ceilings, has been opened up to expand the space. A video camera and hand-held white lights hover above their faces. Shenai music plays on a boom box. Nothing has been rehearsed or explained to them beforehand. A cluster of mashis and meshos surround them, telling them continually what to do, when to speak or stand or throw flowers at a small brass urn. The priest is a friend of Moushumi's parents, an anesthesiologist who happens to be a Brahmin. Offerings are made to pictures of their grandparents and his father, rice poured into a pyre that they are forbidden by the management of the hotel to ignite. He thinks of his parents, strangers until this moment, two people who had not spoken until after they were actually wed. Suddenly, sitting next to Moushumi, he realizes what it means, and he is astonished by his parents' courage, the obedience that must have been involved in doing such a thing.

It's the first time he's seen Moushumi in a sari, apart from all those pujos years ago, which she had suffered through silently. She has about twenty pounds of gold on her—at one point, when they are sitting face to face, their hands wrapped up together in a checkered cloth, he counts eleven necklaces. Two enormous paisleys have been painted in red and white on her cheeks. Until now, he has continued to call Moushumi's father

Shubir Mesho, and her mother Rina Mashi, as he always has, as if they were still his uncle and aunt, as if Moushumi were still a sort of cousin. But by the end of the night he will become their son-in-law and so be expected to address them as his second set of parents, an alternative Baba and Ma.

For the reception he changes into a suit, she into a red Banarasi gown with spaghetti straps, something she'd designed herself and had made by a seamstress friend. She wears the gown in spite of her mother's protests—what was wrong with a salwar kameeze, she'd wanted to know—and when Moushumi happens to forget her shawl on a chair and bares her slim, bronze shoulders, which quietly sparkle from a special powder she's applied to them, her mother manages, in the midst of that great crowd, to shoot her reproachful glances, which Moushumi ignores. Countless people come to congratulate Gogol, saying they had seen him when he was so little, asking him to pose for photographs, to wrap his arms around families and smile. He is numbly drunk through it all, thanks to the open bar her parents have sprung for. Moushumi is horrified, in the banquet room, to see the tables wreathed with tulle, the ivy and baby's breath twisted around the columns. They bump into each other on her way out of the ladies' room and exchange a quick kiss, the smoke on her breath faintly masked by the mint she is chewing. He imagines her smoking in the stall, the lid of the toilet seat down. They've barely said a word to each other all evening; throughout the ceremony she'd kept her eyes lowered, and during the reception, each time he'd looked at her, she'd been deep in conversation with people he didn't know. He wants to be alone with her suddenly, wishes they could sneak off to her room or his, ignore the rest of the party as he would when he was a boy. "Come on," he urges, motioning toward the glass elevator, "fifteen minutes. No one will notice." But the dinner has begun, and table numbers are

being called one by one on the loudspeaker. "I'd need someone to redo my hair," she says. The heated silver chafing dishes
are labeled for the American guests. It's typical north Indian
fare, mounds of hot pink tandoori, aloo gobi in thick orange
sauce. He overhears someone in the line saying the chickpeas
have gone bad. They sit at the head table in the center of the
room, with his mother and Sonia, her parents and a handful
of her relatives visiting from Calcutta, and her brother, Samrat, who is missing out on his orientation at the University of
Chicago in order to attend the wedding. There are awkward
champagne toasts and speeches by their families, their parents'
friends. Her father stands up, smiling nervously, forgets to raise
his glass, and says, "Thank you very much for coming," then
turns to Gogol and Moushumi: "Okay, be happy." Forks are
tapped against glasses by giggling, sari-clad mashis, instructing
them when to kiss. Each time he obliges them and kisses his
bride tamely on the cheek.

A cake is wheeled out, "Nikhil Weds Moushumi" piped across
its surface. Moushumi smiles as she always smiles for a camera,
her mouth closed, her head tilted slightly downward and to the
left. He is aware that together he and Moushumi are fulfilling
a collective, deep-seated desire—because they're both Bengali,
everyone can let his hair down a bit. At times, looking out at
the guests, he can't help but think that two years ago he might
have been sitting in the sea of round tables that now surround
him, watching her marry another man. The thought crashes
over him like an unexpected wave, but quickly he reminds himself that he is the one sitting beside her. The red Banarasi wedding sari and the gold had been bought two years ago, for her
wedding to Graham. This time all her parents have had to do
is bring down the boxes from a closet shelf, retrieve the jewels from the safety deposit box, find the itemized list for the
caterer. The new invitation, designed by Ashima, the English

translation lettered by Gogol, is the only thing that isn't a left-over.

Since Moushumi has to teach a class three days after the wedding, they have to postpone the honeymoon. The closest they come is a night alone in the DoubleTree, which they are both dying to leave. But their parents have gone to great trouble and expense to book the newlywed suite. "I have got to take a shower," she says as soon as they are finally alone, and disappears into the bathroom. He knows she is exhausted, as he is — the night had ended with a long session of dancing to ABBA songs. He examines the room, opening drawers and pulling out the stationery, opening the minibar, reading the contents of the room service menu, though he is not at all hungry. If anything, he feels slightly ill, from the combination of the bourbon and the two large pieces of cake he'd had because he had not had any dinner. He sprawls on the king-sized bed. The bedspread has been strewn with flower petals, a final gesture before their families withdrew. He waits for her, flipping through the channels on the television. Beside him is a bottle of champagne in a bucket, heart-shaped chocolates on a lace-covered plate. He takes a bite out of one of the chocolates. The inside is an unyielding toffee, requiring more chewing than he expects.

He fidgets with the gold ring she'd placed on his finger after they'd cut the cake, identical to the one he'd placed on hers. He'd proposed to her on her birthday, giving her a diamond solitaire in addition to the hat he'd bought for her after their second date. He'd made a production out of it, using her birthday as an excuse to take her to a country inn for the weekend, in a town upstate on the banks of the Hudson, the first trip they'd taken together that wasn't to her parents' place in New Jersey, or to Pemberton Road. It was springtime, the velvet hat out of season by then. She'd been overwhelmed that he'd remembered it all this time. "I can't believe the store still had it," she said. He didn't tell her the truth about when he'd bought the hat. He'd presented it to her downstairs, in the dining room, after a Châteaubriand that had been carved for them at the table. Strangers turned to admire Moushumi when the hat was on her head. After trying it on, she'd put the box away under her chair, not noticing the smaller box lost among the tissue. "There's something else in there," he'd been forced to say. In retrospect he decided that she had been more shocked by the hat than by his proposal. For while the former was a true surprise, the latter was something expected—from the very beginning it was safely assumed by their families, and soon enough by themselves, that as long as they liked each other their courtship would not lag and they would surely wed. "Yes," she'd told him, grinning, looking up from the hatbox before he'd even had to ask.

She emerges now in the snow-white terry-cloth hotel robe. She has taken off her make-up and her jewels; the vermilion with which he'd stained her part at the end of the ceremony has been rinsed from her hair. Her feet are free of the three-inch heels she'd worn as soon as the religious part of the wedding was over, causing her to tower over almost everyone. This is the way he still finds her most ravishing, unadorned, aware that it is a way she is willing to look for no one but him. She sits on the edge of the mattress, applies some blue cream from a tube to her calves and the bottoms of her feet. She'd massaged the cream onto his own feet once, the day they'd walked across the Brooklyn Bridge, causing them to tingle and go cold. And then she lies against the pillows, and looks at him, and puts out a hand. Underneath the robe he expects to find some racy lingerie—back in New York he'd glimpsed the pile of things she'd received for her shower in the corner of her bedroom. But she is naked, her skin smelling, a little too intensely, of some sort of berry. He kisses the dark hair on her forearms, the prominent collarbone, which she had once confessed to him is her favorite part of her body. They make love in spite of their exhaustion, her damp hair limp and cool against his face, the rose petals sticking to their elbows and shoulders and calves. He breathes in the scent of her skin, still unable to fathom that they are husband and wife. When would it sink in? Even then he does not feel fully alone with her, half waiting for someone to knock on the door and tell them how to go about things. And though he desires her as much as ever, he is relieved when they are through, lying naked side by side, knowing that nothing else is expected of them, that finally they can relax.

Afterward they open up the champagne and sit together on the bed, going through a large shopping bag full of cards with personal checks inside them. The checks have been given to them by their parents' hundreds of friends. She had not wanted to register for gifts. She told Gogol it was because she didn't have the time, but he sensed that it was something she couldn't bring herself to face the second time around. It's fine with him, not to have their apartment crammed with a dozen crystal vases and platters and matching pots and pans. There is no calculator, and so they add up the figures on numerous sheets of the hotel stationery. Most of the checks have been written out to Mr. and Mrs. Nikhil and Moushumi Ganguli. Several are written to Gogol and Moushumi Ganguli. The amounts are for one hundred and one dollars, two hundred and one dollars, occasionally three hundred and one dollars, as Bengalis consider it inauspicious to give round figures. Gogol adds up the subtotals on each page.

"Seven thousand thirty-five," he announces.

"Not bad, Mr. Ganguli."

"I'd say we've made a killing, Mrs. Ganguli."

Only she is not Mrs. Ganguli. Moushumi has kept her last name. She doesn't adopt Ganguli, not even with a hyphen. Her own last name, Mazoomdar, is already a mouthful. With a hyphenated surname, she would no longer fit into the window of a business envelope. Besides, by now she has begun to publish under Moushumi Mazoomdar, the name printed at the top of footnoted articles on French feminist theory in a number of prestigious academic journals that always manage to give Gogol a paper cut when he tries to read them. Though he hasn't admitted this to her, he'd hoped, the day they'd filled out the application for their marriage license, that she might consider otherwise, as a tribute to his father if nothing else. But the thought of changing her last name to Ganguli has never crossed Moushumi's mind. When relatives from India continue to address letters and cards to "Mrs. Moushumi Ganguli," she will shake her head and sigh.

They put the money toward a security deposit for a one-bedroom apartment in the Twenties, off Third Avenue. It's slightly more than they can comfortably afford, but they are won over by the maroon awning, the part-time doorman, the lobby paved with pumpkin-colored tiles. The apartment itself is small but luxurious, with built-in mahogany bookcases rising to the ceiling and dark, oily, wide-planked floors. There is a living room with a skylight, a kitchen with expensive stainless-steel appliances, a bathroom with a marble floor and walls. There is a Juliet balcony off the bedroom, in one corner of which Moushumi sets up her desk, her computer and printer, her files. They are on the top floor, and if one leans far enough to the left outside the bathroom window it's possible to see the Empire State Building. They spend a few weekends taking the shuttle bus to Ikea and filling up the rooms: imitation Noguchi lamps, a black sectional sofa, kilim and flokati carpets, a blond wood platform bed. Both her parents and Ashima are at once impressed and puzzled when they come to visit for the first

time. Isn't it a bit small, now that they are married? But Gogol
and Moushumi aren't thinking of children at the moment, certainly not until Moushumi finishes her dissertation. On Saturdays they shop together for food at the farmers' market in
Union Square, with canvas bags over their shoulders. They buy
things they are not certain how to prepare, leeks and fresh fava
beans and fiddleheads, looking up recipes in the cookbooks
they've received for their wedding. From time to time when
they cook they set off the fire alarm, which is overly sensitive,
and they bang it into silence with the handle of a broom.

They entertain together on occasion, throwing the sorts
of parties their parents never had, mixing martinis in a stainless-steel shaker for a few of the architects at Gogol's work or
Moushumi's graduate student friends at NYU. They play bossa
nova and serve bread and salami and cheese. He transfers the
money in his bank account over to hers, and they have pale
green checks with both their names printed in the corner. The
pass code they decide on for their ATM card, Lulu, is the name
of the French restaurant where they had their first meal together. They eat most nights side by side on the stools at the
kitchen counter or at the coffee table, watching TV. They make
Indian food infrequently—usually it's pasta or broiled fish or
take-out from the Thai restaurant down the block. But sometimes, on a Sunday, both craving the food they'd grown up eating, they ride the train out to Queens and have brunch at Jackson Diner, piling their plates with tandoori chicken and pakoras
and kabobs, and shop afterward for basmati rice and the spices
that need replenishing. Or they go to one of the hole-in-the-
wall tea shops and drink tea in paper cups with heavy cream,
asking the waitress in Bengali to bring them bowls of sweet yogurt and haleem. He calls every evening before leaving the office to say he is on his way home, asks if he needs to pick up
lettuce or a loaf of bread. After dinner they watch television,

as Moushumi writes out thank-you cards to all their parents' friends, for the checks they had needed twenty different slips to deposit. These are the things that make him feel married. Otherwise it's the same, only now they're always together. At night she sleeps beside him, always rolling onto her stomach, waking up every morning with a pillow pressed over her head.

Occasionally, in the apartment, he finds odd remnants of her life before he'd appeared in it, her life with Graham—the inscription to the two of them in a book of poems, a postcard from Provence stuffed into the back of a dictionary, addressed to the apartment they'd secretly shared. Once, unable to stop himself, he'd walked to this address during his lunch break, wondering what her life had been like back then. He imagined her walking along the sidewalk, carrying grocery bags from the supermarket that was on the next corner, in love with another man. He doesn't feel jealous of her past per se. It's only that sometimes Gogol wonders whether he represents some sort of capitulation or defeat. He doesn't feel this always, just enough to nag at him, settling over his thoughts like a web. But then he looks around the apartment for reassurance, reminding himself of the life they've set up together and share. He looks at the photograph taken at their wedding, in which matching garlands hang from their necks. It sits in a tasteful leather frame on top of the television set. He wanders into the bedroom, where she's working, kissing her on the shoulder, drawing her to bed. But in the closet they now share is a garment bag containing a white dress he knows she would have worn a month after the Indian ceremony that had been planned for her and Graham, a second ceremony before a justice of the peace on Graham's father's lawn in Pennsylvania. She had told him about it. A patch of the dress is visible through a plastic window in the garment bag. He'd unzipped it once, glimpsed something sleeveless, to the knee, with a plain round neck, reminding him of a tennis dress. One day he asks her why she still keeps it. "Oh that," she says with a shrug. "I keep meaning to have it dyed."

In March they go to Paris. Moushumi is invited to give a paper at a conference at the Sorbonne, and they decide to make a vacation out of it, Gogol arranging to take the week off from work. Instead of staying in a hotel, they stay in an apartment in the Bastille which belongs to a friend of Moushumi's, a male friend named Emanuel, a journalist, who is on holiday in Greece. The apartment is barely heated, minuscule, at the top of six steep flights of stairs, with a bathroom the size of a phone booth. There is a loft bed just inches from the ceiling, so that sex is a serious hazard. An espresso pot nearly fills the narrow two-burner stove. Apart from two chairs at the dining table, there is no place to sit. The weather is raw, cheerless, the sky white, the sun perpetually hidden from view. Paris is famous for such weather, Moushumi tells him. He feels hidden himself; men on the streets stare at Moushumi constantly, their glances lingering plainly, in spite of the fact that Gogol is at her side.

It is his first time in Europe. The first time he sees the sort of architecture he has read about for so many years, admired only in the pages of books and slides. For some reason, in Moushumi's company, he feels more apologetic than excited. Though they journey together one day to Chartres, and another to Versailles, he has the feeling she'd rather be meeting friends for coffee, attending panels at the conference, eating at her favorite bistros, shopping at her favorite stores. From the beginning he feels useless. Moushumi makes all the decisions, does all the talking. He is mute in the brasseries where they eat their lunches, mute in the shops where he gazes at beautiful belts, ties, paper, pens; mute on the rainy afternoon they spend together at the d'Orsay. He is particularly mute when he and

Moushumi get together for dinners with groups of her French friends, drinking Pernods and feasting on couscous or choucroute, smoking and arguing around paper-covered tables. He struggles to grasp the topic of conversation—the euro, Monica Lewinsky, Y2K—but everything else is a blur, indistinguishable from the clatter of plates, the drone of echoing, laughing voices. He watches them in the giant gilt-framed mirrors on the walls, their dark heads leaning close.

Part of him knows this is a privilege, to be here with a person who knows the city so well, but the other part of him wants simply to be a tourist, fumbling with a phrase book, looking at all the buildings on his list, getting lost. When he confesses his wish to Moushumi one night as they are walking back to the apartment, she says, "Why didn't you tell me that in the first place?" and the next morning she instructs him to walk to the Métro station, have his photo taken in a booth, get a Carte Orange. And so Gogol goes sightseeing, alone, while Moushumi is off at her conference, or as she sits at the table in the apartment and puts the final touches on her paper. His only companion is Moushumi's *Plan de Paris*, a small red guide to the arrondissements, with a folded map attached to the back cover. On the last page, Moushumi writes in a few phrases for his benefit: *"Je voudrais un café, s'il vous plaît."* *"Où sont les toilettes?"* And she warns as he's walking out the door, "Avoid ordering a café crème unless it's morning. The French never do that."

Though the day is bright for a change, it is particularly cold, brisk air stinging his ears. He remembers his first lunch with Moushumi, the afternoon she'd dragged him to the hat store. He remembers the two of them crying out in unison as the wind blasted their faces, a time too soon for them to cling to each other for warmth. He walks now to the corner, decides to get another croissant at the boulangerie where he and Moushumi go every morning to buy breakfast. He sees a young couple standing in a patch of sunlight on the sidewalk, feeding each other pastries from a bag. Suddenly he wants to go back to the apartment, climb into the loft bed and forget about sightseeing, hold Moushumi in his arms. He wants to lie with her for hours, as they did at the beginning, skipping meals, then wandering the streets at odd hours, desperate for something to eat. But she must present her paper at the end of the week, and he knows she will not be roused from her task of reading it aloud, timing its duration, making small marks in the margin. He consults his map and for the next few days he follows the routes she has charted for him with a pencil. He wanders for miles along the famous boulevards, through the Marais, arriving after many wrong turns at the Picasso Museum. He sits on a bench and sketches the town houses in the Place des Vosges, walks along the desolate gravel paths in the Luxembourg Gardens. Outside the Académie des Beaux-Arts he wanders for hours through the shops selling prints, eventually buying a drawing of the Hôtel de Lauzun. He photographs the narrow sidewalks, the dark cobblestone streets, the mansard roofs, the ancient, shuttered buildings of pale beige stone. All of it he finds beautiful beyond description, and yet at the same time it depresses him that none of it is new to Moushumi, that she has seen it all hundreds of times. He understands why she lived here for as long as she did, away from her family, away from anyone she knew. Her French friends adore her. Waiters and shopkeepers adore her. She both fits in perfectly yet remains slightly novel. Here Moushumi had reinvented herself, without misgivings, without guilt. He admires her, even resents her a little, for having moved to another country and made a separate life. He realizes that this is what their parents had done in America. What he, in all likelihood, will never do.

On their last day, in the morning, he shops for gifts for his in-laws, his mother, Sonia. It is the day Moushumi is presenting her paper. He had offered to go with her, to sit in the audience and listen to her speak. But she told him that was silly, why sit in the middle of a roomful of people speaking a language he doesn't understand when there was still more of the city he could see? And so, after shopping, he sets off, alone, for the Louvre, a destination he's put off until now. At the end of the day he meets her at a café in the Latin Quarter. She is there waiting for him behind a glassed-in partition on the sidewalk, wearing a dark red lipstick, sipping a glass of wine.

He sits down, orders a coffee. "How was it? How did it go?"

She lights a cigarette. "Okay. Over with, at any rate."

She looks more regretful than relieved, her eyes lingering over the small round table between them, the veins in the marble bluish, like those in cheese.

Normally she wants a full account of his adventures, but today they sit silently, watching the passers-by. He shows her the things he's bought, a tie for his father-in-law, soaps for their mothers, a shirt for Samrat, a silk scarf for Sonia, sketchbooks for himself, bottles of ink, a pen. She admires the drawings he's done. It is a café they've been to before, and he feels the slight nostalgia it is sometimes possible to feel at the end of an extended stay in a foreign place, taking in the details that will soon evaporate from his mind: the surly waiter who has served them both times, the view of the shops across the street, the green and yellow straw chairs.

"Are you sad to be leaving?" he asks, stirring sugar into his coffee, drinking it back in one gulp.

"A little. I guess a little part of me wishes I'd never left Paris, you know?"

He leans over, takes both her hands in his. "But then we would never have met," he says, with more confidence than he feels.

"True," she acknowledges. And then: "Maybe we'll move here one day."

He nods. "Maybe."

She looks beautiful to him, tired, the concentrated light of the dying day on her face, infusing it with an amber-pink glow. He watches the smoke drift away from her. He wants to remember this moment, the two of them together, here. This is how he wants to remember Paris. He takes out his camera, focusing it on her face.

"Nikhil, please, don't," she says, laughing, shaking her head. "I look awful." She shields her face with the back of her hand.

He still holds up the camera. "Oh, come on, Mo. You're beautiful. You look great."

But she refuses to indulge him, moving her chair out of view with a scrape on the pavement; she doesn't want to be mistaken for a tourist in this city, she says.

A Saturday evening in May. A dinner party in Brooklyn. A dozen people are gathered around a long, scratched-up dining table, smoking cigarettes, drinking Chianti from juice glasses, sitting on a series of backless wooden stools. The room is dark apart from a domed metal lamp hanging from a long cord, which casts a concentrated pool of light on the table's center. An opera plays on a battered boom box on the floor. A joint is being passed around. Gogol takes a hit, but as he sits there, holding his breath, he regrets it—he is already starved. Though it's close to ten o'clock, dinner has yet to be served. Apart from the Chianti, the only offerings so far are a loaf of bread and a small bowl of olives. A blizzard of crumbs and pointy violet olive pits litter the tabletop. The bread, like a hard, dusty cushion, is full of prune-sized holes and has a crust that hurts the roof of Gogol's mouth when he chews.

They are at the home of Moushumi's friends Astrid and

Donald. It's a brownstone under renovation; Astrid and Donald, expecting their first child, are in the process of expanding their domain from a single floor of the house to the top three. Thick plastic sheets hang from rafters, creating transparent, temporary corridors. Behind them, a wall is missing. Even at this hour, guests continue to arrive. They enter complaining of the cold that has persisted this far into spring, of the stinging, bothersome wind that tosses the treetops outside. They remove their coats, introduce themselves, pour themselves Chianti. If it happens to be their first time in the house they eventually drift from the table and troop up the stairs, to admire the pocket doors, the original tin ceilings, the vast space that will eventually become the nursery, the distant, sparkling view of Manhattan visible from the top floor.

Gogol has been to the house before, a bit too frequently in his opinion. Astrid is a friend of Moushumi's from Brown. The first time he'd met Donald and Astrid had been at his wedding. At least that's what Moushumi says; he doesn't remember them. They were living in Rome the first year that Gogol and Moushumi were together, on a Guggenheim that Astrid had gotten. But they've since moved back to New York, where Astrid has begun teaching film theory at the New School. Donald is a moderately talented painter of small still lifes of single, everyday objects: an egg, a cup, a comb, suspended against brightly colored backgrounds. Donald's rendition of a spool of thread, a wedding present to Gogol and Moushumi, hangs in their bedroom. Donald and Astrid are a languidly confident couple, a model, Gogol guesses, for how Moushumi would like their own lives to be. They reach out to people, hosting dinner parties, bequeathing little bits of themselves to their friends. They are passionate spokespeople for their brand of life, giving Gogol and Moushumi a steady, unquestionable stream of advice about quotidian things. They swear by a certain bakery on Sullivan Street, a certain butcher on Mott, a certain style of coffeemaker, a certain Florentine designer of sheets for their bed. Their decrees drive Gogol crazy. But Moushumi is loyal. She regularly goes out of her way, and thus out of their budget, to buy bread at that bakery, meat at that butcher.

He recognizes a few familiar faces tonight: Edith and Colin, who teach sociology at Princeton and Yale, respectively, and Louise and Blake, both Ph.D. candidates, like Moushumi, at NYU. Oliver is an editor at an art magazine; his wife, Sally, works as a pastry chef. The rest are painter friends of Donald's, poets, documentary filmmakers. They are all married. Even now, a fact as ordinary, as obvious, as this astonishes him. All married! But this is life now, the weekend sometimes more tiring than the workweek, an endless stream of dinner parties, cocktail parties, occasional after-eleven parties with dancing and drugs to remind them that they are still young, followed by Sunday brunches full of unlimited Bloody Marys and over-priced eggs.

They are an intelligent, attractive, well-dressed crowd. Also a bit incestuous. The vast majority of them know each other from Brown, and Gogol can't ever shake the feeling that half the people in the room have slept with one another. There is the usual academic talk around the table, versions of the same conversation he can't participate in, concerning conferences, job listings, ungrateful undergraduates, proposal deadlines. At one end of the table, a woman with short red hair and cat's-eye glasses is talking about a Brecht play she'd once acted in in San Francisco, performed fully in the nude. At the other end, Sally is putting the finishing touches on a dessert she's brought, intently assembling layers and covering them with glistening white meringue that shoots up like a dense thicket of flames. Astrid is showing a few people paint chips, which she's lined up in front of her like tarot cards, versions of an apple green she and Donald are considering for the front hallway. She wears glasses that might have belonged to Malcolm X. She eyes the paint chips with precision; though she seeks the advice of her guests, she has already made up her mind about which permutation of the shade she will choose. To Gogol's left, Edith is discussing her reasons for not eating bread. "I just have so much more energy if I stay off wheat," she maintains.

Gogol has nothing to say to these people. He doesn't care about their dissertation topics, or their dietary restrictions, or the color of their walls. In the beginning these occasions hadn't been quite so excruciating. When Moushumi had first introduced him to her crowd he and she would sit with their arms around each other, their fellow guests a footnote to their own ongoing conversation. Once, at a party at Sally and Oliver's, they'd wandered off to make quick, giddy love in Sally's walk-in closet, piles of her sweaters looming over them. He knows that that sort of insular passion can't be sustained. Still, Moushumi's devotion to these people puzzles him. He looks at her now. She is lighting a Dunhill. Her smoking hadn't bothered him initially. He liked it, after sex, when she'd lean over the bedside table and strike a match, and he would lie beside her, listening to her exhale in the quiet, watching the smoke drift up over their heads. But these days the stale smell of it, in her hair and on her fingertips, and in the bedroom where she sits typing, slightly disgusts him, and from time to time he can't help but have a fleeting vision of himself, tragically abandoned as a result of her mild but persistent addiction. When he'd admitted his fear to her one day, she'd laughed. "Oh, Nikhil," she'd said, "you can't be serious."

She is laughing now, nodding intently at something Blake is saying. She seems animated in a way he doesn't remember her having been in a while. He looks at her straight, smooth hair, which she's had cut recently so that it flips up at the ends. The glasses that only emphasize her beauty. Her pale, pretty mouth. He knows that the approval of these people means something to her, though what exactly he isn't sure. And yet, as much as Moushumi enjoys seeing Astrid and Donald, Gogol has recently begun to notice that she is gloomy in the aftermath, as if seeing them serves only to remind her that their own lives will never match up. The last time they'd gone home after one of Astrid and Donald's dinner parties, she'd picked a fight with him as soon as they'd walked in the door, complaining about the noise on Third Avenue, about the sliding doors on the closets that always fall off the rails, about the fact that it's impossible to use the bathroom without being deafened by the exhaust fan. He tells himself that it's the stress—she's been studying for her orals, holed up in her carrel at the library until nine o'clock most nights. He remembers how it was studying for his licensing exam, which he failed twice before passing. He remembers the sustained isolation it had demanded, speaking to no one for days at a time, and so he doesn't say anything. Tonight he'd held out the hope that she'd use her orals as a reason to decline the invitation to Astrid and Donald's. But by now he's learned that there is never a question of saying no when it comes to them.

It was through Astrid and Donald that Moushumi had met her former fiancé, Graham; Donald had gone to prep school with him, and he had given Moushumi's number to Graham when he'd moved to Paris. Gogol doesn't like to think about the fact that Moushumi's connection to Graham persists through Astrid and Donald, that through them Moushumi has learned that Graham lives in Toronto now, is married and a father of twins. Back when Moushumi and Graham were together they'd made a foursome with Donald and Astrid, renting cottages together in Vermont, time-shares in the Hamptons. They try to incorporate Gogol into similar plans; this summer, for example, they are thinking of renting a house on the coast of Brittany. Though Astrid and Donald have welcomed Gogol heartily into their lives, sometimes he has the feeling they still think she's with Graham. Once Astrid even called him Graham by mistake. No one had noticed except Gogol. They had all been a little drunk, but he knew he'd heard correctly, toward the end of an evening much like this one. "Mo, why don't you and Graham take some of this pork loin home," Astrid had said as they'd been clearing the dishes. "It's great for sandwiches."

At the moment, the guests are united in a single topic of conversation, talking about names for the baby. "What we want is something totally unique," Astrid is saying. Lately Gogol has started to notice a trend: now that they inhabit this world of couples, dinner party small talk gravitates to the naming of children. If a woman at the table happens to be pregnant, as Astrid is now, the subject is inevitable.

"I always liked the names of popes," Blake says.

"You mean John and Paul?" Louise asks.

"More like Innocent and Clement."

There are nonsensical names, like Jet and Tipper. These elicit groans. Someone claims to have once known a girl named Anna Graham—"Get it? Anagram!"—and everyone laughs.

Moushumi argues that a name like hers is a curse, complains that no one can say it properly, that the kids at school pronounced it Moosoomi and shortened it to Moose. "I hated being the only Moushumi I knew," she says.

"See now, I'd have loved that," Oliver tells her.

Gogol pours himself another juice glass of Chianti. He hates contributing to these conversations, hates listening. A number of name books are passed around the table: *Finding the Perfect Name, Alternative Baby Names, The Idiot's Guide to Naming Your Baby.* One is called *What Not to Name Your Baby.* Pages are folded down, some with stars and checks in the margins.

Someone suggests Zachary. Someone else says she once had a dog named Zachary. Everyone wants to look up his or her own name to see what it means, is by turns pleased and disappointed. Both Gogol and Moushumi are absent from these books, and for the first time all evening he feels a hint of that odd bond that had first drawn them together. He goes over to where she's sitting, takes one of her hands, which have been resting flat on the surface of the table, her arms extended. She turns to look at him.

"Hey there," she says. She smiles at him, temporarily leaning her head on his shoulder, and he realizes that she's drunk.

"What *does* Moushumi mean?" Oliver asks on the other side of her.

"A damp southwesterly breeze," she says, shaking her head, rolling her eyes.

"Sort of like the one outside?"

"I always knew you were a force of nature," Astrid says, laughing.

Gogol turns to Moushumi. "Really?" he says. He realizes that it's something he'd never thought to ask about her, something he hadn't known.

"You never told me that," he says.

She shakes her head, confused. "I haven't?"

It bothers him, though he's not quite sure why. But it's not the time to dwell on it. Not in the middle of all this. He gets up to go to the bathroom. When he is finished, instead of returning to the dining room, he walks up a flight of stairs, to check out the renovations. He pauses at the doors to a series of whitewashed rooms with nothing but ladders in them. Others are filled with boxes, stacked six or seven deep. He stops to inspect some blueprints spread out on the floor. He remembers that when he and Moushumi were first dating they'd spent an entire afternoon, in a bar, drawing a plan of the ideal house.

He'd argued for something modernist, full of glass and light, but she'd wanted a brownstone like this one. In the end they'd designed something implausible, a town house of poured concrete with a glass facade. It was before they'd slept together, and he remembers how they'd both grown embarrassed when deciding where the bedroom should go.

He ends up in the kitchen, where Donald is only now beginning to prepare spaghetti alle vongole. It's an old kitchen from one of the former rental units, which they're using until their new one is ready. Dingy linoleum and appliances lining a single wall remind Gogol of his former place on Amsterdam Avenue. On the stove is an empty, gleaming stainless-steel stockpot so large that it covers two burners. Salad leaves are in a bowl covered with dampened paper towels. A heap of tiny pale green clams no larger than quarters soak in the deep porcelain sink.

Donald is tall, wearing jeans and flip-flops and a paprika-colored shirt whose sleeves are rolled up to just above his elbows. He is handsome, with patrician features and swept-back, slightly greasy, light brown hair. He wears an apron over his clothes, and is busily plucking leaves from an excessively large bunch of parsley.

"Hey there," Gogol says. "Need any help?"

"Nikhil. Welcome." Donald hands over the parsley. "Be my guest."

Gogol is grateful for something to do, to be occupied and productive, even in the role of sous-chef to Donald.

"So, how are the renovations going?"

"Don't ask," Donald says. "We just fired our contractor. At this rate our kid will already have moved out by the time the nursery's ready."

Gogol watches as Donald begins to remove the clams from their bath, scrubbing the shells with something that looks like a tiny toilet bowl brush, then tossing them one by one into the stockpot. Gogol pokes his head into the pot and sees the vongole, their shells uniformly parted in a quietly foaming broth.

"So when are you guys moving out to this neighborhood?" Donald asks.

Gogol shrugs. He has no interest in moving to Brooklyn, not in such proximity to Donald and Astrid, anyway. "I haven't really considered it. I prefer Manhattan. Moushumi does too."

Donald shakes his head. "You're wrong. Moushumi adores Brooklyn. We practically had to kick her out after the whole Graham thing."

The mention of the name pricks him, deflates him as it always does.

"She stayed here with you?"

"Right down the hall. She was here for a couple of months. She was a real mess. I've never seen anyone so devastated."

He nods. This was something else she'd never told him. He wonders why. He hates the house suddenly, aware that it was here, with Donald and Astrid, that she spent her darkest hour. That it was here she'd mourned for another man.

"But you're much better for her," Donald concludes.

Gogol looks up, surprised.

"Don't get me wrong, Graham's a great guy. But they were too alike somehow, too intense together."

Gogol does not find this observation particularly reassuring. He finishes plucking the last of the parsley leaves, watches as Donald grabs a knife and chops them, expertly and swiftly, a hand held flat over the top of the blade.

Gogol feels incompetent all of a sudden. "I've never quite figured out how to do that," he says.

"All you need is a really good knife," Donald tells him. "I swear by these."

Gogol is sent off with a stack of plates, a bunch of forks and knives. On his way he pokes his head into the room down the hall where Moushumi had stayed. It's empty now, a drop cloth on the floor, a tangle of wires poking out of the center of the ceiling. He imagines her in a bed in the corner, sullen, emaciated, a cloud of smoke over her head. Downstairs, he takes his place beside Moushumi. She kisses his earlobe. "Where did you wander off to?"

"Just keeping Donald company."

The name conversation is still going full force. Colin says he likes names that signify a virtue: Patience, Faith, Chastity. He says his great-grandmother was named Silence, something nobody wants to believe.

"What about Prudence? Isn't Prudence one of the virtues?" Donald says, coming down the stairs with a platter of spaghetti. The platter is lowered onto the table to scattered applause. The pasta is served, the plates passed around.

"It just feels like such a huge responsibility to name a baby. What if he hates it," Astrid frets.

"So he'll change it," Louise says. "By the way. Remember Joe Chapman from college? I heard he's a Joanne now."

"God, I would never change my name," Edith says. "It's my grandmother's."

"Nikhil changed his," Moushumi blurts out suddenly, and for the first time all evening, with the exception of the opera singers, the room goes completely quiet.

He stares at her, stunned. He has never told her not to tell anyone. He simply assumed she never would. His expression is lost on her; she smiles back at him, unaware of what she's done. The dinner guests regard him, their mouths hanging open in confused smiles.

"What do you mean he changed his name?" Blake asks slowly.

"Nikhil. It wasn't the name he was born with." She nods, her mouth full, tossing a clamshell onto the table. "Not his name when we were kids."

"What name were you born with?" Astrid says, looking at him suspiciously, her eyebrows furrowed for effect.

For a few seconds he says nothing. "Gogol," he says finally. It has been years since he's been Gogol to anyone other than his family, their friends. It sounds as it always does, simple, impossible, absurd. He stares at Moushumi as he says it, but she's too drunk to absorb his reproach.

"As in 'The Overcoat'?" Sally asks.

"I get it," Oliver says. "Nick-olai Gogol."

"I can't believe you've kept this from us, Nick," Astrid chides.

"What in the world made your parents choose that name?" Donald wants to know.

He thinks back to the story he cannot bring himself to tell these people, at once as vivid and as elusive as it's always been: the capsized train in the middle of the night, his father's arm sticking through a window, the crumpled page of a book clutched in his fist. It's a story he'd told Moushumi, in the months after they'd first met. He'd told her of the accident, and then he'd told her about the night his father had told him, in the driveway at Pemberton Road. He'd confessed to her that he still felt guilty at times for changing his name, more so now that his father was dead. And she'd assured him that it was understandable, that anyone in his place would have done the same. But now it's become a joke to her. Suddenly he regrets having ever told Moushumi; he wonders whether she'll proclaim the story of his father's accident to the table as well. By morning, half the people in the room will have forgotten. It will be a tiny, odd fact about him, an anecdote, perhaps, for a future dinner party. This is what upsets him most.

"My father was a fan," he says finally.

"Then maybe we should call the baby Verdi," Donald muses, just as the opera surges to its closing bars, and the tape ends with a click.

"You're not helping," Astrid says, petulant, kissing Donald on the nose. Gogol watches them, knowing that it's all in jest—they're not the type to do something so impulsive, so naive, to blunder, as his own parents had done.

"Relax," Edith says. "The perfect name will come to you in time."

Which is when Gogol announces, "There's no such thing."

"No such thing as what?" Astrid says.

"There's no such thing as a perfect name. I think that human beings should be allowed to name themselves when they turn eighteen," he adds. "Until then, pronouns."

People shake their heads dismissively. Moushumi shoots him a look that he ignores. The salad is served. The conversation takes a new turn, carries on without him. And yet he can't help but recall a novel he'd once picked up from the pile on Moushumi's side of the bed, an English translation of something French, in which the main characters were simply referred to, for hundreds of pages, as He and She. He had read it in a matter of hours, oddly relieved that the names of the characters were never revealed. It had been an unhappy love story. If only his own life were so simple.

IO

1999

O N THE morning of their first anniversary, Moushumi's parents call, waking them, wishing them a happy anniversary before they've had the chance to say it to each other. In addition to their anniversary, there is something else to celebrate: Moushumi successfully passed her orals the week before, is now officially ABD. There's a third thing worth celebrating but which she hasn't mentioned—she's been awarded a research fellowship to work on her dissertation in France for the year. She'd applied for the grant secretly, just before the wedding, simply curious to see if she'd get it. It was always good practice, she'd reasoned, to strive for such things. Two years ago she would have said yes on the spot. But it's no longer possible to fly off to France for the year, now that she has a husband, a marriage, to consider. So when the good news came she decided it was easier to decline the fellowship quietly, to file away the letter, not to bring it up.

She's taken the initiative for the evening, making reservations at a place in midtown, which Donald and Astrid have recommended. She feels a bit guilty for all these months of studying, aware that with her exams as an excuse, she has ignored

Nikhil perhaps more than necessary. There were nights that she told him she was at her carrel in the library when really she'd met Astrid and her baby, Esme, in SoHo, or gone for a walk by herself. Sometimes she would sit at a restaurant alone, at the bar, ordering sushi or a sandwich and a glass of wine, simply to remind herself that she was still capable of being on her own. This assurance is important to her; along with the Sanskrit vows she'd repeated at her wedding, she'd privately vowed that she'd never grow fully dependent on her husband, as her mother has. For even after thirty-two years abroad, in England and now in America, her mother does not know how to drive, does not have a job, does not know the difference between a checking and a savings account. And yet she is a perfectly intelligent woman, was an honors student in philology at Presidency College before she was married off at twenty-two.

They've both dressed up for the occasion—when she emerges from the bathroom she sees that he is wearing the shirt she's given him, moss-colored with a velvet Nehru collar of slightly darker green. It was only after the salesman had wrapped it that she'd remembered the rule about giving paper on the first anniversary. She considered saving the shirt for Christmas, going to Rizzoli and buying him an architecture book instead. But there hasn't been the time. She is wearing the black dress she'd worn the first time he'd come to dinner, the first time they'd slept together, and over it, a lilac pashmina shawl, Nikhil's anniversary present to her. She still remembers their very first date, liking the slightly untamed look of his hair as he'd approached her at the bar, the dark pine stubble on his cheeks, the shirt he'd worn with green stripes and thinner stripes of lavender, the collar beginning to fray. She still remembers her bewilderment, looking up from her book and seeing him, her heart skipping, feeling the attraction instantly, powerfully, in her chest. For she had been expecting an older version of the boy she remembered, distant, quiet, in corduroy jeans and a sweatshirt, a few pimples dotting his chin. The day before the date, she'd had lunch with Astrid. "I just don't see you with some Indian guy," Astrid had said dismissively over salads at City Bakery. At the time Moushumi had not protested, maintaining apologetically that it was just one date. She'd been deeply skeptical herself—apart from the young Shashi Kapoor and a cousin in India, she had never until then found herself attracted to an Indian man. But she'd genuinely liked Nikhil. She'd liked that he was neither a doctor nor an engineer. She'd liked that he'd changed his name from Gogol to Nikhil; though she'd known him all those years, it was a thing that made him somehow new, not the person her mother had mentioned.

They decide to walk to the restaurant, thirty blocks north of their apartment, four blocks west. Though it's dark already, the evening is pleasantly warm, so much so that she hesitates under the awning of their building, wondering if the pashmina is necessary. She has nowhere to put it, her evening bag is too small. She lets the shawl drop from her shoulders, gathers it up in her hands.

"Maybe I should leave this upstairs."

"What if we want to walk back?" he says. "You'll probably need it then."

"I guess."

"It looks nice on you, by the way."

"Do you remember this dress?"

He shakes his head. She's disappointed but not surprised. By now she's learned that his architect's mind for detail fails when it comes to everyday things. For example, he had not bothered to hide the receipt for the shawl, leaving it, along with change emptied from his pocket, on top of the bureau they share. She can't really blame him for not remembering. She herself can no longer remember the exact date of that evening. It had been a Saturday in November. But now those landmarks in their courtship have faded, have given way to the occasion they are now celebrating.

They walk up Fifth Avenue, past the stores that sell Oriental carpets, unfurled in illuminated windows. Past the public library. Instead of proceeding to the restaurant, they decide to wander up the sidewalk for a while; there are still twenty minutes before their reservation. Fifth Avenue is eerily uncluttered, only a handful of people and cabs in a neighborhood usually choked with shoppers and tourists. She comes here seldom, only to buy make-up at Bendel's, or to see the odd movie at the Paris, and once, with Graham and his father and stepmother, to have drinks at the Plaza. They walk past the windows of closed shops displaying watches, luggage, trench coats. A pair of turquoise sandals causes Moushumi to stop. The shoes are arranged on a Lucite pedestal, glowing under a spotlight, the gladiator-style straps festooned with rhinestones.

"Ugly or beautiful?" she asks him. It is a question she poses to him often, as they leaf together through apartments featured in *Architectural Digest* or the design section of the *Times* magazine. Often his answers surprise her, convincing her to appreciate an object she would have otherwise dismissed.

"I'm pretty certain they're ugly. But I would have to see them on."

"I agree. Guess how much they cost," she says.

"Two hundred dollars."

"Five. Can you believe it? I saw them featured in *Vogue*."

She begins to walk away. After a few paces she turns back and sees that he's still standing there, bent down to see if there's a price tag on the bottom of the shoe. There is something at once innocent and irreverent about the gesture, and she is reminded, forcefully, of why she still loves him. It reminds her of how grateful she'd felt when he'd reappeared in her life. By the time she'd met him she'd begun to fear that she was retreating into her former self, before Paris—untouched, bookish, alone. She recalled the panic she'd felt, all her friends married. She'd even considered placing a personal ad. But he had accepted her, had obliterated her former disgrace. She believed that he would be incapable of hurting her as Graham had. After years of clandestine relationships, it felt refreshing to court in a fish-bowl, to have the support of her parents from the very start, the inevitability of an unquestioned future, of marriage, drawing them along. And yet the familiarity that had once drawn her to him has begun to keep her at bay. Though she knows it's not his fault, she can't help but associate him, at times, with a sense of resignation, with the very life she has resisted, has struggled so mightily to leave behind. He was not who she saw herself ending up with, he had never been that person. Perhaps for those very reasons, in those early months, being with him, fall-ing in love with him, doing precisely what had been expected of her for her entire life, had felt forbidden, wildly transgressive, a breach of her own instinctive will.

They can't find the restaurant at first. Though they have the exact address, written on a slip of folded paper in Moushumi's evening bag, it leads them only to a suite of offices in a town house. They press the buzzer, peer through the glass door into the empty, carpeted foyer, at a big vase of flowers at the foot of the stairs.

"It can't be this," she says, putting her hands up to the glass, shielding either side of her face in order to block out the glare.

"Are you sure you wrote down the address right?" Gogol asks.

They wander partway up and down the block, look on the other side. They return to the town house, looking up at the darkened windows for signs of life.

"There it is," he says, noticing a couple emerging from a basement door below the steps. There, in an entryway lit by a single sconce, they find a plaque nailed discreetly into the facade of the building bearing the restaurant's name, Antonia. A small fleet gathers to welcome them, to tick their names off a list at a podium, to lead them to their table. The fuss feels unwarranted as they step into a stark, sunken dining room. The atmosphere is somber, vaguely abandoned, as the streets had been. There is a family eating after the theater, she guesses, the two small daughters in absurdly fancy dresses with petticoats and large lacy collars. There are a few wealthy-looking middle-aged couples in suits. A well-dressed elderly gentleman is dining alone. She finds it suspicious that there are so many empty tables, that no music plays. She'd been hoping for something more bustling, warmer. Given that it's subterranean, the place seems surprisingly vast, the ceilings high. The air-conditioning is too strong, chilling her bare legs and arms. She wraps the pashmina tightly around her shoulders.

"I'm freezing. Do you think they'd turn down the AC if I asked?"

"I doubt that. Would you like my jacket?" Nikhil offers.

"No, it's okay." She smiles at him. And yet she feels uncomfortable, depressed. She is depressed by the pair of teenaged Bangladeshi busboys who wear tapestry waistcoats and black trousers, serving them warm bread with silver tongs. It annoys her that the waiter, perfectly attentive, looks neither of them in the eye as he describes the menu, speaking instead to the bottle of mineral water positioned between them. She knows it's too late to change their plans now. But even after they place their order, a part of her has a nagging urge, feels like standing up, leaving. She had done something similar a few weeks ago, sitting in the chair of an expensive hair salon, walking out after the apron had been tied behind her neck, while the stylist had gone to check on another client, simply because something about the stylist's manner, the bored expression on her face as she'd lifted a lock of Moushumi's hair and studied it in the mirror, had felt insulting. She wonders what Donald and Astrid like about this place, decides it must be the food. But when it arrives, it too disappoints her. The meal, served on square white plates, is fussily arranged, the portions microscopically small. As usual they trade plates partway through the meal, but this time she doesn't like the taste of his so she sticks to her own. She finishes her entree of scallops too quickly, sits for a very long time, it seems, watching Nikhil work his way through his quail.

"We shouldn't have come here," she says suddenly, frowning.

"Why not?" He looks approvingly around the room. "It's nice enough."

"I don't know. It's not what I thought it would be."

"Let's just enjoy ourselves."

But she is not able to enjoy herself. As they near the end of the meal, it occurs to her that she is neither very drunk nor full. In spite of two cocktails and the bottle of wine they'd shared she feels distressingly sober. She looks at the hair-thin quail bones Nikhil has discarded on his plate and is faintly repulsed, wishing he'd finish so that she could light her after-dinner cigarette.

"Madam, your shawl," one of the busboys says, picking it up from the floor and handing it to her.

"Sorry," she says, feeling clumsy, unkempt. Then she notices that her black dress is coated with lilac fibers. She brushes at the material, but the fibers cling stubbornly, like cat hair.

"What's the matter?" Nikhil asks, looking up from his plate.

"Nothing," she says, not wanting to hurt his feelings, to find fault with his costly gift.

They are the last of the diners to leave. It's been wildly expensive, far more than they'd expected. They put down a credit card. Watching Nikhil sign the receipt, she feels cheap all of a sudden, irritated that they have to leave such a generous tip though there had been no real reason to fault the waiter's performance. She notices that a number of tables have already been cleared, chairs placed upside down on their surfaces.

"I can't believe they're already stripping the tables."

He shrugs. "It's late. They probably close early on Sundays."

"You'd think they could wait for us to leave," she says. She feels a lump form in her throat, tears filming her eyes.

"Moushumi, what's wrong? Is there something you want to talk about?"

She shakes her head. She doesn't feel like explaining. She wants to be home, crawl into bed, put the evening behind her. Outside, she's relieved that it's drizzling, so that instead of walking back to the apartment as they'd planned they can hail a cab.

"Are you sure nothing's wrong?" he says as they are riding home. He's beginning to lose patience with her, she can tell.

"I'm still hungry," she says, looking out the window, at the restaurants still open at this hour—brashly lit diners with specials scrawled on paper plates, cheap calzone places with sawdust-coated floors, the type of restaurants she would never think to enter normally but which look suddenly enticing. "I could eat a pizza."

Two days later, a new semester begins. It's Moushumi's eighth semester at NYU. She is finished with classes, will never in her life take a class again. Never again will she sit for an exam. This fact delights her—finally, a formal emancipation from studenthood. Though she still has a dissertation to write, still has an adviser to monitor her progress, she feels unmoored already, somehow beyond the world that has defined and structured and limited her for so long. This is the third time she's taught the class. Beginning French, Mondays, Wednesdays, and Fridays, a total of three hours a week. All she's had to do is look ahead in her calendar and change the date of the class meetings. Her biggest effort will be to learn her students' names. She is always flattered when they assume she herself is French, or half-French. She enjoys their looks of disbelief when she tells them she is from New Jersey, born to Bengali parents.

Moushumi's been given an eight A.M. section, something that had annoyed her at first. But now that she's up, showered, dressed, walking down the street, a latte from the deli on their block in one hand, she's invigorated. Being out at this hour already feels like an accomplishment. When she'd left the apartment, Nikhil had still been asleep, undisturbed by the persistent beeping of the alarm. The night before, she'd laid out her clothes, her papers, something she had not done since she was a girl preparing for school. She likes walking through the streets so early, had liked rising by herself in semidarkness, liked the sense of promise it lent the day. It's a pleasant change from their usual routine—Nikhil showered, in his suit, flying out the door as she's just pouring herself a first cup of coffee. She's thankful not to have to face her desk in the corner of their bedroom first thing, surrounded as it is by sacks full of dirty clothes they keep meaning to drop off at the laundry but get around to only once a month, when buying new socks and underwear becomes necessary. Moushumi wonders how long she will live her life with the trappings of studenthood in spite of the fact that she is a married woman, that she's as far along in her studies as she is, that Nikhil has a respectable if not terribly lucrative job. It would have been different with Graham—he'd made more than enough money for the both of them. And yet that, too, had been frustrating, causing her to fear that her career was somehow an indulgence, unnecessary. Once she has a job, a real full-time tenure-track job, she reminds herself, things will be different. She imagines where that first job might take her, assumes it will be in some far-flung town in the middle of nowhere. Sometimes she jokes with Nikhil about their having to pick up and move, in a few years, to Iowa, to Kalamazoo. But they both know it's out of the question for him to leave New York, that she will be the one to fly back and forth on weekends. There is something appealing to her about this prospect, to make a clean start in a place where no one knows her, as she had done in Paris. It's the one thing about her parents' lives she truly admires — their ability, for better or for worse, to turn their back on their homes.

As she approaches the department she sees that something is wrong. An ambulance is parked on the sidewalk, the doors at the back flung open. Static crackles from a paramedic's walkie-talkie. She peeks into the ambulance as she crosses the street, sees the resuscitative equipment but no people. The sight causes her to shudder nevertheless. Upstairs, the hallway is crowded. She wonders who's hurt, whether it's a student or a professor. She recognizes no one, only a group of bewildered-looking freshmen bearing add-drop forms. "I think someone fainted," people are saying. "I have no idea." A door opens and they are told to make way. She expects to see someone in a wheelchair, is startled to see a body covered by a sheet, being carried out on a stretcher. A number of onlookers cry out in alarm. Moushumi's hand goes to her mouth. Half the crowd is looking down, away, shaking their heads. From the splayed feet at one end of the stretcher, wearing a pair of beige flat-heeled shoes, she can tell that it's a woman. From a professor, she learns what happened: Alice, the administrative assistant, had fallen suddenly by the mailboxes. One minute she was sorting campus

mail, the next minute she was out cold. By the time the para-
medics had arrived she was dead from an aneurysm. She was in
her thirties, unmarried, perpetually sipping herbal tea. Moushumi had never been particularly fond of her. There had been
a brittle quality to her, something unyielding, a young person
who carried about her a premonition of old age.

Moushumi feels sick at the thought of it, of a death so sudden, of a woman so marginal and yet so central to her world.
She enters the office she shares with the other TAs, empty now.
She calls Nikhil at home, at work. No answer. She looks at her
watch, realizes he must be on the subway, on his way to work.
Suddenly she's glad he's unreachable—she's reminded of the
way Nikhil's father had died, instantly, without warning. Surely
this would remind him of that. She has the urge to leave campus, return to the apartment. But she has a class to teach in half
an hour. She goes back to the Xerox room to copy her syllabus and a short passage from Flaubert to translate in class. She
pushes the button to collate the syllabus but forgets to push the
button for staples. She searches in the supply closet for a stapler, and when she fails to find one, goes instinctively to Alice's
desk. The phone is ringing. A cardigan is draped over the back
of the chair. She opens up Alice's drawer, afraid to touch anything. She finds a stapler behind paper clips and Sweet'N Low
packets in the drawer. ALICE is written on masking tape stuck
to the top. The faculty mailboxes are still half-empty, the mail
piled in a bin.

Moushumi goes to her mailbox to look for her class roster.
Her box is empty, so she roots through the bin for her mail. As
she picks up each piece of mail, addressed to this or that faculty
member or TA, she begins putting it into the appropriate box,
matching name to name. Even after she's found her roster, she
continues, completing the task Alice left undone. The mind-
lessness soothes her nerves. As a child she always had a knack

for organization; she would take it upon herself to neaten closets and drawers, not only her own but her parents' as well. She
had organized the cutlery drawer, the refrigerator. These self-
appointed tasks would occupy her during quiet, hot days of her
summer vacation, and her mother would look on in disbelief,
sipping watermelon sherbet in front of the fan. There are just
a handful of items left in the bin. She bends over to pick them
up. And then another name, a sender's name typed in the upper left-hand corner of a business-sized envelope, catches her
eye.

She takes the stapler and the letter and the rest of her things
into her office. She shuts the door, sits at her desk. The envelope is addressed to a professor of Comparative Literature
who teaches German as well as French. She opens the envelope. Inside she finds a cover letter and a résumé. For a minute she simply stares at the name centered at the top of the
résumé, laser-printed in an elegant font. She remembers the
name, of course. The name alone, when she'd first learned it,
had been enough to seduce her. Dimitri Desjardins. He pronounced Desjardins the English way, the *s*'s intact, and in spite
of her training in French this is how she still thinks of it. Underneath the name is an address on West 164th Street. He is
looking for an adjunct position, teaching German part-time.
She reads through the résumé, learns exactly where he's been
and what he's done for the past decade. Travels in Europe. A
job working with the BBC. Articles and reviews published in
Der Spiegel, Critical Inquiry. A Ph.D. in German literature from
the University of Heidelberg.

She had met him years ago, in her final months of high
school. It was a period in which she and two of her friends, in
their eagerness to be college students, in desperation over the
fact that no one their own age was interested in dating them,
would drive to Princeton, loiter on the campus, browse in the

college bookstore, do their homework in buildings they could enter without an ID. Her parents had encouraged these expeditions, believing she was at the library, or attending lectures—they hoped she would go to Princeton for college, live with them at home. One day, as she and her friends were sitting on the grass, they were invited to join a student coalition from the university, a coalition protesting apartheid in South Africa. The group was planning a march on Washington, calling for sanctions.

They took a chartered overnight bus to D.C. in order to be at the rally by early morning. Each of them had lied to their parents, claiming to be sleeping over at one another's homes. Everyone on the bus was smoking pot and listening to the same Crosby, Stills, and Nash album continuously, on a tape player running on batteries. Moushumi had been facing backward, leaning over and talking to her friends, who were in the two seats behind her, and when she turned back around he was in the neighboring seat. He seemed aloof from the rest of the group, not an actual member of the coalition, somehow dismissive of it all. He was wiry, slight, with small, downward-sloping eyes and an intellectual, ravaged-looking face that she found sexy though not handsome. His hairline was already receding, his hair curly and fair. He needed a shave; his fingernails needed paring. He was wearing a white button-down shirt, faded Levi's with threadbare knees, pliable gold-framed spectacles that wrapped around his ears. Without introducing himself he began talking to her, as if they were already acquainted. He was twenty-seven, had gone to Williams College, was a student of European history. He was taking a German course at Princeton now, living with his parents, both of whom taught at the university, and he was going out of his mind. He had spent the years after college traveling around Asia, Latin America. He told her he probably wanted to get a Ph.D., eventually.

The randomness of all this had appealed to her. He asked her what her name was and when she told him he had leaned toward her, cupping his ear, even though she knew he had heard it perfectly well. "How in the world do you spell that?" he'd asked, and when she told him, he mispronounced it, as most people did. She corrected him, saying that "Mou" rhymed with "toe," but he shook his head and said, "I'll just call you Mouse."

The nickname had irritated and pleased her at the same time. It made her feel foolish, but she was aware that in renaming her he had claimed her somehow, already made her his own. As the bus grew quiet, as everyone began to fall asleep, she had let him lean his head against her shoulder. Dimitri was asleep, or so she thought. And so she pretended to fall asleep too. After a while she felt his hand on her leg, on top of the white denim skirt she was wearing. And then slowly, he began to unbutton the skirt. Several minutes passed between his undoing of one button and the next, his eyes closed all the while, his head still on her shoulder, as the bus hurtled down the empty, dark highway. It was the first time in her life a man had touched her. She held herself perfectly still. She was desperate to touch him too, but she was terrified. Finally Dimitri opened his eyes. She felt his mouth near her ear, and she turned to him, prepared to be kissed, at seventeen, for the very first time. But he had not kissed her. He had only looked at her, and said, "You're going to break hearts, you know." And then he leaned back, in his own seat this time, removed his hand from her lap, and closed his eyes once again. She had stared at him in disbelief, angry that he assumed she hadn't broken any hearts yet, and at the same time flattered. For the rest of the journey she kept her skirt unbuttoned, hoping he would return to the task. But he didn't touch her after that, and in the morning there was no acknowledgment of what had passed between them. At the demonstration he had wandered off, paid her no attention. On the way back they had sat apart.

Afterward she returned to the university every day to try to run into him. After some weeks she saw him striding across campus, alone, holding a copy of *The Man Without Qualities*. They shared some coffee and sat on a bench outside. He had asked her to see a movie, Goddard's *Alphaville*, and to have Chinese food. She had worn an outfit that still causes her to wince, an old blazer of her father's that was too long for her, over jeans, the sleeves of the blazer rolled up as if it were a shirt, to reveal the striped lining inside. It had been the first date of her life, strategically planned on an evening her parents were at a party. She recalled nothing of the movie, had eaten nothing at the restaurant, part of a small shopping complex off Route 1. And then, after watching Dimitri eat both of their fortune cookies without reading either prediction, she had made her error: she had asked him to be her date to her senior prom. He had declined, driven her home, kissed her lightly on her cheek in the driveway, and then he never called her again. The evening had humiliated her; he had treated her like a child. Sometime over the summer she bumped into him at the movies. He was with a date, a tall freckled girl with hair to her waist. Moushumi had wanted to flee, but he'd made a point of introducing her to the girl. "This is Moushumi," Dimitri had said deliberately, as if he'd been waiting for the opportunity to say her name for weeks. He told her he was going to Europe for a while, and from the look on the date's face she realized that she was going with him. Moushumi told him she'd been accepted at Brown. "You look great," he told her when the date wasn't listening.

While she was at Brown, postcards would arrive from time to time, envelopes plastered with colorful, oversized stamps. His handwriting was minuscule but sloppy, always causing her eyes to strain. There was never a return address. For a time she carried these letters in her book bag, to her classes, thickening her agenda. Periodically he sent her books he'd read and thought she might like. A few times he called in the middle of the night, waking her, and she spoke to him for hours in the dark, lying in bed in her dorm room, then sleeping through her morning classes. A single call kept her sailing for weeks. "I'll come visit you. I'll take you to dinner," he told her. He never did. Eventually the letters tapered off. His last communication had been a box of books, along with several postcards he'd written to her in Greece and Turkey but not managed to send at the time. And then she'd moved to Paris.

She reads Dimitri's résumé again, then the cover letter. The letter reveals nothing other than earnest pedagogical intent, mentions a panel Dimitri and the professor to whom it's addressed attended some years ago. Practically the same letter exists in a file on her computer. His third sentence is missing a period, which she now carefully inserts with her finest-nibbed fountain pen. She can't bring herself to write down his address, though she doesn't want to forget it. In the Xerox room, she makes a copy of the résumé. She sticks it in the bottom of her bag. Then she types up a new envelope and puts the original in the professor's mailbox. As she returns to her office, she realizes there's no stamp or postmark on the new envelope, worries that the professor will suspect something. But she reassures herself that Dimitri could easily have delivered the letter personally; the idea of him standing in the department, occupying the same space she occupies now, fills her with the same combination of desperation and lust he's always provoked.

The hardest part is deciding where to write down the phone number, in what part of her agenda. She wishes she had a code of some sort. In Paris she had briefly dated an Iranian professor of philosophy who would write the names of his students in Persian on the backs of index cards, along with some small, cruel detail to help him distinguish among them. Once he read the cards to Moushumi. Bad skin, one said. Thick ankles, said another. Moushumi can't resort to such trickery, can't write in Bengali. She barely remembers how to write her own name, something her grandmother had once taught her. Finally she writes it on the *D* page, but she doesn't include his name beside it. Just the numbers, disembodied, don't feel like a betrayal. They could be anybody's. She looks outside. As she sits down at her desk, her eye travels upward; the window in the office reaches the top of the wall, so that the rooftop of the building across the street stretches across the bottom edge of the sill. The view induces the opposite of vertigo, a lurching feeling inspired not by gravity's pull to earth, but by the infinite reaches of heaven.

At home that night, after dinner, Moushumi hunts among the shelves in the living room she and Nikhil share. Their books have merged since they've gotten married, Nikhil has unpacked them all, and nothing is where she expects it to be. Her eyes pass over stacks of Nikhil's design magazines, thick books on Gropius and Le Corbusier. Nikhil, bent over a blueprint at the dining table, asks what she's looking for.

"Stendhal," she tells him. It's not a lie. An old Modern Library edition of *The Red and the Black* in English, inscribed to Mouse. Love Dimitri, he'd written. It was the one book he'd inscribed to her. Back then it was the closest thing she'd ever had to a love letter; for months she had slept with the book under her pillow, and later, slipped it between her mattress and box spring. Somehow she managed to hold on to it for years; it's moved with her from Providence to Paris to New York, a secret talisman on her shelves that she would glance at now and again, still faintly flattered by his peculiar pursuit of her, and always faintly curious as to what had become of him. But now that she's desperate to locate the book she's convinced that it won't be in the apartment, that maybe Graham had taken it by mistake when he'd moved out of their place on York Avenue, or that it's in the basement of her parents' house, in one of the boxes she'd shipped there a few years ago, when her shelves were getting too full. She doesn't remember packing it from her old apartment, doesn't remember unpacking it when she and Nikhil moved in together. She wishes she could ask Nikhil if he's seen it—a small green clothbound book missing its dust jacket, the title embossed in a rectangle of black on the spine. And then suddenly she sees it herself, sitting in plain view, on a shelf she'd scanned a minute ago. She opens the book, sees the Modern Library emblem, the dashing, naked, torch-bearing figure. She sees the inscription, the force of the ballpoint pen he'd used slightly crimping the other side of the page. She'd abandoned the novel after the second chapter. Her place is still marked by a yellowing receipt for shampoo. By now she's read the book in French three times. She finishes Scott-Moncrieff's English translation within days, reading it at her desk in the department, and in her carrel in the library. In the evenings, at home, she reads it in bed until Nikhil comes in to join her—then she puts it away and opens something else.

She calls him the following week. By then she's dug up the postcards, saved in an unsealed, unmarked manila envelope in the box where she keeps her tax returns, and read them, too, amazed that his words, the sight of his handwriting, still manage to discombobulate her. She tells herself she's calling an old friend. She tells herself the coincidence of finding his résumé, of stumbling upon him in this way, is too great, that anyone in her position would pick up the phone and call. She tells herself he could very well be married, as she is. Perhaps all four of them will go out to dinner, become great friends. Still, she doesn't tell Nikhil about the résumé. One night in her office, after seven o'clock when only a janitor roams the halls, after a few sips from the small bottle of Maker's Mark she has stashed at the back of her file cabinet, she calls. A night Nikhil thinks she's working on revisions for an article for *PMLA*.

She dials the number, listens as it rings four times. She wonders if he'll even remember her. Her heart races. Her finger moves to the cradle, ready to press down.

"Hello?"

It's his voice. "Hi. Dimitri?"

"Speaking. Who's this?"

She pauses. She can still hang up if she wants. "It's Mouse."

They begin seeing each other Mondays and Wednesdays, after she teaches her class. She takes the train uptown and they meet at his apartment, where lunch is waiting. The meals are ambitious: poached fish; creamy potato gratins; golden, puffed chickens roasted with whole lemons in their cavities. There is always a bottle of wine. They sit at a table with his books and papers and laptop pushed to one side. They listen to WQXR, drink coffee and cognac and smoke a cigarette afterward. Only then does he touch her. Sunlight streams through large dirty windows into the shabby prewar apartment. There are two spacious rooms, flaking plaster walls, scuffed parquet floors, towering stacks of boxes he has not yet bothered to unpack. The bed, a brand-new mattress and box spring on wheels, is never made. After sex they are always amazed to discover that the bed has moved several inches away from the wall, pushing up against the bureau on the other side of the room. She likes the way he looks at her when their limbs are still tangled together, out of breath as if he'd been chasing her, his expression anxious before relaxing into a smile. Some gray has come into Dimitri's hair and chest, some lines around the mouth and eyes. He's heavier than before, his stomach undeniably wide, so that his thin legs appear slightly comic. He recently turned thirty-nine. He has not been married. He does not seem very desperate to be employed. He spends his days cooking meals, reading, listening to classical music. She gathers that he has inherited some money from his grandmother.

The first time they met, the day after she called him, at the bar of a crowded Italian restaurant near NYU, they had not been able to stop staring at each other, not been able to stop talking about the résumé, and the uncanny way it had fallen into Moushumi's hands. He had moved to New York only a month ago, had tried to look her up but the phone is listed under Nikhil's last name. It didn't matter, they agreed. It was better this way. They drank glasses of prosecco. She agreed to an early dinner with Dimitri that night, sitting at the bar of the restaurant, for the prosecco had gone quickly to their heads. He had ordered a salad topped with warm lambs' tongue, a poached egg, and pecorino cheese, something she swore she would not touch but ended up eating the better part of. Afterward she'd gone into Balducci's to buy the pasta and ready-made vodka sauce she would have at home with Nikhil.

On Mondays and Wednesdays no one knows where she is. There are no Bengali fruit sellers to greet her on the walk from Dimitri's subway stop, no neighbors to recognize her once she turns onto Dimitri's block. It reminds her of living in Paris—for a few hours at Dimitri's she is inaccessible, anonymous. Dimitri is not terribly curious about Nikhil, does not ask her his name. He expresses no jealousy. When she told him in the Italian restaurant that she was married, his expression had not changed. He regards their time together as perfectly normal, as destined, and she begins to see how easy it is. Moushumi refers to Nikhil in conversation as "my husband": "My husband and I have a dinner to go to next Thursday." "My husband's given me this cold."

At home, Nikhil suspects nothing. As usual they have dinner, talk of their days. They clean up the kitchen together, then sit on the sofa and watch television while she corrects her students' quizzes and exercises. During the eleven o'clock news, they have bowls of Ben and Jerry's, then brush their teeth. As usual they get into bed, kiss, then slowly they turn away from each other in order to stretch comfortably into sleep. Only Moushumi stays awake. Each Monday and Wednesday night, she fears that he will sense something, that he will put his arms around her and instantly know. She stays awake for hours after they've turned out the lights, prepared to answer him, prepared to lie to his face. She had gone shopping, she would tell him if he were to ask, for in fact she had done this on her way home that first Monday, halting her journey back from Dimitri's in midstream, getting out of the subway at 72d Street before continuing downtown, stopping in a store she'd never been in, buying a pair of the most ordinary-looking black shoes.

One night it's worse than usual. It's three o'clock, then four. Construction work has been taking place for the past few nights on their street, giant bins of rubble and concrete are moved and crushed, and Moushumi feels angry at Nikhil for being able to sleep through it. She's tempted to get up, pour herself a drink, take a bath, anything. But fatigue keeps her in bed. She watches the shadows that the passing traffic throws onto their ceiling, listens to a truck wailing in the distance like a solitary, nocturnal beast. She is convinced she will be up to see the sun rise. But somehow she falls asleep again. She is woken just after dawn by the sound of rain beating against the bedroom window, pelting it with such ferocity that she almost expects

the glass to shatter. She has a splitting headache. She gets out
of bed and parts the curtains, then returns to bed and shakes
Nikhil awake. "Look," she says, pointing at the rain, as if it were
something truly extraordinary. Nikhil obliges, fully asleep, sits
upright, then closes his eyes again.

At seven-thirty she gets out of bed. The morning sky is clear.
She walks out of the bedroom and sees that rain has leaked
through the roof, left an unsightly yellow patch on the ceiling
and puddles in the apartment: one in the bathroom, another in
the front hall. The sill of a window left open in the living room
is soaked, streaked with mud, as are the bills and books and papers piled on it. The sight of it makes her weep. At the same
time she's thankful that there's something tangible for her to be
upset about.

"Why are you crying?" Nikhil asks, squinting at her in his
pajamas.

"There are cracks in the ceiling," she says.

Nikhil looks up. "They're not too bad. I'll call the super."

"The rainwater came right through the roof."

"What rain?"

"Don't you remember? It was pouring rain at dawn. It was
incredible. I woke you."

But Nikhil doesn't remember a thing.

A month of Mondays and Wednesdays passes. She begins to
see him on Fridays as well. One Friday she finds herself alone
in Dimitri's apartment; he goes out as soon as she arrives, to
buy a stick of butter for a white sauce he is making to pour over
trout. Bartók plays on the stereo, expensive components scattered on the floor. She watches him from the window, walking down the block, a small, balding, unemployed middle-aged
man, who is enabling her to wreck her marriage. She wonders
if she is the only woman in her family ever to have betrayed her

husband, to have been unfaithful. This is what upsets her most
to admit: that the affair causes her to feel strangely at peace,
the complication of it calming her, structuring her day. After
the first time, washing up in the bathroom, she'd been horrified by what she'd done, at the sight of her clothes scattered
throughout the two rooms. Before leaving, she'd combed her
hair in the bathroom mirror, the only one in the apartment.
She'd kept her head bent low, glancing up only briefly at the
end. When she did she saw that it was one of those mirrors that
was for some reason particularly flattering, due to some trick of
the light or the quality of the glass, causing her skin to glow.

There is nothing on Dimitri's walls. He is still living out of
a series of mammoth duffel bags. She is glad not to be able to
picture his life in all its detail, its mess. The only things he's
set up are the kitchen, the stereo components, and some of his
books. Each time she visits, there are modest signs of progress.
She wanders around his living room, looks at the books he is
beginning to organize on his plywood shelves. Apart from all
the German, their personal libraries are similar. There is the
same lime green spine of *The Princeton Encyclopedia of Poetry
and Poetics*. The same edition of *Mimesis*. The same boxed set of
Proust. She pulls out an oversized volume of photographs of
Paris, by Atget. She sits on an armchair, Dimitri's only piece
of living room furniture. It was here that she'd sat the first
time she'd visited, and he'd stood behind her, massaging a spot
on her shoulder, arousing her, until she stood up, and they'd
walked together to the bed.

She opens up the book to regard the streets and the landmarks she once knew. She thinks of her wasted fellowship. A
large square of sunlight appears on the floor. The sun is directly
behind her, and the shadow of her head spreads across the thick,
silken pages, a few strands of her hair strangely magnified, quiv-
ering, as if viewed through a microscope. She leans back her

head, closes her eyes. When she opens them a moment later the sun has slipped away, a lone sliver of it now diminishing into the floorboards, like the gradual closing of a curtain, causing the stark white pages of the book to turn gray. She hears Dimitri's footsteps on the stairs, then the clean sound of his key in the lock, slicing sharply into the apartment. She gets up to put the book away, searching for the gap in which it had stood.

11

GOGOL wakes up late on a Sunday morning, alone, from a bad dream he cannot recall. He looks over at Moushumi's side of the bed, at the untidy pile of her books and magazines on the end table, the bottle of lavender room spray she likes to squirt sometimes on their pillows, the tortoiseshell barrette with strands of her hair caught in its clasp. She's at another conference this weekend, in Palm Beach. By tonight she'll be home. She claimed she'd told him about the conference months ago, but he doesn't remember. "Don't worry," she'd said as she was packing, "I won't be there long enough to get a tan." But when he'd seen her bathing suit on top of the clothing on the bed, a strange panic had welled up inside of him as he thought of her lying without him by a hotel pool, her eyes closed, a book at her side. At least one of us isn't cold, he thinks to himself now, crossing his arms tightly in front of his chest. Since yesterday afternoon the building's boiler has been broken, turning the apartment into an icebox. Last night he'd had to turn the oven on in order to tolerate being in the living room, and he'd worn his old Yale sweatpants, a thick sweater over a T-shirt, and a pair of rag-wool socks to bed. He throws back the comforter and the extra blanket he'd placed on top of it in the middle of the night. He couldn't find the blanket at first, nearly called Moushumi at the hotel to ask where she kept it. But by then it was nearly three in the morning, and so, eventually, he'd hunted it down himself, found it wedged on the top shelf of the hall closet, an unused wedding gift still in its zippered plastic case.

He gets out of bed, brushes his teeth with freezing-cold water from the tap, decides to skip shaving. He pulls on jeans and an extra sweater, and Moushumi's bathrobe over that, not caring how ridiculous he looks. He makes a pot of coffee, toasts some bread to eat with butter and jam. He opens the front door and retrieves the *Times,* removing the blue wrapper, putting it on the coffee table to read later. There is a drawing for work he must complete by tomorrow, a cross section for a high school auditorium in Chicago. He unrolls the plan from its tube and spreads it out on the dining table, securing the corners with paperback books he grabs off the bookcase. He puts on his *Abbey Road* CD, skipping ahead to the songs that would have been on side 2 of the album, and tries to work on the drawing, making sure his measurements correspond to the principal designer's notes. But his fingers are stiff and so he rolls up the plan, leaves a note for Moushumi on the kitchen counter, and goes in to the office.

He's glad to have an excuse to be out of the apartment, instead of waiting for her, at some point this evening, to return. It feels milder outside, the air pleasantly damp, and instead of taking the train he walks the thirty blocks, up Park Avenue and over to Madison. He is the only person at the office. He sits in the darkened drafting room, surrounded by the desks of his coworkers, some piled with drawings and models, others as neat as a pin. He crouches over his table, a single pool of light from a swinging metal lamp illuminating the large sheet of paper. Tacked to the wall over his desk is a tiny calendar showing the entire year, which is coming once again to a close. At the end of the week, it will be the fourth anniversary of his father's death. Circled dates indicate all his deadlines, past and future. Meetings, site visits, conferences with clients. A lunch with an architect who's interested, possibly, in hiring him. He's eager to move to a smaller firm, to have some domestic commissions, to work with fewer people. Next to the calendar there is a postcard of a Duchamp painting he has always loved, of a chocolate grinder that reminds him of a set of drums, suspended against a gray background. Several Post-it notes. The photograph of his mother and Sonia and himself at Fatehpur Sikri, salvaged from his father's refrigerator door in Cleveland. And next to this, a picture of Moushumi, an old passport photo he'd found and asked to keep. She is in her early twenties, her hair loose, her heavy-lidded eyes slightly lowered, looking to one side. It was taken before he'd begun to date her, when she was living in Paris. A time in her life in which he was still Gogol to her, a remnant from her past with little likelihood of appearing in her future. And yet they had met; after all her adventures, it was he whom she had married. He with whom she shared her life.

Last weekend was Thanksgiving. His mother and Sonia and Sonia's new boyfriend, Ben, had come, along with Moushumi's parents and brother, and they had all celebrated the holiday together in New York, crowded together in Gogol and Moushumi's apartment. It was the first time he had not gone either to his parents' or to his in-laws' for a holiday. It felt strange to be hosting, to assume the center of responsibility. They had ordered a fresh turkey in advance from the farmers' market, planned the menu out of *Food & Wine*, bought folding chairs so that everyone would have a place to sit. Moushumi had gone out and bought a rolling pin, made an apple pie for the first time in her life. For Ben's sake they had all spoken in English. Ben is half-Jewish, half-Chinese, raised in Newton, close

to where Gogol and Sonia grew up. He is an editor at the *Globe*.
He and Sonia met by chance, at a café on Newbury Street. Seeing them together, sneaking into the hallway so that they could
kiss freely, holding hands discreetly as they sat at the table,
Gogol had been oddly envious, and as they all sat eating their
turkey and roasted sweet potatoes and cornbread stuffing, and
the spiced cranberry chutney his mother had made, he looked
at Moushumi and wondered what was wrong. They didn't argue, they still had sex, and yet he wondered. Did he still make
her happy? She accused him of nothing, but more and more
he sensed her distance, her dissatisfaction, her distraction. But
there had been no time to dwell on this worry. The weekend
had been exhausting, getting their various family members to
the apartments of nearby friends who were away and had given
them keys. The day after Thanksgiving they had all gone to
Jackson Heights, to the halal butcher so that both their mothers could stock up on goat meat, and then to brunch. And on
Saturday there had been a concert of classical Indian music up
at Columbia. Part of him wants to bring it up with her. "Are
you happy you married me?" he would ask. But the fact that he
is even thinking of this question makes him afraid.

He finishes up the drawing, leaves it pinned on his desk to
be reviewed in the morning. He's worked through lunch, and
when he steps out of his office building it is colder, the light fading rapidly from the sky. He buys a cup of coffee and a falafel
sandwich at the Egyptian restaurant on the corner and walks
south as he eats, toward the Flatiron and lower Fifth Avenue,
the twin towers of the World Trade Center looming in the distance, sparkling at the island's end. The falafel, wrapped in foil,
is warm and messy in his hands. The stores are full, the windows decorated, the sidewalks crammed with shoppers. The
thought of Christmas overwhelms him. Last year they went to
Moushumi's parents' house. This year they'll go to Pember-

ton Road. He no longer looks forward to the holiday; he wants only to be on the other side of the season. His impatience makes him feel that he is, incontrovertibly, finally, an adult. He wanders absently into a perfume store, a clothing store, a store that sells only bags. He has no idea what to get Moushumi for Christmas. Normally she drops hints, showing him catalogues, but he has no clue as to what she's coveting this season, if it's a new pair of gloves or a wallet or new pajamas she'd like. In the maze of stalls in Union Square that sell candles and shawls and handmade jewelry, nothing inspires him.

He decides to try the Barnes and Noble at the northern edge of the square. But staring at the immense wall of new titles on display he realizes he has read none of these books, and what was the point of giving her something he hadn't read? On his way out of the store he pauses by a table devoted to travel guides. He picks up one for Italy, full of illustrations of the architecture he had studied so carefully as a student, has admired only in photographs, has always meant to see. It angers him, yet there is no one to blame but himself. What was stopping him? A trip together, to a place neither of them has been—maybe that's what he and Moushumi need. He could plan it all himself, select the cities they would visit, the hotels. It could be his Christmas gift to her, two airplane tickets tucked into the back of the guide. He was due for another vacation; he could plan it for her spring break. Inspired by the thought, he goes to the register, waits in a long line, and pays for the book.

He walks across the park toward home, thumbing through the book, anxious to see her now. He decides to stop off at the new gourmet grocery that's opened on Irving Place, to buy some of the things she likes: blood oranges, a wedge of cheese from the Pyrenees, slices of soppresata, a loaf of peasant bread. For she will be hungry—they serve nothing on planes these days. He looks up from the book, at the sky, at the darkness gathering, the clouds a deep, beautiful gold, and is momentarily stopped by a flock of pigeons flying dangerously close. Suddenly terrified, he ducks his head, feeling foolish afterward. None of the other pedestrians has reacted. He stops and watches as the birds shoot up, then land simultaneously on two neighboring bare-branched trees. He is unsettled by the sight. He has seen these graceless birds on windowsills and sidewalks, but never in trees. It looks almost unnatural. And yet, what could be more ordinary? He thinks of Italy, of Venice, the trip he will begin to plan. Maybe it's a sign that they are meant to go there. Wasn't the Piazza San Marco famous for its pigeons?

The lobby of the apartment is warm when he enters, the building's heat restored. "She just got back," the doorman tells Gogol with a wink as he walks past, and his heart leaps, unburdened of its malaise, grateful for her simple act of returning to him. He imagines her puttering around the apartment, drawing a bath, pouring herself a glass of wine, her bags in the hallway. He slips the book he will give her for Christmas into the pocket of his coat, making sure it's well concealed, and calls the elevator to take him upstairs.

12

I T IS the day before Christmas. Ashima Ganguli sits at her kitchen table, making mincemeat croquettes for a party she is throwing that evening. They are one of her specialties, something her guests have come to expect, handed to them on small plates within minutes of their arrival. Alone, she manages an assembly line of preparation. First she forces warm boiled potatoes through a ricer. Carefully she shapes a bit of the potato around a spoonful of cooked ground lamb, as uniformly as the white of a hard-boiled egg encases its yolk. She dips each of the croquettes, about the size and shape of a billiard ball, into a bowl of beaten eggs, then coats them on a plate of bread crumbs, shaking off the excess in her cupped palms. Finally she stacks the croquettes on a large circular tray, a sheet of wax paper between each layer. She stops to count how many she's made so far. She estimates three for each adult, one or two for each of the children. Counting the lines on the backs of her fingers, she reviews, once more, the exact number of her guests. Another dozen to be safe, she decides. She pours a fresh heap of bread crumbs on the plate, their color and texture reminding her of sand on a beach. She remembers making the first batches in her kitchen in Cambridge, for her very first parties, her husband at the stove in white drawstring pajamas and a T-shirt, frying the croquettes two at a time in a small blackened saucepan. She remembers Gogol and Sonia helping her when they were small, Gogol's hand wrapped around the can of crumbs, Sonia always wanting to eat the croquettes before they'd been breaded and fried.

This will be the last party Ashima will host at Pemberton Road. The first since her husband's funeral. The house in which she has lived for the past twenty-seven years, which she has occupied longer than any other in her life, has been recently sold, a Realtor's sign stuck into the lawn. The buyers are an American family, the Walkers, a young professor new to the university where her husband used to work, and a wife and daughter. The Walkers are planning renovations. They will knock down the wall between the living and dining rooms, put an island in the kitchen, track lights overhead. They want to pull up the wall-to-wall carpeting, convert the sun deck into a den. Listening to their plans, Ashima had felt a moment's panic, a protective instinct, wanting to retract her offer, wanting the house to remain as it's always been, as her husband had last seen it. But this had been sentimentality speaking. It is foolish for her to hope that the golden letters spelling GANGULI on the mailbox will not be peeled off, replaced. That Sonia's name, written in Magic Marker on the inside of her bedroom door, will not be sanded, restained. That the pencil markings on the wall by the linen closet, where Ashoke used to record his children's height on their birthdays, will not be painted over.

Ashima has decided to spend six months of her life in India, six months in the States. It is a solitary, somewhat premature version of the future she and her husband had planned when he was alive. In Calcutta, Ashima will live with her younger brother, Rana, and his wife, and their two grown, as yet unmarried daughters, in a spacious flat in Salt Lake. There she will have a room, the first in her life intended for her exclusive use. In spring and summer she will return to the Northeast, dividing her time among her son, her daughter, and her close Bengali friends. True to the meaning of her name, she will be without borders, without a home of her own, a resident everywhere and nowhere. But it's no longer possible for her to live here now that Sonia's going to be married. The wedding will be in Calcutta, a little over a year from now, on an auspicious January day, just as she and her husband were married nearly thirty-four years ago. Something tells her Sonia will be happy with this boy—quickly she corrects herself—this young man. He has brought happiness to her daughter, in a way Moushumi had never brought it to her son. That it was she who had encouraged Gogol to meet Moushumi will be something for which Ashima will always feel guilty. How could she have known? But fortunately they have not considered it their duty to stay married, as the Bengalis of Ashoke and Ashima's generation do. They are not willing to accept, to adjust, to settle for something less than their ideal of happiness. That pressure has given way, in the case of the subsequent generation, to American common sense.

For a few final hours she is alone in the house. Sonia has gone with Ben to pick up Gogol at the train station. It occurs to Ashima that the next time she will be by herself, she will be traveling, sitting on the plane. For the first time since her flight to meet her husband in Cambridge, in the winter of 1967, she will make the journey entirely on her own. The prospect no longer terrifies her. She has learned to do things on her own, and though she still wears saris, still puts her long hair in a bun, she is not the same Ashima who had once lived in Calcutta. She will return to India with an American passport. In her wallet will remain her Massachusetts driver's license, her social se-

curity card. She will return to a world where she will not sin-
gle-handedly throw parties for dozens of people. She will not
have to go to the trouble of making yogurt from half-and-half
and sandesh from ricotta cheese. She will not have to make her
own croquettes. They will be available to her from restaurants,
brought up to the flat by servants, bearing a taste that after all
these years she has still not quite managed, to her entire satisfaction, to replicate.

She finishes breading the final croquette, then glances at her
wristwatch. She is slightly ahead of schedule. She sets the platter on the counter next to the stove. She takes a pan out of the
cupboard and pours in the oil, several cupfuls, to be heated in
the minutes before her guests are expected. From a crock she
selects the slotted spatula she will use. For now, there is nothing left to be done. The rest of the food has been prepared, sitting in long CorningWare pans on the dining room table: dal
coated with a thick skin that will rupture as soon as the first of it
is served, a roasted cauliflower dish, eggplant, a korma of lamb.
Sweet yogurt and pantuas for dessert sit on the sideboard. She
eyes everything with anticipation. Normally cooking for parties leaves her without an appetite, but tonight she looks forward to serving herself, sitting among her guests. With Sonia's
help the house has been cleaned one last time. Ashima has always loved these hours before a party, the carpets vacuumed,
the coffee table wiped with Pledge, her dimmed, blurry reflection visible in the wood just as the old television commercial
used to promise.

She roots through her kitchen drawer for a packet of incense.
She lights a stick by the flame of the stove and walks from room
to room. It's gratified her to go to all this effort—to make a final, celebratory meal for her children, her friends. To decide on
a menu, to make a list and shop in the supermarket and fill the
refrigerator shelves with food. It's a pleasant change of pace,

something finite in contrast to her current, overwhelming, on-going task: to prepare for her departure, picking the bones of the house clean. For the past month, she has been dismantling her household piece by piece. Each evening she has tackled a drawer, a closet, a set of shelves. Though Sonia offers to help, Ashima prefers to do this alone. She has made piles of things to give to Gogol and Sonia, things to give to friends, things to take with her, things to donate to charities, things to put into trash bags and drive to the dump. The task both saddens and satisfies her at the same time. There is a thrill to whittling down her possessions to little more than what she'd come with, to those three rooms in Cambridge in the middle of a winter's night. Tonight she will invite friends to take whatever might be useful, lamps, plants, platters, pots and pans. Sonia and Ben will rent a truck and take whatever furniture they have room for.

She goes upstairs to shower and change. The walls now re-mind her of the house when they'd first moved in, bare except for the photograph of her husband, which will be the last thing she will remove. She pauses for a moment, waving the remains of the incense in front of Ashoke's image before throwing the stick away. She lets the water run in the shower, turns up the thermostat to compensate for the terrible moment when she will have to step onto the mat on the bathroom floor, un-clothed. She gets into her beige bathtub, behind the crackled sliding glass doors. She is exhausted from two days of cook-ing, from her morning of cleaning, from these weeks of pack-ing and dealing with the sale of the house. Her feet feel heavy against the fiberglass floor of the tub. For a while she simply stands there before tending to the shampooing of her hair, the soaping of her softening, slightly shrinking fifty-three-year-old body, which she must fortify each morning with calcium pills. When she is finished, she wipes the steam off the bathroom mirror and studies her face. A widow's face. But for most of her

life, she reminds herself, a wife. And perhaps, one day, a grandmother, arriving in America laden with hand-knit sweaters and
gifts, leaving, a month or two later, inconsolable, in tears.

Ashima feels lonely suddenly, horribly, permanently alone,
and briefly, turned away from the mirror, she sobs for her husband. She feels overwhelmed by the thought of the move she
is about to make, to the city that was once home and is now in
its own way foreign. She feels both impatience and indifference for all the days she still must live, for something tells her
she will not go quickly as her husband did. For thirty-three
years she missed her life in India. Now she will miss her job at
the library, the women with whom she's worked. She will miss
throwing parties. She will miss living with her daughter, the
surprising companionship they have formed, going into Cambridge together to see old movies at the Brattle, teaching her
to cook the food Sonia had complained of eating as a child. She
will miss the opportunity to drive, as she sometimes does on
her way home from the library, to the university, past the engineering building where her husband once worked. She will
miss the country in which she had grown to know and love her
husband. Though his ashes have been scattered into the Ganges, it is here, in this house and in this town, that he will continue to dwell in her mind.

She takes a deep breath. In a moment she will hear the beeps
of the security system, the garage door opening, car doors closing, her children's voices in the house. She applies lotion to her
arms and legs, reaches for a peach-colored terry-cloth robe that
hangs from a hook on the door. Her husband had given her the
robe years ago, for a Christmas now long forgotten. This too
she will have to give away, will have no use for where she is going. In such a humid climate it would take days for such a thick
material to dry. She makes a note to herself, to wash it well and
donate it to the thrift shop. She does not remember the year

she'd gotten the robe, does not remember opening it, or her reaction. She knows only that it had been either Gogol or Sonia who had picked it out at one of the department stores at the mall, had wrapped it, even. That all her husband had done was to write his name and hers on the to-and-from tag. She does not fault him for this. Such omissions of devotion, of affection, she knows now, do not matter in the end. She no longer wonders what it might have been like to do what her children have done, to fall in love first rather than years later, to deliberate over a period of months or years and not a single afternoon, which was the time it had taken for her and Ashoke to agree to wed. It is the image of their two names on the tag that she thinks of, a tag she had not bothered to save. It reminds her of their life together, of the unexpected life he, in choosing to marry her, had given her here, which she had refused for so many years to accept. And though she still does not feel fully at home within these walls on Pemberton Road she knows that this is home nevertheless—the world for which she is responsible, which she has created, which is everywhere around her, needing to be packed up, given away, thrown out bit by bit. She slips her damp arms into the sleeves of the robe, ties the belt around her waist. It's always been a bit short on her, a size too small. Its warmth is a comfort all the same.

There is no one to greet Gogol on the platform when he gets off the train. He wonders if he's early, looks at his watch. Instead of going into the station house he waits on a bench outside. The last of the passengers board, the train doors slide to a close. The conductors wave their signals to one another, the wheels roll slowly away, the compartments glide forward one by one. He watches his fellow passengers being greeted by family members, lovers reunited with entangled arms, without a word. College students burdened by backpacks, returning for

Christmas break. After a few minutes the platform is empty, as is the space the train had occupied. Now Gogol looks onto a field, some spindly trees against a cobalt twilight sky. He thinks of calling home but decides he is content to sit and wait awhile longer. The cool air is pleasant on his face after his hours on the train. He'd slept most of the journey to Boston, the conductor poking him awake once they'd reached South Station, and he was the only person left in the compartment, the last to get off. He had slept soundly, curled up on two seats, his book unread, using his overcoat as a blanket, pulled up to his chin.

He feels groggy still, a bit lightheaded from having skipped his lunch. At his feet are a duffel bag containing clothes, a shopping bag from Macy's with gifts bought earlier that morning, before catching his train at Penn Station. His choices are uninspired—a pair of fourteen-karat gold earrings for his mother, sweaters for Sonia and Ben. They have agreed to keep things simple this year. He has a week of vacation. There is work to do at the house, his mother has warned him. His room must be emptied, every last scrap either taken back with him to New York or tossed. He must help his mother pack her things, settle her accounts. They will drive her to Logan and see her off as far as airport security will allow. And then the house will be occupied by strangers, and there will be no trace that they were ever there, no house to enter, no name in the telephone directory. Nothing to signify the years his family has lived here, no evidence of the effort, the achievement it had been. It's hard to believe that his mother is really going, that for months she will be so far. He wonders how his parents had done it, leaving their respective families behind, seeing them so seldom, dwelling unconnected, in a perpetual state of expectation, of longing. All those trips to Calcutta he'd once resented—how could they have been enough? They were not enough. Gogol knows now that his parents had lived their lives in America in spite of what was missing, with a stamina he fears he does not possess himself. He had spent years maintaining distance from his origins; his parents, in bridging that distance as best they could. And yet, for all his aloofness toward his family in the past, his years at college and then in New York, he has always hovered close to this quiet, ordinary town that had remained, for his mother and father, stubbornly exotic. He had not traveled to France as Moushumi had, or even to California as Sonia had done. Only for three months was he separated by more than a few small states from his father, a distance that had not troubled Gogol in the least, until it was too late. Apart from those months, for most of his adult life he has never been more than a four-hour train ride away. And there was nothing, apart from his family, to draw him home, to make this train journey, again and again.

It had been on the train, exactly a year ago, that he'd learned of Moushumi's affair. They were on their way up to spend Christmas with his mother and Sonia. They had left the city late, and outside the windows it had been dark, the disturbing pitch-black of early winter evenings. They were in the middle of a conversation about how to spend the coming summer, whether to rent a house in Siena with Donald and Astrid, an idea Gogol was resisting, when she'd said, "Dimitri says Siena is something out of a fairy tale." Immediately a hand had gone to her mouth, accompanied by a small intake of breath. And then, silence. "Who's Dimitri?" he'd asked. And then: "Are you having an affair?" The question had sprung out of him, something he had not consciously put together in his mind until that moment. It felt almost comic to him, burning in his throat. But as soon as he asked it, he knew. He felt the chill of her secrecy, numbing him, like a poison spreading quickly through his veins. He'd felt this way on only one other occasion, the night he had sat in the car with his father and learned the rea-

son for his name. That night he'd experienced the same bewilderment, was sickened in the same way. But he felt none of
the tenderness that he had felt for his father, only the anger,
the humiliation of having been deceived. And yet, at the same
time, he was strangely calm—in the moment that his marriage
was effectively severed he was on solid ground with her for the
first time in months. He remembered a night weeks ago; looking through her bag for her wallet, to pay the Chinese food delivery man, he'd pulled out her diaphragm case. She told him
she'd gone to the doctor that afternoon to have it refitted, and
so he'd put it out of his mind.

His first impulse had been to get out at the next station, to be
as physically far from her as possible. But they were bound together, by the train, by the fact that his mother and Sonia were
expecting them, and so somehow they had suffered through
the rest of the journey, and then through the weekend, telling
no one, pretending that nothing was wrong. Lying in his parents' house, in the middle of the night, she told him the whole
story, about meeting Dimitri on a bus, finding his résumé in
the bin. She confessed that Dimitri had gone with her to Palm
Beach. One by one he stored the pieces of information in his
mind, unwelcome, unforgivable. And for the first time in his
life, another man's name upset Gogol more than his own.

The day after Christmas she left Pemberton Road, with the
excuse to his mother and Sonia that a last-minute interview
had fallen into place at the MLA. But really the job was a ruse;
she and Gogol had decided that it was best for her to return to
New York alone. By the time he arrived at the apartment, her
clothes were gone, and her make-up and her bathroom things.
It was as if she were away on another trip. But this time she
didn't come back. She wanted nothing of the brief life they'd
had together; when she appeared one last time at his office,
so that he could sign the divorce papers, she told him she was

moving back to Paris. And so, systematically, as he had done for his dead father, he removed her possessions from the apartment, putting her books into boxes on the sidewalk in the middle of the night for people to take, throwing out the rest. In the spring he went to Venice alone for a week, the trip he'd planned for the two of them, saturating himself in its ancient, melancholy beauty. He lost himself among the darkened narrow streets, crossing countless tiny bridges, discovering deserted squares, where he sat with a Campari or a coffee, sketching the facades of pink and green palaces and churches, unable ever to retrace his steps.

And then he returned to New York, to the apartment they'd inhabited together that was now all his. A year later, the shock has worn off, but a sense of failure and shame persists, deep and abiding. There are nights he still falls asleep on the sofa, without deliberation, waking up at three A.M. with the television still on. It is as if a building he'd been responsible for designing has collapsed for all to see. And yet he can't really blame her. They had both acted on the same impulse, that was their mistake. They had both sought comfort in each other, and in their shared world, perhaps for the sake of novelty, or out of the fear that that world was slowly dying. Still, he wonders how he's arrived at all this: that he is thirty-two years old, and already married and divorced. His time with her seems like a permanent part of him that no longer has any relevance, or currency. As if that time were a name he'd ceased to use.

He hears the familiar beep of his mother's car, spots it pulling into the parking lot. Sonia is sitting in the driver's seat, waving. Ben is next to her. This is the first time he's seeing Sonia since she and Ben have announced their engagement. He decides that he will ask her to stop off at a liquor store so he can buy some champagne. She steps out of the car, walking toward him. She is an attorney now, working in an office in the Hancock building. Her hair is cut to her jaw. She's wearing an old blue down jacket that Gogol had worn back in high school. And yet there is a new maturity in her face; he can easily imagine her, a few years from now, with two children in the back seat. She gives him a hug. For a moment they stand there with their arms around each other in the cold. "Welcome home, Goggles," she says.

For the last time, they assemble the artificial seven-foot tree, the branches color-coded at their base. Gogol brings up the box from the basement. For decades the instructions have been missing; each year they have to figure out the order in which the branches must be inserted, the longest ones at the bottom, the smallest at the top. Sonia holds the pole, and Gogol and Ben insert the branches. The orange go first, then the yellow, then the red and finally blue, the uppermost piece slightly bent under the white speckled ceiling. They place the tree in front of the window, drawing apart the curtains so that people passing by the house can see, as excited as they were when they were children. They decorate it with ornaments made by Sonia and Gogol in elementary school: construction paper candlesticks, Popsicle-stick god's-eyes, glitter-covered pinecones. A torn Banarasi sari of Ashima's is wrapped around the base. At the top they put what they always do, a small plastic bird covered with turquoise velvet, with brown wire claws.

Stockings are hung on nails from the mantel, the one put up for Moushumi last year now put up for Ben. They drink the champagne out of Styrofoam cups, forcing Ashima to have some, too, and they play the Perry Como Christmas tape his father always liked. They tease Sonia, telling Ben about the year she had refused her gifts after taking a Hinduism class in college, coming home and protesting that they weren't Christian. Early in the morning, his mother, faithful to the rules of

Christmas her children had taught her when they were little, will wake up and fill the stockings, with gift certificates to record stores, candy canes, mesh bags of chocolate coins. He can still remember the very first time his parents had had a tree in the house, at his insistence, a plastic thing no larger than a table lamp, displayed on top of the fireplace mantel. And yet its presence had felt colossal. How it had thrilled him. He had begged them to buy it from the drugstore. He remembers decorating it clumsily with garlands and tinsel and a string of lights that made his father nervous. In the evenings, until his father came in and pulled out the plug, causing the tiny tree to go dark, Gogol would sit there. He remembers the single wrapped gift that he had received, a toy that he'd picked out himself, his mother asking him to stand by the greeting cards while she paid for it. "Remember when we used to put on those awful flashing colored lights?" his mother says now when they are done, shaking her head. "I didn't know a thing back then."

At seven-thirty the bell rings, and the front door is left open as people and cold air stream into the house. Guests are speaking in Bengali, hollering, arguing, talking on top of one another, the sound of their laughter filling the already crowded rooms. The croquettes are fried in crackling oil and arranged with a red onion salad on plates. Sonia serves them with paper napkins. Ben, the jamai-to-be, is introduced to each of the guests. "I'll never keep all these names straight," he says at one point to Gogol. "Don't worry, you'll never need to," Gogol says. These people, these honorary aunts and uncles of a dozen different surnames, have seen Gogol grow, have surrounded him at his wedding, his father's funeral. He promises to keep in touch with them now that his mother is leaving, not to forget them. Sonia shows off her ring, six tiny diamonds surrounding an emerald, to the mashis, who wear their red and green saris.

"You will have to grow your hair for the wedding," they tell Sonia. One of the meshos is sporting a Santa hat. They sit in the living room, on the furniture and on the floor. Children drift down into the basement, the older ones to rooms upstairs. He recognizes his old Monopoly game being played, the board in two pieces, the racecar missing ever since Sonia dropped it into the baseboard heater when she was little. Gogol does not know to whom these children belong—half the guests are people his mother has befriended in recent years, people who were at his wedding but whom he does not recognize. People talk of how much they've come to love Ashima's Christmas Eve parties, that they've missed them these past few years, that it won't be the same without her. They have come to rely on her, Gogol realizes, to collect them together, to organize the holiday, to convert it, to introduce the tradition to those who are new. It has always felt adopted to him, an accident of circumstance, a celebration not really meant to be. And yet it was for him, for Sonia, that his parents had gone to the trouble of learning these customs. It was for their sake that it had come to all this.

In so many ways, his family's life feels like a string of accidents, unforeseen, unintended, one incident begetting another. It had started with his father's train wreck, paralyzing him at first, later inspiring him to move as far as possible, to make a new life on the other side of the world. There was the disappearance of the name Gogol's great-grandmother had chosen for him, lost in the mail somewhere between Calcutta and Cambridge. This had led, in turn, to the accident of his being named Gogol, defining and distressing him for so many years. He had tried to correct that randomness, that error. And yet it had not been possible to reinvent himself fully, to break from that mismatched name. His marriage had been something of a misstep as well. And the way his father had slipped away from them, that had been the worst accident of all, as if the preparatory work of death had been done long ago, the night he was nearly killed, and all that was left for him was one day, quietly, to go. And yet these events have formed Gogol, shaped him, determined who he is. They were things for which it was impossible to prepare but which one spent a lifetime looking back at, trying to accept, interpret, comprehend. Things that should never have happened, that seemed out of place and wrong, these were what prevailed, what endured, in the end.

"Gogol, the camera," his mother calls out over the crowd. "Take some pictures tonight, please? I want to remember this Christmas. Next year at this time I'll be so far away." He goes upstairs to get his father's Nikon, still sitting on the top shelf of Ashoke's closet. There is practically nothing else there. No clothes hang from the rod. The emptiness upsets him, but the weight of the camera is solid, reassuring in his hands. He takes the camera into his room to load a fresh battery, a new roll of film. Last year he and Moushumi slept in the guest room, on the double bed, with its folded towels and a fresh bar of soap on top of the dresser, what his mother always left out for guests. But now that Sonia is here with Ben, the guest room is theirs, and Gogol is back in his room, with a bed he's never shared with Moushumi, or with anyone.

The bed is narrow, covered by a solid brown quilt. He can reach up and touch the frosted white light fixture suspended from the ceiling, filled with dead moths. The stains of Scotch tape once attached to his posters are visible on the walls. His desk was the folding square card table in the corner. Here he had done his homework under the dusty black gooseneck lamp. There is a thin, peacock blue carpet on the floor, slightly too large so that one side curls up against the wall. The shelves and drawers are mostly empty. Unwanted, miscellaneous things are in boxes already: essays written in high school, under the name Gogol. A report done in elementary school on Greek and Roman architecture, Corinthian and Ionic and Doric columns copied from an encyclopedia onto tracing paper. Cross pen-and-pencil sets, records listened to twice and then abandoned, clothes that were too large, too small—that never seemed worth transporting to the increasingly cramped apartments he inhabited over the years. All his old books, the ones he read by flashlight under the covers, and the ones required for college, only half-read, some with yellow USED stickers on the spines. His mother is going to donate them all to the library where she works, for their annual book sale in the spring. She has told him to go through them, make sure there's nothing he wants for himself. He pokes through the box. *The Swiss Family Robinson. On the Road. The Communist Manifesto. How to Get into an Ivy League School.*

And then another book, never read, long forgotten, catches his eye. The jacket is missing, the title on the spine practically faded. It's a thick clothbound volume topped with decades-old dust. The ivory pages are heavy, slightly sour, silken to the touch. The spine cracks faintly when he opens it to the title page. *The Short Stories of Nikolai Gogol.* "For Gogol Ganguli," it says on the front endpaper in his father's tranquil hand, in red ballpoint ink, the letters rising gradually, optimistically, on the diagonal toward the upper right-hand corner of the page. "The man who gave you his name, from the man who gave you your name" is written within quotation marks. Underneath the inscription, which he has never before seen, is his birthday, and the year, 1982. His father had stood in the doorway, just there, an arm's reach from where he sits now. He had left him to discover the inscription on his own, never again asking Gogol what he'd thought of the book, never mentioning the book at all. The handwriting reminds him of the checks his father used to give him all through college, and for years afterward, to help him along, to put down a security deposit, to buy his first suit, sometimes for no reason at all. The name he had so detested, here hidden and preserved—that was the first thing his father had given him.

The givers and keepers of Gogol's name are far from him now. One dead. Another, a widow, on the verge of a different sort of departure, in order to dwell, as his father does, in a separate world. She will call him, once a week, on the phone. She will learn to send e-mail, she says. Once or twice a week, he will hear "Gogol" over the wires, see it typed on a screen. As for all the people in the house, all the mashis and meshos to whom he is still, and will always be, Gogol—now that his mother is moving away, how often will he see them? Without people in the world to call him Gogol, no matter how long he himself lives, Gogol Ganguli will, once and for all, vanish from the lips of loved ones, and so, cease to exist. Yet the thought of this eventual demise provides no sense of victory, no solace. It provides no solace at all.

Gogol gets up, shuts the door to his room, muffling the noise of the party that swells below him, the laughter of the children playing down the hall. He sits cross-legged on the bed. He opens the book, glances at an illustration of Nikolai Gogol, and then at the chronology of the author's life on the facing page. Born March 20, 1809. The death of his father, 1825. Publishes his first story, 1830. Travels to Rome, 1837. Dies 1852, one month before his forty-third birthday. In another ten years, Gogol Ganguli will be that age. He wonders if he will be married again one day, if he will ever have a child to name. A month from now, he will begin a new job at a smaller architectural practice, producing his own designs. There is a possibility, eventually, of becoming an associate, of the firm incorporating his name. And in that case Nikhil will live on, publicly celebrated, unlike Gogol, purposely hidden, legally diminished, now all but lost.

He turns to the first story. "The Overcoat." In a few minutes his mother will come upstairs to find him. "Gogol," she will say, opening the door without knocking, "where is the camera? What's taking so long? This is no time for books," she will scold, hastily noting the volume open against the covers, unaware, as her son has been all these years, that her husband dwells discreetly, silently, patiently, within its pages. "There is a party downstairs, people to talk to, food to be taken out of the oven, thirty glasses of water to fill and line up on the sideboard. To think that we will never again all be here together. If only your father could have stayed with us a bit longer," she will add, her eyes growing momentarily damp. "But come, see the children under the tree."

He will apologize, put the book aside, a small corner of a page turned over to mark his place. He will walk downstairs with his mother, join the crowded party, photographing the people in his parents' life, in this house, one last time, huddled on the sofas, plates held in their laps, eating with their hands. Eventually, at his mother's insistence, he will eat as well, seated cross-legged on the floor, and speak to his parents' friends, about his new job, about New York, about his mother, about Sonia and Ben's wedding. After dinner he will help Sonia and Ben scrape bay leaves and lamb bones and cinnamon sticks from plates, pile them on the counters and two burners of the stove. He will watch his mother do what his father used to do toward the end of every party, spooning fine-leaf Lopchu tea into two kettles. He will watch her give away leftovers in the cooking pots themselves. As the hours of the evening pass he will grow distracted, anxious to return to his room, to be alone, to read the book he had once forsaken, has abandoned until now. Until moments ago it was destined to disappear from his life altogether, but he has salvaged it by chance, as his father was pulled from a crushed train forty years ago. He leans back against the headboard, adjusting a pillow behind his back. In a few minutes he will go downstairs, join the party, his family. But for now his mother is distracted, laughing at a story a friend is telling her, unaware of her son's absence. For now, he starts to read.